APACHE AMBUSH

Schermer and Moriarity were angling downwash to hit the shelter of the bend. Schermer almost made it. Then he fell, hit at least a dozen times. Moriarity took three strides and caught a .50 caliber Springfield slug in the forehead. The back of his head flew into Bourke's face when the Irish sergeant leaped out to try and grab the youth. The bullet hit the sergeant's hat, sent it cartwheeling, and sent the sergeant reeling with it. The slug had ripped his scalp in passage, smashing him to his knees with shock, blinding him with sudden blood.

As he staggered up he heard a familiar voice yelling at him to "Swing up! Swing up!" and saw the blurred form of the small horseman bearing down upon him.

It was the Coyote, their Apache scout.

But whose side was he on this time?

WILL HENRY

CHIRICAHUA

LEISURE BOOKS   NEW YORK CITY

For Philip Durham and Everett Jones,
true friends of the West and of the
Western story.

A LEISURE BOOK®

May 2008

Published by special arrangement with Golden West Literary Agency.

Dorchester Publishing Co., Inc.
200 Madison Avenue
New York, NY 10016

ISBN 10: 0-8439-6130-9
ISBN 13: 978-0-8439-6130-0

Printed in the United States of America.

10 9 8 7 6 5 4 3 2

AUTHOR'S NOTE

This work is proposed in tribute to Peaches, and to the Apache Scouts of the United States Cavalry, Arizona Territory. It does not pretend to document either the history of the scouts or of the territory, but rather to honor in spirit a wild, free way of life, vanished forever with Crook's conquest of the fighting Chiricahua, truly the last of the Apaches.

Prologue

The Chiricahua Apache, during General George Crook's first tour in Arizona Territory, were of all the Apache bands curiously exempted from the general's command and control. This was doubly odd in that these Indians—famed Cochise's wary people—were easily the least tractable, most troublesome of all the Apache.

However, when Crook was returned to command in the early summer of 1882, stationed then at Whipple Barracks, Prescott, not San Carlos Reservation as most assume, he was given the Chiricahua, called "Cherry Cows" by the Arizonans, to watch over.

When they heard of this the hotheads, the *hesh-kes*, or ritual killers among nonreservation Chiricahua began at once to agitate upon the reservation. In October, 1882, they succeeded, through a vicious compost of lies about Crook's secret intention to banish all the Chiricahua people to the dreaded Florida hot country, in provoking an outbreak of the entire tribe. In the dark of a storming night, seven hundred ten men, women, and children fled San Carlos for the legendary sanctuary of their wild people in the Sierra Madres mountains of Old Mexico.

An unwilling hostage-prisoner of this flight was a young White Mountain Apache named Pa-nayo-tishn, The Coyote Saw Him. Known also as Tzoe among his White Mountain family, he was called "Peaches" by the hard-bitten white cavalrymen whom he insistently beseeched to permit him to train as a regimental Apache scout. To the hour of his taking by the retreating Chiricahua, however, there is no record of his enlistment at San Carlos, or indeed of his residency there. History has only his own subsequent word for who he was and where he came from, before fate put her dark finger upon him.

He always maintained that he was not a Chiricahua, but married to two Chiricahua women, by both of whom he had children. He had lived in peace, he vowed, with his old mother in the hills not far from San Carlos, harboring but one ambition, cherishing but one dream—to be an enlisted scout for the United States Cavalry.

If the military command in Arizona Territory would not hear his yearning plea, Ysun, the god of his ancient fathers, took heed and compassion.

Late in March, 1883, two bands of killer Chiricahua swept up out of the Mexican mountain fastnesses to raid in Arizona. The leaders were the dread Geronimo, with fifty men, and an unknown new young *hesh-ke* named Chatto, or Chato, from the Spanish *chato*, or Flat Nose, with twenty-six men.

In the course of this terrible six-day raid, scores of whites and friendly Apache Indians died in southeast Arizona, while five hundred cavalry troops scoured their every trail and reported position without once blooding them.

The sole Chiricahua casualties were one man, shot down by employees of the Total Wreck Mine, whose severed head was on display at Fort Apache until it rotted, and one man captured by U.S. troops in a manner officially described in the journals of Lieutenant Britton Davis and not elsewhere substantiated.

The singularity of the latter incident, however, lay with the identity of the captive.

He was the White Mountain friendly, Pa-nayo-tishn, known as Peaches.

This is his story as the very, very old men still tell it in the lovely White Mountains of Arizona, Apacheland today as it was one hundred years ago, and it is an Indian story from first to last. Where it may agree with the history books of the white man, the old Apaches will shrug and grin and say, "Well, even the white man cannot lie all the time."

But they will tell you the strange and moving story of Pa-nayo-tishn who, as Peaches, guided General George Crook's troopers to the secret camps of the Chiricahua in Mexico and broke the power of the *hesh-kes* for all time among his people, returning them to peace.

Also, as Peaches, he is dismissed with two or three lines or a paragraph in most documentive texts, sometimes with faded photograph, sometimes without. But then the Apache have no word for fame, and they do not write history books. They only tell stories, if one will listen, and buy a little *tizwin* and tobacco.

This is such an Apache story.

Pima Bend

1

The whiskey-raddled bum at the far corner table of the Tecolote Saloon came awake. Blearily, he stared after the exodus of late afternoon customers running for the dirt street outside. What the hell was going on?

Abandoned, the drunk made valiant effort to arise and follow the rush, which now included the barkeep. Three veering staggers toward the slatted doors, however, and he was down again. This time no chair awaited him, and no table. He was met by the beery sawdust of the plank floor and the contents of the bar-end spittoon that his flopping arm overturned, lacquering his mustache and gaping mouth with a stagnant patina of brown rice-paper butts and cheroot juice.

He lay in this state until Hayes Jacobs, the bartender, returned from the flanks of the street crowd. Hayes, who prided himself on his housekeeping, hauled the drunk out through the swinging doors. "Here, you, Clooney Borrum!" he called to the Negro swamper and stablehand next door. "Dump this one in the trough and hold him under till he stops bubbling."

The black man knuckled sweating forehead. "Yes sir, Mister Hayes, sure enough."

Clooney Borrum, if no longer young, had little difficulty hoisting the bone-thin drifter into the watering trough. There, he swished him to and fro with the practiced indifference of defleaing a dog or dipping a ticked sheep.

"Whee-ooo!" was his sole comment.

Regardless of the vagrant's foul odor, however, and in disobedience of the instructions to hold him under, the big Negro surfaced the man repeatedly and with gentle care to bring him around without getting water in his lungs. In

3

result and presently, the drunk sat up in the trough and said, "Jesus H. Christ, where at am I?"

"Where at you is," answered Clooney Borrum, "is wallering in the middle of the town horse trough, boss. You tooken on enough booze to bog a mallard duck."

"All right," mumbled the drifter. "What town?"

"Pima Bend, boss."

"God amighty," said the man, making no effort to get out of the trough. "I thought I'd died and now I know I have. Pima Bend. Ain't that hell spelt backwards?"

"And sideways," said the Negro.

"Hold it there. You forgot the 'boss'."

"Yes sir, sure enough I did, boss."

"Keep forgetting it," advised the drifter. "I ain't the boss of nobody."

"Onliest difference is," murmured the black swamper, "nobody's the boss of you, neither."

The drunk frowned, lost the thread, lay back gratefully in the green-scummed water of the trough. "The hell with it," he said. "Wake me up at noon, mister. I got me a mislaid steeldust horse to locate and some Mexican miles to lay away from this here burg. How far did I get from Fort Gila?"

"Day's ride," said the swamper. "Long one."

The ragged drunk settled lower still into the tepid scum of the tank. "Ahhh!" he exhaled. "Clean sheets!"

And sank beneath the murky waters of the Pima Bend horse trough, snoring bubbles.

The man came awake with a cold sweat start.

His vision swam, then steadied.

He lay on a rude cot staring up at an adobe ceiling whitewashed that peculiar hoosegow gray familiar to him these latter days of his years.

"Ah, Christ," he groaned. "In again."

He sat up on the cot. The effort split his head nose to skullbase. Dropping weakly to all fours he crawled across the cell. He did not look where he was going but when he got there, there was the washstand and the clay olla and the galvanized tin basin. A man learned from experience. The real shaker would have been if the washstand had not been there when he got to it. Gingerly, he sloshed the contents of the olla over the enormous throbbing that was his head, then he collapsed and lay on the mud floor until enough conscious will returned for him to flop over upon his back and start yelling to be turned loose.

Directly, the deputy, a pink-eyed youth with lank blond hair and a bad complexion, lounged in.

"What the fuck," he said, "you caterwauling about?"

The drifter studied his jailer through pain-raw eyes. He had seen the kind time without number. The pimply kid with the low-slung gun and the copied bad-man slouch was as familiar to him as the crockery pitcher on the bench-legged washstand. Wincing, he tried closing his tortured eyes. Christ. They felt gritty as fish eggs dropped in bank sand and then put back. And his head was cracking open again, this time around the hatband crease, ear to ear. Oh, Jesus H. Christ, that goddamned bottle. Would it ever let him be?

"Listen," said the kid deputy. "Don't yell no more like that, you hear? You do, I'm going to come in here and bend a Colt barrel acrost your hat. You savvy?"

"Jesus, yes," groaned the prisoner. "Kid, for God's sake give me a hand up in here." He gestured helplessly from the floor. "I'm still so goddamned roostered I can't get up on my hind legs to crow."

"Shit," said the youth. "You crow once more in my jail, old man, you're going to wish you never heard of a dungheap to get up on. Now you *callate pronto*."

"Yes sir," grated the ashen-faced prisoner. "Could I please see the sheriff, Mister Deputy?"

"Sure," conceded the youngster, ego reached. "Just go yonder to the window. He's the fat old bastard ordering the crowd around."

"The crowd?" groped the prisoner. He had vague recall of patrons milling out of the Tecolote Saloon and of blurringly seeing, over their heads, the passage down Main Street of a lurching coach, short on horses and leaning all wrong. "What crowd, boy?"

"That crowd, you damned souse." The deputy pointed again to the cell's lone window. "Next door. Out front of the livery there. Where the Fort Gila stage is parked." He lifted thin upper lip. "It's the one pumped plumb full of them Cherry Cow Apache arrows," he specified disgustedly. "As if you would know or give a shit."

Turning, he tough-walked his way into the outer office, slamming the cellblock door. Deputy W.K. Suggins, Jr. did not care for old drunks and has-been drifters. They were all hard-wintered and humped in the loin, using their back for a mattress and their belly for a blanket. Old men stunk. All of them.

Alone, the drunk crawled to the wall of his cell and put the flat of his back to its rough plaster. Hunching himself up onto his feet, he was at once and rushingly ill, vomiting all down his front. The purging cleared his vision, however. He could see the cell window now. Going around the wall, back flat so that he would not fall again, he reached the ancient handwrought Spanish bars. Gripping them, he peered forth into the summer dusk. Suddenly, he straightened, slurring a curse.

Goddamn them, the deputy was right. Those *were* Apache arrows, Chiricahua or otherwise, driven into that parked Fort Gila coach. Yes, by God, and so were they Apache shafts sticking in the poor damned horses being taken out of harness and led away for shooting. And those were likewise Apache arrows—three of them—in the slack body of the shotgun rider being slid carefully down off the driver's box and fed into the canvas sack held by Clooney Borrum and Hunker Larsen, the blacksmith with whom the drifter had left his steeldust gelding before buying the first bottle for the boys.

"Dirty murdering red bastards—!" he began to yell.

Then the grimed fingers loosened their hold on the iron bars of the cell window. The voice thickened to a rotgut mush, trailed away unintelligibly. The emaciated body slid peacefully down the whitewashed wall, came to snore once more upon the earthen floor of the Pima Bend jail. It still lay there, immured in the nauseous cake of its own fly-encrusted filth, when old Sheriff Jules Hoberman stamped into the cellroom with his bleached-haired deputy and said, "For God's sake, Pinky, what's died in here?"

In the outer office the deputy duly explained that the fetid prisoner was white, male, no papers on him, about forty-odd years old and "looking like he didn't have the pressure to pee a hole in a dust puddle."

Moreover, he was the same rummy that Hayes Jacobs had pitched out of the Tecolote and the same bum that had ridden into town that morning on the good gaiting steeldust that he, Suggins, and the sheriff himself had agreed looked like he had been ridden long and put away lathered.

"You know," said the deputy. "The one we telegraphed Fort Gila about as to having been stole from anywheres over thataway."

"Oh," said Jules Hoberman. "Yeah."

He was thinking of other things. His good supper and plump Mexican wife waiting for him at home. The bad news that the army had shot and killed Nah-tez up at Fort Gila. The unreasonable dollar-fifty price Doc Slattery had charged him for pulling that infected wisdom tooth for his fat thirteen-year-old daughter. The fact that Ranger, his bluetick hound puppy, had the epizootic and wouldn't eat. Real things. Counting things.

"Well," said the deputy, "I picked up our answer from old Piney Newbold down to the telegraph office. You got yourself a horsethief, Mister Hoberman."

"Oh?"

"Yup. That steeldust gelding was took from Steinhower's place night afore last. He's a race horse, and old man Steinhower says he will pay fifty bucks to get him back." W.K. Suggins twisted thin lips. "That's twenty-five each, sheriff," he said. "I can take him back over to the fort in the morning and collect."

The old lawman looked him over carefully.

"How long you been my deputy, Pinky? Four year this spring?"

"Yes, sir, something on that order."

"And how long since we been splitting private ree-ward money down the middle, fifty-fifty, territory sheriff and pimple-ass deputy?"

Young Suggins' acned face writhed.

"Damn it all, Mister Hoberman, we got to start sometime. I ain't going to work for twelve dollars a week forever. Got to be some incentual pay somewheres along the line."

Jules Hoberman pulled faded walrus mustache, frowned with the pain of human greed and unnatural ambition.

"Pinky," he said, "I vow to God that if I could do it lawful, I would put you aboard the next stage west and pray you never made it home to Pima Bend again." Again the lugubrious tug at weathered mustache. "Only trouble is, there ain't going to be no next stage west."

"There ain't?" The deputy scowled, hitching at low-slung gunbelt. "You mean they ain't going on to Sifford Wells tomorrow?"

"Not tomorrow, nor the next day neither."

"Who says?"

"U.S. Cavalry says. They telegraphed me from the fort when I had Piney report this here Apache run on the stage.

Told me to hold the stage here and let nothing through for Tucson. Territory's closed till the Chiricahuas quiets down."

"The hell it is!" countered a heavy voice from the street door.

Old Jules glanced up. "The hell what is, T.C.?" he said.

"The hell my stage line is shut down to Tucson."

"Oh."

"Oh, your sweet ass," said T.C. Madden, half owner and general super of Southwest Stagelines west of El Paso. "I got fifteen thousand in gold coin aboard that busted-up Concord and it's going to Tucson if I have to ride the box myself."

"Ain't you talking a little rough, T.C.?"

"I ain't talking, I'm telling."

Jules Hoberman moved around his desk. "You ain't auger-ing with me, T.C. It's the U.S. government."

Madden, a stager since he could hold six lines in two hands, kicked shut the street door.

"Get that goddamn deputy out of here," he growled. "Me and you are going to the mat."

"Go ahead on, Pinky," said the old lawman, shoulders sagging. "Get that horsethief around to the pump. Make him strip and soap. Hose off his clothes. Don't say what he's being heldt for."

The deputy left, and the stage line super laid it on the sheriff's table: Southwest was facing bankruptcy; if the gold to guarantee its payroll didn't get to Tucson in forty-eight hours, the creditors would take over the line. "That line is T.C. Madden's life," the big man concluded, face set like canyon rock. "That gold is going to Tucson. On schedule."

"Meaning," said Jules Hoberman, "That this shot-up coach is going on to Sifford Wells?"

"We've sold the tickets," was all that burly T.C. Madden said.

They chewed it a little more, but it still came out full of craw gravel. The sheriff said they would sort it out later, that he right now had a scared-stiff town to quiet down. Killing Nah-tez had been a hell of a mistake. Of course that did not mean Chatto would attack Pima Bend. But some of the citizens were spreading the rumor that he might. Right as they talked, they could both hear the sporadic gunfire of the jumpy ones blasting away wildly at the darkening sage out past chicken shed or privy. It was plain that, as sheriff, he had to get on down the street and be seen calm and in charge. Otherwise somebody was going to shoot somebody in the ass and blame it on the Indians and get Chatto and his Cherry Cows in a meaner corner than they had already put themselves.

"For closers," old Jules said, "I want you should savvy it straight that the cavalry order stands. That coach ain't going to Sifford Wells with or without you. Now I mean it, T.C. You make one move up Main Street with that rig, and I'll cut your lead team in two with Double Ought buck. Need be, I'll switch to bird shot for you."

"Sheriff," said Madden, "you do your job, I'll do mine." The blue Irish eyes were hard, the heavy jaw set. "We'll see who gets paid first."

"None of that. I want your word on it, T.C."

"Word, hell, did I ever lie to you? You won't see that coach move anyplace but into the repair shed."

Old Jules followed the big man outside. Both stood a moment looking through the night.

"*Cuidado*," said the grizzled lawman.

"Me?" said Madden. "Take care? With that damned Chatto? You know how I feel about that Indian, Jules."

Hoberman's wrinkled mouth lines deepened.

"T.C.," he said, "you got a dead shotgun rider in the ice house and two winged passengers down to Doc Slattery's office right now. Your driver's tooken an arrow through the leg and lost a quart of blood from another one slicing half his belly open. You want to see your whole damned manifest dug in on boot hill?"

"Not tonight," grunted Madden and moved off down Main toward the stage station.

The lawman watching after him, knowing the big stager from cowboying days long before the one put on the star and the other picked up the ledger quill, began to growl. "Goddamn him, he'll try it; no, goddamnit, he'll do it."

He started after the super, but his deputy came up just then with the dripping prisoner, and the sheriff held up to inspect the man.

"Good job," he said, sniffing the air cautiously some ten feet upwind. "Take him on in. Give him a pot of coffee and a seegar. Watch things. I'm going downtown for a walk around, then home to supper."

W.K. Suggins hitched gunbelt lower yet on narrow hips. "You don't need to worry about nothing with me in charge, Mister Hoberman."

"You in charge is what I worry about," said the old sheriff wearily. "You look sharp now. Cavalry patrol due in some time along after midnight. Call me down."

"You mean you ain't coming back after supper?"

The old man, already four strides gone, stopped short. "I'm going to bed. You got that?"

"You mean to sleep?"

Jules Hoberman did not reply. Instead, he started on through the Arizona night. Turning patient face to velvet first stars above, he nodded and made recitation to no one in particular.

"The Lord pours in the brains of some with teaspoons," he said. "And still gets his arm joggled, even so."

2

The street blinds were drawn. The only illumination in the rear office of Southwest Stagelines' Pima Bend division office was the stub of a candle in the tin coffee cup on T.C. Madden's desk.

In the front office of telegrapher P.W. "Piney" Newbold, the sounding receiver was silent. In the street window, between downed blind and dusty, cracked glass, a quickly hand-lettered sign announced that *"Southwest Co."* was closed temporarily *"By Order of the Sheriff."*

No light at all shone in the repair shed where Clooney Borrum had parked the battered Concord. Nor were the ready-stock corrals facing Main Street lit by their customary lone street lamp. "Long as we're shut down," Madden had said to Jules Hoberman, coming by on his Main Street walkdown, "we may as well go dark." The weary lawman had agreed with a grunt, and, only moments later, the waiting super saw him trudging back up Main on his way home to whatever of man contentment he found in the company of his Mexican *mujer*, his fat daughter, and his sick dog. Instantly, Madden swung about to pass the order to Piney Newbold, his ticket agent as well as Pima Bend's telegrapher.

"All right, Hoberman's heading for the hay. Get everybody in here. Rustle your butt."

Piney literally scurried to do his employer's bidding. He had worked for Southwest the entire chancy span of its existence, and, if he was not ready to expire for the company, he would at least sweat for it to the last gland. Within minutes, the summoned group stood along the walls of the smokily lit inner office. Present were Lars "Hunker" Larsen, brawny immigrant blacksmith and chief wagon mechanic for Southwest; Clooney Borrum, black wizard with all things horseflesh; Feeny Gleason, night man in the livery barn; Madden; and Newbold. The subject was urgent, short-fused on time and burning, and federally illegal:

The running of the U.S. Cavalry quarantine to Sifford Wells and Tucson.

Madden was the inquisitor: "Hunker, will your repaired rig roll the distance?"

"She will, mister."

"Clooney, you found six good head of sound stock to pull her?"

"Six to pull and two spare head to tie on the boot. Likewise that good gelding of the poor man up to the jailhouse, iffen you wants to take him along on loan."

"Forget the gelding. He's a stole horse."

"Right sad to hear that, Mister T.C. I know that poor feller seen better days. He's a good man, sure."

Madden ignored the colored swamper. "Piney, we got to leave somebody behind to mind the store. You know, stall old Jules and likely his pimple-faced deputy. Only one can handle that job is you. You agree?"

"There's no choice, T.C. Feeny certainly can't do it."

"Well, yeah, goddamnit, there's Feeny. I don't want to take him along and I don't dast to leave him behind. What the hell we going to do with him? Any ideas?" His protruded jaw challenged the listeners. "Come on, come on. We got to get shut of here before the damn cavalry shows up. You get anything more on them, Piney?"

"Line's been cut," said the operator. "Nothing since they said a patrol was on its way."

"Son of a bitch. Well, how about Feeny?"

No one answering, Feeny, the problem employee, spoke unexpectedly in self-behalf. "I got to do something, Mister Madden. Company's been powerful kind to me. Leave me ride extry gun up on top."

"*You?*" Madden was taken short. "Hell, you'd bounce off on your ass first rock we hit. Anybody else?"

"Inside, then!" persisted the stablehand desperately. "Please, Mister Madden. I ain't never shot at no live Injun.

Got me one of them Civil War Spencer's sawed-off. She's a bull's-ass special, honest to Christ!"

"Bull's-eye, bull's-eye," winced Piney Newbold.

"He shoots pretty good, mister," said Hunker Larsen. "I will watch him for you." He never called T.C. Madden anything but "mister," and the super never corrected him.

"All right, Feeny," he said. "Go and get your damn Spencer and for God's sake don't let nobody see you."

Feeny Gleason, hound-sad eyes fired with visions of riding inside gun on a real run, fled the room wordlessly, using the darkened back hallway. Good God, he was going to get to carry a gun with the Apache out; he was going to get to shoot himself a filthy redskin!

"Now, Piney," said T.C. Madden, "I'll drive and that leaves us needing only a shotgun man. Hunker will keep the rig rolling. Clooney will hold the horseflesh together. You cover us here. And every man jack of you will get one hundred gold cash and bonus pay of twenty per month extra. We can do it; we will!" He paused, bulldog face shadowing. "Who the goddamned hell can we get to ride shotgun? With Charley Broadus killed and Petey Goheen sliced up and bled half out, it ain't going to be simple. Not even for gold pay."

There was a stir from the hallway leading to the rear door which Feeny Gleason had just exited. They all thought it was the stablehand returning but it was not. "Did I hear gold?" said W.K. Suggins, Jr., lounging in from the darkened hall in his gunfighter's slouch. He stood lip curled. It was intended as a grin but came out a grimace, and T.C. Madden growled like a grizzly with his foot caught in a baitpan trap jaw.

"You heard gold," he said. "How much else did you hear?"

"All I need," answered the deputy. "You just hired your shotgun rider."

"You're crazier than hell," said Madden.

"Sure I am," agreed the pimpled lawman. "That's why you're going to pay me double. Two hundred on the counter."

"Suggins, you're bluffing."

"Try me."

Clooney Borrum shook dark head. "Don't you do it, Mister Madden, sir. I hearn something scuffling in the hallway arter Mister Feeny left. Could have been this one."

"Blackmail," said T.C. Madden, staring down the deputy. "Pure and uncut."

"Bullshit," snarled W.K. Suggins. "Just plain natural brains.

I had enough and to spare of Pima Bend." He looked around at the others. For a moment the pink-rimmed eyes seemed to appeal for mutual misery. "I aim to go all the way to Los Angeles and smell them orange trees. Two hundred in gold will see me there and any place else I want to ramble. Sure was lucky I dropped down here on my own to impound that there horsethief's steeldust." As quickly as the pimpled face had turned pleading, it was again a mask of derision. "Son of a bitch, you never know what you're going to stumble onto if you keep your pistol cocked."

Madden had never broken his blue-iced stare at the young lawman. "You had better keep yours cocked, Suggins," he said.

"Oh, my," answered the youth, recoiling. "I am scairt shitless." The skinny blotched hand slid like a coiling snake, flicked, really, and in it appeared the old-model army Colt. The big hammer spur was back, and W.K. Suggins, Jr. was grinning mirthlessly. "She's cocked," he said. "How about that shotgun job?"

Madden would fight a bulldog barehanded. He would free-fall a wild gorilla and give him top-hold. He was, as the saying went, a man with he-hair on his brisket. But he was not a fool; he knew the deputy.

"All right, Pinky," he said. "But remember it. I will."

The deputy moved his wrist and the big Colt was back in its leather. "I'll go along up to the jail and get my scatter gun," he blinked. "You can count out my pay while I'm gone." He started out, but Clooney Borrum put out a tentative black hand to touch his gun arm.

"Mister Pinky, sir—"

The deputy whirled, jerking the arm away from the swamper's touch. "Don't you never do that again, you black fucker," he whispered. "Not never."

"Yes, sir. Didn't mean no harm, sir." Clooney slunk back, but his concern would not permit him to relinquish the question. "Could you tell me, please, Mister Pinky—what is that horse-thieving charge going to mean in the law? They going to hang the man for it?"

Suggins glared at the Negro swamper a long moment then turned and went out silently. T.C. Madden spoke into the stillness. "They won't hang him, Clooney," he promised. "They don't do that anymore. Not legal anyways. He'll draw five years in Yuma likely."

"Yumer?" breathed the black man, awed. "Oh, Gawd, I

purely hopes not. I done a year there, Mister T.C. It like to kill me, too—just one little old year."

"You did a year, Clooney," said Piney Newbold accusingly. "For what?"

Clooney Borrum shook his head. "They never toldt me," he said. "That's how come I never toldt you."

T.C. Madden looked at the other white men. His thick hand went to the shoulder of the anxious Negro.

"It comes out even, Clooney," he said. "Piney."

"Yes, T.C."

"How many tickets we sell this run?"

"Five. Four canceled."

"That leaves one. Go and get him and give him his money back. Go wide around. Both ways."

"It's not a he, T.C."

"All right, goddamnit, go get her. Hop your ass!"

"It's really her and her kid," said Piney Newbold, not moving for the door.

"*Kid?*" gritted Madden. "*What* kid for Christ's sake?"

"The one this lady passenger's going to have in two days," the ticket agent said. "If we're lucky."

"Jesus Christ almighty!" exploded Madden. "A pregnant female? Nobody told me that. Where in the hell did she come from? It don't matter. She can't go on."

The plain anxiety of Piney Newbold deepened. "She claims she can, though. Says she's agoing sure. Says she has got to make it to Tucson, and she will."

"Well," snapped T.C. Madden. "She don't, and she ain't. You tell her that."

The assistant manager, Pima Bend Division, mopped sweaty forehead, pulled steel-rimmed spectacles down on long thin nose, stood a little taller than his five feet four inches.

"Mister Madden," he said, "we can't do that. Her ticket's punched and paid for."

T.C. Madden, forty-eight hours from losing everything, including the eleven years of his life he had put into Southwest Stagelines, flinched visibly.

The little telegrapher nodded, knowing where the conversation had come:

When Southwest Stagelines sold a ticket, that ticket carried the implied and implicit guarantee that its purchaser would arrive at destination for which passage had been booked "in good and sound condition and not out of pocket."

In another way of saying it, and a final way, when a passenger on Southwest bought a ticket for Tucson, he would get there if Southwest did—and what went for hes, went for shes; no backouts, no moneybacks.

"She goes," said T.C. Madden. "Goddamnit."

3

The Indians sat on the big hill above Pima Bend watching the town and smoking their corn-shuck cigarets. It was shortly after 8:00 P.M. Behind the hill three young boys out on their first raid tended the ponies. The men were waiting for the leader to advise them beyond this quiet hillside.

In the Apache fashion, the waiting was given over to recounting the day's work. Do-klini, a man very large for his squat people, had put the arrow across the driver's belly. His brother of the same mother, Dust Devil, a small man, had killed the second man atop the stagecoach. Dust Devil had used a rifle. There was some joking at Do-klini's old-fashioned bow. Also of the odd long-sleeved underthing the big arrow shooter had taken from the horse rancher killed up near the fort. It looked funny for a man to wear such a garment in the full of summer, when all of the rest of them rode only in their breechcloths and thigh boots.

"I think," said Noche, "that Do-klini is trying to become a white man."

Bosque thought this sally worth a chuckle.

Another brave, Nevado, old White Hair, so named for his prematurely snowy mane of hair, believed differently. He was a lonely man much preoccupied with tribal law and the ways of his people in sterner times. It was wrong, he frowned, for any Chiricahua to dress in a manner to imitate the hated White Eyes. It was immoral and dangerous. To give in anywhere to the white man was one more step in the death march of the Apache. Indeed, Do-klini ought not to be permitted to wear that strange red underthing.

The sixth warrior, Tubac, inclined to this harsh view of the enemy. And with present bitter Chiricahua cause. "Aye," he said. "How can we make a joke of such a thing when, even now, Nah-tez, who tried to halt our raid by going in peace to speak of honorable terms, is prisoner at Fort Gila? Remember, Nah-tez went there to speak for peace. Peace for all the Chiricahua. Remember, too, that it was the soldiers who asked Nah-tez to come in to the fort and sign a paper for us all."

He paused, frowning deeper still.

"It was only a trap the same as always. And they very nearly caught our leader, too. Only because he was wary and refused at the last instant to go in with his brother does he ride free with us tonight."

"And remember, they very nearly got all of us, anyway," continued Tubac angrily. "Or have you *tontos* forgotten those soldier bullets whizzing all around us when we broke to run for our ponies after they seized Nah-tez?" He drew down the mid-thigh reach of his soft-tanned riding boots. His fellows leaned close in the darkness to see the ugly inch-deep furrow still bleeding under its forming clot. "That is not the bite of a deer fly," growled Tubac. "I agree with White Hair. Do-klini is a fool, and we are fools for letting him be a fool."

The hulking brave, Do-klini, as good-natured as his wild and cunning people came, defended himself by indirection, the classic Indian way.

"There is no real cause to grow serious," he said to Tubac. "Peace or war, Nah-tez hates the white man. They will not get anything out of him."

"We all hate the white man," scowled Bosque. "I think Tubac is right. Your head is hollow as an old hornet's nest."

Do-klini was something approaching the Apache version of a barracks-room lawyer. He saw beauty in all things, especially when the price of the seeing was only a good lively Indian argument with himself appearing as defendant and friendly words flying all around instead of soldier lead.

"Oh, I am not so sure about that hating thing," he shrugged. "For example, I felt no hate when we went after that stagecoach this afternoon. You know, the one we ran right into that town down there." He pointed at the lights of Pima Bend, introducing the settlement itself as prima facie evidence of his own veracity. "I felt no hatred, either, when I was putting my arrows into that man who was riding up on the top driving the horses. Was not his friend shooting with his rifle at me? Moreover, we are not at war now. Nah-tez will be all right up there at the fort. He is a talker. They will listen to him. They will let him go. There will be peace. You will see. Love will come again."

"Love!" snorted Dust Devil. "How about that knife you put into that old horse rancher up there by the fort this morning? You know, after the soldiers jumped us and we got away and then needed fresh horses and stopped at that ranch to get them? Were you thinking love things, brother, when you killed that old man?"

"That was different!" said Do-klini indignantly. "I wanted his long-sleeved beneath-clothes. There is not another Apache with a buttoning-hole in the back of his pants to make dung through!"

"Bah!" interrupted White Hair, turning from Do-klini. *"Jefe,"* he said, appealing to the leader. "It is time for you to decide how we shall ride from here."

The leader did not reply at once. He had been having a dark-mind time since the raid on the ranch near Fort Gila. It had to do with something told him by the old Apache workhand at the ranch. This *anciano* had crawled out from under a hayrick after the killings to speak with the leader. He had told the latter something bad, but the leader had not then told them what it was.

So they waited now for him to speak.

As they did so, the moon rose, etching the brooding chief like the figure on a minted coin of silver. He was of average size for an Apache, short, squat, powerful. The eyes were level in set and widely spaced beneath a broad brow. The nose seemed broken by some accident of the past, giving him his spreading nostrils and indeed his very name. The mouth was narrow-lipped, large, a second line of straightness to match the fierce eyes. The face was a classic Chiricahua face, the only surprise in it the unexpected youthfulness of the man behind its unforgiving mask: Chatto, or *Chato* in the Spanish, "Flat Nose," next only to Geronimo in wildness and in war.

The young chief spoke now. "There is nothing to decide," he said, his voice deep. "He who spoke for us is dead."

There was an insucking of startled breaths.

"Nah-tez dead?" It was old Nevado, incredulously.

"Yes. Do not say his name again."

"Will you say how it was?"

"The soldiers killed him after we ran away. They said he tried to run also. They put him in the prison at the fort and he would not stay there. It is only a rude hut remember. No place for a Chiricahua chief."

"Do you believe it?"

"That he is dead, yes."

"But the other?"

"You mean the manner of his killing?"

"That is my meaning; that he really tried to escape."

"What does it matter now? We told him not to go down there. We said, 'Wait up at your own camp and thus make the soldiers come talk there.' How many of our people have been killed talking peace at the lying white man's place? I still cannot believe we let him go there."

"But you believe he is dead?"

"The old man at the ranch told me. The Apache. He heard it at the fort only the hour before we came."

Softly, Noche, Dust Devil, Do-klini, and the three remaining braves beyond White Hair, commenced to intone the Apache chant for the dead. They did not use the name of the great chief. Once the chant of the dead had been sung, no Apache would say aloud that name again. When the singing was done, the soul of the departed was consigned. Nah-tez, peace chief of all the Chiricahua people, literally would be no more.

White Hair, always a religious but cautious man, prayed only until the chanters were well into their doleful ritual, then said quietly to Chatto, "What will we do now? There is sure to be a war again. I don't mean raiding. A real war. Like in the old days."

"Yes." Chatto's deep voice came more quickly. It held the altered tone of decision, of necessity, even of urgency. "We must go back and gather up our women who are following us and run for our home in Mexico. The raid is over. We must do our best to escape. But, if we fail, we will still have our women."

White Hair nodded. "By this time perhaps you will have more than your woman following us," he said. "I suspect the child has come by now."

Chatto shook his turbaned head.

"She promised to keep him within her until I came," he said. "But we did not count on those soldiers jumping us after we left the women. If they had not shot so many of our horses, we would not have gone to that ranch to steal new ones."

"No," said his companion. "Nor killed those five people. Now the soldiers will be after us harder than ever. Yes, and more of them, also."

"Well, that is why we struck at the stagecoach, to draw off the soldiers from our women."

"And there you have more white men killed."

"Only to save our women."

"Yes, I suppose."

"You do not think they were too close to the women?"

"No, no. I did not say that. The one or two on the stage were fine. We had to do that."

"It is the five at the ranch, then. You think Lucero did not need to do that?"

"Just the men," said White Hair. "The old man and his son, yes."

"But not the son's woman and the two children?"

"No, he was wrong to do that."

"Lucero is my friend," Chatto frowned. "I trust him. He thought it must be done. You do not leave people behind to talk to the soldiers."

"Lucero does not," corrected White Hair.

Chatto did not answer him. Instead, he turned to the other men, instructing them to seek their mounts at the picket line behind the ridge. "We will ride until first light," he said. "We and the women should not have far to go to find each other by then."

The seventh brave, who had not spoken a word in all of the watching of the town, now answered for his companions. He was a barrel-chested, murderous-looking, tall Apache, strikingly handsome and graceful. Like Chatto, he spoke in a resonant bass and with natural dignity.

"As far as we must go, we shall go," he said.

Chatto put his small hand on the tall man's shoulder. "*Schichobe*," he said. "Old friend."

"Yes," said Lucero. "I hope it is a man-child."

"I will name it for you," promised Chatto. "Let us go over the ridge now."

There was a slight, blurred stirring of the night's shadows and the hill north and west of Pima Bend stood empty in the glare of the early spring moon.

Only the rocks were there, and the sandstone, and the mesquite and salt juniper and the silence.

The Fort Gila Rocks

4

The cavalry patrol waited in the Fort Gila rocks. Their two scouts, Bobbie and Peaches, had led them there after finding the camp of the Apache women abandoned only minutes before their arrival in the predawn of that day.

"They must come this way," Bobbie had told Lieutenant Kensington. "The tracks of their men follow the stage road, but the women will ride wide of that road and will come through this cut in the rocks."

Bobbie was an older scout from San Carlos reservation. He was a fullblood Mescalero and had no love for the Chiricahuas they pursued. In the corps of the Apache Scouts employed by the cavalry, he wore a sergeant's chevrons. Kensington listened to him.

The other scout's name was Pa-nayo-tishn, The Coyote Saw Him, known to the white man as Peaches. He was not an enlisted regular, as was Bobbie, but a volunteer with a most strange and recent history. He claimed to have escaped, within the week, from the raiding band of Chatto, having been an unwilling member of that band with invaluable information for his white friends of the cavalry regarding the location of the legendary Apache stronghold in the Sierra Madre of Mexico. Chatto, he told the captain commanding at Fort Gila, had just come up from Mexico, and, if the army would listen to Peaches, he could guide them back to the secret fortress on the retreating trail of Chatto. As a token of his trustworthiness, he offered to go right then with the cavalry after his former fellows, and it was upon this basis that Captain Herritt had sent him with Kensington's patrol.

This Indian, of course, the lieutenant did not trust.

Nor did he for one moment believe his fantastic tale of being held in the Mexican Sierra Madre stronghold against his will. Much less did he accept the idea that he had accompanied the bloody band of such a brigand and murderer as Chatto just so that he might escape at first opportunity to warn his white friends of the cavalry against Chatto and, even more than that, against the dreaded Geronimo. Kensington was more than busy chasing Chatto. He did not care to hear anything about Geronimo. Moreover, all of the army reports concerned Chatto and his reputed twenty-six Chiricahua killers. None had mentioned the older and far better known Geronimo.

Peaches continued to insist that not only was Geronimo up from Mexico, but that he had with him "two times the men" of Chatto. The little Indian also insisted that he himself was no Chiricahua but a friendly White Mountain Apache married to two Chiricahua women, having families with both and, hence, a real knowledge of the Chiricahua.

Captain Herritt had seen some truth here and, on a soldier's hunch and from a shortage of otherwise available Indian scouts at Fort Gila, had decided to put him under Mescalero Bobbie's charge. He was of course not entered upon the roles, nor in any way added to the record.

Presently, neither Bobbie nor Peaches was with the soldiers in the rocks. Both were still trailing the wary Chiricahua women. There were five women following their menfolk raiding ahead. Unusual on such a raid, one of the women was melon-big with child to come. Accordingly, it came many times to the mind, and heart, of volunteer Peaches to warn the women of his wives' people. But always the fierce eyes of the San Carlos-trained Bobbie were upon him. Moreover, Peaches well knew that the warrior squaws must be captured in order to discourage the wildly killing Chiricahua men under Chatto.

Well, it would turn out all right. Risky as always in such matters, surely. For the soldiers would get mean and cross waiting in the ovenbake of those rocks. Some of them, perhaps, might fire when they were told to hold fire. But this officer with them was no fuzz-chin boy. He would hold them safely. If Bobbie and Peaches did their part, staying to the rear of the women so that they would be captured when the soldiers rose up from the rocks calling for surrender, then it would be all right. The women could always get away later, slip off from the reservation and go home.

And taking them prisoner now would surely bring their

menfolk to give up the wartrail and go home as well, so holding the peace a little longer.

As an Apache who had gone over to the white man, young Peaches knew that the future of his wild people was foredoomed. The fighters, like these eleven Chiricahuas from whom he had deserted before the bloody business of the Steinhower killings, were admirable men, true Apaches. Yet they were what the tame Indians like Peaches called "crazies." Their minds were twisted. They did not understand the final power of the white man. Peaches did. Bobbie did. All of the Apache scouts, enlisted or irregular, understood it; still Peaches worried.

The worst had been when, just as they discovered the camp of the Chiricahua women that dawn, he had heard the wailing birth cry of an Indian infant. Peaches knew then that the melon-big woman had delivered her child, and that it was a man-child. Still, he knew he could not trust Bobbie with that which he, Peaches, wanted to do: go into the camp of the women and arrest them, guaranteeing them no harm.

Now he and the Mescalero pressed very closely behind the traveling women. The trail was easy to follow because of the birthing blood dropped by the new mother. Ordinarily, the band would have waited a few hours for the mother to gain strength and clot the blood. But these were Chiricahuas, the wildest of the wild; Peaches knew and Bobbie knew that their presence behind the women had been sensed. The quarry was nervous. They gave no time to the mother but beat their thin ponies with hand, heel, and stick, keeping them on the lope. The woman must either ride as hard or fall behind. Somehow it made Peaches proud that she chose to stay up with the band and to bleed for her child in this way. He even made the mistake of saying as much to Bobbie.

The Mescalero gave him a look that was not good.

"Chiricahua cub!" he said in a whispered hiss. "I would take it from her like a wolf whelp from a cutbank den."

Peaches stared at him disbelievingly.

"You would club a man-child of our people?"

Again Bobbie glared at him with black and burning eye. "The Chiricahua are not *my* people," he said.

Peaches fell silent. But now he knew that something bad was happening. He wanted to go at once wide around the women and get to the soldiers and see what they were doing. Indeed, after a few more rods of hand walking the mounts up the sandy wash just behind the nervous band ahead, he suddenly stopped. His pleasant face did not glow now but was dark with his fears.

"I am going quick and see the soldiers do not do anything wrong. I smell *dah-eh-sah* here; I smell death."

He swung up on his pony, holding red hand over the small brute's belling nostrils to prevent it from nickering or even blowing out noisily. The Mescalero immediately cocked his rifle. "Get down," he said, making the order by handsign, aiming the weapon with it.

"Shoot me," answered Pa-nayo-Tishn, called Peaches, "and the women will be gone."

Bobbie knew he could not fire. He leaped to strike at his comrade, however, with upraised, clubbed rifle. Peaches kicked him full in the face and, as he recoiled, drove downward into the Mescalero's coiled headband with the butt of his own weapon. Bobbie fell sideways into the sand, still holding the reins of his pony.

Peaches called down to him, "Forgive me, my brother," and lashed his own mount up out of the arroyo.

He was too late.

The Chiricahua women had reached the rocks.

Peaches saw the rifle fire bloom its smoke blossoms. He saw the ponies of the ambushed women staggering to the smash of the .50 caliber guns. In a little minute it grew quiet up there.

The volunteer scout sat and watched the soldiers come out of the rocks and prowl the bodies of the downed horses, finishing the ones that were yet alive.

A woman, still breathing, crawled from under a badly wounded companion. She got to her feet, dazed, not trying to run, only standing there calling in Apache for kindness, for capture. A nearby trooper put his gun's muzzle in her belly and shot her. She went slowly to the ground. Her friend beneath whom she had lain tried to reach her, comfort her. Another soldier, stepping over a dead horse, shot the second woman. Her soft moaning ceased with the ricochet of the trooper's bullet. Then and truly Peaches heard no more sound from up there.

But ah! below him in the track of the sandy dry wash winding down from the rocks of the ambush, there came a sliding of pebbles. It was the fifth Chiricahua woman. Her stricken eyes looked up in that instant and saw the mounted scout above her. They stared at one another. After a time of three breaths, Peaches slid his old rifle into its scabbard. The woman, newly born man-child at breast, passed on down the arroyo. Not once did she look back. Nor did she give any sign to the White Mountain scout.

Peaches waited, giving her time to find Bobbie and the tethered pony of the Mescalero. Then he rode down and put the slack body of the other scout over the withers of his own mount and led the burdened animal up the pebbled sands of the wash out upon the bouldered flat of the ambush. When he came up to them, the soldiers were sitting on the rocks smoking and talking in the loud relief that always follows a very bad thing. Most of them were quiet, though, in a little time, and the rest of the talking stopped when Peaches rode up and slid the body of Bobbie to the ground.

"What the hell happened to him?" rasped the sergeant, striding over from his conversation with the lieutenant. "Did he get hit?"

"No. Pony slip in rocks fall bad," answered Peaches. "Bobbie hit head hard. Pony run off quick." The diminutive scout shrugged. "Peaches can't help."

"Dumb Mescalero bastard," said the sergeant, examining the bloody headband. "He'll live." He stood up, eying Peaches, as the lieutenant came over. "Anything else?"

"Nothing else," said the Apache.

"All right," said Kensington to his sergeant. "Mount them up; we're losing time. Peaches."

"Yes, Loo'ten'an Kens'ton."

"Take Bobbie back to the fort. We will never head this bunch now. Tell Captain Herritt we are going on to Pima Bend as ordered. Bring a detail back here to get rid of these bodies. Then you will come on and rejoin. We shall still be in Pima Bend if you follow my directions. If you do not follow those directions, you will be arrested and hung."

He tried staring down the small Apache.

"Am I perfectly understood?"

"Peaches be there," answered the White Mountain scout; he did not drop his eyes.

Kensington took the men out of the rocky flat at a smart trot. They were up the incline and gone out through the pass, westward, before Peaches broke his dark eyes away from them to glance far down the arroyo-cut slope to the east. Down there, too small in the distance for any save Apache vision, a crawling dot paused against the skyline of the backing ridge.

If the tiny mounted figure waved, Peaches could not be sure. He only knew that he waved to her.

Then she was gone.

"Go far," said Peaches softly. "And do not ever stop." Then he, too, was gone from that place and only *dah-eh-sah* remained there.

5

"We go out through the sagebrush." Madden hooked a thumb toward the emptiness west of the single line of false fronts huddling along Pima Bend's Main Street. "Once away, we cut back. Hit the road maybe five miles out. We go till daybreak, laying over at the Wells. Same thing next night. Sunup should show us Tucson."

He turned to the pale girl passenger.

"Running at night, ma'am," he said, "we miss the Indians, mainly. They favor the day." He spun about on the assembled crew. "All right, Feeny. You and Hunker see the lady aboard. Keep a sharp eye out."

Striding forward, Feeny Gleason took his first command. He had donned over bib overalls a fringed buckskin coat of the Buffalo Bill Cody style. In his low-crowned sodbuster's hat a hastily red-painted turkey feather drooped moltingly. The Civil War Spencer hung by an ancient harness belting from one shoulder. On the other shoulder a cavalry cartridge bandoleer containing seven verdigrised rounds of ammunition gave him balance and completed his Indian fighting outfit.

"Foller along right smart," he ordered the lone and anxious passenger, walking with his knocked knees bent painfully outward so that he might seem properly bowed of leg. "We got hell to harrow twixt here and Sifford Wells, ma'am. Remember, stay down low when the arrers commences to fly, and always—"

"Feeny!" Madden bawled. "Get out of here!"

He took a deep, deep breath. "Clooney," he said. "We can't wait no more for the deputy. You're going to have to ride shotgun." The Negro stableman blanched. Madden picked up the tin cup and blew out the stub of candle flickering in it. "Don't fret now," he said. "You'll do just fine."

The black swamper did not answer. He felt his way along the rear hall, slipped out into the wagon yard.

Madden, waiting to hear the door close, went out through

the telegraph room. Piney was there pretending to be working on the books. The super said a loud goodnight and exited the street door. As the latch clicked behind him, he heard another click; this one from the handcuff snapped upon his thick right wrist.

"Let's go," said old Jules Hoberman.

Madden gathered himself instinctively, ragingly.

But the old man had been and seen the elephant a few times. He had heard the cactus owl hoot and the chaparral bird sing at midnight. The bore end of his .45 Colt felt big as a posthole auger against the smallribs of T.C. Madden.

I reckon you know I don't pack this thing for ballast, T.C.," he said. "Come easy."

Halfway across the wagon yard on his way to the repair shed and the waiting, loaded Concord, Clooney Borrum drew up to sudden halt.

It was a windstill night. Pima Bend echoed with emptiness, its citizens Indian-scared off the street. The gruff voice from out in front of the stage office carried easily to the startled Negro. At once, he bent low and ran for the mud wall of the loose stock corral fronting Main. He was in time to see the old sheriff and T.C. Madden walking past. They were bound for the jail, and old Jules was telling Mr. T.C. how it went against his grain to lock up an old friend, but that it was the safest way that he knew to keep the Fort Gila stage in the repair shed: The hired help was surely not going to make any Apache runs without owner T.C. Madden to boss the job and, moreover, if T.C. would quit gritting his teeth and let down he could avoid a bad case of handcuff wrist for both of them. "You know," said the grizzled lawman, "that you and that damn coach ain't going noplace until the U.S. Cavalry says so. So why don't you slack off?"

Crouching behind the wall, Clooney Borrum knew near panic as he slunk along following the two men.

Mr. T.C. in jail? The shotgun deputy missing? All that gold money aboard and ready to go? And who was there now to get that limpy old Concord down to Tucson in time? Sweet Jesus, was Mr. T.C. going to lose his stage line, after all?

Well, clearly he was. He plainly had to lose it; unless—unless—

The panic was real now.

Dear Lord God, it was up to Clooney Borrum to do it, or

it was up to nobody! Could Feeny Gleason or Hunker Larsen drive a six-horse hitch through the moon-spraddled shadows of a pothole *mal-país* jack-rabbit road? Could either of them even ride shotgun up top? How about the passengers? Whee-ooo, roll on Jordan! One little bitty old bad-scared white girl about to bust wide with her first kid? Good and kind Jesus, wasn't there anybody but Clooney Borrum to do it? A black man? A nigger? Taking a white man's stage to Tucson without his say? No sir. God help Clooney Borrum and God help Mr. T.C. and the Southwest Stageline, but it had to be a white man *somewheres* to boss that run.

As the impossibilities multiplied in Clooney's mind, he came to the end of the mud wall and brought up with a jolt against the adobe of the jailhouse; the thudding of his notably hard head on the ancient mud bricks drew an interested spectator to the cellblock's one window. There was a moment of mutual moonlight peering. "Is that you?" said the prisoner, low-voiced.

"Is that you?" countered Clooney Borrum, as carefully.

Both men laughed. Not much. Surely not loud. But a small quiet inside laugh shared by the hard-driven.

"Where at is the deputy?" inquired the practical Clooney. "We ain't see'd him."

"Good reason," said the drifter. "He's in the cell next to me. Sleeping peaceful as a dead calf. Sheriff come back and caught him hassayampa-ing me about getting paid two hundred in gold to shotgun your boss's Tucson run through the Injun country. Sheriff had to cold-cock the kid when he flashed his fancy draw. That old man's a pistol. He would haul hell out of its shuck."

A heartbeat of the summer night pulsed between them.

"What's your name, friend?" asked the prisoner.

"Clooney Borrum. What they call you?"

The prisoner laughed.

"Anything they want to," he said.

"Suits me," whispered Clooney.

Again the awkward silence and then the prisoner's voice altered.

"Listen, Mister Clooney Borrum, I'm into the high water way over my hocks. I need help and need it fast."

"I knows your trouble," said the black swamper. "Five years in Yumer. I cain't he'p you."

The drifter gripped the bars. "Sure," he said. "Maybe I can

help you. Man can see you're carrying double, too. It don't hurt to share the load."

Clooney looked hard at him. For a reason he never knew, nor paused to puzzle over, he told the drifter straight out what the trouble was, and, when the story was done, the bone-thin horsethief understood it.

"Alls you need," he said, "is a shotgun guard."

"What we needs," said Clooney Borrum, "is a white man up top to boss things."

He could hear the prisoner's breath suck sharply in. The voice changed timbre yet again.

"I ain't working right now," he said.

"You?" The Negro swamper stared.

"Get me out and you've got your shotgun man *and* your white man. Ponder that, friend Clooney."

Clooney pondered it, and pondered it again, and came upon the hard rock hidden in it.

"Iffen I could get you out, I could get Mr. T.C. out likewise. Then you just a hossthief agin."

The prisoner, desperate, began to plead. He was interrupted by an angry rising of the voices in the jail's outer office, a curse, a scuffle, a knocking over of furniture—and silence. The cellblock door opened to admit lampshine and the figure of Sheriff Jules Hoberman, puffing some, dragging the unconscious body of his friend T.C. Madden across the block and into cell three. The drifter, away from his window instantly, heard the old man grunt, "Sorry, T.C., the horsethief's got the only room with a view." Then cell three was locked, and, unexpectedly, the lawman limped over to the drifter's cage. "You *did* steal that horse?" he said.

"Yes sir."

The old man nodded, started away, turned around,

"Goddamnit," he said. "Why for'd you do it?"

There was not any answer, and he did not expect any. He went on out. The drifter sprang for the window. "Clooney! Clooney Borrum! You still there?"

"Right here. But I gots to go. Old sheriff on a rompage sure now. Goodbye, Mister Nobody."

But, even as he spoke, the desk lamp in the outer office was turned down to night-low. Both men heard the door latch open and shut. Clooney raced for the front of the jail. Jules Hoberman was just locking up for the night and for sure this time. He put the big key ring on its belt hook behind the ancient .45 and, with a sigh that Clooney thought blew dust off the jail-door window ledge, headed finally for home.

Whee-ooo. Here was some kind of opportunity but a black man could not say just what kind.

Maybe the best thing was to go home like the sheriff.

Nobody could blame a nigger for that.

"Clooney! Clooney, man! You still out there?"

The swamper moved mechanically to obey the pleading summons, then stopped short. He did not want to talk to the white man again. He sorrowed for him, but there was nothing Clooney Borrum could do for him, nor for anybody. The Pima Bend jail was locked up tight, and Mr. T.C. and all that Clooney cared about was locked up tight inside it. What in hell could he possibly do for a horsethief?

"Clooney, friend? Please—!"

Clooney could not bear that final sound. It was too desperate and, Lord God, he knew what desperate was. He had at least to go and listen to the poor devil. After all, he *was* a white man and he had called Clooney Borrum "mister." More, too. Clooney remembered that one year of his own in Yuma Prison.

At the cell window the prisoner's thin arm came out through the bars and seized his shirt.

"Try the bars," he said. "Take aholdt of them firm and give them a wrench twistingways."

Clooney did what he was told to do—he always had—and he could feel what the prisoner meant; the whole frame of the old Spanish metalwork was loose in its mud socket. But not Clooney Borrum nor any other ordinary human being was going to just rip that old ironwork out of there. It was still time to go. Sadly he turned away, once more starting off across the corral.

But the drifter was not thinking of human strength, only of human will.

"Clooney," he called after him. "You got to have a spare team and a set of leather drag tugs."

The swamper came about in disbelief. "Sweet Jesus," he gasped. "You ain't going to pull the hull contraption out'n there!"

"No sir," said the prisoner soberly. "You are."

Clooney Borrum moved slowly back to the cellblock window. He stared up at the thin, bearded drifter. His mind labored over all that had brought him to his moonlit prison window and all that would go out of his life with Southwest Stagelines.

Presently the slope went out of his big shoulders.

He threw back his head, filled his broad chest with the hot, dry air of the desert night. Clooney Borrum had made up his mind. All doubts were done with. He felt like a full man for the first time in weary memory. He knew what he was going to do—what he had to do—shown the way by a drifter, a drunk and a horsethief.

"Thank you, Mister Shotgun Rider," he said, and turning, raced the moonshadows across the silent corral to the repair shed.

6

The eleven Apaches, the boys riding tall as the men, came down out of the cedar brakes along the mesa and sent their little horses at a lope along the Indian track down the narrow valley. The sun was an hour high and they had been pressing hard since first pink light.

Somewhere soon they should meet the women.

This was the path.

Apaches had traveled it from time out of memory. A white man might know of it, but if he did he would avoid it. Ahead lay a dike of red rock rising cross-valley. For a few minutes the turbaned horsemen could not see the far side. They never did get to see it. Just short of the dike's crest, they pulled in their snorting mounts.

Silhouetted against the red sun, the lone figure of a horseman appeared without warning.

The wind lay behind the stranger. The ponies of the war party backed and belled nostrils. In a moment they flicked ears, nickered in a glad way. This was a friend; they smelled an Indian horse and an Indian horseman up there on the rise of the redstone dike.

But Chatto's eyes were keener than the noses of his whickering mustangs. That was not a horseman. It was a woman. Chatto's woman. And in her arms the war leader could see the cradled form of the newborn—his man-child that he would name Lucerito.

With a glad cry, very rare for him, never heard before even by old White Hair, the renegade put his pony up the slope toward his woman and their child. On the crest, the woman sat as if a part of the rock beneath her. No answering cry came from her wide lips. She still said no word of greeting when Chatto slid his mount to a halt beside her, and she moved only to give over to her younger mate the man-child for which, due to the difference in their years, they had prayed so hard.

Chatto received the babe, watching as he did so the eyes and the vacant face of his woman. He felt the stiffness of the tiny form within his strong hands, and he knew.

"A man-child?" he said gently to his wife.

"Yes, and beautiful," she answered.

Chatto looked down, parting the swaddling blanket to see the face of his son. It was not there. Where it would have been had passed a .50 caliber bullet of the soldiers.

The stillness upon the slope was a felt agony.

Chatto raised his eyes and gazed at his woman in mute compassion. Gently, his dark hands re-covered the pitiful form he held. He turned his horse and went back down the slope, the woman following him upon the pony of the Mescalero, Bobbie. The men pulled aside from the trail letting their leader pass. They did not look at the woman and only once looked at their leader with his small son in his arms. But they remembered it always in their hearts.

Chatto was weeping.

7

Clooney came panting across the loose stock corral reining the spare team at the trot. It was but the work of a moment for him to pass the straightbar, a short pipe, in through the cell bars to the prisoner.

The latter placed the straightbar parallel to the cell window casement, across the vertical run of the cell bars. Clooney then passed him the hook of the drag chain, which the prisoner snugged over the straightbar, saying tensely, "Ease the team into it." He retained his grip on the bar until Clooney noodled the nervous team into just taking up the slack in the tugs and the drag chain. There was a bad moment when the hook slipped, but then it caught and the straightbar bit into the cell bars and the prisoner ducked back. "Let 'em go," he said to Clooney Borrum.

"Hee-yah!" the latter ordered his team, and the coach horses squatted and dug in and hit their breastbands and

collars with a smack and pop that literally exploded the cell
bars, ancient iron frame and all, out of the moldering adobe
of the Pima Bend jail.

A cascade of the big mud bricks spilled out in wake of the
flying window, and the prisoner virtually walked out through
the wall.

"Lay on them lines," he said to Clooney Borrum. "Deputy's
stirring in yonder and so is your Mister T.C. One of them's
bound to holler for the old sheriff—likely the deputy to lick his
hand and make up."

The white horsethief and the black stablehand ran as one
after the plunging team. Frantically, they dodged the bounding whiffletrees, drag chain, and hook. "Got's to slack off,"
panted the team's driver. "I ain't run no furlong on this pace
since'st I were sot free. Whar at's the big haste?" The
sprinting prisoner gasped back that the big haste was wherever the wise old pecko of a sheriff might be. "Maybe he's
went home like you say and maybe he ain't," puffed the
white man. "Lay it to them bays and don't look back!"

"Praise Gawd," answered Clooney. "Here we is."

He hauled back on the team and his companion saw that
they had reached the repair shed. Only one half of the
double-hung door was opened. Into this space Clooney now
gee-ed his team. The liberated horsethief followed on faith,
stumbling in the blind darkness.

Clooney halted the team, calming the excited horses with
that power that was his over their kind. He shut the half
door. Rasping a sulphur match on the seat of his overalls, he
palm-cupped it, lit the nearside coach lantern, trimmed it
instantly to a small blue flutter.

"Psstt!" he signaled, and Hunker Larsen loomed out of the
barn's bat-cave interior. "This here's the new shotgun man,"
he told the blacksmith. "He ain't Mister Pinky, but he will
hafter set in for him."

Hunker studied the squinting, bearded figure huddled by
the barn door. He nodded acceptance, saying nothing.

Clooney fastened the spare team to coach's rear.

"Say, partner," the drifter said, remembering suddenly.
"Where at's my steeldust and forty-dollar saddle?"

"Sweet Jesus, you wants to steal him *agin*?"

"Why not? It's the same five years in Yuma."

"That's so. But Mister T.C. say to leave the steeldust be,
and that's moreso."

The drifter, looking at the ready-loaded coach, the

hooked-on teams, the sputtering brass running lantern; as suddenly recalled something else far more important than the stolen race horse: He was out of jail.

"God," he shivered. "You done it, Clooney friend."

"Mister Hunker," called the black swamper. "You please to run back the smithy door all the way."

The blacksmith nodded again and was gone.

Clooney reached into the empty baggage boot of the Concord to produce a 10-gauge L.C. Smith doublegun, which he tossed to the drifter. "She's bored cylinder and cylinder," he said. "Both sides crammed full of buckload. Fires the front trigger fust. Owner didn't leave no will. Reckon she's yourn."

The drifter bobbed his shaggy head. "Reckon I thank you," he said nervously. "Hadn't we best light out?"

For answer, Clooney blew out the coach lantern. A square of starlight smeared the rear blackness of the big shed. Hunker Larsen was opening the slide-back door that led out through the airy ramada of his lean-to smithy. The starlight limned the coach. Hunker's thick-muscled form appeared, entering the right-hand door of the stage. Feeny Gleason's voice greeted him. Then stillness.

Clooney Borrum and the stranger ran up opposite sides of the coach, swung up to its driver's box, so anxious they banged heads resoundingly.

Both cursed, then both laughed the small inside laugh they had shared at the cellblock window.

"We swarmed that like two striped-ass Barbary apes looking for the same place to shit," said the white man, and the black man laughed again.

"Sure enough we did, Mister Somebody," he said.

He gathered the lines, eased off the stick of the setbrakes. In low tones he instructed his companion to "hang tight on," adding some gibberish in animaltalk for the horses. The horses responded as if the heavy lines in the stableman's grasp were marionette strings, as if they were lightly bobbing puppets restrained by silken threads. But the big coach was moving, and not by any gossamer twines; it was rolling.

How the six-horse hitch was actually gotten unsnaked and put straight out through smithy ramada into back-of-town sagebrush and salt bush flat was a thing of higher horse learning than the drifter knew. All he understood of it was that, a moment after Clooney yelled "low bridge!" they were away from Pima Bend running under nothing but the Arizona stars. For the first time the situation assumed the form of reality for the nameless horsethief.

"You know something, Mister Clooney Borrum?" he laughed excitedly to the swaying black driver. "We might really make it. We're almost free—!"

Clooney Borrum did not answer him. He only tightened the lines, braced manured work boots the harder on the pitching dash. He had been almost free a long time.

8

The Fort Gila patrol, a dozen men, the old first sergeant, and the senior lieutenant rode on from their morning's work in the rocks with a medium-bad case of Apache nerves building in the watchful ranks.

They had no native scout remaining, dared not put out troopers on flank for fear of having them picked off. Another officer would have quit with the women. But H.C. Kensington had orders cut for Pima Bend. The risk of the Chiricahua men discovering their murdered dead and hurricaning up from behind deterred him not at all. And he was right, damn him. They made noonhalt, rode on, saw nothing, struck the river at dark, raised the Bend a scant hour after moon-up, and were safe.

For himself, Lieutenant Kensington felt very right with his cavalry world. It was only 9:00 P.M., grand time down from Fort Gila. Encountering the Chiricahua women so early in the day had been hunter's luck. Not encountering their men subsequently had been more of the same. Hornets' nest business, you know. But give the red devils twenty-four hours to sing their morbid chants and burn their pagan *hoddentin* powder in the funeral fires—or whatever other red nonsense they went through for their dead—and they would quit buzzing. Kensington knew them, the sneaking cowards.

And he would get them.

When they had quieted down, of course.

A frown, the bare trace of a moment's doubt, interrupted the absolute sureness of the sunburned face.

Six years wise to the ways of the Apache, Kensington had been twice passed over for promotion and did not understand it. The reprimands he had been given for that affair in the San Pete range and the one down at Cow Springs were certainly not warranted. A man was trained and paid to be a soldier. The duty and obligation of the soldier was to seek and destroy the enemy and/or to maintain the peace, whichever. In cases where that enemy had violated all terms of the peace and was, in fact, upon the wartrail the no-quarter rule applied sub rosa, and every officer upon the frontier knew that it did. Why then single out Lieutenant Kensington? Both reprimands had stated, "for over-zealous prosecution or failure to follow implicitly departmental policy in face of granted provocation," which meant simply that a good officer had pressed his duty to the fullest limit of opportunity against a merciless, and a murderous, foe. That this pressing had embarrassed his immediate commanders with those idiots in the Indian Bureau, those sob-sisters and weeping-hearts safely back in Washington, D.C., who knew nothing of the bloody truth in Arizona Territory, seemed entirely beside the military point to the aging lieutenant. A man did his duty.

The frown eased. The moment's slumping of the ramrod seat was banished with the return of certainty.

This time it was different.

Apache women who rode in the field with their warriors were fair game by all rules, published or sub rosa.

Such casualties, unlike those incurred in attacking an established rancheria or mapped encampment, required not even a uniform report. You made your count of the bodies, sent back for your burial detail, pushed forward your patrol, and commenced savoring your new grade.

Captain Harry Kensington.

Grand, just grand.

Or perhaps Captain Henry C. Kensington. Yes, a bit more of the Academy "ring" to that, eh? Ha, ha.

No, wait. It still did not have that horse soldier sound to it. That magic something-in-a-name that caught the fancy of the eastern press, ensnared the loyalty and devotion of the damned civilian imagination that, in the unfair end of it all, made or broke the career officer on the Indian frontier.

Like "Yellow Hair" Custer.

Or "Redbeard" Crook.

Say! how about H.C. "Wild Horse Harry" Kensington? Then, later, when it was unadorned General Kensington, people would know it was not just *some* General Kensington, but General Wild Horse Harry Kensington, by God!

That was it.

No possible question about it.

The officer's laugh of relief burst happily.

Old soldier, First Sergeant Emmett Bourke, riding at his elbow, glanced up, startled. He had never heard the lieutenant laugh, happily or otherwise.

"Sir?" he said, to be saying something.

"Bourke," the officer answered, "do we have a United States marshal's office here in Pima Bend?"

"No sir. Only the local sheriff."

"What's his name?"

"Hoberman, sir."

"Is he a good man, sergeant?"

By this, Bourke understood the officer to be inquiring if the particular lawman was for or against the U.S. military. It was not, in the context of time and place, an idle query.

"Yes sir. Very good man, sir. Little old, but on the job."

They were coming out of the sagebrush now, columning right with the wheel ruts of the stage road to pick up Main Street and the kerosene lights of the town. The column leader nodded in pleased acknowledgment of the answer to his question, stiffened spine, threw back squared shoulders.

"Pick up the canter," he told the sergeant, touching spurs to his own mount. "This is the United States Cavalry riding in."

9

The morning, begun with the finding of Chatto's woman and the dead man-child, was wasted following the cold track of the cavalry patrol into Pima Bend. Now, the sun noon-high, the Chiricahua men sat once more upon the hills above the town pondering their luck; the soldiers must have entered the settlement the previous night within the same hour that the Indians had departed to rendezvous with their women.

But their luck was about to change. Pa-nayo-tishn, The Coyote Saw Him, came riding squarely under their guns as they rested. It would never have happened save that sun and wind were against the volunteer scout. He caught neither rifle barrel glint, nor pony smell.

"*Hola,*" Chatto called out to him in Spanish, the second tongue of their people. The young chief eased off the hammer of his rifle, not smiling. "You live because you let my woman live," he said.

Peaches thanked him, indicating no fear.

"My two wives are Chiricahua, as you know," he told Chatto. "My own firstborn was also of this moon. I know your man-child is dead. I weep with you."

"We should kill him," said Lucero passionately.

"Yes," agreed Dust Devil. "He has ridden with us and deserted us. If we let him go, he will lead them after us. Kill him. I am sorry, Coyote," he apologized to Peaches. "But these are bad times for us."

"Kill him," voted Noche, cocking his rifle.

"Kill him," echoed Bosque, who had never uncocked his weapon.

Burly Do-klini put cedar shaft to his bow of Comanche ironwood. "Well," he sighed, "for myself I like him. Why do we not encourage him to tell us a little before we kill him? He has been skulking around that soldier fort up there. He must know much we do not."

Old Nevado, old White Hair, cocked his head.

Do-klini had a way getting down to things.

"Yes," the older brave said. "Go ahead, Coyote. Tell us what you have learned up there." He paused, studying the white man's scout, waiting. His rifle was not even in his hands, but Peaches knew this old man and trusted him. He told a straight-tongue story:

Bobbie, the Mescalero whose hatred had put the Chiricahua women and children under the guns of the cavalry, was dying of the head injuries Peaches had given him with the metal-shod butt of his old long rifle. If he did die, Peaches would be judged for murder. It was especially bad for him because the captain up at the Fort knew he had been with Chatto. It made the captain look bad, so the captain had talked over the wires with Redbeard Crook at San Carlos about what to do with Peaches. Peaches had not waited to learn what Redbeard said, however. He had his orders to report in the field to his own officer, Lieutenant Kensington, and so he had fled confinement and here he was. If his friends, the Chiricahua, would speak with Chatto's woman they would know that Coyote was their friend, really, and then they would permit him to go on.

"Estune," he pleaded with the woman. "Tell them."

Estune was not her real name. It meant only one who was a mature matron, a married or settled female. The woman received the plea with no show of emotion. Her features had not changed in expression since the ambush rocks. But she now uttered her first word in all of that tortured time of the day's ride, and the word was clear, "*anh*, yes," and the life of Peaches was saved.

Chatto, overruling Lucero and the others, spoke with him who was a half brother through his Chiricahua wife.

"*Sikisn*," he said in his deep voice, "Brother. If you will tell me that you will not lead the soldiers after us any more this time, you may go on. What is your answer?"

Peaches in truth had no answer, yet before he might admit as much, or frame some life-prolonging lie, he was paroled by a higher authority.

Two of the three youth warriors along with the party, presently assigned guard among the boulders below the rest-halt site, came into view dragging a frightened woman of the town. She proved to be the half-breed wife of Piney Newbold out looking for her people and asking upon capture by the alert young men to see Chatto at once and to warn him.

The young guards had thought to cut her throat, but the creature's mention of Chatto had saved her.

It developed further to the captive's benefit that her mother had been a Chiricahua of Mexican birth known to both Noche and Bosque. As with the damned Coyote from Fort Gila, let this half-blood she-wolf of their people tell her tale before any more talk of throat slitting. Start with the woman. She had even later news than the little peach-cheeked white man's scout.

Chatto looked into the Pima Bend woman's eyes a long moment and then grunted, "*Anh*, go ahead."

The woman's story brought them all to leaning farther forward on their haunches.

Did they think the stagecoach they had shot full of arrows and rifle-bullet holes was still below in the repairing barn of the stage line company? Did they calm their concerns as to the whereabouts of the strong cavalry patrol by imagining that it yet rested in bivouac hidden by some buildings of the town? Or, indeed, had gone back up to Fort Gila? Was it, finally, a disillusion of their wishful thoughts that the white men stupidly believed the attack upon the stagecoach had been the work of some other Chiricahua? Or that the towns-people were not fully aware of the true identity of the raiders? Well, then, let them listen: The stagecoach was gone in the dark of the night before, racing for Sifford Wells and bound, the following night, for Tucson and final safety; the cavalry had departed in the same darkness, resting but a few hours in the loose stock corral of the stage line before taking the track of the stagecoach to arrest it and return it to Pima Bend; the leader of the raiders and of the killers up near Fort Gila was known by repaired telegraph wires to be none other than the cousin of her own mother's sister among the American Chiricahua—did they all know such a man, one known as Chatto, Flat Nose?

And did Chatto know that he would be arrested for the killings he had done, and he would be dealt with by white man's justice in such matters? Strung up into the air by a rope about his neck to kick until *dah-e-sah* released him? Or at very merciful least sent away for all of his remaining life to that place of imprisonment far to the east from whence no Apache had returned?

The woman had heard this from both the cavalry officer and the town's old-man-of-the-law, she claimed. Now she did not know anything of the stern-looking pony soldier chief but she could tell them all that Sheriff Hoberman did not twist the truth.

"You all know old Jules," she had concluded.

Again Chatto studied her eyes and the lines of her broad half blood's face.

"*Anh*," he growled. "We know him, but how do you know all of this that you tell us? And how do we know that you know it?"

The woman was still much afraid but spoke with her eyes steady and the lines of the face firm.

. "My husband is the second chief at the stage lines," she said. "What he tells me, I tell you. That is all."

Here the scout Peaches moved forward.

"Not quite all," he said to Chatto. "She forgot to tell you that her husband is also the telegraph man in this town—the one who talks over the wires all the time to Fort Gila and even to San Carlos."

"Ahhhh!" said Chatto.

The young guards were commended and sent back to their watch below. A council of the seven grown men was called, the woman of Chatto attending it without demur. Peaches and the wife of Piney Newbold were bound to stunt cedars nearby. The Chiricahua talked animatedly for ten or twelve minutes.

At one time the argument halted while a member came over to ask the Newbold woman what she wanted? What had brought her to come and look for Chatto and the

Chiricahua party? To this, the townswoman had answered that she was tired of the white man's living and wished to go home, to live with the Chiricahua again, down in Pa-gotzin-kay, the Stronghold, south in old Mexico. "*Chin-da-see-lee,*" she told the council member in remembered Apache. "I have the homesickness."

A second interruption occurred when another man came over to inquire of Peaches if he would prefer to ride on with them or to be shot where he was?

The question was fairly put, and the volunteer army scout understood that it was. He also understood that his reply must not be insincere. "Tell the council that I am not homesick," he instructed carefully, "but that I will not try to escape. Also that, since my medicine brought me to this camp of my brothers, it is telling me that I must stay with them, that I have no choice but to ride on with them as a Chiricahua brother by marriage."

The man to whom he gave the message looked puzzled.

"What does your answer mean?" he frowned.

Peaches grew even more careful. "It means that I do not wish to be shot in this place. My medicine is bad here. It tells me *dah*, no. Ride on, ride on—!"

Now the man thanked him and departed. Almost at once the council broke up. The tall wife of Chatto came moving gracefully past Peaches, saying, "You will not die here." The men following her cut both the small Apache scout and the Pima Bend woman free. A spare mount was brought up for the woman. The party swung at once to saddle. Chatto and his wife, with the handsome bachelor Lucero, led the way. The gait was a long rolling lope. Peaches looked over at Do-klini, his trail companion and guard.

"What was the vote?" he said.

"Na-koo-say," answered the friendly brave.

Peaches knew what that meant. He looked up at the position of the sun and down at the quality of the horses of the Chiricahua war party. The answer was bad. The council had decided for *zas-tee*, the kill. They were going after the nearest isolated white people, and they had the time and the horses to beat the darkness to the chosen victims: the cavalry patrol that had murdered Chatto's man-child and which now must be resting with the recaptured stagecoach at Sifford Wells, hard by the secret Apache waterhole called Na-koo-say.

But Peaches was an Apache, a son of the desert. He knew

well the ultimate dogma of his harsh environment—survive. The white people of the stage line, as well as the soldiers of his patrol, were beyond his simple help. He could only look after Pa-nayo-tishn, The Coyote Saw Him.

"*Enthlay-sit-daou*," he said gravely to Do-klini. "You are a wise and calm person. Thank you."

"It was not any considerable thing, Coyote," the big Chiricahua shrugged. "Cover its tracks in your memory."

Querecho Mesa

10

W.K. Suggins, Jr. was sitting up and taking nourishment. It was a cup of cold black coffee brewed hours ago for the vanished horsethief. But old Jules was too busy straightening out his rudely awakened town to do any fancy cooking for the inmates. Pima Bend, the metropolis of the White Mountains, was not accustomed to being routed out of a sound sleep at 9:00 P.M. of an ordinary weeknight. After all, how often did a cavalry patrol, a jail bust-out, and a stagecoach stealing arrive at one and the same time?

With the jailhouse locked up tight and the old sheriff home snoring his wheezy head off?

And up to a hundred bloodthirsty Cherry Cow Apaches swarming the city limits?

And the U.S. of A. Cavalry saddling up again, right then, only a couple of rest-hours after they had pulled in from Fort Gila? Saddling up to go on after the rustled stagecoach and bring it safe-back before the Indians beat them to it? Beat them to it and finished up the job they had started by killing shotgun messenger Charley Broadus and gut-shooting the driver, little Petey Goheen? Mister, that was a full-house night in any man's territorial town!

W.K. Suggins, Jr., straining to see what he might of the lively street from his number two cell, winced ashen-faced to the staggering pains in the bones of his lumpy skull where old Jules had stretched him for nothing at all. Goddamn the old devil, he would get his!

For Christ's sake, what had W.K. done that was outside the law? Gone out and got a better paying job? Shit, he had told the old bastard he was going to have to do that. That no man could live on what Pima Bend wanted to pay a deputy. Shit again. There was no law on the Arizona books that he

42

had broken. No way in the whole of the territory that he could be held more than overnight.

Well, shit, there wasn't.

What was the old fart going to charge him with?

Trying to take the stage to Tucson?

Turning in his badge for two hundred dollars and a chance to see those California oranges?

Like hell he was.

W.K. was innocent and, by God, he would make that old man eat dogshit before he was through with him.

"Goddamn him—" he began, speaking over-shoulder to his cellblock companion in number three cell, "I'll—"

He broke off, realizing for the first time that number three cell was empty, its door swinging wide. Man, he had been belted harder than he thought. Last time he had looked, Madden had been in there shaking his head and growling threats against the political future of Sheriff Jules Hoberman that made even W.K. blush. Now he was gone, obviously let and not busted out, too.

Son of a bitch. What did that mean?

The deputy got his answer from the source, from old Jules Hoberman, just then entering the cellblock. The lawman had his jailhouse key ring out and Suggins's quick-draw gun rig hanging over the other arm. He opened number two cell, tossed the gun rig to W.K., and said, plainly distressed, "Pinky, there's hell to pay; I got to trust you."

"You don't got to do nothing for me," snarled the deputy, buckling on and tying down his rig. "I'm in business for myself right from here."

"No," said the old man, frowning, "no you ain't."

"The shit I ain't," said W.K., settling the rig.

Old Jules only shook his head.

"What you are," he explained, "is duly deputized sheriff whiles I'm away. You want to look that up in the books after I'm gone, you do it. You're going to find you ain't a legal limb to lean on. Comes down to Territory Sheriff and the power to deputize under plain-and-present danger-times, there ain't no appeal."

W.K. spread his legs. "The shit there ain't," he said, gun hand flexing.

"Pinky," sighed the old lawman, "you know any other word but shit?"

The deputy eyed him. He could not handle this old man in his mind. He knew he was not quick enough for him. He was like an old dog-wolf. Maybe he could no longer hamstring a full-grown bull, but he could sure as hell put down a yearling from behind—and had.

"Shit," said W.K. Suggins, Jr.

"Likely," nodded old Jules. "Now you listen to me."

The instructions were that W.K. would watch the town while old Jules accompanied the cavalry after the missing Tucson stage. Reason for old Jules going along was to watch T.C. Madden. Reason for the stage line super going along was that he had fifteen thousand dollars of his life's savings in gold aboard that coach, and, one hell of a lot more to the point in Jules Hoberman's mind, Madden knew that road to Sifford Wells—and the Indian country all about it—a day's ride better than the next man to him in such knowledge. Reason for old Jules going to shepherd the paroled stage line super, rather than W.K. Suggins, Jr., was that old Jules could trust old Jules.

"It ain't no use to argue it, Pinky," he said. "I don't rightly hunger after the job, you know. But that damned stiff-ass lieutenant from up to the fort he don't know a foot of the way west of here, and he ain't got his Apache scouts along. One's been sent back and the other ain't caught up yet. That plainly leaves one man down thisaway can guide them hoss soldiers through to Sifford Wells by dark." He paused, weary of the burden of W.K. Suggins, Jr., but remembering that the boy was a fast gun and did know the town. "I'm giving you a chance, kid," he said. "You'd better take it."

W.K., on the angry point of snarling out what Jules Hoberman could do with his sheriff's badge and his Pima Bend chances, heard something of a sudden which went through him in a nerve-jangling way that nothing else ever had.

There were a lot of horses out there in the loose stock corral being handled around by their cavalry riders. Some were spitting out bits, others bunching to the saddle, still others blowing out bellies against the cinchstrap. In the process, some of them were making complaints in horsetalk, as some always did, grunting, nickering, even whinnying full-out.

Over in the deserted repair shed of Southwest Stagelines, a forgotten and impounded stranger, stabled there to be out of the way of the regular work stock in the livery barn, and lonesome for his kind, heard the cavalry horses being readied unwillingly for departure. The lean beautiful head went up, the thin-veined wide nostrils flared. Race-bred and restless, the steeldust was ready to go—and his high piercing neigh answered as much to the balky military mounts.

And over in the cellblock of the Pima Bend jail, the nerve ends of Deputy Sheriff W.K. Suggins, Jr. were ajangling like chain lightning. There had appeared in his rebellious brain another and more desperate chance than any dreamed by old Jules Hoberman or the legal law.

"Mister Hoberman," he heard himself saying piously. "I been a damn fool and don't deserve what you've did for me. I'll do my level best whiles you're away."

Old Jules eyed him suspiciously, but he was out of time and deputies. Outside, the "mount-ups" were being sung out, and the U.S. Cavalry was moving.

"All right," he said reluctantly.

He went out through the front office, picking his Winchester from its wall hooks, still mumbling.

W.K. Suggins, Jr. waited only until he saw, through the broken-out cellblock wall, the old lawman limp into view and leg-up rheumatically on his homely roan to side the impatient lieutenant, already mounted with T.C. Madden, at the head of the forming column of U.S. troops.

Then the deputy held up another counting of seconds while the "forward ho!" was bellowed out by the veteran first sergeant, and the cavalry horses pounded on the lope out through the gate of the mud-walled loose stock corral to "column left!" on another roar from the sergeant down the wagon ruts of Main Street, westwardbound.

He was running for the stage line repair shed and the lonesome, race-bred steeldust gelding, before the dust of the departure resettled in the loose stock corral or the jingle of military bit and spur chains died away down Main.

Shit, oh shit! thought W.K.

What in the name of God had he been doing hating the old sheriff for beating him out of a measly two hundred dollars.

There was fifteen thousand in that goddamn Concord coach!

And it was hidden in two special panels under the passenger benches where no naked-ass Indian would ever in a *hundred* stage station burn-outs think to look for it. If he could get to that coach after the Indians and before the U.S. Cavalry—

"Shit!" burst out the pink-eyed deputy and ran the harder

and more desperately for the shed and the steeldust race
horse that was going to win him all of the oranges in
California.

11

Once away from earshot of Pima Bend, Clooney guided
the creaking Concord down into Coyote Wash and sneaked
his teams along its dry, smooth-sanded course like the very
animals of its name. The horses were held to a walk, only the
crunch of pebbles and the occasional fracture of larger stone
disturbed the quiet. Now and again an iron wheel rim would
scrape the exposed bedrock, squealing drily. Inside the old
coach, Hunker Larsen talked in his slow way with the excited
girl passenger, calming her, reassuring her. When Feeny tried
interpolating some of his more colorful ideas of the night's
work, with particular emphasis on the murdering redskins,
the big blacksmith put an elbow the size of a fence post stub
into his ribs, and that was that.

Atop the Concord all went well. Black driver and white
shotgun rider kept their dual vigils until well away and back
on the road, then sighed together.

It was a night to put old memories back in heart and mind
for the thankful horsethief. The moon sailed along with the
rocking sway of the old Concord. The teams were cool and
moving easy. Clooney Borrum drove them as though his
fingers ran all the way down the lines from wheelers to
leaders right through the swing team in between. Not a
wasted motion. Not an empty word. Man and animals at one
with each other and with the arid land about them. Rolling
through the desert night with only a soft snuffling here, a
clop of shod hoof in the dust of centuries there, a headtoss to
make snaffle-ring or roller-bit music thrown in for tempo-lilt
along the way. Free, in God's name, thought the drifter. Oh,
thank Jesus for that.

Jesus and Clooney Borrum.

"Clooney friend," he said, softly so as not to disturb the
night or break the rhythm of the horses. "I reckon speechmak-
ing time is here."

"For what?" asked the Negro stablehand.

"Five years in Yuma not being did."

"It ain't why I bust you out."

"No?"

The Negro was silent a moment, thinking. "No," he said. "I done it bercause I ain't never had no friend before."

"My God."

"Well, I ain't. It's different with a white man. White man's got lots of friends. Nigger he ain't none."

"One," corrected the drifter.

"Yes sir," said Clooney Borrum. "That's why you free."

He guided the hitch over a particularly potholed stretch of the stage road, seeming to feel where rock or dip or downright gully waited to break wheel spoke or spring axle.

"Question is," he continued, "why is I here?"

"Reckon you told me, didn't you?" frowned the drifter. "Your Mister Madden done said tickets had been sold and the stage would go. Likewise, if the stage didn't go, the stage line would go under. Less all that gold money got to Tucson, it would. That's what you said."

"Wasn't me said it," denied the Negro. "It were Mister Piney. He say oncst the ticket's punch and pay fer, the passenger got to be deliver. He say it print right on the back side of the ticket. Company g'arantee. Yes sir."

"The hell. We ain't no passengers this here run."

"Oh yes we is. I ain't told you but there's one."

"One passenger?"

"Two, really. Little old bitty knocked-up gal going to shuck that baby out any bounce."

"A girl? Going to have a baby?"

"Well, it better be a baby."

"My God, where's she from?"

"Don't know."

"Well, where's she bound?"

"Ticket's punched for Tucson."

"Tucson. Think she'll make it?"

"Iffen we does."

"You figure we will?"

Clooney clucked to the horses, looked all about them over the moonlit duskiness of the summer night.

"Depends," he said.

"On what?"

Again the powerful Negro surveyed the sweep of the desert. He looked back to the disappearing hills of the river at Pima Bend. He looked ahead to the rising escarpment of Querecho Mesa, over whose sandstone spine they must pass and descend to reach Sifford Wells.

"Injuns," he said. " 'Paches."

"That," said the drifter cheerfully, "is what a educated feller would call a redumbrancy."

"A whichso?" scowled Clooney.

"Well," explained the much-traveled horsethief, "it's sort of like saying the same thing twicet. You know, like iffen you say Injun out here, you done already said Apache."

"Whee-ooo! ain't that grand. How you spell that?"

The drifter spelled it for him, or spelled something for him, and the black man spelled it back at him, whatever it was, and straightened on the driver's box beside his new white friend.

"It's a right prideful feeling," he announced. "I thanks you for it. Yes sir."

"For what?" puzzled the drifter.

"That new word," answered the Negro. "Now I got two of them."

"Two words, for Christ's sake?"

"No sir, two *fancy* words: quality folks talk."

"Oh?" said the drifter. "What's the other one?"

Clooney Borrum sat even straighter on the jolting box of the Sifford Wells stage. "Redolize," he said.

"Redolize?" repeated his white companion.

"Yes sir. You know. What you was doing in the horse trough, er, I mean what you was doing that got you throwed inter the trough, 'sides your being drunk, that is."

"I was redolizing?" said the drifter.

"Yes sir, you truly was. I ain't never smelt nobody stunk no worse."

"Well, all right," shrugged the drifter. "Now we both got two six-bit things to say. Hope I can remember yours."

"Ain't nothing to it," said Clooney proudly. "Just say 'stink' instead."

They fell silent, then, and the stage ghosted on up the long pull to the top of old Querecho. Here there was a blowing-out halt for the horses, and Clooney put the fresh team from the back of the coach in place of the lathered leaders, tying the tired horses on behind. During the halt, the lady passenger was helped out of the coach by big Hunker Larsen. Feeny Gleason, red feather still drooping valiantly, walked with the young woman on watchful guard against the desert stillness, Spencer carbine ever ready, untrained eye darting ceaselessly for sign of hated redskin. The drifter got down and stretched his legs also. He kept apart from the others, helping Clooney with the horses. Two times the girl passed very near him, but he turned away ashamed of his ragged garb and rough beard, thinking painfully of any possible redolizing he might be doing, as well. But the night breeze, working rightly for a moment, brought *her* scent to him and oh! she smelled wonderful, like the one good woman he had known ten thousand miles back along his life, and those memories of heart and mind were stirred once more.

"Board!" called Clooney Borrum, low-voiced.

The reverie was broken, and the dusty moon sailed on. Over the level pull of the table-top mesa they made excellent time, the roadbed being also superior here.

They ran an hour, then two, the small talk waning.

After a twenty-minute stretch of hoof-drumming and thorobrace swaying in total silence, the drifter looked over at his black companion.

"You know something, partner," he said. "I'm scairt to death."

The Negro driver let the teams out another wrap of the lines.

"Move over," he answered. "You got company."

The drifter laughed his soft laugh. "That all you got to offer, Clooney friend?"

"You wants advice to go with it?"

"Reckon so. You ain't missed a head-shot all night."

Clooney nodded, letting out the willing horses yet a little more, scanning the mesa ahead, narrow-eyed.

"Don't never look back," he said. "You might see something."

"Been looking back and been seeing things," muttered the drifter. "Must be the moonbeams or the dustsmell or something. Oh, man, it was a night just like this one."

Clooney could tell that he wanted to talk, wanted to get it out, but you had to let a man take his own gait going down the back road. "Mmmmm," was all he said.

The drifter rambled at first. He was "circling it," coming into it from upwind. Clooney let him get it done his own way. Remembering could hurt you bad. Clooney knew all about that.

He did not, the confessed horsethief admitted, recall much of the creative part of the past day in Pima Bend. In the first place any man riding into a strange town on a borrowed horse and stopping longer than to ask directions to the Mexican border was already as lost as a blind dog in a butcher shop. When that same man was thirty-eight years old, making the town with daylight, then by noon having his nose stuck tight in the bottle, well, he was really looking to get his saddle sacked and sent home to his kin. The wonder was it took all day long.

He did recall, the drifter frowned, that, along about sundown, all the lifelong friends he had made since forenoon and the start of his bottle-buying for the house had evacuated his table and left him lonely as an unloaded polecat. At the same time, his money being gone and his credit run out with the hocking of his six gun and saddle gun to host the last few rounds, the management of the Tecolote Saloon was giving him ten minutes to get his feet under him and depart of his own free, white, and old-enough-to-vote will.

Considering his options under this arrangement, he had seen them as two in number: Some other drunken bum would wander in with a new bankroll and take up furnishing the rotgut-and-tumblers where he had left off; the nigger swamper from over at the stage line livery stable would show up and help him to remember where he had parked the stolen steeldust.

He had already decided to go for the second travel plan, providing the nigger showed up. He would climb on that rangy, cat-fast gelding and shake the bedbugs of whatever burg he was in from his blanket roll forever.

"Onliest thing was," he annoted sadly to Clooney Borrum, "you didn't show up."

"No," said Clooney. "It was you done that. Feet fust and your head stuck in the spittoon."

"Yes," nodded the drifter. "And redolizing something fierce."

"Well, go ahead on with it," suggested the Negro driver. "Ain't you ever going to quit sniffing the bait and dab in your paw and spring it? You wasn't borned no hossthief. I knows quality. You cain't cover it up with no ragged clothes. Quality's got a smell morest powerfuller than any stink you done meanwhile lay onto yourself. How come you to get yourself so plumb cultus?"

"Strong drink," said the drifter. "Red-eye rotgut."

"Sure enough whiskey will make a man bad," Clooney agreed. "But what make a good man take to bad booze?" He paused, eying his white companion. "They's allus a reason, Mister Hossthief. What's yourn?"

The drifter turned away from the Negro driver's steady

regard. He was narrow-eying the silver-lit mesa, traveling through bloodshot eye and whiskey-blurred memory to that other summer night so much like this one, but so very long ago.

"The Apaches," he said at last and softly.

Clooney gathered lines, whistled to his teams. Ahead the stage road disappeared over the sharply cut edge of Querecho Mesa. The horses slowed to a walk resting for the bad downgrade to come.

"Go ahead on," said Clooney.

The drifter nodded, no longer watching the desert.

Life could grow malodorous, he said, and even smell a little, too, when a man had been putting down on the red and seeing the ball drop black ever since his wife and child left him. It was not, he maintained seriously, that he blamed the Indians—all of them—for what he had done to himself through those afteryears. But a man could have personal and terrible reasons for taking to liquor that he would not care to advertise, nor to defend, nor to lay face-up on life's table for just anybody to study. He knew, he said, the words coming through suddenly clenched teeth, that the day would come—or the night—for collecting his due-bill on the red brother. Somewhere, somehow, he would meet up again with the particular Indians of his three-year search. When he did, they would learn what the soft long hair of one white man's wife and baby were worth to—

The drifter abruptly stopped talking. He had started to say a name, *his* name, and Clooney Borrum understood that he had caught himself.

"I ain't axt you who you is," he said. "You knows who you is. Man don't never forget his name."

"I can remember hers," said the drifter, voice so murmured Clooney had to lean to hear. "It was Aura Lee."

"That's a purty name," the Negro driver said. "It one of the most purtiest name they is. They was a old song we uster hum. You 'members?"

In a crooning bass, lullabye-sweet, lover-sad, the stable-hand began to sing:

> As the blackbird in the spring,
> 'Neath the willow tree . . . .
> Sat and piped, I heard him sing,
> Singing Au—ra—Lee.

Clooney held two beats and, singing baritone harmony, the drifter joined him beautifully:

> *Au-ra-Leel Au-ra-Leel Maid of golden hairl*
> *Sunshine came along with thee,*
> *And swallows in the air* . . . .

The voices trailed off. The road swung left into the full cast of the moon. The drifter was not a man who could cry, but Clooney saw the look on that face and heard the catch in the words, and he knew.

"*I remember*," the drifter said.

"Me, too."

"You had a woman like that, Clooney friend?"

"Every man do."

"Yeah. Clooney—"

"Hmmm?"

"What happen to yours?"

"Field cap'n whupt her with the hoe handle. She was heavy with my chile. Just a chile herse'f; only old enought, no more. Likely you wouldn't call her nobody's woman. Just a chile, just a chile."

The drifter shook shaggy head, denying it.

"She was your woman, Clooney."

"Die in the night," the Negro said. "Give up the dead baby fust, then slip away grabbing holdt my hand."

"Clooney."

"Yes sir."

"You kill the field captain?"

Clooney Borrum shook up his horses. The drop-off of the Querecho Mesa Grade lay twenty rods ahead.

"Never even learnt his name," he said quietly. He eyed the white man. "You going to ask that Injun his name whens you cotch up to him?"

The drifter answered him as quietly.

"I know his name," he said. "It's Chatto." He paused while the surprise of the name sent its chill through Clooney Borrum. "Comes out Flat Nose in Spanish, they tell me."

Almost unconsciously Clooney edged away from the white man.

"I *knows* what it comes out in Spanish," he said. "You knows what it comes out in 'Pache?"

The drifter indicated that he did not, and the Negro driver

hauled back on the lines, setting the teams for the Querecho Grade.

"Dead people," he said. "White ones."

The six-horse hitch sat back on its hocks, braking against the roof-steep downpitch of the stage road. The big Concord rode up on the haunches of the wheelers; the noses of the swings were into the cruppers of the leaders. It seemed an even gamble that the coach would go over the side. But the drifter only tightened his grip on the handholds and on the steel breech of the cylinder-bored L.C. Smith, voice still soft.

"I know," he said. "I remember."

Thirty minutes later they were down off the mesa.

Ahead, no light and no life showing within the black darkness of its mud-walled silhouette, was Sifford Wells.

"Made it!" chortled Clooney Borrum, reining sweated teams into a trot out onto Big Dipper Flat. Then, the fact that the way-lantern was not burning at the station's gate drew a belated frown. "Mebbe," he added.

Beside him he sensed the shotgun rider straightening and heard the metallic clinkings of the L.C. Smith's outside hammers being cocked. He slowed the trotting teams, reached beneath his seat for the company Winchester. "Any idees?" he asked the white man.

"Hold 'em in close to the corral wall going by," the drifter said. "Keep talking out loud right on in."

Clooney whistled to his horses, slapped them with the lines. "You want that talk in Injun, Mex, or White Eye?" he said.

"Whichever," answered the drifter laconically.

Clooney nodded, gathering the lines and wrapping them lightly on the dashhook, freeing both hands for the Winchester. "Reckon I'll use American," he said. "Arter all, them's American 'Paches, ain't they?"

"Yeah," said the drifter, hipping the L.C. Smith. "Whistle 'em a chorus of *Stars Bangled Banner*."

12

Knowing where the stage road ran, T.C. Madden knew as well where it did not run and, where, accordingly, short-cuttings might be made by men on horseback. As with the railroads later, the early coach routes were restricted as to type of terrain, degree of grade, crown drainage, flood-wash, all the mundane problems of wheeled traffic. Madden understood that. But he was also a cowboy in youth, and still one in spirit, and he knew equally what a mounted man ought to be able to negotiate handily that would wind up any Concord, Murphy, spring bed, Celerity, buckboard, surrey, shay, trap, post chaise, Studebaker, mud wagon, lumber buggy, Owensboro dray—anything on wheels—right square down in the gully, sideover and the spokes still spinning.

The stage line super took Lieutenant Kensington's patrol wherever the road did not go. He led the way by kit-fox trails and wild-pig runs that any Apache would detour. In broad daylight and traveling lazy. But Madden was thinking of his fifteen thousand dollars and his stage line and those Chattoled Chiricahuas who had already come within one arrow shot of ruining him on the Fort Gila leg. If, in the process of beating the Indians to his twenty-five-hundred-pound, twelve-hundred-fifty-dollar heavy Concord, he put a couple of U.S. cavalrymen over the side, too bad.

T.C. Madden was not in the cavalry business.

The final condition that slowed his outrageous quick-cuts was that of his old friend Sheriff Jules Hoberman. Jules had not been doing too many such owlhoot cross-country exercises of recent late, and neither had his corn-fed roan. Both were blowing foam and caked between the cheeks before two hours were pounded under.

The old man was not the law out here—Kensington was—and could not order the pace. Yet the officer's men and horses had already made a long run that day down from Fort Gila, so presently Sergeant Bourke rode up beside the panting Madden, saluting.

"Begging your pardon, sir," he said gruffly. "But the lieutenant says if you don't slack off and take a more Christian route, he will have your mount neck-roped to the sheriff's and the two of you sent back under guard. The lieutenant says he can follow the stage road quite nice without any line supers to wipe his nose."

Madden had a reply prepared that would singe the hair in any horse soldier's ears, but he saved it. An instant and wild Irish thought had seized him.

"Ah, can he now, the bright lad," he said to the patient noncom. "All right. The road's over there forty rods south. You can't miss it. I will just go my own way and be no more trouble to you."

Before the astonished sergeant could react, Madden had

spun his horse about and galloped him off north. Bourke
dared not fire after him, nor even shout. All he might do is
what he did, spur back to Kensington and the halted column
and make his report. Surprisingly, the lieutenant took it in
better stride than the old sheriff. The sheriff vowed that the
stage line super had done them a little coyote, Indian talk for
a damned dirty trick, and that, if they found the road forty
rods south, or a hundred and forty rods south, he would buy
all the oats from there back to Pima Bend.

Which was precisely where he, Jules Hoberman, was going
right then and instanter.

They would never find Madden that night, nor the damned
stage road short of daylight and field-glass weather. As for
himself, he could hit the river by the set of the stars and
then follow it down to the town and goodnight and the hell
with all of them.

Kensington let him go convinced it was good riddance.

As for the daft stage line owner, he would not get far. Nor
was he of any importance to Kensington. All the lieutenant
wanted was to rescue that wayward coach full of poor, lost
citizens—including an imminent mother-to-be, what luck! After that, he could hope and pray that Chatto and his damned
Chiricahua murderers were following him and would fall
upon the station to get at him.

What a grand splash that would make in the eastern
papers. Lord God, Harry Kensington, it could be a clean
jump clear over captain, all the way to the gold oakleaves.

Lowly lieutenant and twelve men ... the local law giving
up and going back ... the stagecoach saved ... the most
sought red criminal in the west killed in dramatic battle at
lone stage station ... his renegade braves scattered ... the
power of the Chiricahua Nation broken forever by Wild
Horse Harry Kensington—Major Wild Horse Harry Kensington. ... Ah! to dream, to dream, damn them all; them and
their prissy-assed, green-eyed reprimands; he would show
them: This was the time ... Now!

"Sergeant Bourke!"

"Yes sir."

"Column left, forty rods. Strike the road, column right.
Move them out."

"Sir, the horses—"

"Damn the horses. Do you hear me, sergeant? I gave an
order."

"Yes sir! Forward ho! Column left."

The weary troopers, half asleep in the saddle, muttered the classic endearments of enlisted men for lieutenants the soldiers' world over. If there ever was a good Indian scrape, with enough dust and noise and hostile lead aflying to let a man get just one trigger-squeeze of decent bead between that bastard's shoulder blades! Ah, well, if wishes were that cheap all the dogfaces would be generals and all the shavetails shot in the back in battle.

The hell with it.

Column left it was, forty rods to the road, and column right. Jolt, jolt, jolt. Rock, rock, rock.

Twenty rods. Thirty rods. Forty rods.

Where in the goddamn hell was the road?

A mile on, a mile back. Quarter right. Quarter left. Column ho. Column halt. Dismount. Mount up. Jolt, jolt, jolt. Rock, rock, rock. Jingle, jingle, jingle. Where was that motherfucker of a road?

The lieutenant did not know, the sergeant did not know, the troopers did not know, the horses did not care.

Column ho. Jolt, jolt, jolt, jingle, jingle, jingle, rock, rock, rock.

13

The steeldust seemed to float beneath the moonlight, trim hooves caressing rather than pounding the desert track of the Sifford Wells stage road. The deputy had never been on a horse like that. Indeed, he had never sat a saddle such as the lightweight one the horsethief used. That bum might be a drunk and a drifter, but he was sure as shit a professional at lifting livestock.

W.K. reined the steeldust down a bit.

He looked back toward Pima Bend.

Christ! they were already out of sight of the town hidden in the bottomgrowth of Four Mile Bend.

My God, this horse was going on to California with W.K. Suggins, Jr. A man could not give up a treasure like the steeldust. Not when the gelding was going to get him to that fifteen thousand dollars ahead of everybody. No wonder the damned horsethief had dawdled and got liquored in Pima Bend. Shit, with a horse like this, all he would have needed to do was get to him. After that, drunk or sober, there was nothing in the Arizona Territory going to head that Texas horse. Why, this horse could drag a man faster than most could carry him. And a site farther, too, likely. He did not seem winded at all yet, just breaking out a light sweat and breathing easy as a whore in the morning.

W.K. could not repress himself.

"Shit!" he yelled exultantly. "We're going to Cal-lif-for-ny-ay!"

With the shout, the horse took off. The deputy let him go. He did not run, he fled through the night. Or flew. W.K. was not much with words. All he knew was that it was like watching somebody else from a distance riding that horse. It was not him, Pinky Suggins. It was a whole new man sitting up there on that steeldust's back. He was outrunning the dust he raised, the river in the valley, the town along the river, everything that the deputy wanted never to see again. It was a full surprise to feel the upgrade of Querecho Mesa come under that soaring roll of a magic gallop.

"Whoa up, whoa up," said W.K., astonished. "My God."

He was going to have to slow himself down, too; he understood that perfectly.

After all, all he had to do was head the cavalry.

As far as the stagecoach was concerned, he knew it would be at Sifford Wells station before daylight.

That old nigger driver would know how to rate his teams to put them into the highwall adobe corral at the Wells within ten minutes of any time he chose, and, with the main idea being to cut down the Indian odds by night-running, the black bastard would damn well choose to pick a time safe ahead of sunup. To W.K. this meant enough of working darkness remaining for him to crawl up on the coach, get the gold out, haul it off and hole it up wherever was best and nearest for later coming back and picking it up.

Of course a damn fool would figure just to sack the two saddlebag pouches the gold was in, one across the withers, one over the rump of the steeldust, and get the hell shut of there. But W.K. was no damn fool. That gold coin, with the heavy leather pouches, would go close to forty pounds each sack, that was, each of the two double-pouch bags. But whether you toted it up two-times-forty, or four-times-twenty, it came out eighty pounds. There was no horse in the world going to carry a handicap like that, race-bred or not. Not far, he would not carry it. Not even with a lightweight jockey like W.K. Suggins up on him. You take and you add W.K.'s hundred and thirty-five pounds to the eighty of the gold and you came out with two hundred fifteen pounds to go a distance of God knew how far.

Just thinking about it made the deputy get down off the steeldust and begin hand-leading him up the steepening grade.

"Hell," he said aloud. "I'll just camp out with the coyotes a spell, then come back with a pack mule and clear out in style. Anybody asks me, I'm just prospecting for gold. Yes sir. I'll even hang me a pick and pan on the pack to make it look good."

He laughed, startling the steeldust, which spooked on him and nearly got free. "Whoa, whoa!" he called, easing him down. "You're my ticket for Californy; punched and paid for by Southwest Stagelines, just like old T.C. says." He paused, gentling the nervous racer, chuckling happily. "Only hell, boy, we ain't going to Tucson. We're making it to Los Angeles, maybe even San Francisco. Christ, anyplace!"

They topped the grade, and the deputy swung back to saddle. He held in the champing steeldust a moment, sighting westward over the moon-white mesa. Nothing. Not a sign. No dust, no anything. Of course, moonlight or not, the cover up on the mesa was so high and thick as to hide the road unless you were right on top of it. So what if the cavalry was out there not moving?

Jesus Christ. Now wait a minute.

The goddamn cavalry must be *behind* him. That fucking steeldust had gone so fast he had headed them before W.K. had cut back into the road four miles out.

That must be it; it had to be.

He wished now that he had not been so lightheaded over the bastard's speed. He could not really recall what pace they had held going wide through the sage out of Pima Bend. Had he run the son of a bitch the whole of the way? Had he slacked him off enough while thinking about his plan for the gold, to let the troops stay ahead of him? If so, he had to remember they had T.C. Madden guiding them. And that T.C. knew more ways than a jack rabbit across that brush-thick mesa. They could have left the road entirely. They might be out there ahead of him anyplace. Off the road, out in the chaparral, a man could see neither them nor their dust.

Shit.

What was he going to do?

The horse nickered softly, side-stepping and rump-bunching beneath him. Goddamn. Had the bastard winded something? He was acting like he had.

Now hold on.

The horse soldiers could not have gotten far enough ahead of him for their dust to be laid. That was, if they were stopped out there to ambush him; no, it just was no way possible. But they might be almighty damned close behind him. That was for sure. And him sitting there atop that antsy steeldust waiting for them in the broad moonlight? Son of a bitch, what had he been thinking of, taking all that time walking the gelding up the grade? That gold, that is what. And he had simply let the cavalry slip out of his mind along the way. Now, goddamnit, where were they?

The steeldust gave him the answer.

The slender neck twisted around, the muscled rump gathered and brought the nervous animal full-about in a nearfoot spin to face the grade behind them.

W.K. grabbed for and luckily got ahold of the moving horse's nostrilbridge, clamping hard down. "Whoa, whoa," he whispered, and in the moment's pause he heard the clank of sabre steel and jangle of bit-chain and blowing out of nostril of climbing horses from below.

Oh, Christ, now what?

He could not stay where he was. If he took off and ran the stage road, straightaway, they would never catch him, but he would tower-up dust enough to force them into trying, and that would put his whole gold plan under pressure whether he won the horse race going away, or not. With T.C. Madden and that smart old sheriff to advise them, they would keep coming on his trail too hot to leave him the time he needed at the other end. It could even push them all into the rear end of the damned Concord before that nigger driver ever got her to Sifford Wells and parked where Suggins could get at the gold and make off before daybreak.

Well, they weren't going to do W.K. Suggins, Jr. out of that fifteen thousand and those California orange trees.

He and the steeldust could rabbit-sneak that mesa top just as good as T.C. Madden or any of them. They would just, right now, vacate into the chaparral and be long lost to view, or pursuit, by the time those worn-down cavalry plugs topped the grade. Then he would find the road again, *ahead of them for sure this time,* and just keep it that way into the Wells. All he had to do was cut back once he and the steeldust had tiptoed wide of the road into the dust-free

rocks of the yonder roughlands. Then just line out on the
gelding's floaty lope and start figuring where to hide the
saddlebags and the fifteen thousand dollars.

"Walk easy, you bastard," he told the gelding, and he put
him into the salt bush and rabbit sage flanking the moonlit
road. They were well lost to sight and sound when the
cavalry troops plodded to the topout site and wearily obeyed
the dismount relayed by Sergeant Emmett Bourke.

The evasive action worked as W.K. had known it must.
The U.S. troopers were still back there at the topout blowing
their horses, when he hit the big roughs and turned the
steeldust for where the road should be.

Only it was not there.

Neither was it the next place that W.K. looked for it. Nor
the next. The heavy brush was way over the head of a horse
and rider, thick as the shinnery catclaw of south Texas. It
was a precious two hours of foul-mouthing and whipsawing
the innocent steeldust gelding before the deputy knew where
he was.

And what he knew was that he did *not know* where he
was.

                              14

Even Apaches, and even Apache horses, must rest in the
summer's midafternoon heat. On the way to Na-koo-say there
was a place, remembered in Peaches' mind from childhood,
called Hoh-shuh Springs. *Hoh-shuh* was an Apache horse-
gentling word. Peaches believed that it came from the white
man's, whoa, but older men than he, and far wiser in tribal
things, insisted it was as Indian as *inchi* for salt, or *ikon* for
flour, or *zigosti* for bread, or even *tu-dishishn*, black water,
for coffee.

In any Chiricahua event, the word came back down the
panting line of moving men and animals that there would be
a halt at Hoh-shuh Springs, just ahead. They had been
staying with the sun very well—making good time on the
trail—and a rest could be afforded where none was sched-
uled. They would boil water for tea and even take time to
eyanh, to eat a little. Moreover, what band of nomads such as
they could forego the ancient bathing place at Hoh-shuh?
Yes, good news! Chatto had said they might stay that long as
to get in the water and splash around.

"It is the woman, you see," said Do-klini to Peaches where they brought up the rear eating dust. "Chatto stops for her. Hah! Do you think he would waste the time to splash around for us?"

"I would doubt it," said Peaches guardedly.

"You would doubt properly," snorted the big brave. "That woman has the power. We boil tea, we eat, we swim in the clear pool, we rest the horses, *for her!*"

"Chatto must love her very much."

"No, I think it is losing the man-child. It is Lucero who loves her very much."

"And she?" risked Peaches. "Who does she love?"

The big man scowled. "Look at Chatto. Look at Lucero."

"I would rather look at that woman," said Peaches honestly. "Even ill from birthing, one can see that she is still as desirable as when she danced *goo-chitalth!*"

"What?" said Do-klini. "The Virgin Dance? That one? Ah, brother, let me advise you, that one never was a virgin. I think she was born with her membrane broken. But I will agree with you, *sikisn*, every time that I look at the deepness of her buttocks and the way those breasts stand out there, Ysun! especially now that there is all that milk for the dead baby and, well, you know how it is, Coyote. It makes a man's *pico* ache just to look at her walk around."

Their conversation involving noble teats and the Apache God, Ysun, was interrupted by Dust Devil riding down the line to say that Chatto wanted him, Dust Devil and big brother Do-klini, his best *nan-tans*, his premier scouts, to go on out ahead and be sure Hoh-shuh was not occupied. Or, if it were, by what people.

The guarding of Peaches was relegated to Tubac, whose normal mean-dog nature had not been moderated by the long and broiling lope from Pima Bend.

"Make a move to leave the trail, one slip of your pony's forefoot," he nodded to the Fort Gila scout. "Please do it."

"No thank you," said Peaches.

"Do not thank me," snapped the surly one. "Thank Chatto's woman. She is saving your life."

"We are all brothers," was all that Peaches could think to say. "Except of course for the sisters."

"Curse the slut!" was what Tubac answered him. "I never liked women on the wartrail. Sisters, bah!"

Peaches, believing the exchange had come as far as it might with profit to his future, permitted the discussion to languish. Before long, Do-klini came pounding back with great news. There was a select party of Chiricahua at the spring ahead of them! It was like a reunion!

A reunion? Pah! it was more like a miracle.

They would never in another hundred raids imagine what Indians were up there at Hoh-shuh Springs.

"Say," he concluded to Peaches, fetching him a friendly punch that nearly unseated him. "Just try to guess who their chief is? I will even furnish you a hint. Nobody rides ahead of him, not even Juh!"

"My God," said Peaches, surprised into English. "*Him?*"

"Yes. He and his people were on their way up to Fort Gila to help Nah-tez. They were ready to help him talk peace, I mean, not to escape or make war." Do-klini waved in the superior way of anyone who has truly important news. "You see they did not know what we know; what Chatto found out from the old Apache."

"And now?" said Peaches.

"And now they know," Do-klini shrugged.

"My God," said Peaches again and looked frightened. Tubac and Dust Devil had ridden away upcolumn, and he was alone with Do-klini. "Will we still rest and swim and eat up there?" he asked. "I mean *now?*"

"Why, more than before!" cried his hulking guard. "I told you, it is a reunion. Especially seeing him. Do you know he has been in Mexico over one year?"

Peaches felt like saying he could wish that "him" would stay in Mexico for a hundred years. There was no Chiricahua in or out of Mexico that he would rather not see at Hoh-shuh Springs. But he knew better than to permit this feeling to impart itself to Do-klini.

"Come on!" shouted the latter. "Let us go up and give him greeting. You know him, do you not?"

"Worse than that," admitted Peaches glumly. "He knows me."

And so it was that he put heel to plodding pony and followed Do-klini up along the line to go and pay his Apache respects to Geronimo.

At that, it had gone better than hoped for. It was now over and the party was readying to move on for Na-koo-say. Geronimo and his fellow Chiricahua war leaders had not all liked Nah-tez, and not one of them but had advised against the peace chief's trust of the government, except as that government was represented by Red Beard Crook, at San Carlos. So it was that Geronimo did not even speak harshly to Peaches, and all attention was devoted to talk of war coming.

Each of the several subchiefs present agreed that Chatto had to go on to Na-koo-say and to his vengeance against the Fort Gila soldiers. Three of the chiefs advised against further harm to the stage line people, as such deaths always attracted more trouble than just killing soldiers. Three others volunteered to go with Chatto, with all their men. But Geronimo, the overlord, if indeed there was such a thing in the Apache order of military society, ruled against this. It was Chatto's wartrail. It belonged to him. It was entirely for him to say.

"Well, brother," one of the subchiefs said to Chatto. "How do you wish that it shall be?"

"*Anh*, yes," grunted Geronimo. "What do you want from us?"

Chatto thought a moment. In the stillness, the men were mounting ponies all about the war leaders. Peaches, never missing a detail, counted eighty-nine Indians in the concourse. Of these, thirty were war-women or young boys along for experience. Fifty-nine were grown men. Of these, again, about forty had superb horses and modern repeating guns, either rifles or revolvers. Chatto seemed to be making the same count. He turned to Geronimo and the subchiefs.

"Give me three men from each of your bands," he said. "Let them say themselves which will come. Is this fair? *Anh? Dah?*"

Geronimo and the others consulted briefly.

Peaches could feel his black Apache bangs, together with the rest of his white man serving scalp, begin to shrink. What he heard was what any self-tamed friend of the cavalry might predict to hear from such bad ones. Chatto and Geronimo were the two hostiles most sought by General Crook. Indeed, of the entire congregation at the historic meeting of the two leaders, there was not so much as a solitary member who might be called well-disposed toward the White Eyes. They were nearly all *hesh-kes*, unreasonable haters, filled with the uncontrollable urge to kill.

"*Anh*, yes, it is fair," Geronimo announced. "Only we think you should select your own men. Less than that and we feel it is not fair."

Chatto made the gesture of deepest respect to the famed warchief. Quickly, he proceeded to pick out his men. Peaches noted that he took only the ones with Winchesters and

Spencer carbines, repeating arms, leaving those with old single-loading guns.

When it was done, he had twenty-one new men from the Hoh-shuh hostiles of Geronimo. With Lucero and his own six other adult-age fighters—the three youths were to be taken back to the Stronghold by Geronimo and the main band—Chatto headed a force of twenty-eight men.

These were all from Pa-gotzin-kay, all wild ones, all with some bloodtie to the dead Nah-tez, even if only from a third cousin of a married brother-in-law back in the time before Cochise and then his father before him.

But, as Peaches had ruefully said, they were all brothers.

The departure was made at once, Peaches guessing it to be about 2:00 P.M. They pushed the horses. In the van went Chatto and his people, the new people following. For the time of this raid they would be of Chatto's tribe. He would be the leader.

Two hours of hellish, weaving heat were relentlessly endured, mercilessly ridden under. At four o'clock, Gila Lookout was reached. The view northward and westward took in all of Querecho Mesa and the vast downplain of Big Dipper Flat. Do-klini pointed excitedly to a great rocky spill on the west face of Querecho, another long hour's ride. "Na-koo-say, Na-koo-say!" he said to Peaches. "*Anh*, yes," answered the friend of the United States Cavalry from Fort Gila. "I have been there."

They rode on, beating the little mustangs now.

Na-koo-say, thought Peaches, his spirits failing; legendary water of his people; pure cold spring gushing downward from its birthplace one brief mile of wild rock to fill the storied desert tanks below—the tanks that spelled life in that bleached land and that, since the white man had walled them in, were called another name:

Sifford Wells.

15

Old Jules found the road by accident only minutes after he had turned back from the strayed cavalry patrol. He thought about going on to Sifford Wells after Madden but then cooled off on that. What the hell? If that overage lieutenant bagged any of them up there at the Wells, he would get old T.C. along with the rest. Besides, why not be honest with himself? He was not on the army's side. The old man laughed aloud. He had done his best, and T.C. had coyoted him for his trouble, as old Jules had very well known he would.

The stage line super had not foxed him for a minute with all that wild-goosing across the arroyos and cutbanks of the mesa, away from the road.

If T.C., wherever he was, did not understand that, then their cowpoke years together had been wasted.

He had deliberately let the super sagebrush the patrol. The only reason he had suggested Madden for their guide was to give himself an excuse to let T.C. out of jail. It had been wrong of him to lock up the super. But then he had been thinking of the other employees or any possible passengers who might make the blockade run with him. Hell, had it just been T.C. and his big Concord coach going to Tucson, old Jules would have helped him harness the teams. But a sheriff of the territory was supposed to look out after *all* the folks in his bailiwick, and, for Sheriff Hoberman of Pima Bend, that had meant corralling his old friend to keep him from killing off innocent people in trying to save his busted stage line—which everybody in the territory knew was busted anyway.

But now he was glad that Madden had made it away and would get to his Concord and his fifteen thousand dollars at Sifford Wells in time to take charge of getting the shipment on down to Tucson.

Once it was ipso facto, or whatever the law called locking the barn door too late, that the coach was gone and on its way, Indians *or* U.S. Cavalry be damned, the only decent thing he could do was try to set the law straight. He only hoped that folks did not figure it out too easy that their sheriff's idea of straightening out his custody arrest of T.C. Madden was to not only turn the big Irishman loose, but then to go along with him and help lose the United States Cavalry up in the roughs of Querecho Mesa. There was an election coming along and he was getting old; if the citizens got the idea that his head vessels were softening up, hell, he would have trouble out-polling even Pinky Suggins.

Funny thing. Just when a man got to where he was really needing the job, and really knowing it, too, he got thrown out on his ass, and some young peckerhead was handed his badge and told to clean up the mess the old bastard had left behind him.

Pinky Suggins cleaning up after Jules Hoberman?

Well, now, wait a bit.

Maybe he had been too hard on the kid. Maybe it was time for him to let a younger man take over. His wife's folks, down in Chihuahua, had a beautiful big horse ranch and had wanted for years for him to come down and run it for them. It would be a great life. A white man down there with strong Mexican kin could live like a king. Why ought he to continue breaking his old ass and agonizing his rheumatics for one hundred forty-five dollars a month and reward money? Sure enough, he would have a serious talk with young Suggins as soon as he got back. He would see how the kid had done with being left in charge, and, if he had handled it halfways good, then Jules would not stand in his way.

He could not recommend Pinky, but the least he could do—and by God so he would—was to give the kid an even-money chance to make it on his own.

Jules Hoberman felt better than he had in a long time. Man, it would be sweet down there in Chihuahua. And, Lordy, Lordy, but he was tired all of a sudden and needing the change. It would be like starting all over again, even at his age. Maria Teresa would be happy, too. Pima Bend had not been busting its butt to be nice to her. A sun-grinner was a sun-grinner to them, even their sheriff's legal-married wife.

Well, the hell with that. His mind was made up and his heart was high. It was a beautiful night, and Jules Hoberman began to do something he had not done, or could not recall doing, in the past fifteen years—whistling a tune. It was *"Jalis-co!"* Its lively yet haunting refrain, more Mexican than serapes and sandals, revived even old Geronimo, his overweight roan saddler. The fat rascal commenced to do a little side-dance in time with his rider's happy rhythm.

Around the blind turn of the narrow ruts just ahead, another horse nickered suddenly.

There was no time for either rider to more than haul back on the reins, and the fat roan was still in his whicker of response to the steeldust's neigh when the sheriff of Pima Bend and his errant deputy came face-to-face on the Sifford Wells stage road.

There was mesquite and smoke-tree shadow just there where W.K. Suggins sat the steeldust. The old sheriff had to lean and squint and say, in the soft Mexican lingua franca of the owlhoot trail, *"Quién es?"*

Where the sheriff was, the moonlight shone white as clean sheets. It lit the old lawman better than daylight, because

there was no sun to look into. The deputy could have
shot him, sure. He loomed up like a skinned horse hung in a
ranch-gate. It would have been like triggering into an issue-
day beef at the Indian agency. And the old man would never
have known.

But Pinky Suggins *wanted* him to know.

There in that suspended second between them, when the
deputy was given the grace note of the chaparral shadows
and the old fool's decency in asking who it was, rather than
blasting first, Pinky had thought of the last link in his plan
for the stagecoach gold.

The only awkward thing in it all along had been the fact
that the steeldust could not pack double, carrying both Pinky
and the gold away at the first swipe. He had been short a
pack animal in the plan. Now he was not. That old roan
might be fat, but toting only eighty pounds of gold coins in
place of the two hundred pounds of sheriff suet he was
saddled with now, well shit! it was perfect.

The thing was the old man could not be left as witness.
Neither would he, Pinky knew, let his deputy ride on for
Sifford Wells. It was cut and dried, and it had to be that
way:

"Why, it's me, Mister Hoberman; hello and goodbye."

He flashed the magnificent draw, and the big gun bucked
and roared in his trained hand and old Sheriff Jules Hoberman went down and out of the saddle as though pole-axed.
He hit the ground with a thud audible above the rolling
echoes of the deputy's single shot and lay without moving
underneath the fat roan.

Pinky knew he had centered him. He guided the steeldust
up to the patient roan, which had scarcely moved to either
gunshot or to fall of rider's heavy body. Leaning over, the
deputy slid out the sheriff's Winchester repeating 44-40,
slammed it into the empty scabbard on the horsethief's lightweight outlaw saddle on the sidling steeldust, hooked the
dragging reins of the roan, and, hopes soaring again, set off
westward on the Sifford Wells road. He had his pack horse
and was better armed than ever with the new Winchester
added to his handgun. As for the fat old bastard lying so
quiet back there in the silver moonlight of Querecho Mesa,
well, he had said he would make him eat dogshit one day.
Now it would have to be coyote shit and by night. But what
the hell? Shit was shit. Old Jules and him were quits. There

was nobody going to grow old putting off on W.K. Suggins, Jr. All he had to do now was get on up to Sifford Wells, still ahead of the cavalry and of the coming daylight, and he was off for California.

Whoa up, wait just a fucking minute. *Still* ahead of the cavalry? If he was still ahead of the horse soldiers, how in shit had the old sheriff gotten ahead of *him?* With the doubt, he checked the steeldust.

My God, could he have missed something?

He could, and he had.

Back in the road where he had left him for dead, old Sheriff Jules Hoberman was lying on his potbelly taking elbow-braced, double-hand aim at the beautifully moonlit space between the skinny shoulder blades of W.K. Suggins, Jr. The grizzled lawman, recognizing his deputy's voice from the smoke-tree shadows, had not waited for the finish of the speech. He had been moving in his faked-up fall from the roan before the thundering gunshot, which seemed to have started him downward, was, in fact, triggered.

Moonlight; it had ambushed a lot of better men than W.K. Suggins, Jr. You had to know how to hold under for moonlight. It was like shooting into water. Everything looked bigger and closer than it was. You held center and what you got was high-noon and off the paper.

Jules Hoberman had looked over the sights of his old seven-inch Single Action Cavalry Model Colt in the pale light of many a moon before this one on Querecho Mesa.

He fired three aimed shots.

The steeldust reared in fright. The old roan broke free and galloped in a circle back through the brush to its owner of fourteen years. The steeldust bunched low down and took off in blind panic up to the stage road, west, squirting diarrhea. Deputy Sheriff Suggins was not in the saddle but was still with the racing horse. His boot was hung in the onside stirrup, his body bounding and thudding along the road to Sifford Wells through the offal of the terrified animal. The gelding was taking him toward California, but Pinky Suggins was not smelling orange trees.

Back in the road, old Jules Hoberman caught up the fat roan. He got stiffly into the saddle, settled himself, looked for a moment after his vanished deputy. Hell, no use shagging after him tonight. The steeldust was running wild, already lost to sight and sound. He would have to get his rifle back next day, or whenever. As far as W.K. was concerned, he could find him easy come daybreak and the buzzards.

"Goodbye, Pinky," he said and turned the old roan for home.

Sifford Wells

16

They came on into the Wells with the horses at the walk. "No use to hang back," Clooney said. "Either they bin here or they ain't." The drifter said, "Yeah. Either that or they been here and still are." To which the tense Negro answered, "You is the cheerfullest hossthief ever I bust out the jail," and the drifter added, "Happy as though I was halfbright; keep 'em walking."

With the last words, he was down off the far side of the stage and slipping on foot behind its shelter into the cover of the high mud wall of the work-stock corral. By the time Clooney had brought the weary teams on up to the front of the station and halted them, the substitute shotgun rider had gone over the wall and in through the rear of the station house to sing out softly from the black rectangle of the front door.

"All clear, Clooney friend. Nothing in here but us hossthiefs."

The Negro wrapped the lines, climbed down.

"Whee-ooo," he said. "Where at did you larn to see in the dark like that?"

"In all them jails, amigo." There was memory in the words. "Ain't never see'd one yet with no light in the cells."

"In Yumer Prison," Clooney said, "there ain't even no winders. Man get like a mine-shaft mule. Cain't see nothing whens they lead him out."

"Up in the Injun nations," the drifter said, still looking all around the silent station, "they got a jail dug underground. Puts you in it like you was buried alive. Dark!" he said. "You cain't find your nose with both hands." He laughed the low laugh once more. "In my business, in or out'n jail, man learns to see in the dark. You know, friend, borrowing hosses ain't percisely something that's did for profit in the daylight."

70

Clooney nodded and went past him to the door of the Concord. "Come on out," he said. "We's here."

A slim white hand appeared, then the delicate face of its owner. "I can't open the door, Mister Driver."

Clooney leaned in closer and heard the sonorous duet of Feeny Gleason and Hunker Larsen at full snore on their opposite benches.

"Here, ma'am, you don't mind a nigger's hand."

Clooney opened the door, offering his gnarled black paw with lifelong diffidence. The girl took it gladly and with a warm kind of confidence that made its dark proprietor feel as though he were home again handing down the elegant ladies from the surreys and traps and chaises of that plantation past he held with such mixed nostalgia.

"Thank you, ma'am." He turned and gestured toward the lounging drifter. "Mister—" He had started to say that Mister so-and-so would see her inside the station, but he broke off remembering his white friend had no name. "The shotgun man will sees you safe inside, ma'am," he finished instead. "Just you goes along now. Old Clooney got to mind his teams." He left Hunker and Feeny asleep in the coach and shuffled up to his tired horses crooning and love-talking to them in his wordless tongue-of-animals.

The drifter was alone with the girl.

"Ma'am—" he said, and then he could say no more. Neither could he move to take her faded carpetbag. He had to just stand there, rooted to his spot in the glare of the dying moon. The girl murmured something kind and picked up the bag, starting on. The drifter took a half step to follow and saw her step falter. She put a hand to her temple, and he knew she had grown faint.

He caught her as she fell, carrying her in his arms into the abandoned station.

Within, he stood at room's center. The moonlight poured in the high-cut front window rifle-slits, barring the floor with white light and black shadow. He could make out the rude bench along the rear wall flanking the fireplace on both sides. Moving around the eating table in room's center, he held the girl a moment longer before putting her down. The light of the white paper moon, washing into pale orange now with the old canteloupe's slide behind the distant shoulder of Mount Piños, fell full on the girl's face.

God! but she was beautiful.

The drifter put his face into her honey-blonde hair, drew

long and wonderingly into his lungs the fragrance and the hauntingness of her.

It seemed to him, of a sudden, as if music played within the verminous squalor of the relay station. He listened and, in the moonlight, he recognized it:

> *Au-ra-Lee! Au-ra-Lee!*
> *Maid of golden hair . . . .*
> *Sunshine came along with thee*
> *And—swallows—in the air.*

He kissed her reverently on the sleeping cheek, lips brushing the wisp of silken hair that strayed there.

Behind him, low-spoken, rough voices warned him of dream's ending: Clooney questioning Hunker and Feeny about having put away the teams, safe-tied. My God, how long had he stood with the girl in his arms? Time enough to unhook and put up eight head of stage horses? Dear Jesus, the years, the years. Had he thought to bring them back by holding onto the poor little unconscious thing? A child-woman possibly brief hours from having her baby in the middle of Apacheria? With the Apaches out and being hard-pushed by the U.S. Cavalry troops?

Christ give them the strength and the brains to do the right thing with this situation. Let him help the girl, God, *this* girl, *this* time, God. Let him do at least that much—for Aura Lee.

When the others tromped in, soft-asking about making a light, the girl was resting on the bench by the fireplace. The drifter was taking a lantern from the mantel and raising its chimney to expose the wick.

"Get the shutters shut and barred, Clooney," he heard himself say. It did not sound like him, but the Negro stable-hand knew who it was, and he felt glad and good.

"Yes *sir!*" he said.

"Hunker." It was still the drifter, still surprising himself.

"Yah, there?" Hunker was surprised too.

"You go along outside." He tossed the blacksmith some empty feed sacks. "Stuff these in any cracks the light shines through. Don't miss a pinhole."

"Yah," said the smith and went.

Feeny stepped forward as the drifter lit and trimmed the wick, set the lantern on the table.

"How about me, mister?" he demanded. "I'm T.C. Madden's regular inside guard."

The drifter studied him.

"All right," he said. "We will let you guard the inside."

"Naw ya don't!" defied Feeny, presenting arms fiercely. "I want outside, where the Injuns is at!"

Clooney Borrum intervened, bending the barrel of the Spencer aside for the safety of all.

"Do what he say," advised the powerful Negro. "We gots to have a white man in charge."

"Well, hell!" raged Feeny, red turkey feather aquiver. "I'm a white man!"

"They's white men and they's white men," explained Clooney. "Get out'n the way."

Hunker knocked at the door and said he was coming in. The drifter threw an old horse blanket over the lantern. The door opened and closed. The drifter uncovered the smoking lantern. The four men squinted at one another. "Meeting's come to order," said Clooney.

"Yeah," said the drifter. "Good thing we ain't no big decisions to make."

"We gots mebbe twenty minutes to daylight." Clooney was scowling. "*That* don't call for no decision?"

"Nope," said the drifter.

He raised his head. For the first time Clooney Borrum noted that his eyes were a light clear steel blue under severe black brows. He spoke quietly.

"If the Apaches had been out there when we come in, they wouldn't have let us come in. If they're out there now, they won't let us come out."

"Hmmmm. It do sort of narrer the choice."

"All depends," qualified the drifter, "on what Apaches we got to deal with."

"I thought you say the deputy done told you in his boast-talk—the Cherry Cows."

"Yeah, he told me. But what Cherry Cows?"

Clooney walled his eyes. "*The* Cherry Cows," he said.

The drifter caught it, and the piercing blue eyes blazed like fire-ice in the pale, whiskered face.

"You saying Chatto?"

"As ever was," answered the black stablehand. Then, carefully, "C-H-A-double-TT-O. 'Cause he don't knows how ter spells it kerrec withs onliest one T."

The drifter's flash of deep hate faded.

"Iffen there's anything makes trouble in the world," he said, "it's a educated nigger."

"No, hell, 'tweren't me!" specified Clooney hurriedly. "It were Mister T.C. He's the one toldt me."

The drifter nodded. The old sly grin lifted one corner of the relaxing mouth.

"And how many T's does me and you both know old Mister Chatto can use to spell his name?" he asked the worried Clooney.

Black man and white looked at one another a wise-eyed moment and said right together:

"As many as he wants to!"

And both laughed their private little desperate laugh and then fell still.

Outside it was growing light. The Apache, if they were out there, would be coming now.

"I'll take the roof," said the sometime drunk, drifter, and horsethief. "Gimme the Winchester."

Clooney tossed him the lever-actioned repeater. The drifter gave him the L.C. Smith. "You put Hunker and Feeny wheres you want them," he told the Negro. He hesitated, watching the black man. "You all right, Clooney friend?" he said.

"I am whens you calls me that," Clooney answered and turned to make his defenses. He placed Feeny at one front rifle-slit window, Hunker at the rear door and near the girl. He took the other front window rifle-slit himself, signaled his readiness to the waiting drifter.

"*Cuidado!*" he called to his white friend.

"I'll take a set at it," said the other and went up the frontier chicken ladder through the traphole to the roof.

17

"Did you hear that shot, sergeant!?"

"No sir," said Bourke, halting his mount.

Kensington wheeled to the half-asleep troopers in strung-out column in the bush behind.

"Did any of you men hear a shot just now?"

During the night the horses had been pushing through very heavy salt cedar, mesquite, rabbitbush, and horse sage cover and making too much of their own noise.

"No sir," answered one man mumblingly. "Never heard nothing, sir."

"I heard a shot." Kensington was flat with the statement. His horse gladly stood, head down, unbidden to move and not volunteering. The lieutenant sat on him scowlingly. Were these men turning on him? They had heard that shot.

Angrily he lashed into them.

Was this their commentary on his leadership? he demanded. Their mule-headed way of letting him know they blamed him for being lost? Were they going to take over his command by sulking on him? Was Sergeant Bourke correct in his stubborn persistence that they must dismount, loosen girths, and wait for seeing daylight? Had they indeed already overused their mounts as Bourke claimed?

Well, of course they had.

God knew they had.

But would Custer or Miles or Crook or O.O. Howard or Phil Kearney or Hancock or even Old Man Harney ever have gotten their Indians by letting up on their horses? Suppose Custer had worried about saving his animals that black midnight of the blizzard before the Washita surround of Black Kettle in '68? Or Preacher Chivington had halted his nightmarch against the Cheyenne at Sand Creek? By God! those were horse soldiers, mister! Horses were what they rode, not what they rested. "Bourke!" he rasped. "We will push on."

"But, lieutenant, sir!"

The veteran's risk of his chevrons was punctuated by a period string of three booming shots. They came from the right rear flank, not overly distant.

"Sergeant Bourke!"

"Yes sir."

"Did you hear *those* shots, sir?"

"Yes sir."

"You men?"

There was a wash of mumbled accent amid ranks, and Bourke took it on his shoulders.

"We all heard the shots, lieutenant. What are your orders?"

"What are my orders *what?*" Kensington snapped.

"Sir. What are your orders, sir."

"You already have the order, Bourke."

"You mean we won't go back? I mean to check the shots, sir?"

Kensington lowered his voice, guarding his words from the troopers. "Damn you, Bourke," he seethed. "What did I tell you?"

"That we would push on, sir."

"That is correct. And where did you just say the shots came from?"

"Behind us, sir."

"And where does our duty lie, sergeant?"

"Our *duty*, sir?"

"Orders were cut for this mission, Sergeant Bourke."

"Yes sir."

"How did they read?"

Old soldier Emmett Bourke furrowed seamy brow.

"To pursue and if possible to punish the Injuns what hit that horse ranch up by Fort Gila."

"What else?"

Bourke frowned again. "To close off the country west of Pima Bend."

"As far as where?"

"Tucson, sir."

"And where is Sifford Wells relay station, Sergeant Bourke?"

"Halfways to Tucson, lieutenant."

"Now is that quite all of the orders, Bourke?"

"Well, yes sir. Excepting for the usual, sir."

"The usual what, sergeant?"

"All due caution took to safety of civilian life and property."

"Is that Concord coach civilian property, sergeant?"

"Yes sir."

"Are those civilian lives on board her?"

"Yes sir."

"Is there not the distinct possiblity, due to Nah-tez having been shot in custody, that those same Indians who attacked the coach this same afternoon may not, indeed very probably will, follow their attack with another this coming morning?"

"You mean on the stage at Sifford Wells, sir?"

"Is there another coach in consideration, Bourke?"

"No sir."

"Well, sir?"

"Well, sir, lieutenant, I would say that, in the light of what you said and even more in light of what you didn't say, yes sir; there's a damned good chance them devils of Chatto's will hit that station."

"Bourke!"

"Yes sir."

"What do you mean, 'in light of what I did *not* say?'"

The sergeant colored. He knew he had gone too far, but he also knew that Kensington had gone too far, as well. If he could keep the beset officer from going any farther—from getting good men killed chasing a set of double bars or golden oakleaves for himself—he intended to take the necessary risk. Emmett Bourke, thirty years enlisted with this month, would rather be a live dogface private than any grade of dead sergeant.

"Them Cherry Cow women and kids, sir."

The stillness of Querecho Mesa hurt the ears. The lieutenant stared through it at his very brave sergeant.

"Bourke."

"Yes sir."

"Would you not be required to in truth take oath in testimony that I gave no order for that shooting?"

Bourke, who had come all the way, and understood he had, answered simply, "Yes sir."

But Kensington would not let it alone.

"And that is all, is it not?" he demanded icily.

"No sir, it ain't," said Sergeant Emmett Bourke quietly. "I would have to tell the court that you didn't give no orders against it, neither."

The dawnwind was freshening. It stirred the smoke trees. Far over across Big Dipper Flat, beyond Querecho Mesa, beyond the skyline upthrust of Mount Piños, the night's moon was, as the Apaches put it, going home.

Lieutenant Harry Kensington put the anger and the fear out of himself. These were his men. They were brave men and good soldiers all. No better fighting noncommissioned officer ever sat the high wishbone pommel, rounded cantle, and open-slot seat of a McClellan saddle than First Sergeant Emmett John Bourke. If they did not, these men of his, understand departmental field policy as opposed to Washington publicity, he must not blame them. The men were his and the mission was his; if he could not command both, he deserved neither.

"Bourke," he said. "We're old soldiers, you and I. Don't discuss this with the men. Pass the order."

"Yes sir," said Emmett Bourke.

"And, Bourke—" He wanted to say thank you, but could not. "Never mind," he waved in dismissal.

The old soldier nodded and saluted. "Yes sir," he acknowledged, then checked his mount and brought him back to the officer's drooping gray. "You're welcome, lieutenant," he said.

The column moved out.

They went by the right flank figuring the shots behind them might have come from some traveler by the stage road. Within minutes they had cut the wagon ruts and columned left for Sifford Wells.

A quarter mile back, first panic forgotten, the steeldust raised delicate head from its roadside grazing. The freshening breeze brought scent of many friends—the same many friends he had winded in the stock corral at Pima Bend. The steeldust was glad. He made a pleased chuckling whicker in his throat and set out to follow the cavalry horses ahead of him.

It was slow work. But he was used to the bumping drag of his burden by now. He kept steadily at it.

18

Just at break of day, the drifter having been upon the roof no more than twenty minutes, there was a stir in the brush southward. Below, the heavy boom of Feeny's Spencer replied at once. The drifter heard the great leaden slug plowing off through the thicket amputating mesquite trunks and piñon limbs and eliciting a bellow of rage from the scrub.

"Lay off, you goddamned idiot! It's me!" And next thing T.C. Madden, on his strapping bay, broke free of the tangle.

"That was you, Feeny!" T.C. roared. "You and your bull's-ass special. I'll flay you alive."

"Better get on in under cover, Mister Madden," the drifter called down. "It's early yet."

Madden, after a night in the boondocks, was not impressed. "Who the hell is that?" he challenged, bulldog chin elevated. "I'm not paying *you!*"

The drifter stood up from behind the low parapet of adobe. "I'm already paid," he said. "I'm out."

"You!" the super yelled. "The goddamned horsethief. Clooney! Clooney Borrum! Where the hell you at, you black scoundrel?"

The Negro stableman waved dusky hand out rifle slit.

"Come along in like the shotgun man say, Mister T.C.," he called. "I'll take your hoss."

Hunker came forward to cover Clooney's post at the thick adobe front wall. Clooney went out quickly and took the reins of the stout bay. Madden quit saddle willingly enough. "Anything happened?" he asked. "No sir," said Clooney. "But like the shotgun man say, she's early."

"Seems like you bought yourself a full share of stock in that shotgun rider," scowled T. C. Madden. "I understand it was you busted him out."

"It were."

Madden's deep-set eyes lit up. The bushy brows arched. "Well, damn your black hide, you done great. You get here with the team stock all sound?"

"Every head of 'em, Mister T.C."

They were still standing outside, the super surveying the pink flush of the silence out beyond.

"Get on inside," said the drifter from above.

Madden stepped out away from the station house, jutting the pitbull jaw again.

"Goddamn," he said. "I don't remember promoting you. Get on down here. I want to see the color of your gills. Hop your horsethieving ass."

The drifter scowled. It was the first time Clooney had seen him look ugly. "Watch your mouth, Mister Madden," he called down in his quiet way. "There's a lady inside."

"Christ, I know that, you damned rummy!" growled T.C. "I sold her her ticket. Get on down here."

The drifter shook shaggy head. The black unshorn hair fell over dirty work shirt collar to brush wide thin shoulders. The fierce blue eyes stared down under the brooding level brows.

"You want to see me, I'm up here," he said.

"Why you—" Madden began, then remembered the lady.

He followed Clooney Borrum inside, and Clooney asked him if he would not kindly look to the poor little girl, as they had all been too busy getting set for the redskins, and none of them were, anyways, fit hands to care for a lady.

"Maybe she's a lady, maybe she ain't," T.C. said uncharitably. "I didn't see no wedding circlet."

"Could be, Mister T.C.," said Clooney. "I wasn't looking for none."

Madden growled something at him and went over to look at the girl. He felt her pulse, opened the lid of one eye, went to the cistern in the cookshack lean-to, and drew a bucket of water. This he employed to lave the girl's face, very gently for all his gruff talk, and presently she was trying weakly to raise herself up and to express her gratitude.

It was growing light swiftly now and the stage line super saw that slender oval of a face and all that long honey-blonde hair and got an idea of the tiny smallness of her in good morning illumination.

Lord, God, he thought, she is prettier than a chestnut filly with four socks and a blaze. When she got the big eyes fully open next moment and he saw they were a dewy-clear gray with charcoal-black lashes, he was gone.

"What is the matter with you ninnies?" he bawled, turning on the cringing crew. "Letting this here poor little thing lay here all alone. She might of died!"

Clooney, just then returning from putting up Madden's bay, heard the last words.

"Mister T.C., kin I see you abouten the hosses. It's important." He smiled for the girl. "Company work, missy."

"All right." Madden knew his eleven-year stableman: Clooney Borrum was the best hand alive with horse stock; he surely did not need T.C. Madden to tell him about his stage teams. Outside, in the corral shed, the Negro unfolded a note and handed it to the super.

"It's from Bill Jimmie," he said. "I know his mark."

T.C. frowned over the note:

Some Tonto and Coyotero here tell me Nah-tez shot—Turnt the stock loose not draw Injuns—Ift enny somebody find whut I writ they git out kwik—Pache come shure—Cherrycow—bad chief same Flat Nose, Injun say.

BIL JIMMIE R.

Bill Jimmie Redsand was a Navajo foundling taught to read and write by T.C. Madden. He was a loyal employee and like a part-son to the childless stage line owner. But Madden knew that, when the Chiricahua went out, all the other Indians in the vicinity for two hundred and more miles went out with them—as far and as fast in the opposite direction as their ponies would carry them.

He did not blame Bill Jimmie.

Moreover he was grateful for the note—left where the Navajo stock tender knew they would find it in the privy of the station—as it told them a lot more than it said.

Friendly Indians had come by and told a brother Indian, even of a disliked fellow-tribal origin, to get out fast. There was only one meaning to this. Those Indians were not guessing where Chatto and the Chiricahua were; they knew.

"Goddamn," said T.C. Madden. "They're aheading here. You showed this to your new shotgun man?"

"No sir. He ain't regular company paid."

Madden bobbed beefy head.

"Maybe not," he agreed. "But he strikes me like a man who will measure sixteen hands under full load. I'll go check his teeth and see he ain't windbroke."

They went back into the station house. The girl was sitting up at the table. She did not look well to T.C. Madden. "Brew her up some black java," he ordered the Negro stableman. "Make enough for all hands," he added. "And fry up some fat back and sheepherder bread. Hell, we ain't no secret to them Cherry Cows no more. Make all the smoke you care to." He squeezed the girl's small hand. "Don't you fret it none, missus," he said. "There ain't no ragtag bunch of Inujns going to jump no four white men and a good nigger, full-armed and ready for them." He patted the hand like a child's. "You and your baby going to get to Tucson. T.C. Madden sold you a ticket, didn't he?" He smiled broadly. "Read your g'arantee again, little lady. Printed right there on the back of the stub. That's all you need."

He was gone, then, up the chicken ladder to the roof and the lookout posted there.

Clooney touched the girl's arm. "Come on, honey chile. You lays yourself back down till old Clooney get the coffee boilt. How that baby feel?"

She put her hands to the child, smiling wanly.

"Strong," she said. "Like a boy."

"I knows," murmured Clooey. "I seen him kick. Man-chile he don't kick like no puny little old gal do."

He made a feed-sack mattress for her and a pillow of his rolled-up work coat. "Hard doings, missus," he apologized, helping her down on the plank bench. "But Mister T.C. done toldt you honest. You going to have that chile in Tucson."

The girl stroked the black hand. "You're a good man, Clooney," she smiled. "Tell your friend he's a good man, too." The smile softened. "He didn't know I was awake when he kissed me. Tell him thanks." The gray eyes shadowed over to a moment's rigid pain, then closed, and the pale hand lay quiet upon Clooney Borrum's gnarled black fingers. The thick lashes did not move.

"So tired, so tired," the girl whispered and was gone in fitful sleep.

Clooney went away from the bench by the fireplace beating fist into palm, wordlessly, desperately.

Mid-room, he stopped.

"Goddamn, Lawd Jesus," he said. "She going ter do it. That baby's a'coming sure. Right squar in the middle of her ticket!"

19

"What you think?"

Madden took back the note of Bill Jimmie from the drifter with the question. The latter shrugged.

"Injun writes purty good."

"You know what I mean."

"Yeah."

Giving the answer, the drifter was sizing up the stage line super. He was glad to see that Madden had brought another late-model Winchester to add to the armament. "You shoot that thing?" he asked.

"I guess. Why?"

"Then we got us a good shake."

"Hell," said Madden. "You can get a good shake out of a saltcellar. And that's full of holes."

"Well, it ain't a bent-up comparison. We're apt to get sieved somewhat."

"Don't be funny. What you make of that note?"

His companion cocked his head. "You know Apaches?"

"Hell, man! I run a stage line. Does a bear shit in the woods? Does a bitch-wolf bite? Course I know Apaches." Madden took a harder look at the stranger. "What's your name, mister?"

"Bum. Drunk. Drifter. Hossthief. Pick your peg and hang my hat on it."

"All right, Mister John Doe Drifter: Keep going."

The other scanned the juniper flat, saw nothing, said nothing. Finally, he resumed. "I know them," he said. "Know them from ten years of hunting and hating. If it's Injun and Apache and lives in the Arizony Territory, I know it." The strange blue eyes bored into Madden's. "You can tell them J.D. Drifter toldt you so."

The Irish super held steady to the look and said, "All right, J.D., go ahead on."

"It's a funny thing about a name." The drifter tipped crumpled Stetson to block the climbing sun. "Man gives up peckering around. Works hard. Gets his name knowed decent. Marries himself a good woman. Has his fust kid; little girl, for this feller had my name—"

The pause to think back went on so long, Madden did not believe he was going on. But he waited.

"Feller worked for the guv'ment, up in the Injun nations. Heldt a marshal's badge. Job took a lot of time away from home. Wife finally got six months with the fust baby—that's the one I spoken on. Tascosa sure wasn't no fit place to start the kid, nor for the mama of it to stay, neither one. Feller up and laid aside his law gear, loaded woman and worldly goods inter a old Studebaker spring wagon, headed south for the sun.

"Wanted to get down where there weren't no toughs. No long rides back with them canvas-covered lumps on the pack horse. No jumping his piece evertime some board squeaked or chair scraped ahind him. Reckoned he would start him a little spread in the Arizony Territory, mebbe grow sort of like with the country. Hell!" The sudden soft laugh startled Madden. "He didn't own enough beef to holdt a barbecue. One old crossbreed whiteface bull. Four open heifers of no breed at all. A old muley cow abouten to drop her calf on the road.

"That was for milk for the baby, case the mama didn't make any, or not enought."

The drifter's face softened.

"Feller figured he was set for anything. Little girl she come along. Corn-tassle hair and morning glory eyes just like the mama. Blowing bubbles and a'grinning evertime she seen the feller or heard him come in.

"It were near a year went by.

"Baby and mama was making it fine. Old horny bull he got a heifer calf out'n every one of them four she-stuff. Damn if old muley cow don't drop twins, likewise both heifers and whitefaces. Feller had him all of a sudden ten whiteface she-stuff, everything wintered through without a wheeze or sneeze. He was asinging with his tail up the livelong day, gladder to be alive and away from killing people than he could explain it to his Lord every night when he goed down on his hunkers longsides the bed wheres the long-hair blonde woman waited for him, and, oh Jesus, the days wasn't long enough, nor the nights, to get all his living and loving done.

"And then the Apaches come."

The end was as abrupt as that, and Madden, for a moment, did not realize it. Then he knew.

"Both of them?" he said, waiting awkwardly.

The drifter nodded, looking away.

"Three years this fall. It's been a long, long ride, and bad. Ain't nothing I ain't did. Nothing I ain't drunk. Or stole. Mostly hosses and for the hell of it; trying to get kilt, I reckon, and trying not to. Long, long ride," he repeated. *"But she's over."*

"You've found your peace," said Madden.

"No," said the drifter, the intense eyes showing their wild flare of lightning. "I've found my Apache."

The line super wheeled about. "My God, you mean Chatto? These here same Cherry Cows wiped you out? My God, man, he ain't hardly old enough to have—"

"He was old enough," said the drifter.

They both sat and let the wind blow and the sun climb. After another smoke, Madden got back to it.

"All right. You know the Apache. I don't."

The drifter spun his cigarette into the sand of the stage yard below. "That's where we was," he said.

"Well, spill it; what you think?"

The drifter leaned the Winchester against the parapet, got up stiffly, stretched the ache of long-bones and cramping back. "They ain't coming this morning; somebody else is, though," he said. He inclined the waterhole-stained sidebrim of his disreputable Stetson toward Querecho Mesa. "The U.S. Cavalry to the rescue."

Madden paled, squinted, and, when he had made out the sun-dance of the dozen black dots against the blinding sand of Big Dipper Flat, cursed helplessly.

The drifter laughed, then the black brows leveled.

"I love 'em," he said. "They're the onliest damn white men in the territory knows the Apaches for what they are and back-shoots them according."

Madden did not return his laugh and his own bushy brows drew down. "You ain't going to love this bunch of the bastards, Mister Horsethief," he said. "They got old Sheriff Jules Hoberman with them. I reckon you can laugh about that all the way back to the Pima Bend jail."

He continued to shade his eyes and scowl into the sun-glare, trying to get a better fix on the incoming cavalry patrol. After a moment, he said over his shoulder, "Hey, I don't hear no laughing. How come?"

When, next instant, he swung about belatedly suspicious, his only answer was the rustle of the morning wind curling roofdust along the parapet.

The drifter was gone.

Little Dipper Wash

20

The drifter did not go down the traphole and the chicken ladder, but over the parapet of the west wall. The drop to the soundless dust of the stage yard was not over ten or twelve feet from his handhold on the rooftop rise. There was no window on the west of the station house, and the corral wall took up at the corner of the house. The drifter ran down along the length of the combined cover knowing exactly where he was going. A dry wash, Little Dipper, cut anglingly past the northwest, rear corner of the station's mud-walled complex. There was no ground cover between wash and relay station, T.C. Madden having selected the alkali hardpan upon which the stop was built for that very reason—no sneak-up growth within snap shot Winchester reach of any of his stopover posts.

Bending double, the fugitive sprinted across the open hardpan. It was dicey going over the edge of the wash at top speed. In that bone-dry country a deer fly could not break wind without raising dust. But when he had made it and raised black eyebrow above wash-edge to check the rooftop, he knew he was safe.

Above, T.C. Madden was just then bellowing down the traphole, "Don't let the bastard get by you down there! Grab him, boys! He's up to something!"

The drifter agreed fervently with that; what he was up to was locating the den-hole of the old she-wolf he had seen go down into the wash with first light. It would be nearby in the cutbank on his side. Wolves were that smart. Dig in right under the nose of the lonely humans—the last place the latter would expect. The hole would be, or had ought to be, within eye-reach.

Question was: Could it be squeezed into?

He had a finger-pinch of time. Nobody would follow him out of the station until the cavalry rode up.

Ahh! Damn! There it was. Where that flash-flooded chunk of sandstone leaned against the salt cedar snag. He scuttled to it. God, it was tiny. Maybe a foot by a foot and a half. And now he could hear the old wolf growling. "Sorry, old girl," he called in to her. "It's a Pecos swap." He got out his matchbox, looked about for drift flotsam that would make smoke. Son of a bitch.

There was nothing burnable within reach of his side of Little Dipper Wash!

He peeled off his shirt. It would do. Greasy, unwashed, worn thin, and flimsy. He tore it into strips, made a loose bundle of it, put a lit match to it. It caught, clear-flamed, singeing his hands. He had to let it get going good, burned hands or not. It did, still not making smoke but just a little dance of heat wrinkles that only an Indian eye would have seen above wash lip.

When he could not hold it longer, he jammed it as far down in the den-hole as his arm would reach. At once, almost, it began to smolder and make smoke. He plastered his hatbrim tight over the hole, leaving only enough airspace at the bottom to make a sucking draft.

He distinctly heard the snarling of the she-wolf rise in pitch and then fade into a whimpering, frightened whine, as the oily smoke reached her.

By God! he had known it. The smoke was going away along the hole, not backing up out of it. It had to be that way. The wolf bitch never lived who would choose a one-entrance den. There was always a back door.

All right, where?

The drifter strained eyesight up the wash, murmuring prayerfully, "Got to be there. Elsewise her backhole is drownded out in high water time." The blue eyes swept to the stage road, where the wash veered south and east, up toward the long uplight of the mesa—up where the water came from.

Aha!

Right across the road, by Christ, just past where the ruins of the old stage station of the Overland Line to Socorro and the Rio Grande lay tumbling over the edge of the wash, rank-grown with rabbitbush and juniper.

The she-wolf came gliding up out of that rear hole with no more noise nor notice than a slide of pebbles and tiny trickle of caving bank no bigger than a snake would make coming out of a gopher-run.

"All right, mama," said the drifter. "Keep a-going and don't come back. I'd still ruther be with you."

Suddenly, acutely, he was aware of the military jingle of bit-chains and saber loops, and a dry, flat voice saying, "Dismount, sergeant. We'll noon here."

Feet first, he went writhing into the wolf den. Whiskey-thin as he was, he made it. It was more of a trick to reach back out and muscle the sandstone slab into covering the entrance hole—smoothing the marks of its movement in the washsand every inch of the way—and still have it in place with a prayer it would pass inspection, by the time he heard, from within his earthen tomb, the sounds of cavalry boots sliding down the cutbank and the God-blessed voice of some old soldier singing out, "Nothing down here, lieutenant. And we can see clean to New Mexico one way and halfway to Sonora the other."

Then the pause, with the lieutenant questioning distantly, and the old soldier insisting, within spitting distance of the sandstone slab and the old salt cedar snag, "No sir, he ain't been thisaway. Wherever he is, sir, he's into the high brush for sure, that's certain."

"Goddamnit!" the drifter heard distinctly in the flat voice of the column commander. "Where is that bloody Peaches?" Then, resignedly, "All right, Bourke. Get back. You've got that cursed wash so stomped up now even Bobbie couldn't find a track in it."

There was more of the mumbled exchange, Madden's voice mixed briefly in, but the drifter wasn't listening to it. He was still free. Thank God for the rock float he had walked on in the wash. For the old wolf going out her back way on the smoked-shirt run. For all of it.

It was crazy and maybe he was crazy with it.

But he had found his hole and he was going to stay in it.

He was, anyway, until nightfall and the chance to steal a horse.

One thing, come cavalry, come old sheriff, come even Chatto and his Cherry Cows: He was not going back to Pima Bend and Yuma Prison, or any other prison, not ever.

Somewhere in the night's passage of the river's bend, or the mesa's moonlight, or in the brief hour of the dawn at Sifford Wells, the wind had changed.

Here in the foul-aired, blind-dark of the wolf burrow he

could not wet and put up his finger to it. But he knew it was blowing. A nigger man had saved him from five years of hell because he called him friend. A girl with yellow hair, and her little baby in her, had rested in his arms and made him hear again, Aura Lee! Aura Lee! He had ridden shotgun on fifteen thousand dollars for nearly forty miles, and all he had thought of was the nightdust and the horsesweat and the desert mountain smell sweet off old Piños and the high country, and the fact he was thirteen hours clean of the whiskey stink and body rot of ten lost years.

The drifter shut his eyes against the darkness. He shook the long black hair that now fell, Indianlike, to naked shoulders. He wished he knew, he wished he knew. Where was that wind ablowing?

He had found Chatto and the Chiricahua at last.

But he had likewise found Clooney Borrum and the yellow-haired girl with her little baby somebody did not want: Where was the wind, in that, for a drifter?

Which way did he follow it?

21

At the station house, Kensington introduced himself and placed in military arrest for return to civil custody, Pima Bend, Arizona Territory, one T.C. Madden, proprietor, and one Clooney Borrum, employee, of Southwest Stagelines. Madden was wanted for violation of terms of parole, Borrum for breaking jail in behalf of one absentia horsethief, name and address unknown.

The stage line owner would also be held to account by the United States Army for violation of quarantine.

Kensington and his men were at the service of the others. He wished to especially assure the young lady of their solicitude and her resulting entire safety.

This done, the officer posted men on the station roof and stock shed roof, both strategic corners of the mud-walled corral compound. The men did two hours on, two off. By noon, all had gotten food and rest. Their mounts, grained and put under shade, had dozed the full five hours of the halt. It was time for decisions.

All of the morning, the lieutenant had not slept.

He had eaten only on the stalk, going from sentry to sentry, continually thinking with his head down and his jaw muscles working. Nothing was moving, the men told him. Only the heat shimmer. That and some mirages playing far to the north where the big flat fanned out into lower country and thicker shimmer yet.

Sergeant Bourke went with him, faithful dog to his master's stride. He was worn down to saying "yes sir" now to everything. Whatever it was of action that the lieutenant arrived at in his toiling mind, Bourke would bark it out for him to the men.

But the thirty-year veteran knew what his officer was pacing about for; he was waiting for Peaches.

He had ridden as far into Apacheland as he cared to do without his native scouts.

The problem meanwhile remained: Where were those Chiricahuas of Chatto's, and what were they waiting for? Surely they had long since found their slaughtered women and children. As surely they had taken the trail of the horse soldiers who had done the bloody work.

It was only thirty miles from Fort Gila to Pima Bend, even if more like forty-five "straightened out." It was another scant forty miles on to Sifford Wells by the stage road running mostly level and uncurled, as the local civilians put it.

All right. But those were all wheeled traffic miles. The Apache, any Apache, knew antelope tracks and coyote runs negotiable to their wiry mustangs that would subtract literal hours from any time Kensington and his men could have made following the road.

The possibility was that the Chiricahua could be watching Sifford Wells at this moment—and waiting.

That had been the net finding of the morning's talks with stage line owner, T.C. Madden, and with his errant coach crew. Madden and the crew and the cavalry had all taken different routes over the mesa, at different hours of the past night; among them they would certainly have flushed out any sizable band of Indians. No, the Apache would have to be ruled out on Querecho Mesa, as well as in the valley on the Pima Bend side north of town, as of the night before. It remained to ascertain as definitely where they were today. *That* noontime. Not yesterday. Not last night. Not even the past, nervously endured morning. But right exactly then.

T.C. Madden, ending the last discussion within the hour, had spelled it out for Kensington and Bourke as clearly as it would ever be spelled out for them.

With a wearily eloquent jab of the thumb toward the stillness and the sunbake beyond the low mud walls, he had said: "They're out there."

The afternoon wore on and, with it, the nerves of Lieutenant Harry Kensington. At 3:00 P.M., he called Bourke to the roof of the station house. He handed his field glasses to the sergeant. "Will you kindly tell me what you see out there, Bourke," he said.

Emmett Bourke studied the desolation and the beauty of the mountain desert. He swung the glasses three hundred and sixty degrees, then swung them again. He gave the glasses back.

"Nothing, sir," he said.

"Exactly!" Kensington was panting with the rooftop heat, flushed, hollow-eyed from exhaustion. "There isn't anything out there—yet."

Bourke waited.

Kensington was glassing the country again, this time up the wash south and east to the rearing west face of Querecho Mesa. "But there is going to be something out there, sergeant," he said very quietly. "Us."

"Sir?"

"We're going out there—*we're going to be out there*—before those devils are."

He said it in the same flat everyday way that he might announce a saddle-up for routine post review, and Bourke just stared at him.

It's the heat, he thought; he can't mean it.

But Kensington meant it.

His reasoning had that near-conviction and mirage argument that mirrored at the same time it mocked clear thinking. The Chiricahua raiders were either in the area, or they were not, he said. As to that, both his own and his first sergeant's experienced surveillance of the country had just once more agreed that nothing resembling an Apache Indian party was on the move within reach of army field glass, nor had been since their arrival at Sifford Wells. The assumption must be that, if they were coming, they had not yet arrived. Immediate derivative of that, Kensington pointed out, was that they, the cavalry, had time to deploy troops to receive the Apache in a manner best conceived to result in a military conclusion unfavorable to Chatto and his Chiricahua murders.

"Do you agree, Bourke?" he snapped. The excitement of his idea was building in him, and the sergeant knew he must be extremely cautious with his reply. He nodded and made a play of using the field glasses again.

"Go on, sir."

They would deploy, Kensington continued, in the big flood-plain of boulders that rose steeply southeast of the station. There was water up there on Querecho, a big spring, Madden had said, which gave rise to the beautiful creeklet that terminated in the deep-rock native tanks over which the stager had built his relay station. It was the only water outside the mud walls of the Sifford Wells compound for forty miles in any direction and a known Apache camping place. If any Indians were moving on the station, they would of rational necessity rendezvous at that big spring up there.

"What I propose, Bourke," the officer concluded, "is to wait for our red friends in their own station, rather than in Madden's. What do you think?"

Bourke tried to gather his sanity within the limits bounded by the chevrons on his sleeves. Go up on that mesa slide, deploy up through those boulders that could hide five hundred Apaches along the way, and *then* set an ambush on a water hole the Indians had been coming to for God knew how many hundreds of years—a place they were bound to know as well as Bourke knew the parade ground at Fort Gila? Completely halted, the old sergeant made the worst possible blunder at retreat.

"These here ain't the women, sir. We got to—"

He realized too late what he had said. Kensington, however, merely nodded quickly.

"Yes, yes. Go on."

Unbelievably, the officer was reading into Bourke's statement only that they would need to go about this kill a bit differently than the other. The sergeant countered lamely, "I was just going to say, sir, that Chatto's bunch will have their scouts out, wheres the women didn't have none."

"And?" said Kensington intently.

"We ain't none, either, sir."

"Ahh!" said Harry Kensington. "A point."

"Yes sir. I surely wish Peaches would show up."

Kensington was looking at the boulder field once more. And the brooding mesa behind it. And the steep face of the mesa where the Apache spring was hidden. He was not using the glasses. He was just looking up there and thinking. Suddenly, he was not so excited.

"Goddamn it!" he said. "We've got to do something. We can't just sit here and let the devils get away."

"Sir."

"Yes, Bourke?"

"What about the stage line folks, sir? And the coach? And Mr. Madden's gold shipment for Tucson?"

"What about them? They're all under arrest. You know that. We'll escort them *and* the coach *and* the gold back to Pima Bend. Now you heard me tell Madden that."

"Yes sir. How about the lady, lieutenant?"

"Goddamn it, Bourke. It is not my fault that she got herself with child, or that she decided she had to get to Tucson to have that child."

"But, sir, she ain't hardly more than a baby herself. Only a kid, sir. And, sir—"

"Yes, yes."

"The darkie, sir, he says she's going to have the baby any minute. Claims she's been gritting her teeth and hiding her pangs since this morning early."

Kensington was neither an insensitive nor an indecent man. Unmarried and barracks-lonely, he was still a man's man and could be reached.

"Are you saying she's in labor, Bourke?"

"No sir. Just panging."

"We will have to let happen what will," the officer decided. "If we don't outthink the Apache, she may never have the child."

"Yes sir. Or wish she didn't."

They fell silent, the sergeant apprehensive, the lieutenant wracking his military intellect for inspiration on out-thinking Chiricahua Indians. He left the roof and returned half a dozen times. The lookout on the roof was changed twice, on the hour. The troopers began preparations for evening mess, "lieutenant's orders," at five-thirty. Kensington was still on the prowl. Still thinking. Still struggling. Never quitting.

In God's name, there had to be a way to get those Indians. Peaches and Bobbie, both of whom had cut sign on the Chiricahua men before finding the track of their women, had told him there were no more than a dozen warriors in the party. He, Kensington, had also twelve men, and the Indian never lived who could fight a white force, man for man. All he had to do was get those devils to come on. To somehow lure them into—

He stopped, head swinging up.

Lure.

Had he said "lure" in his mind?

That was it!

Lure. Lure and trap. Set the trap and lure them into it. Then, snap! But wait. Trap? Aha, bait! Bait the trap. Then set it and let it go snap.

Bait? What did he have of bait to use?

He was in the common room of the station house walking from rifle-window to rifle-window.

Bait, bait, bait. Something they would pounce on a sight faster than they would twelve U.S. cavalrymen in full patrol detail. Something they would grab and then find out they had twelve U.S. cavalrymen snapping down on them. Bait, decoy, lure.

T.C. Madden came in from the outside, fuming about his Concord and its arrest and what the Governor down in Tucson was going to hear about Lieutenant Harry C. Kensington. The army had no right, no goddamned right at all, to conspire in the bankruptcy of a civil stage line. Holding back that gold from going on to Tucson that night was a crime. The Governor of the territory would sure as hell think it was, anyway, seeing as how he owned thirty-four per cent of the stock in Southwest Stagelines, Incorporated and Limited, by God.

Kensington had heard it all before and many several times earlier in the day.

But this time it was different. This time they were not talking about a Concord coach in illegal transit of a military quarantine area. This time they were talking about something entirely aside and singular.

"Mister Madden, sir." The officer's voice was its old flat arid self again. "How would you like your coach to go on to Tucson this evening?"

Madden continued his complaint another ten words, then spun around. "What did you say?" he demanded.

"I'm going to help you," said Lieutenant Kensington. "Your coach is going on to Tucson—with full military escort. Make your arrangements, sir."

Madden blinked, blew out like a startled horse, stampeded

out the rear door bawling for Hunker to begin the hooking-up; he had his clearance for Tucson!

So he had.

And Harry Kensington his Apache bait.

22

Peaches had guessed the pony time closely. It was just after five o'clock in the afternoon when the augmented Chiricahua party reached Na-koo-say, above Sifford Wells. It was not a happy camp. Chatto and Lucero still argued the problem of the two prisoners. The leader kept referring and deferring to his wife in the matter, which did not make things better.

War-women who went with their men had equal vote in trail councils, true. But they were never leaders. It galled more than fierce Lucero that Chatto was leaning on his woman. It was dangerous to have outsiders such as Peaches and the Pima Bend woman in camp. Perhaps Lucero should be listened to.

But then they all remembered the poignancies of that sad day begun with the burial, the immediate swift burial as required by the fearful custom of their people, of their leader's firstborn and only son. It was White Hair whose words spoke it for them all:

Chatto, he said, had left a part of his heart back there in the rocks where they had met his woman. Ysun himself—the veteran used the ancient name for Yosen—knew what part of her Chatto's woman had left back there with her mutilated man-child.

"He is not leaning on the woman, you fools," the elder warrior glared. "He is permitting her to lean on him. He is giving her something to live on."

Lucero was not there, being as always in the shadow of Chatto and Chatto's woman. The next complainer of any ranks was fat-paunched Tubac, a surly man given neither to charity nor to nonsense of any other kind. His word held weight.

"Very well," he said. "Those two will be safe here. The woman will not dare run away, and we have Coyote tied up tight to that cottonwood. Who would free him?"

"The vultures, perhaps," grinned Do-klini.

"The vultures free us all," growled White Hair. "I will tell Chatto we vote with him."

"Yes," said Do-klini, the unconscious philosopher. "Unless the counsels of the soft hand upon the penis and the tickling fingers underneath the stones have turned his mind from killing altogether."

"*Cochel*" snapped White Hair. "The woman still bleeds from the breeching. The child came wrong and she has not rested since. She may die if the bleeding does not halt. And you think of coupling?"

Do-klini made indignant gesture of denial. "You mistake my meaning, old bad-tempered dog. I was only saying that, with a woman, no decision is safe. Especially that one. You know she is no ordinary person."

"I know she does not think about what you think about all the time." White Hair's dark eyes blazed. "Just because Ysun hung that great jackmule's *pico* upon you does not make you any authority on women. You don't know anything about them. You never took the time from playing with yourself with both hands to find out."

Do-klini was grinning again. "Ah," he said, "I know something about that one. Why do you think Lucero hangs around Chatto's fire all the while? He is handsome enough to have all the women he wants from any band he wants. Aye, and she is older than he by more than a few summers. Chatto is a fool. I'm not so sure that was his man-child."

"Gossip," said Noche, getting up quickly.

"Old woman's talk," grunted Bosque, following his comrade to his feet.

"I wonder?" said Tubac and led the march around the gushing pool of Na-koo-say to tell the war leader they were ready and to let the captives live *until*.

Neither Peaches nor the Pima Bend woman missed a word, spoken or implied, in their stay of execution.

In separate ways, each was Chiricahua.

If the woman was so by only half of her blood, then the cavalry scout was even more so by virtue of his marriage into the band. By Apache law, all allegiance, all real property, all future of any kind belonging to the man went to the woman, and the tribe of the woman, with the wedding vows. He could not even again live with his own band, whatever it might have been, but must stay only with the people of his wife and mother-in-law. He became in effect what his wife was, and so in very real terms Peaches was no longer White Mountain but Chiricahua.

In this way he and the wife of Piney Newbold understood their danger: She was fat and soft from settlement living and would hold them back in flight; he was a keen trail reader who would remember every stone of that flight. Question: Would the Chiricahuas of Chatto need a fat city woman or a self-professed volunteer cavalry scout to help them retreat from the killings to come at Sifford Wells?

Peaches, for one, did not believe they would.

He waited only until the Chiricahua men were around the spring untying their ponies.

"Missus," he said to the Newbold woman, holding his voice low and in English. "You better think hard, much hard. Them people kill us they come back."

The woman's eyes widened. And Peaches had made a bad misjudgment. She at once cried out in excellent Apache to the mounting party across the spring that the cavalry scout was trying to trick them, trying to get her to betray them, to free him so that he might find the soldiers and lead them to this place.

"He means to do it while you are gone!" she cried. "Remember, he is Coyote. He can make those ropes fall off his wrists and his ankles with his medicine!"

This was not an empty charge.

Coyote was second only to Owl in the bad-animal signs of the Apache people. Bû was the worst, of course, but Pa-nayo was even craftier. And Chatto was very religious. He believed in the old signs.

"Do not delay now, *jefe!*" cried White Hair. "The light is going. Do not listen to this liar. She is half white. Don't forget that. Cut her throat is my advice. Or jerk her tongue out and smoke it for Ysun."

Chatto came back around the spring.

He looked into Peaches' eyes.

He looked into the eyes of the white man's wife whose mother had been a Mexican Chiricahua.

"One of you has lied," he said.

"It is him! It is him!" screeched the woman.

In that his bonds would permit him, Peaches shrugged. "If I am Coyote and can make the ropes fall off, ask the woman what need I have of her to free me?"

All of the others, the Hoh-shuh Springs hostiles as well as

the original Fort Gila raiding party, now came moving around the water of the Na-koo-say to stand silently.

"We have found the liar," Chatto said.

Do-klini seized the woman from behind, strangling her. Tubac and Bosque each secured a flailing arm. Noche took her legs at the knee, one in the muscled crook of each arm. Chatto slid out the knife.

When it was done, the leader went back around the spring to his pony. His seven men and his woman and the twenty-one Chiricahua brothers followed, mounting up as he did. "*Ugashé*, we go," Chatto told them, and they grunted, "*Ugashé, ugashé*," deep-voiced, and they were gone. Almost at once, all sound went with them.

Peaches, gauging the clear green sky of spring evening, did not like it. Too much killing light remained. If he could not get free to reach the people at Sifford Wells, Chatto would fall upon them without warning. If Peaches' patrol were there, it would be a fight. If the stagecoach people were alone, it would be a massacre.

There was a single chance—the woman.

She was on her hands and knees now like an animal. She moved jerkily along the flinty ground making the terrible suck-and-gagging noises such poor wounded ones uttered— the only sounds they would ever again utter. It came to Peaches, watching her, what she was looking for—her tongue—her tongue—she wanted to put it back.

"*Mujer!*" he called to her, seeing the terrible bleeding from her mouth. "Please, I will help you look. But I need my knife to be free or I can't help you. *Mujer!*"

Chatto had cut too deeply. This one was going to die. Sometimes they did that. But she would live long enough, if he could only attract her attention, get past the agony of her hurt into her crazed brain.

He repeated her name, trying English, Spanish, Apache.

At the last words she responded, swinging stricken face up to stare at him, the blood and clots vomiting from the corners of the pitiful mouth.

"My knife!" cried Peaches. "It is hidden under the stirrup fender of my saddle. Left side. The pony is tied. You can reach him. If I have the knife, I can save your life. Think of that. *Get the knife!*"

Somehow she understood. Somehow she got to the pony of the frightened scout and found the hideout blade beneath the fender. Somehow she started back toward the bound captive with the weapon. And then she fell.

Peaches sucked in his breath; life was so close.

And death.

"Please, missus!" he pleaded. *"Jesus Christ—!"*

The woman heard him. She looked up.

The monstrous gargle welled once more in her throat. She strangled upon it, vomiting. Peaches closed his two eyes. It was all done. Ysun, the old Apache God, was not there. Nor was the white man's Jesus Christ the Lord.

It was only Pa-nayo-tishn.

And Mrs. Piney Newbold.

He heard a sound. A scraping over flinty pebbled scarpment soil. He opened his eyes. The woman was at his feet holding up the blade toward his bound hands. Straining, he could reach it, and he took it from her.

She slid down and lay across his *n'deh b'keh*, his curl-toed Apache boots. She quivered a little and was still. Peaches said something for her to Ysun and also to the Lord Jesus and twisted violently in his bonds to bring the hideout knife against the rawhide thongs.

Five minutes later the camp stood empty.

Except for Mrs. Piny Newbold, who would wait in it forever.

23

Life in a cutbank wolf burrow through midday of an Arizona springtime was, the drifter decided, not just precisely prime doings.

At first, since it had worked and he was free, he had thought himself smart as a bunkhouse rat to figure out such a hole. Along about noon, losing lots of sweat and having no water to put it back he began to wonder. He tasted the perspiration and found it salty as licking Lot's wife. A desert man and a dry-range man, he knew he could not lose all that water and salt and wind up alive. He was already panting like a rundown dog just to get enough air to keep his heart pounding. He knew he had to have more. With the sun overhead and no sign of the Apache, he took the chance and wedged back the sandstone slab which blocked the entrance.

Ahh! It was hotter than bullet-mold lead and just about as heavy, but it was fresh and it was air. Almost at once, his breathing slowed, pulse rate dropped, the flush of building heat exhaustion cooled. He would be all right now. But he would have to have some water soon.

In fact, he would have to have it long before sundown brought the darkness that would cover his resignation from Southwest Stagelines. Unconsciously, he commenced scanning the surrounding parch-growth of stunted juniper and high country chaparral looking for hopeful sign of a seep from the Apache spring up above.

Again, he breathed, Ahh! For again he had seen something as welcome as the taste of the outer air.

Up there where the old she-wolf had come out of her back door in those crumbling Overland ruins, there was a splash of bright greenery that could only come from being locally fed. It was a little rash of bunchy salt grass not worth a Mexican nickel for feed, but, sure as a mustang horse apple would be full of mesquite beans, it was not growing along those old adobe walls *inside* their moldered foundations waiting for it to rain. That grass, bunch-salt or not, was getting water from below. And it was doing it in one little spot not bigger than a sheetmetal stocktank. A cistern? An old, old, caved-in and forgotten station-house cistern dug down to underwash groundwater thirty years gone by the Overland company?

Well, brother, it had better be.

There was not another solitary sign of more moisture than a dog-fox might leave by a leg-hoist on the trot and not stopping to scrape.

It was at this relieved point that the drifter realized that the bend of the wash around the Southwest compound would not permit him to bank-sneak up to the old Overland ruins. The wash made an S-twist going over the stage road that would reveal him in full to any of the horse soldiers on the roof for at least forty feet. It was no good. His options were shrinking with his stomach, which was already so shriveled up it would not chamber a pinto bean. If he could not find water where he was, he would have to go where he knew it was—inside the station compound, green and cool and sparkling clear in the old Apache tanks at Sifford Wells.

God it was hot lying there in that wolf hole on his naked belly. It was hot enough to raise a blood blister on a rawhide bootsole. Things for him were getting touchy as a teased snake, but he would need to keep his thinking straight and to hang onto his cards like an Indian to a whiskey jug. He dare not let go for a minute. Faint heart never filled an inside straight, as they said, and he would be damned if he was going to stampede as though he had bought a ticket to hell and was running to catch the first train out of the depot.

No sir.

They might strap him on his horse toes-down, but he was not going to help them do it.

If worse came to worst, he could go in and get his drink by leave of the U.S. Cavalry. It was a far ways better than just laying there in that bad-aired varmint run waiting to get his halo gratis.

What in the name of Christ was he doing in the wolf hole anyway? The old sheriff was not a bad sort. He might give a man a break on the way back. Especially a man that had tried to help his friend Madden get his coach and gold payment down to Tucson. And Madden would sure as hell put in a word for him. Maybe even give him a full-time job. My God, it did not have to be too late to try again. Other men had done it.

The drifter actually started to wriggle out of the foul heat of the burrow, then he thought of Yuma Prison and stopped wriggling.

Ah, Jesus, a man had to go the full distance of his guts before he would buy a drink at that price.

"I'll make it," he said softly aloud. "By God, I will."

Suddenly the thought came to him. That old smart bitch-wolf had not gone up the wash to get to the Overland ruins. Now, wait. That was the heat getting to his head talking. Crawl up there through the hole? A full-grown man? Squirm and squiggle his bony frame where a sixty-pound wolf had gone? But now hold on. Maybe it was not the heat making his head swim. That damned old bitch had gotten up there powerful quick. It was almost as if she had galloped through that burrow, not snaked along it on her bellyfur. Well, Lord, ten times double ought zero was still straight cipher. Happen a man crawled far enough around the teacup, he just might find the handle. Even starting from ten lengths back of scratch. What was it they said? You don't pick up the walnut, you never find the pea?

Scuttling backward like a six-foot sandcrab, the drifter wormed along the burrow. Soon his kicking feet found waving room, and he was into the denning room proper and could turn about and get his breath and go head first from there on. In five minutes, no more, he saw the light at the other end of the hole.

The Lord had done it for him.

Some high water from the past had flooded out the upper escape hole and poured a volume of water under great pressure through the burrow, gutting it out its full length in places so much so that the drifter could get up on his hands and knees and scramble at full speed. The old wolf's rear door, when reached, was too small, and he would have to hand-claw his way out of it, but he could manage that: he could because all around up there near the surface the ground was damp and cakey, and he knew he had been right about the seepage from the Apache spring up on the mesa's flank; he was not going to have to buy his drink of water at the price of five years in Yuma Prison.

It was 6:15 P.M. The sun's edge squinted over the forks of old Piños' saddle-backed landmark ridge. The desert was in its evening hush, that strange, green-skied time between day's end and night's beginning. Within the stock corral at Sifford Wells station, T.C. Madden readied his big Concord. He counted the gold behind the underseat panels. He checked each whiffletree, tug, snap, ring, and buckle of the six-horse hitch's harness rigging personally. Behind him moved his black shadow; Clooney Borrum, double checking his beloved Mr. T.C. and his equally beloved, softly nuzzling, six picked horses. Hunker Larsen was in the station house getting the girl ready. Feeny was running proud liaison to the roof; at that instant standing on the chicken ladder bringing very latest intelligence from the staging yard.

"Mister Madden says he's near all set. Wants to learn iffen you-all are likewise?"

Kensington instructed Bourke to get rid of the messenger and the sergeant pushed Feeny's head back down through the traphole with ungentle bootsole and stern advice to, "Pop it up again and I will kick it off your goddamned shoulders. Yeah, we're about set here."

The sergeant returned to the officer, squatting beside him at the parapet. For the final time they studied the silence out toward Piños and the last sunwink and up toward the red-dyed crags and cedar clumpings that hid Na-koo-say from Sifford Wells.

"All right," said Kensington suddenly. "Let's go."

In the yard behind the station house, screened from any Indian view up on Querecho Mesa, the coach stood parked to Kensington's orders. Sergeant Bourke came out the rear door, stayed carefully in under its ramada roof. "Are you ready to board your passengers, sir?" he called out to Madden.

"All set!" waved the latter, feeling his Irish rise.

By God in Heaven, he was going to make it on down to Tucson. Those damned miserable spalpeens of crooked sons of banking bitches would get their blood money, and that lovely little tyke of a yellow-haired unwed lady-girl would get to have her baby where she wanted it, after all.

If Madden could remember any of the saints, he would surely be praising them at this time. Instead, he called up to Clooney, now mounted on the driver's box. "Go along easy at first, Clooney man. We don't want to raise any undue dust till we're well away and the light's gone."

"Yes sir, Mister T.C. I wishes we had us that hossthief back again. What we gonner use for a shotgun man?"

Madden laughed. "Young feller I knew name of Thomas Carlysle Madden used to ride a fair West Texas smoothbore for the old Jim Burch line," he said. "I reckon he can still swing on a running redskin grouse."

This was several times too involuted for Clooney to unravel right off. While he was trying, Madden saw Bourke returning, this time in soldierly stride. He went quickly and opened the onside door of the coach, expecting the mother-to-be, Hunker, and Feeny to be following the sergeant.

But they were not.

There were only First Sergeant E.J. Bourke looking very grim indeed and, behind him, eight troopers of the Fort Gila patrol, also very grim, also armed to the shoulder straps with revolver, carbine, sabre, and double cartridge bandoliers slung crosswise, Sonora-style. In their van came Lieutenant Harry C. Kensington not looking grim, at all, but flushed and eager and brimming with that U.S. Cavalry *something* that went with buglers blowing the charge, sabres out and swinging, and somewhere the valiant shouting, "Forward ho—!"

The old sergeant drew up, still grim.

"These here are your passengers, Mister Madden," he said. "You've got a full load. Pull out."

24

The drifter found his water at the bottom of the abandoned Overland cistern too thin to plow, too thick to drink, in his rangeman's view, but just right for chewing the juice out of and thus, staying alive.

Sundown, 6:15 P.M., found him in fit condition, anxious for prowling dusk, meanwhile thinking hard on his choices, if any.

It was the girl who bothered him mainly. She and Clooney Borrum. The others could go to hell, or back to Pima Bend, whichever. But the girl was only a child like his own Aura Lee had been, with the same long yellow hair and flecky deep blue eyes. And it was not that she was going to have that baby that prisoned his mind into fears for her. It was that she was so young and so like his own lost darling.

He still could not believe that she was gone. Or that only three brief years had passed since that terrible other sunset. It all refused to hang together in his memory. Theirs had not been just another older man and young girl frontier settlement match. The seventeen years difference in their ages was what had made it all so wonderful; him being a man long-grown and she only a kid willing and excited and purely happy to have him above any other man. And knowing what she was doing too. Why, she had been way more like twenty-seven than seventeen. But that was Tascosa and those other endless summers gone, and he had been thirty-four acting like seventeen. Jesus, Jesus, what love they had known.

He wondered about this girl. What love had she known? What kind of a love could it have been that would let her have the baby without the band?

The drifter dug deep into his possibles pocket, an extra little hideout place he had handsewn himself into the front slash of his disintegrating Levi's. The wedding circlet glowed even in the gloom of the weed-grown, timbered-over cistern. He held it folded in his two hands a moment, yearning back. Then he put it way and said softly, "Come on, sundown. Get dark, get dark—"

In the rear yard of the station, T.C. Madden stood stunned, speechless. The eight troopers were boarding his heavy Concord for Tucson. His fifteen thousand dollars in gold coin remained under the passenger seats. His employees sat atop the driver's box. But Hunker Larsen was in the station house with the girl, and he, Madden, was standing there with his Irish mug shut tight and watching a damned popinjay of an overaged lieutenant of U.S. Cavalry shanghaiing his legal property, with not one ticket punched or paid for and God knowing if the run would get two hundred yards from Sifford Wells—beyond Winchester iron-sight range—before the Cherry Cows jumped it.

And he called himself an Irishman?

A hand the size of a smoked elk ham fell not too gently on the shoulder boards of Lieutenant Harry C. Kensington. "Just a goddamned minute," bellowed Madden belatedly. "We ain't through talking!"

Kensington came about on one heel, white-faced.

"Sergeant," he said to Bourke. "Finish loading the men." He took Madden's arm. "Come over here, Mister Madden," he said, indicating the rear door ramada, out of earshot of his command. Madden went with him, not white-faced but red-faced. "Now, sir," said the officer, "you will understand my position. A military commander has always to try to think what the enemy will do, then act in accordance with that projection in mind. And he must always anticipate. He must always act before the enemy. If he cannot act, whether through tactical indecision or simple personal cowardice, he endangers not only his command but, as well, all those civilian lives and properties that the situation has thrust into his custody. I have my orders, sir, duly cut at Fort Gila, given me by Captain Herritt, executed to the letter so far and to be executed to the letter right now. They are to close off the Indian country between Pima Bend and Tucson; to pursue and, if possible, severely punish the hostiles of the Chiricahua chief, Chatto; and, in such process, to protect and defend the civilian community to the full limit of my resources. Do you, sir, finally understand that?"

Madden understood it with such clear vehemence that Kensington had to shout up Bourke and put the Irishman in physical restraint. Pinioned by Bourke's four troopers, the stage line owner still managed to convey his own civilian position with enough authority to cause the cavalry commander to again take pause. "All right, sergeant," he said. "Release him. Back to your loading."

He then carefully explained to Madden that he had no desire whatever to have his actions reviewed per virtue of any civil lodgments of dereliction of duty charges against his, Kensington's, conduct in the field.

"You know my orders, sir," he said. "Now you force me to reveal my plan for implementing those orders."

Speaking with intense conviction, a conviction that Madden, himself as confirmed an Indian-hater as the territory held, must be affected by, the cavalryman unfolded his strategy. It was simple. It was brutal. It was beautiful. He was going to kill a lot of Indians or, in terms better suited to the eastern newspaper mentality, a lot of Indians were going to get themselves killed.

It would work as follows:

The coach would depart with his eight heavily armed men within. Sergeant Bourke and his four troopers would ride out front in obvious escort of the continuation of the Tucson run The Indian assumption of necessity would be that the coach held the same passenger load as of the day previous, or at very least a similar civilian cargo. Certainly, they would never suspect the Concord to be packed with pony soldiers. They would see but five troopers with the coach. Knowing the patrol's original strength to be fourteen—twelve men, the sergeant, and the lieutenant—the devils would think that the officer was staying at the station with the major force. They would have to assume that he, in his ignorance of their fury over their dead women, believed five soldiers to be sufficient—with whatever other guns might be inside, plus the two company men on top the coach—to guarantee that no twelve Cherry Cows, no matter what their motivation, would jump the Tucson-bound Concord.

The Apaches would be further deluded, Kensington continued, by the fact that the escort was riding out in front of the coach, rather than behind it, where any knowledgeable frontier officer would have it.

He had done, he assured Madden, everything that he could, to pull the bastards out of the chaparral. If they were in fact out there, as Madden himself had said he believed them to be, then surely Kensington's ruse of using the baited stage as a lure would work.

It had to work, providing they took the bait.

The bait was poisoned.

They would get such a dose of lead and at such a point-blank range that the only survivors of their attack would be the horses which bore them into it.

There was some risk, certainly, to the driver and shotgun rider. But they did not know the danger to be any more real than that they had willingly run the night before in bringing the stage to Sifford Wells. Their loyalty was to T.C. Madden, to Southwest Stagelines, and to getting that gold down to Tucson for their employer.

Lieutenant Harry C. Kensington had precisely the identical devotion.

If Madden did not believe him, listen to this:

Should the Indians not materialize and attack prior to darkness, the coach would be turned about, brought back to Sifford Wells. If they did attack, as Kensington believed they must, then the coach would be returned even more promptly to Sifford Wells. In either event, the Concord would be permitted, indeed, ordered, to proceed with all due haste to Tucson, bearing its original passengers from Pima Bend, plus any wounded sustained in the fight, and fully guarded by all troops fit for duty. In short, T.C. Madden could not lose.

All he had to do was stay at the station with the suffering unwed girl and the brawny blacksmith and wait out the certainty of the cavalry's trap.

There was no possibility in Kensington's professional view, including his six years in Apacheria, that the Indians would fall upon a station they must presume to be heavily guarded.

Not, in God's name! when they could jump a stagecoach with but five soldiers guarding it, outside the station. In summation, Lieutenant Kensington proposed that Mr. T.C. Madden must agree and asked him to so state, now and quickly.

"Bourke!" he called. "Over here, please."

The old sergeant came over, and Kensington said to Madden, "Sir, I have explained to you our situation and what the cavalry proposes to do about it: Will you please say, now with this witness, that you do or do not agree with my estimation of the danger and my means of combating it?"

T.C. Madden nodded. "Sergeant," he said to Bourke, "forget all the fancy talk. The lieutenant has told me he will take my coach on down to Tucson tonight, win or lose with the damned Injuns. That includes all my company people and the passenger that paid for her ticket punched Pima Bend to Tucson. Long as the cavalry understands that, *in front of you*, by God, I agree."

Bourke looked at his officer, who nodded quickly, and Bourke said to Madden, "Yes sir, the cavalry understands." Then, most uneasily, "The coach is loaded, lieutenant."

Harry Kensington took a deep breath. He looked around at the high country stained red and gold with the late, last of the sun. This was the moment. He knew it. They all must have felt it. Crook, Custer, One-Arm Howard, Bearcoat Miles, all of them. Jesus!

"All right," he said quietly to his anxious noncom. "Let's move out, Bourke."

Peaches, sneaking afoot down the far, western side of Little Dipper Wash, was vastly worried. Not being able even to hand-lead his pony on a swift walk without raising fatal telltale dust on that late, still summer evening, he had hidden the little mustang in a covert up the wash. Now, nearing the Sifford Wells station, he watched intently the eastern bank of the wash where, surely, Chatto would come down from Na-koo-say. The wash itself, great litter of boulderfield to the contrary, would not screen a force on horseback from rooftop lookouts at the stage station. At the self-same time, neither could that Indian force ride or walk their mounts without, no less than Peaches, putting up enough hoof-drag to dust the still air warningly.

And the pseudo San Carlos scout could see no dust.

Damn!

Where were they?

They had started out before Peaches with an urgency of mounting up and clearing out of the campsite that indicated they meant to attack directly.

As in all such uncertain circumstances, the Indian act was to hide up until such time as circumstances gave reason to travel on once more with knowledge of the way ahead. Accordingly, when the Apache Scout drew near the place where the stage road went over Little Dipper Wash, westward, his dark eye cast about for that hide-up that native caution indicated to be prudent as of *ahora mismo*, right now, as the Mexicans put it.

It was thus he scuttled across the wash just above the road, where a peculiar cross-channel bristle of stunt cottonwoods gave cover. And it was thus, since the roots of the thick greenery took life from the seep that fed the old Overland stage cistern, that he came to that same cistern, simply by following the tree cover. Once into the weed-clogged ruins, the caved-in timbers of the cistern top had to suggest to him the same thing they would suggest to any hunted creature—concealment, with its time to think, what next?

It was only when he lowered himself with great care down through the sun-bleached timbers, great care not to change their original caved-in arrangement, that he discovered the cistern to be occupied.

As a matter of rude fact, his moccasined feet were seized on the reaching dangle, and he was whipped down into the brackish refuge with a back-flat thump which knocked the Indian wind completely out of his thick Apache chest. When he could breathe again, and thus move again, he found his own skinning knife to be held to his throat but not by his own hand.

"*Quién es?*" gritted the white man's voice. "*Amigo o enemigo?*"

"Goddamn," said Peaches. "Put knife more far away."

Surprised by the English, the drifter eased the big blade from his guest's jugular but did not offer to return the weapon. "Christ," he said. "A educated Injun?"

"Name Peaches," whispered the captive. "San Carlos cavalry scout," he lied instantly. "Reach feel neck-tag."

All of the enlisted scouts at San Carlos wore numbered metal identification tags. Peaches had prudently thought to borrow that of the Mescalero Bobbie, knowing its life-saving value. These frontier-day dog tags were the only guarantee of safe conduct for red-skinned males in an Arizona where any Indian and all Apache Indians were made instant "good Injuns," unless otherwise and unquestionably identified. The drifter, in his three-year trailing of Chatto and the Chiricahua, had of course learned this fact of the never-ending warfare between red man and white in the lonely reaches of Apacheria.

But he was also aware that hostiles had been known to kill San Carlos scouts and appropriate their security badges as a means of getting up close to white victims.

While checking quickly to make sure the Indian beneath him did indeed wear a tag, he did not then release him or put up the knife.

"All right," he said. "You got to do better than that, Injun. What's holding this here blade next your juggler's vein ain't no friend of the Apaches. You *comprende* that, you little bastard?"

"Sure," answered Peaches very soberly. "Peaches your friend. Look for patrol warn about Chiricahua."

"What patrol?" said the drifter tensely. "You name it right Peachy, and otherwise pray fast."

"Loo'ten'an Kens'ton," said the Apache. "Sarjen Broke. My soldiers. Fort Gila. Chase Chiricahua kill ranch people up fort way. Chiricahua catch me."

The drifter decided Kens'ton and Broke were close

enough. He had heard the names from Madden at the station, even though no mention had been made of any Apache scout with the patrol. He put the knife in his own belt.

"You got away from the Cherry Cows and you're trying right now to get back to your patrol, is that right?"

"Yes."

"That Chatto's bunch?"

"Yes."

"They coming down here?"

"Peaches think yes. They say yes."

"When?"

"Now. Ten minute. One hour. Before sun go home."

"Sun's already goed home," said the drifter. "Just looked out and watched her dip ahint old Piños."

"Yes. Peaches mean light to shoot. Before light go."

"Yeah, hell, I know what you mean."

The two men were silent. Both cocked heads listening to the stillness above them. A little wind was rising. They could hear it lisping in the salt grass overhead.

"You hate 'Pache Injun bad?" said Peaches.

"They kilt my wife and baby," answered the drifter.

The San Carlos impostor nodded. "This day yesterday," he said, "my soldiers kill four 'Pache wife, one baby."

"That's different," rasped the white man. "They was at war. They had it coming."

Peaches nodded. "Yes," he said. "Them Injuns."

"Murdering bastards, all of them," said the white man. He hesitated, awkward over what he had said. "You know what I mean," he explained lamely. "Iffen you didn't, you wouldn't be no cavalry scout fighting your own kind."

Again the small Apache nodded.

"I fight you side," he said. "Me, you, friend."

The drifter denied it, voice rising. "Me and you ain't nothing!" he snapped. "You better understand that, you little red-assed shithead. You and me—"

"Shh!" whispered the Apache. The white man and he could make out one another dimly now, eyesight adjusted to the cistern's gloom. "Horses come," he said. "Be no more talk. Listen."

"Injun hosses?" breathed the drifter.

Peaches listened through a second break of silence, then shook his black bangs. "Stagecoach," he answered. "Pulling horses. Hear sand and wheel."

The drifter could hear absolutely nothing save the sibilant whistling of the light evening breeze. Then he did hear it. Wheel grind. Harness sounds. Beat of hooves driving dust-holes in the deep sand.

"Cavalry too," said Peaches. "Four, five maybe."

Again the white man did not hear the sounds until moments passed. "My God, yeah," he said. "They're coming this way. Heading west. Christ! Tucson."

"Christ up there," said Peaches pointing unsmilingly upward. "Teach 'Paches good San Carlos."

The drifter looked at him in quiet desperation.

"You ever find Him up there," he told the Indian, "you guide me the way, will you?"

"Sure," grinned the would-be San Carlos scout, confidently. "Me you friends. Peaches guide."

"How in God's name you figure we're friends?"

"Easy thing; you don't kill me."

"Oh, Christ," said the drifter. "Come on."

Both men glided up the fallen timbers of the ancient cistern. At the top, they bellied into the salt grass commanding view over the straggle of low-growing cottonwood brush of the Sifford Wells crossing of Little Dipper Wash. They were in time to see Sergeant Bourke and four troopers put their mounts down the cut of the bank's wash ahead of the big Concord.

"Sarjen Broke," whispered Peaches. "Lieutenant Kens'ton stay station eight men. Bad thing damn."

"Good thing mebbe!" said the drifter, a sudden thought coming to him of farther fields and final safety for hunted horsethieves. "You sure Kensington and them others ain't follering the coach?"

"Not follow. Only Sarjen Broke, four man."

"Yeah," breathed the drifter. "And that sweet big Concord with the little gal in it and the baggage boot empty as your Injun head. Christ, Christ!"

Peaches said nothing. He knew his head was not empty, but what the white man had just said did not fill it up any either. A little girl and a baggage compartment without any baggage in it did not add up to answering where Chatto and the Chiricahua had gone. That was the only question in Peaches' Indian head. And it was the one that would determine everybody's head there at Sifford Wells on that long sundown evening of the green sky and the summer stillness of the good shooting light.

At wash's brink, the big Concord lumbered into view.

Peaches could feel the white man's body tensing.

"No go out there!" he warned. "You stay Peaches."

The drifter gathered himself for the run.

"Peachy," he said. "You stay your place, I'll stay mine. We'll see who gets to Tucson the fustest."

25

Peaches watched the white man go.

He saw him get into the cottonwoods and wait for the sergeant and four soldiers to go on up out of the wash. He saw him then run out as the big stagecoach slowed to pull through the heavy sand of the wash. He saw the white man use the dust of the wheels to hide his dash out behind the coach, his swing-up, his opening of the baggage boot, and his disappearance within the boot, all in a moment. Then the coach was up out of the wash and gone westward from Peaches' sight.

The Apache Scout hesitated.

He ought to go right back underground and stay in the old cistern until full dark gave him his chance to sneak into the stage station and rejoin his patrol commander.

That would be the smart thing. The Indian thing.

But the other thing was that Peaches still did not know where the Chiricahua were, and that was his real business. He was a loyal volunteer scout of the U.S. Cavalry. He was proud of the metal tag worn about his neck, even though it was not his. His first duty lay in finding the reinforced band of Chatto. Then he could run like the coyote of his name through sage and salt bush to the station to warn Lieutenant Kensington.

Anh, yes, it was decided.

Peaches snaked through the bunch grass and weeds of the Overland ruins. He came to the highest corner of standing mud wall that yet remained. There was in this corner a fantail of fallen roof timbers overlaced with dead and live weedstalks big enough to hide an antelope fawn or a medium-sized *javelina* wild pig or a small Apache cavalry scout. It provided even enough cover that Peaches might stand up crouched within it and be hidden while seeing out over the adobe foundation.

When he had done so, however, he wished that he had

not. Or wished that he were some other loyal volunteer, in some other part of Apacheria, attached to some other field force than that of Harry C. Kensington.

With that one stabbing sweep of his keen vision in the clear green light of evening, Pa-nayo-tishn—called Coyote by his people, known to the white man both by his White Mountain family name, Tzoe, and his Fort Gila nickname, Peaches —had found where the Chiricahua were.

Both places.

One suddenly revealed rise of swiftly moving pony dust lay to the east of Little Dipper Wash; one lay to the west. The eastern one, closest to Peaches' hiding place, was bearing down on the strangely deserted-looking stage station. The western one, half a mile beyond the wash, was circling north in a halfmoon to cut off the departed stagecoach. Chatto had split his forces.

And Peaches was caught in the middle.

He was badly frightened. This time the Chiricahua would kill him if they found him. Estune, Chatto's strange, sloe-eyed woman, would not save him another time, nor would the *hesh-kes* listen to her, if she tried.

Peaches by any other name, Pa-nayo-tishn, Coyote, or Tzoe, was dead unless he got away.

His fast good cavalry pony was just up the wash, well hidden and waiting. The Chiricahua would for the next few minutes be preoccupied in their twin assaults on station and stage. There was nothing in the Indian world that Peaches could now do to help his officer caught in the station compound at Sifford Wells. His clear duty was to get away and bring help. There was time for that if Captain Herritt had sent more troops down to Pima Bend in support of Lieutenant Kensington.

The chances were excellent that the captain had done just that. Red Beard Crook would have ordered it from San Carlos by the telegraph wires.

All right, Peaches would run for Pima Bend.

Right now. Goddamn.

Ugashé, go!

The next moment only the evening wind moved among the weeds and fallen timbers of the old Overland ruins on the banks of Little Dipper Wash.

The Coyote had run away.

Nine Soldier Gulch

26

Lucero, with all twenty-one of the new Chiricahua, attacked the coach one mile west of Little Dipper Wash at 6:35 P.M. He came in knifing between Bourke's advance escort and the following Concord. He came from the west, where the road hooked north to negotiate a lateral of the wash. The soldiers, looking always south, never saw him until his Chiricahua were virtually upon them. More, Lucero had them come with no whoops and no wolf cries—running their mustangs flat-out and holding fire as well as voices.

Bourke, hearing the thudding of all those unshod pony hooves on the earth behind him, whirled his mount in time to see that his detachment was already cut off from the coach, and to see, as well, that some half dozen of the Apache horsemen were being waved after him by Lucero—to keep him cut off. The veteran sergeant had not spent thirty years in the cavalry to be a useless hero in the end. He made no effort to reach the coach but sought at once the nearby outbreak of sandstone and red rocks which his eye told him was the only fort-up he could beat the six red horsemen to and still put out rifle fire in defense of his own command.

He made the rocks by a bullet whistle, which sieved his hatbrim, and a chorus of wicked, whining ricochets which screamed around in the tumble of his hasty fort like banshees wailing. He and his men, all miraculously unhurt, could hear the lead splash and could see the lead splash all about them. They did not have to look to know that the red men had Winchesters or other repeaters. "Men," said Bourke, levering his Spencer, "stay down and pick your shots. You, Werner," he called to the fourth trooper back in the rocks with the horses. "You let them mounts get free and we're did for." He turned back to the three white-faced youngsters lying with

114

him in the forward rocks. "All right, boys," he said calmly. "When you see a good shot, take it."

The men nodded and held their fire. The Indians, off their horses and under cover, kept pouring in the general fusillade of those to whom ammunition was in prodigal supply. That, and continually moving forward to improve their positions behind their fire.

"We can't let them hold us here," Bourke said. "We got to get set to get out'n here. Lookit yonder." The three men followed the point of his hand toward the stage road, only a few rods distant.

They were not so young in the service they could not see it happening.

The coach was beginning to career. Indians were slipping off their own horses to get down between the teams cutting lines. The Negro driver, within seconds, had nothing to hold his animals in. They were running straightaway on their own panicky instincts, still harnessed and taking the coach with them, but with red riders on their backs now.

The shotgun rider on top was emptying his old Spencer down into them with no visible result. Other Indians rode up behind the coach, transferred to its boot, swarmed its top. The first of these came at the shotgun man. The Negro driver saw him and yelled warning. The shotgun man turned in time to fire his Spencer, flashburn close, into the face of the Apache. It was Feeny Gleason's last, best shot at getting his filthy redskin, and he did not make it. The hammer fell with a sickening clink on an empty chamber, and the attacking brave shot Feeny three times in the head and kicked his dying body off the rolling coach.

Clooney Borrum, knowing he was next, and seeing two more Apaches coming up over the rear of the coach to make certain of the knowledge, stood up on the swaying box, knees braced on the dash. His bass shout of assurance went out to the lineless horses which he loved so much, "*hoh-shuh, hoh-shuh!*" and, not waiting to learn if they heard him, or cared, he yelled at lungtop, "Gee! Gee! Gee!"

His horses heard him. And they answered him. They went at once out of their headlong senseless gallop into a squealing, hard-right turn, careening the coach and throwing the three crawling Apaches from its top. Life spared, Clooney tried straightening the teams by voice again and could not. Now they were back under control of the redmen astride their sweating backs, and they must go where the screeching Indians directed them.

What, in these uncounted seconds, the eight troopers inside the coach with Lieutenant Harry Kensington were able to do went unnoted by red man or white. Thrown together and continually jerked around within the narrow confines of the cab, their rifle fire out-window was without visible effect. Reloading proved literally impossible owing to bounding bodies and lurch of vehicle. Kensington never once lost control in the melee, calling repeatedly for "steady fire, men, steady fire," not seeing, or not able to understand that what he commanded was no longer an effective body of troops but a driverless hearse outwardbound toward the last bugler blowing retreat and the tolling of the sunset gun that he would never hear. Lieutenant Harry C. Kensington, two times struck in the breast, blinded by a hanging scalp wound, was not seeing the bloodied limbs and blanched faces of his men; he was seeing grand blocks of newsprint:

> Heroic veteran cavalry officer fights off notorious Apache chief in Arizona Territory.... Lieutenant H.C. Kensington late Thursday met and defeated the red flower of the Chiricahua Nation while guarding a stagecoach rushing a young mother-to-be from a wilderness relay station to medical help in Tucson, capital of the territory.

In the coach, men vomited, men cried out, men wept, men prayed, men died. In the rocks where Bourke lay other men cursed, fired desperately, were hit, knew mortal fear.

> ... With but twelve men the gallant Kensington held off many times his number of the savage Chiricahua.... Chief of the band was the murderous Chatto, said to be named from the Spanish, *chato*, or Flat Nose....

There was smoke in the coach and the smell of flesh and burned powder and a growing agony of silence. From the rocks the old sergeant called on God, kept his men low.

> ... In a special release, General George Crook issued highest commendation for bravery beyond the call. Until Kensington got upon the trail, Crook said, young Chatto was thought by the Indians to have "bigger medicine" than the white

man, a fact that made his resistance particularly a peril to the frontier community and virtually demanded his destruction. . . .

It is expected that Chatto's death at the hands of Kensington's heroic few will bring an end, at last, to Apache depredation in Arizona. . . .

ALL EASTERN PAPERS PLEASE COPY—

From their rocks, Bourke and his men saw the Apaches drive the stage teams off the brink of the tributary gully. They saw the Indian riders jump. They saw the Negro driver jump. The coach went over the edge, came to crunching, overturned stop in mid-gully. The old Concord split like a dried gourd, spewing wounded and hale, alike, out upon the rocky sand of the side wash.

The stage horses thrashed and squealed in a trapping web of harness and coach-twisted wagontongue. The cavalrymen stumbled to their feet dazed, bewildered.

From the brink of the deep lateral wash above, the Apache marksmen now executed them in a timed volley of merciless fire. The Indians stood dismounted, rifles braced, and shot in deliberate, aimed sequence. They did not cease until all movement ceased among the blue-clad forms below. Then it was quiet, and they slid down the steep bank and came in among the dead and the dying to complete the grisly work by hand and blade.

In his redoubt beyond the stage road and overlooking the gully, Sergeant Bourke was ill—but not so ill that he failed to note that the Chiricahua who pinned down his small troop were likewise distracted by the soldier killing in the gully beyond the road. As he watched, he saw black smoke begin to roil up from the Concord and he knew the Indians had fired it, their traditional signal of fight's end and victory.

"Werner," said Bourke, "get 'em up here. Mount up, boys." The ashen-faced young troopers got to saddle. "Not a word now, and I'll shoot the first mother's son of you that touches off a shot," he promised. "Straight out and through them and head back for the station. Follow me."

The five troopers went out of the rocks as suddenly and soundlessly as the Chiricahua had come down on the Concord and on themselves only minutes gone. The six Apache scattered before them and did not find their ponies in time to pursue with close purpose. Bourke was away with his four men in a good race for life to the mud walls of Sifford Wells station. He knew and his four men knew that all were dead in the crossroad gully. They did not even look at the place in passing it; they only leaned the flatter to their galloping mounts' necks, praying the harder for themselves.

The six pursuing them peeled away at the bank unable to withstand the curiosity to see what lay below. They slid their little mustangs to halt on the gully's brink, peering downward where their fellows were beginning the mutilations and the hair-takings.

"See there," said an interested brave, pointing. "All of them are dead and the wheels of their wagon are still turning."

His companions nodded slant-eyed agreement.

It was a true thing.

One of them said, "Do you see that officer who killed our women and children?" A comrade only waved and answered, "Yes, that is the one. You see there? The one Lucero has just grabbed the hair of? No, no, over there. Lucero and that fighter of ours are arguing. See them?"

"Ah, yes, now I do," said the other man. "Come on. We'd better go tell Lucero that our soldiers got away."

"No," counseled an older, wiser man. "Let us wait until Lucero has taken his hair. Then he will be happier with us."

"Yes," agreed another old campaigner. "Besides, those men of ours will not get far."

"*Unhuh!*" cried the other. "Of course. I had forgotten Chatto back there."

They waited a moment, loading their guns, tightening saddle cinches. Then they swung up and went down into the gully, making wolf yelps to their fellows.

27

Chatto came in upon the station in quite another manner than Lucero upon the stagecoach. The young chief's purpose was to hold the main body of cavalry and the killer lieutenant behind the walls until the coach was disposed of and his Chiricahua main force returned to him by Lucero. Chatto had taken the less attractive of the missions for one reason— the officer. Estune rode with him still, looking for the soldier who had murdered her man-child. He could not trust Lucero with the lieutenant. Lucero might go into the station without waiting and try to kill the lieutenant for himself. Chatto had

sensed this. And it made him jealous and angry. He knew
what his own men were saying about the real father of his
man-child.

So he and Estune and old Nevado and the five true
brothers of his own band whooped in toward the silent relay
station, firing their guns and yelling their Apache throats
hoarse to imitate a greater attack than they were mounting.

Within the mudbrick fortress, Madden and Hunker Larsen
manned the two front window rifle-slits. Behind them, the
girl-mother groaned and fought back her pain and fear. She
had lost her water now and was bleeding slightly and had
blinding pain. Something was wrong. The two men knew it,
but they did not understand what it was. Over-shoulder, they
kept telling her it would be all right. That she was young and
small and she would stretch to it. "Bear down, bear down,
lady," Hunker said in his slow, dumb way. "Push hard."

The big smithy had been married once and delivered his
settlement wife of four children. Madden felt good from this.
If Hunker told the little kid that she was going to be all
right, she would be all right. The Swede was not bright, but
he remembered what he knew. On the frontier that was
oftentimes more important than being smart. So T.C. Madden, whose Irish heart panged him with every cry from the
suffering girl, cursed the yelling advance of the Chiricahua
and advised Hunker on what he, Madden, knew about—
fighting Indians.

"Hold fire, Hunk," he said. "Hold fire."

"Yah sure," answered the hulking smithy.

They each had Winchesters, and, if they levered them well
and shared the timing of their shots, they could make their
two rifles seem like four or five to the first charge of the
Chiricahua. Later, the devils would smell out what the true
garrison was. But, hell. By that time Kensington would be
back with the cavalry, and then the red bastards would see.

"He'll sure hear them shots," Madden said, low-voiced.

"Yah? Who?" said Hunker Larsen.

"The cavalry!" rasped Madden. "That damned smartass
lieutenant. He's got to be hearing this here gunfire of theirs."

"Yah. Suppose he keeps running?"

"I suppose that's funny to a Swede," growled Madden.
"Watch your slit and don't shoot until I do."

"Yah sure."

"Yah, shit," breathed Madden guardedly, swiftly looking to
the girl by the fireplace. "Hold on, honey," he said. "They

always sound like ten times the number. It ain't going to harm us, all that Injun yammer. You'll see." His only answer was a fierce gasp of gut-pain, a tortured cry smothered in writhing arms.

Outside, in the last of the heavy chaparral before the stage road across from the station, Chatto suddenly set his horse back on its hocks. The little animal sprayed sand and pebbles, slid to a halt, splay-footed. Estune, Nevado, and the other men brought up their wiry mounts as abruptly. "What is it?" asked the old brave.

"Stay back!" shouted Chatto. "Keep to the cover."

Do-klini and Dust Devil scowled at one another. Noche and Bosque shared a similar grimace. Tubac, the lone one, made his own scowl and said it for them all.

"What the devil is the matter with you?" he demanded of Chatto. "Are you listening to your woman again? Or is it that damned old man? Why do you make us slide our ponies like this at the last minute?"

Chatto did not seem angered. His young face was smooth. Serene almost. He was certain he was right.

"Think of it a bit," he advised. "Do you suppose that officer who killed our women is some fool? Do you think he would like anything better than to have everyone of us ride into him in a bunched-up herd like we are? Riding into his eight soldiers and himself? With the mud wall in front of them and with ourselves in front of the mud wall? Think about it."

The braves exchanged scowls for nods. This was why Chatto was a chief while so young. He thought about things before he did them. That is what made chiefs.

"What I wish you to do," the leader continued, "is to spread out each way, staying in the brush and pounding the ponies back and forth to appear four times ourselves. Fire your guns all you like. Yell a lot and raise much dust by spinning and reversing. Make them shoot. The woman and myself, we shall remain here. The officer is mine, remember. I stay here to watch for him. All right?"

The braves split three-and-three, Tubac riding with Noche and Bosque, old Nevado going with happy big Do-klini and serious small Dust Devil. All raised their rifles when Chatto asked them if it were agreeable. In a moment they were racing and firing wildly back in the chaparral. They indeed sounded as four times themselves, but no single round cracked from the rifle-slits of the station, nor did any weapon's barrel protrude over the rooftop parapet to thunder down.

Very quickly, Chatto raised the wolf howl, calling the men in again.

"Something is not as we think it here," he said.

"I believe it," answered old Nevado, old White Hair. "What will we do?"

Chatto held up a hand for silence.

"Think about it a moment," he ordered.

The men nodded and scowled and reined-about their lathered and restless ponies. Into this brownknit meeting of no voices came a harsher sound by far than their own camouflaging fire. It was the stacatto barking of many Winchesters and the hollow-booming replies of at least a dozen big-caliber pony soldier Spencer carbines.

"*Santa!*" burst out Nevado. "Too many soldier guns up there. Lucero has them all!"

The woman of Chatto looked at the young chief and said in her throaty low voice, "You have been tricked."

Chatto did not deny it. Nor did he take time to establish the nature of his deception. "*Ugashé!*" he shouted, spurring his pony for the stage road over Little Dipper Wash. Five of his six braves spurred after him. The sixth waited. When Estune, Chatto's woman, also wheeled her mount to follow her master, Nevado seized her arm and held her back.

"No," he said. "We will wait here. You are not well yet, daughter. And I am too damned old."

For the first time the tall woman smiled.

It was like a sunrise calm in the autumntime, yet smoky and warm. It gave her bronzed face a singular fleeting beauty, then she was without emotion again.

"*Anh,*" she nodded. "We shall watch the station."

"Good," agreed old Nevado. "Fire a few shots for me into those rifle-slits, will you kindly, daughter? Just to let them know we are out here. I would like the time to make a smoke."

The woman fired her nickel-plated Winchester like a man, from the hip, levering it without conscious aiming. As she emptied the magazine, four or five shots broke mud chips from the narrow slots of each front window. She reloaded while the old man rolled his corn-husk cigarette.

"You are a wonderful woman," he said, pausing. "I think, if I were ten years younger, neither that homely cub Chatto nor that sneering *hesh-ke* Lucero would have sired your dead man-child."

The woman said nothing, waiting, listening.

There was a sudden stillness from beyond the Little Dipper Wash. No rifle, neither pony soldier nor Chiricahua, broke the spring dusk. There came no sound either of war yelping or cavalry commanding words, thin with the distance through that heavy silence.

"It is over," said Nevado.

The tall woman shook her head. "*Dah*, no," she said. "Listen."

The crash of the rifle fire that came then was not from far over where Lucero had caught the stagecoach. It was from just beyond the wash, where Chatto had only now ridden; and his woman Estune struck her pony with her whip and shouted to it, "*Ugashé—!*" But again old Nevado's hand was quicker and stronger than hers. It pinioned the headstall of her pony, jerking the animal back.

"No," he said. "No! You must not go up there!"

She cut at him with the whip, cursing. With his free hand he seized the lash and wrapped it around his forearm, pulling the quirt from her grasp and throwing it down. At once, she was off her pony, running afoot with the Winchester into the heavy brush.

The old warrior watched after her a moment, then got down off his mount and made himself a new cigarette.

Squatting in the shadow of a mesquite tree older than himself, he leaned against the gnarled bole and drew in the delicious smoke.

"Ahh!" he said to his hipshot mustang. "What the hell? Who really cares? Do you, little horse?"

The ewe-necked paint shook brushy mane, stomped unshod hoof, whickered softly.

"Exactly my own view," nodded its master and sucked noisily and with deep Indian contentment upon the second cigarette.

28

Bourke and his four men lashed their mounts along the stage road. Behind them, all sign of Indian pursuit had ceased. The sergeant knew, however, that it was only an act of God that they had survived the fate of their fellows in the

Concord coach. He knew, as well, that the devils would be after them. Perhaps they already were, riding by some side wash to intercept the five cavalrymen who had gotten away from the massacre.

In the process of thanking that God who had saved them, Emmett Bourke and his men, bunched like jockeys coming into the stretch run, broke around the last bend in the road before Little Dipper Wash.

There was no time then to do anything. Chatto and his five braves were bunched in the same manner and running the same turn—going the other way.

It was a smashing, jolting collision of horseflesh and rider. Animals squealed and reared, some staggered, some broke through cleanly for both sides. Two Indians and two soldiers were knocked off their mounts. Both parties made initial reaction effort to rescue their unhorsed members. Again the luck of the field went equally. Bourke and Werner each picked up a man set afoot, as did Do-klini and Dust Devil for the Chiricahua. The sergeant's force labored on for the dry wash. Chatto shouted for Tubac to go after the soldiers with all the braves and to get the sergeant. He, Chatto, would ride on, alone, and see to the lieutenant.

The now remounted Apaches wheeled back for the wash, yelping and firing on the heels of the fleeing cavalrymen. But their God was still with the white men. They came to the wash well ahead of Tubac's pack, Bourke shouting them on with the glad news that they were as good as inside the walls. The Apache fire was wild, and their small ponies had lost too much ground to the rested service horses. "Hold 'em steady, boys!" he barked above the thudding of the horses' hooves and the panting labor of their breathing. "We've got the bastards headed!"

But Bourke was wrong; the bastards had him headed.

At least one of them did.

Chatto's woman came running on foot to the brink of the wash opposite them. She had a shining Winchester in her hands. Seeing the cavalrymen riding at her, she threw herself into cover beside the stage road and commenced firing from the ground. The fire was aimed and it was accurate. Werner was shot dead out of his saddle, his mount lunging on over the wash. One more man was badly hit. Bourke, giving up all thought of riding through such a barrage, not believing it could all come from the Apache squaw, yelled for his survivors to take cover! at the same time reining his own mount for the only retreat available: a drift-jam of higher country small logs and rootsnags behind them on the west bank. They were into it so quickly that the Chiricahuas of Tubac, coming from the west, overrode them and had to keep going for the squaw's side. They made this temporary safety before Bourke or his remaining troopers might put out any fire into their disappearing rears. The sergeant heard the Indian woman scream, "Fools" at the surprised warriors, and then both sides recovered and the fight was on.

Bourke knew from the first that it was hopeless.

They must, even dying, get out of that driftlog pile. They had let their horses go and were in bad shape afoot. Werner's body lay out in the wash. One gone. Young Peabody was bent over holding in his guts with his hands and crying. He had bullets through both arms and could not lift a rifle or revolver. As Bourke noted this, a third bullet ricocheted off a bone-hard driftwood chunk and went throught Peabody's spine. Two gone.

And three left.

Himself, Schermer, and Dennis Moriarity.

Across the wash, he heard the Apache squaw curse and tell her fellows she was out of ammunition for the shiny Winchester. None of them used the same gun. As well, they, the men, were getting low on loads.

He repeated this news to his remaining troopers, and Schermer, the older of them, said, "All right, for Christ's sake; let's go, Sarge. We ain't never going to be given a better chance."

Bourke shook his head, looking for another way.

"Without horses," he said, "it ain't no chance at all. Leave me think, leave me think."

"Sarge.'" It was the kid, Dennis, Bourke's company pet and Irish mascot. "Dutch is right. We got to go."

"Reload, kid," said Dutch Schermer. "We *are* going."

"Hold it!" snapped Bourke. "That's an order!"

The men hesitated. Into the pause came a yelping and yipping of Chiricahua voices behind them, up toward where Lieutenant Kensington and their eight friends lay. Some of the devils were coming back. A handful, only, to judge from the voices. But, Jesus God, they already had one handful of the bastards on the other bank. Between them and the station. Now these new ones coming up behind?

"Shove your orders," snarled Schermer. "Come on, kid—!"

Bourke made a grab for young Moriarity, but too late. He

was over the driftlog barricade and running with the older trooper. They were angling downwash to hit the shelter of the bend that enclosed Sifford Wells station. Schermer almost made it. From where he fell, hit at least a dozen times, his glazing eyes could see the mud walls of the loose-stock corral, and safety. Moriarity took three strides from the driftlog jam and caught a .50 caliber Springfield slug in the forehead. The back of his head flew into Bourke's face when the Irish sergeant leaped out to try and grab the youth in a desperate lunging tackle. The scarcely slowed Springfield bullet hit the sergeant's hat, sent it cartwheeling, and sent the sergeant reeling with it. The slug had ripped his scalp in passage, smashing him to his knees with shock, blinding him with sudden blood.

It was as he staggered up that he heard the familiar Apache voice yelling at him to, "Swing up! Swing up!" and saw, through streaming blood as he wheeled about, the blurred form of the small horseman bearing down upon him from upwash.

It was Peaches.

The Coyote had circled and come back.

Nevado raised his head? What was that? Ysun forgive him, he had nodded over that second cigarette! All he knew now was that there was a lot of new firing up at the wash, and he could hear Estune yelling bad words at the others up there. In a moment, he knew more.

Here came a familiar pony, double-mounted and working hard beneath the load. Why, it was that damned runt scout from Fort Gila. That white-loving little traitor with the boy's face and the pleasant sunny smile, whom they had left tied tightly to that tree up there at Na-koo-say. Well, you never could trust a White Mountain. Those *Dest-chins*, those Red Dust people of this slinking little chubby Coyote, riding yonder there with the horse soldier sergeant up behind him and making along the stage road for the gates of the relay station, they were a bad lot, altogether.

Old Nevado, old White Hair, did not hurry to rise and reach his saddle-scabbard and his old rifle.

Even when he saw Do-klini and the others beating their ponies in pursuit of the flagging mount of the pudgy runt scout, he did not hasten himself. Indeed, Madden had opened the compound gates and let the fugitives gallop through, then slammed the gates in the face of the Apache pursuers, before

Nevado got his old gun out. Then, of course, he had to load it.

He was still trying to get an ill-fitting shell into it when Estune burst from the brush on foot and face dark with anger. "Why did you not shoot them?" she accused, running at the same time for her tethered pony and spare ammunition belt. "You had them right under your nose and riding double on a tired pony!"

By this time, the covering fire of Hunker Larsen sprayed into the five braves retreating from the corral gates, letting Madden, Peaches, and Bourke get around behind the station house, unscratched. The humiliated tribesmen at once joined Chatto's woman in harassing poor old Nevado, needing someone to blame when the leader returned.

Finally, the old man picked up his gun and said quietly. "I would have hit you, firing at them. I can arrange the same thing right now, if you wish."

His fellows, of a sudden, were not so censorious.

Mumbling threats in the manner of the guilty, they took out their ire on the adobe walls of the station house, putting up a great fusillade just in case Chatto should come riding back and catch them idle.

Their fire was hotly returned by those inside the station. This proving uncomfortable so close in, the Chiricahuas withdrew deeper into the brush and spread themselves apart, as well. Estune and Tubac could rant all they wished. Let them get hit if that was what truly they sought. For the rest of them, the situation would keep until Chatto got back and told them what to do.

Unhuh, the hell with it.

In the gully where the wheels of the overturned Concord no longer spun, the last of the hair-taking went forward. Behind the stooping braves, the coach burned lickingly, the flames working toward the covered boot, the black smoke of the varnish and upholstery rolling over the grisly field. It was here that Chatto galloped down the bank to interrupt Lucero in the scalping of the dead lieutenant. The young chief was furious. Lucero knew at once that he had made a bad mistake, but he did not let go of the officer's dark hair nor of his scalping knife. Chatto, beyond himself with his rightful anger *and* his impugned honor, did a very rare thing for an Indian. He struck Lucero with his hand, knocking the subchief to the ground. In the moment that Lucero was dazed, Chatto leaned down and ripped the partially cut away scalp from the officer's skull and fastened the trophy to his own belt.

"Get up," he said to Lucero. "Do whatever it is that you will do."

It was a confrontation: naked, total.

In the mind of Lucero there was murder. But in his hand there was only the scalping knife. And Chatto held a rifle. The subchief came slowly to his feet.

He stood a moment looking at Chatto. Then he turned about and strode to his pony. Mounting up, he spurred the little animal up out of the gully. He took a westward course along the stage road for Tucson. He did not once look back. When he was gone, Chatto ordered the remaining Chiricahua *hesh-kes* to find their ponies and to follow him, Chatto. Heavy firing and some Apache cries could be heard back at the stage station. *Ugashé*, it was time to go.

Two of the hostile *hesh-kes*, prying to get the baggage boot open before the flames reached it, did not want to break off their looting. "A moment, *jefe*," one of them called. But Chatto had no moments for them. He repeated his order and, reluctantly, they gave way and went to their horses. When that Chiricahua spoke such words in that voice, even *hesh-kes* moved quickly.

After a long, long time of silence had closed in behind the Indian departure, the bonnet of the baggage boot raised slowly upward, and the drifter, coughing on the greasy smoke, peered forth.

29

In the history of Arizona's dark and bloody ground, her past of cavalry and Apache, it would be called Nine Soldier Gulch, or the Kensington Massacre, depending on whether its minstrels were red men, or white.

In the time and the case of the nameless horsethief now gazing in disbelief at the carnage, it was a battleground still smoking, still smelling of blood and of the hot excrement of excited horses. It had happened. He was there. The sole white survivor.

The bodies of the eight troopers had been stripped bare. Their grossly white forms lay a sickish hue in the fading twilight, looming obscenely against the red rock and gray

sand. Not all had been scalped. Only the ones with nice hair.
Some had been otherwise cut, some sprawled unmarked save
for blade or bullet that had brought the end. All looked like
wax figurines to the drifter. Not real. Not men. Not soldiers.
Just things in a dusk-ridden landscape.

No, he thought, crawling out of the boot, crouching in the
lee of the smoldering coach. I know what they look like. I
remember that bear I shot for his pelt on Tonto Rim that
winter to make a coat for Aura Lee. When he was skinned
out he was as white as the troopers. He did not look like a
bear, at all, anymore. These men did not look like men any
more. They looked like skinned bears. He shivered in the
heavy heat.

He the saw the ninth man, also, where Chatto had dropped
him after taking his hair. The ninth trooper had not been
stripped, a mark of honor to him by the Chiricahua. He was
an officer. The shoulder boards were stark in the thickening
gloom. This would be Kensington, the lieutenant. And these
others would be what was left of Peaches' Fort Gila patrol.

No, wait. There had been twelve troopers, plus a sergeant.
So somewhere, in some other gully, were four more men and
a noncommissioned officer named "Broke." But wait again.
Maybe not. Maybe Sergeant Bourke and his four good men
were still alive and had made it back into the station. If they
had, there would be a goodly force back there. Five U.S.
cavalrymen and an Apache enlisted scout, added to Madden
and Hunker Larsen, was some firepower put behind thick
walls.

Maybe, too, Feeny and Clooney Borrum had made off
through the brush afoot and were back there.

For certain, or nearly certain, the yellow-haired girl had
not been on the stage: She was back there; she had to be
back there.

There had been no one on that stage but the nine soldiers
who lay at last ghoulish salute in the sand of the lateral gully,
one mile west of Little Dipper Wash.

It was early dark now. Leaving time.

The drifter searched among the waxen soldiers for a jacket
with not too much blood on it and found a good one. He put
it on to cover his own luminous white skin. Nothing showed
up in night darkness like a white man with no shirt on. He
felt uncomfortable, uneasy, wearing the jacket. But he blend-
ed with the sage and the chaparral and the sandstone.

Searching for a weapon, he had less luck. The Indians had

taken everything, of course. But then, in the last instant of
turning away, he saw the button of a scabbard protruding
from beneath the fallen Concord. Crawling into the interior
through a charred window, he found he could not budge the
wedged scabbard, but the blade gave within it. In half a
minute he had worked it loose and had thirty-two inches of
cold cavalry steel in his hand. Taking charcoal from the
scorched chassis of the Concord, he smeared the blade, his
hands and face, and he was ready.

A last thought, even in all that grimness, caught his one-
time-lawman's fancy. A quick look below the pungently
smoking horsehair seat cushions showed the panels intact.
They rolled back easily, just as Clooney had told him. He saw
the twin saddlebags and tugged at each, and both were still
heavy with their treasure.

My God, he thought, fifteen thousand dollars.

And what if, in the end, they were all dead but him? Who
would then come for the money? Madden's ghost? Some live
fat banker from Tucson, or Los Angeles? Taking what was
only Madden's? Or his own?

He took the gold out of the paneled recesses beneath the
seats, lugged it up the gullybrink, and buried it in a marked
place above highwater and away from the stage road. Then
he and his charcoaled sabre were finally done, finally down
to it.

Which way would he go?

He could win free if he so willed. Going west on foot,
following the Tucson road and playing in any kind of luck,
whatever, he would come to a place that kept a horse or
three—or even a mule from some Mexican of the *monte*—
and another dawn would see him below Tucson, and below
Fort Huachuca, in Sonora past Nogales and still going free.
That was west.

East was Sifford Wells and the yellow haired girl.

But there was something else back there.

There was Aura Lee and all those murdering Chiricahua
Apaches, and there was Chatto back there.

"All right," said the drifter to the night and to his memories. "I'm coming."

Chatto ordered his combined force into seige position
around Sifford Wells station. It was full dark, the moonblaze
beyond the distant mesas advising of old Luna's rise. There
would be full and bright moonlight within the hour. The

young chief called a council of his leading men. The place was within the standing tumble of the old Overland ruins. Here they might have the small fire so dear to Apache hearts and so central to Apache spirits in dark-mind times. The defenders of the station house could not fire into this ancient redoubt owing to the remaining walls and a rise, also, of sandstone bedrock which blocked the line from the station.

The summoned Chiricahua were just assembling when the drifter arrived at Little Dipper Wash, having traveled down the lateral tributary gully of the Kensington Massacre. This side wash spilled into the main wash opposite the entrance to the wolf burrow that had spared the horsethief capture earlier in the day. It was his plan to use the den-hole only as a landmark to target his crossing of the big wash, since the hole's position was nearest the walls of the station compound. But, from his view up the wash, the Overland ruins were worn low, letting him see the gathering of dark figures coming in to sit about the small flame of the councilfire.

Ah, how a man would love to hear what those bastards were plotting. Yet to attempt a crawl-up on the ruins with the chaparral sheltering at least twenty Chiricahua, counting only the number that had wiped out Kensington and his men, well, it was not the sort of nightwork that paid well for a white man.

You would have no way of guessing around which next juniper or sage clump you would belly into one of Lucero's killers. Or even one of Chatto's original bunch, hardly less *hesh-kes* than the subchief's new recruits, whoever they were. Given present complaints, there was *no* Apache going to stop and palaver the time of moonrise with a White Eye creeping around in Indian brush with a U.S. Cavalry jacket on and an issue horse-soldier sword in one hand. Not quite.

But, about to slide down the bank for his sprint over the main wash, the drifter took one more look.

Those Indians were getting worked up, up there.

Gestures were broadening, guttural voices rising.

Damn!

It could mean the lives of everyone in Sifford Wells station to learn what was being said in those Overland ruins.

He had been a lawman operating with the gun long enough up in the Indian Nations to learn that the man who knew ahead of time what the other fellow was intending to do was the one who came home with the other one in that canvas sack slung across the pack mule.

So he knew that, to do the most he could for the folks trapped in the station, he should try to sneak that Apache councilfire. Try to learn what they were up to. But, Christ, there was another side to that, too. Suppose they nailed him? Then no information at all would get into the stage station. More, the professional gun that he still was would not be added to the firepower presently defending what had brought him this far back—the yellow-haired girl and her baby.

Still more, he already had information they could not have about the strength of the enemy.

Hidden as he had been in the blind darkness of the baggage boot, it had been a matter of wild, topsy-turvy glimpses taken when the boot-top was jounced open a bit before the crash of the Concord. After the crash, he could only breathe shallow and pray deep. But he had seen enough to know that there were one hell of a lot more Indians with Chatto and Lucero than Madden had told him or than Lieutenant Kensington had obviously thought there were. He ought to go up there right now and scout that big bunch of redskins, so the people in the station could know their real situation and thus prepare for it. But the hell with that. He was already doing his full share just to have come back at all. For a drunk and a drifter and a horsethief, there were limits to being noble. He would just go into the station and forget about any such brave journeys.

He went across the wash in a running walk, sighting on the stunt tree that marked the wolf's den, knowing the bank was good and high there. It was blinky dark down in the wash proper, and, with the firelight in their eyes, the Indians at the Overland ruins meeting would not see the white man in his army-blue coat, and they did not. He was at the wolf hole crouched and ready to bombard up over the bank—after a cautious peek over its caving brink—across the short level of alkali flat to the station's rear wall. He knew he could vault that structure, as it was precisely the same as most ranchers in the territory used to keep their prize horse stock in at night. He had gone over a hundred such in his life on the owlhoot trail, following Chatto and the Chiricahua, and needing always the best and freshest of horses to even stay within a week of the red bastards.

But suddenly the drifter knew he was not going up that bank and over that alkali flat. A stifled cry came through the early night from the station. It was the girl. She was having

that baby. Or worse, she was dry-trying to have it, and it was
not coming right.

If a man were to do everything that he could to help her,
he would *have* to scout those Indians. In so doing he might
learn something, anything, that would result in easing her
fear and terror over where she was and what was going to
happen to her; then maybe she could let down and the baby
would come naturally.

It was not much of a hope, God knew.

It was just only better than him going in with nothing to
bring of news or information that would uplift her, making
just one more dumb hand in there to add to the ones already
helpless to quiet her or to bring the baby alive.

He dropped to his knees, squeezed into the wolf burrow.
In the denning room, he left the cavalry jacket and sabre and
his boots. This time he would not be hiding from old sheriffs
or over-aged lieutenants. He would be six feet underground
and ten feet overground from the Indian he had sworn to
find and kill.

On a windstill summer night.

One creak of cistern timber, one sliding of wolf burrow
sand, one dislodged pebble worming out the very small exit
at the other end, would mean that Chatto would find *him;*
leaving Aura Lee alone forever.

30

Peaches and Madden and Bourke came in through the rear
door of the station house. All three lay back against the stout
adobe wall of the building for a hard-breathing moment, as
though unable to believe it had happened, that the scout and
the sergeant were alive. Then Madden puffed back to his
window.

Starting to follow him past the fireplace, the Indian heard
the girl groan. Bourke nodded, and Peaches went to the
white mother and bent over her. She saw the dark Apache
face and drew back, terror in her wide eyes.

But he touched her gently, saying, "*Schicho*, lady," and she
saw the kindness and the bronze calm of the young face, and
she touched him back. He smiled shyly.

"My name Peaches. Cavalry scout San Carlos," he told
her, watching Bourke. "Got two wife plenty kid each one.
Know things. You let Peaches see, feel?"

"What the hell you think you're doing?" huffed T.C. Madden leaving his window. But Emmett Bourke, from the other window, said sharply, "Leave him do it, Madden. Injuns knows these things like he says. Get back to your window and stay there, or take the roof guard."

"You taking charge?" Madden jutted broad jaw.

"You rather?" said Bourke quietly.

"Hell no. Sorry. Got to tell you, sarge, my nerves ain't what they was when I built this line."

"Let the Swede take the roof then. You stay below. Last thing we need up top is nerves."

"Hunker's the man for you," grinned Madden. "Ain't a nerve in his whole carcass. And he shoots good."

The blacksmith departed for the ladder. Bourke turned to Peaches, who was waiting on him. "Go ahead," he told the Apache. "The super and me can keep the Injuns interested, can't we, super?"

"Sure, hell," said Madden. "Take care of the little lady, redskin. I didn't mean no insult to you."

Peaches asked the girl to let him feel her stomach, then examined where the baby was trying to come. He gave his belt pouch to the groaning mother, saying, "Bite hard when hurt hard. You fine be all right." Going over to Bourke at his window, he whispered, "Baby come all wrong. Bad thing. Need woman help."

Madden, overhearing him, moved over from his window.

"Yeah, shit," he glared. "We'll send for a midwife from Tucson right off." He was frightened. As the other men, he was touched by the unwed mother's plight, by her courage, her smallness, her utter aloneness. He finished with a growl. "Crazy Injun bastard."

"He may be a bastard," said Emmett Bourke. "But he ain't crazy. Not hardly. I know what he means. He's talking about Injun help. Apache medicine."

"Well, fine, why didn't you say so," said Madden scathingly. "We got plenty of that. Right outside."

"I know," Bourke answered mutteringly. "And that might as well be in Tucson, too."

Behind them the yellow-haired girl contorted to a deep spasm, screamed sobbingly. It was a terrible sound to helpless men. Unbearable. Demoralizing.

"Peaches," said the old sergeant. "Go and help her all you can. You must know some tribe medicine."

The small Apache shook his head.

"Peaches scout U.S. Cavalry," was all he said.

From the cistern in the Overland ruins the drifter could not only hear all of the Chiricahua conference but see it in good part. His guess that its forces were divided proved correct. The younger fighters of the Hoh-shuh Springs men were inclined to favor the departed *hesh-ke* Lucero and his more spartan view of total war on the white man. At the same time, these younger men were plainly careful with Chatto, whose personal reputation for murder was untarnished. Nonetheless, there was open grumbling of a split-up of the two parties.

The trouble seemed to be the confrontation up at Nine Soldier Gulch. The Hoh-shuh Spring Chiricahua did not understand its origins, and, Lucero not being there to speak for himself, they were demanding of Chatto to know what was the truth. It would seem to them, one spokesman said, that the hair had rightfully gone to the man who had killed its wearer, Lucero.

Chatto and his woman looked at each other here, yet neither spoke. Old Nevado made bid to speak for the leader. He stated bluntly that there was talk among Chatto's own band that fathership of the man-child of Estune was in question, with the suspicion pointing at a liaison between Lucero and the squaw of Chatto. Nevado, for himself, felt Chatto to be the aggrieved party; it was not for the young chief to speak, but for his woman to do so. Who else might know the real thing of it?

The drifter held his breath, watching Estune.

He had never seen an Indian woman like this one. An angular face, oval at the same time, with an oriental slant of luminous eyes but an almost highborn white quality of feature. The neck was long, not short like the Apache necks. The shoulders, although squared and straight, were not broad and thick as were the Apache shoulders. She was long and pantherish of limb, with a slender body featuring large high breasts with notable nipple-thrusts, wide hips like a white woman but no fat on them, and legs, too, of a hard firmness no settlement female ever knew. Casting back into his days in the Indian Nation, where all the northern tribes—Sioux, Cheyenne, Arapahoe, Ute, Pawnee, and Absaroka—passed in nomadic turn, he thought mainly of the latter band, the Crows, handsomest of the Plains Indians. This woman looked like a Crow. She was, the drifter decided, either a slave woman or the offspring of a captive. No squat southern tribe ever gave the original blood to this elegant warrior woman who was Chatto's wife.

The woman now arose from her place.

"I confess what I have done," she said. "Chatto so wanted the child, yet his seed would not grow. My heart never departed his side, only my body."

The Chiricahua men sat as though turned to stone.

Tribal law was beyond mitigation. If the breach were admitted, the guilt was presumptive. The penalty was set: The nose was cut off, an ear even, or two ears; in all cases the husband of the adulteress enforced the law.

If he did not, or would not, the burden was upon him, and his reputation, among those of the old ways, was forfeit. Pity was unknown, cruelty ingrained. The law was the law, said those of the older times.

But the times were changing.

The drifter thought the pausing and waiting for Chatto to bring out the knife would never end. He watched the other Chiricahua, particularly the three Hoh-shuh members, Na-tishn, Durango, and Gah-chilzin who, with Chatto, Estune, and old Nevado, made up the six of the council meeting.

Into that pause, startling the hidden white man as severely as the intent Indians about the fire, stepped a seventh Chiricahua. He was unbidden and had ridden his pony hard to be there. He towered in the outer jump of the flames' uncertain pattern. Bigger than any of them, fiercer than all; Lucero, the magnificent, the lordly, the returned.

Fearing precisely what had happened, the subchief said, he had come back to claim his woman. If any would now touch Estune with the knife, he would die by Lucero's rifle. Other than that, he and the woman would go in peace. They would make a new life and make a new man-child. Lucero did not hold with the old ways, nor did the woman. She had given herself to Lucero and he was taking her. If any should doubt, ask Estune.

Again, the graceful tall woman arose. The drifter felt once more the thrill of her. The animal power.

"My brothers will understand," she said, "that I am only a woman. I do not want my nose taken away. I know the old laws, but I am not brave enough. I will go with Lucero." She looked about at them all and, last of all, at Chatto, into his eyes. "You will know with which man my heart truly remains; ask yourselves."

She turned to go with Lucero, and no man moved to block her way. But into the little silence came a piercing woman's cry of labor from the white man's station across the road, and Estune stopped short.

Another cry came, higher and of deeper agony.

"A mother knows that crying out," the squaw said. "The baby comes as my man-child came, the behind presenting itself. She will lose the child."

"What has that to do with us?" demanded Lucero.

"I want the child. My milk is hurting me."

"It may be a girl-child."

"I do not care; a girl sucks as hard as a boy."

"They are all going to die over there."

"I do not care about them. Only the white girl's baby. It must live. It is mine, in trade for my man-child. I must have it."

Lucero saw no merit in this overwrought squaw's talk and said as much to Estune in anger. But Chatto spoke softly, unexpectedly.

"We will get it for you if we can, Estune."

Lucero wheeled upon the squaw, not believing she would hold to such a delusion.

"Then you are staying, even to lose your nose?"

"Yes, even that."

Lucero was incredulous. "The land is full of unwanted children. Come with me. We will find a hundred."

"I want only this one."

Chatto spoke again. The voice was still subdued but not weak. It was as though he saw, in the eyes of Estune, a thing none of the others could see.

"I say the same thing," he contended. "This child is Estune's child. A child for a child." For the first time he raised his eyes to look at Lucero. "It does not matter who sired the man-child; it was Estune's body in which it grew, she alone gave it birth."

Here old Nevado intervened testily. "Well, where does all this leave us? Who is staying with Chatto, and who is going with the damned *hesh-ke?*" He was glaring at Lucero when he said it, not the other young men from Hoh-shuh Springs, and so it was Lucero's to answer.

"Old man," he said, "I will kill you."

"As I said," nodded Nevado. "A damned *hesh-ke.*"

One of the young fighters from Hoh-shuh Springs stood up. "Durango goes with Lucero," he said. Another of the three *hesh-kes* arose. "As does Na-tishn," he added. Gah-chilzin, the last of them, thought it over a bit longer. Then he too arose. "Well," he said, "I like Chatto, always have. But we have killed too many soldiers today. Other soldiers will be out looking for them. When they find what we did, we had all better be in Mexico." He turned to Lucero. "You *are* going there?" he frowned.

Lucero nodded quickly. "All of the chiefs at Hoh-shuh Springs are going there," he said. "They all told me this. They said, 'Make your killing and get away quickly.' They said, 'Red Beard Crook is back and he will never quit the trail.' They said, 'Go to Pa-gotzin-kay and stay there; we will all be together.'"

Now Chatto stood up, young face scowling.

"We all know what was said at Hoh-shuh Springs," he rumbled, deep-voiced. "We all heard Geronimo and just as well as you did. I go to Pa-gotzin-kay myself."

"Ah!" pointed out Durango. "But Lucero goes tonight. You delay to get that baby for your untrue woman. You may stay here forever."

"He will," growled Na-tishn, "if Red Beard catches him here."

Gah-chilzin, the thinker, was convinced.

"Nonetheless," he said, surprisingly, "I will stay with Chatto. His brains are better than Lucero's."

Chatto thanked him with a look. It was Lucero's moment. But again old Nevado robbed him of it.

"I want to know one other thing that is important," the white-haired elder said. He turned to Chatto, a harshness in his voice as would befit a keeper of the people's past. "What about the woman's nose?"

The young warchief was caught. To weaken was to risk power with his fighting men. He was the husband of the adulteress. He alone must say how it would go for her. But Chatto was not afraid.

"I believe her," he said, low-voiced. "I will not take her nose. Rather, I will do all that I may to bring her the white woman's child. It will be our own child then. The child of Lucero is dead. And from this camp forward Lucero lives no more for me." He made an ancient Apache sign with his two hands, indicating that an enemy may go, that, indeed, he has ceased literally to exist. Lucero received the sign and, after a

dark-faced hesitation, returned it. Now they existed no more
for each other. They would never speak again, the one to the
other, nor camp in the same camp.

In the last breath, Durango announced that he would go
and take a vote among the Hoh-shuh hostiles as to who would
ride with the *hesh-kes* tonight and who might care to stay
with Chatto to go through with tomorrow's foolish business
of getting a lot of innocent Apaches killed so that Estune
might have the white girl's baby to replace her own.

This being agreeable to Chatto, the *hesh-ke* departed to
return shortly with eight other discontented ones. Leading
these, Lucero now quickly mounted up and was gone. Across
the peaks and mesas old Luna was just showing her first
red-dusted brightness of the night.

Into this hushed pause fell another, and yet another, burst-
ing cry of dry labor from the tortured young white mother
in the station beyond the stage road, and Chatto's untrue but
beloved woman wheeled about.

"*Ugashé!*" she cried. "We must go *now!*"

And Chatto made the sign to Nevado and Gah-chilzin, and
the drifter was alone with the popping embers of the councilfire and with the information he had come for, and then
some.

The yellow-haired girl had a chance now.

Its name was Estune.

31

Going through the wolf burrow to the denning room, the
drifter re-donned cavalry jacket and his boots, leaving the
long sabre because in simple truth he forgot the weapon in
his concern for the white party.

Its people were in a plenty cultus place.

His fear would not leave that fact alone. He kept turning
it in his mind as he crawled on out of the den entrance to
survey the alkali flat beyond the wash.

It looked scarily like an Apache trap to him.

Inside the station you had the poor girl with her baby
coming. You had Madden, Hunker, possibly five cavalrymen
counting the sergeant, maybe the scout Peaches, maybe even
Feeny and Clooney; too many maybes.

Outside, in the Chiricahua ranks, were ten Hoh-shuhs under Gah-chilzin, six Chattos under Chatto, plus the warrior

woman Estune, a total of nineteen fighting-age Apaches, all with modern repeating weapons, except for the eccentric brave with the Comanche bow-and-arrows.

It could be a seige, a starve-out. There were too many Indians to ride out through, and it could not be done with the girl anyway. But there might also be too many defenders forted-up solidly in the station compound for that many Apache to storm straightaway. The massacred troops in the gully might not be found for days. The same went for any cavalry in force following up the Kensington patrol. Those Indian devils from the Hoh-shuh Springs meeting, scattering and raiding their ways into Mexico and the fabled hideaway of the Apaches in the old Sierra Madre, would draw off all the troops in Arizona. Relief might never come from Fort Gila or down Tucson-way. Or it might come too late. If those Indians were willing to gamble on either of the latter likelihoods, the people inside Sifford Wells station were deep in trouble. Everything depended on making a deal.

He was running across the alkali flat now and over the mud wall of the compound. Dropping to earth inside the walls, he disturbed the animals in the covered horse shed and was met by a chorus of low whickerings.

God! he had forgotten all those cavalry mounts.

What an added bait for the Indians to take the station! Eight, no nine, big fresh U.S. horses, belonging to the dead Kensington and his men. Then the strapping bay saddler of Madden's. The spare coach team. Plus whatever horses Sergeant Bourke's survivors might have gotten back with, and the pony of the scout Peaches had he rejoined his patrol inside the walls. There could be fifteen, sixteen head of prime horses in that shed and the corrals beyond it. And the ponies of the Apache were pretty well run down and needing rest. All those prime mounts could be a critical factor in any Indian bargaining or thinking. Damn it to hell. There was always some hair in the butter that a fellow had not counted on finding there.

The horses becoming quiet, he went on to the rear door of the station and knocked sharply. He was challenged by a familiar Apache voice in English, "Who the hell out there?" and he told the scout it was his friend from the old Overland cistern. "I forgot my cigarettes, Peachy," he called back. "Open up and leave me come in."

By this time Bourke was at the door admitting him.

Introductions were brief and to the meaning of the hour.

The Irish veteran sized up the newcomer in one glance as a hand that would do. The drifter told his twin stories of the Kensington Massacre in Nine Soldier Gulch, and of the trouble between Chatto and Lucero and the Chiricahua meeting in the Overland ruins, with all its over and undertones. He concluded with the dramatic decision of the squaw that she would have the white girl's baby in repayment of the loss of her own child, and Chatto's agreement to attack with full vigor toward getting the newborn for her. When he told of the woman's instinctive guess that the baby was coming bad and that the white mother needed help that only she, the Indian mother might provide, Peaches at once said that the greatest danger for them all lurked in any agreement with the Chiricahua.

"Indian think different," he informed the drifter. "With other Indian no lie. With white man all lie."

The drifter only shrugged.

"Cain't see we got any choices, Peachy. We don't make a deal with that damn squaw, little missy here—" He broke off, realizing the girl had quieted and was listening intently. "Well, no use her suffering like she is," he finished. "Them redskins know everything about things like this. I say get the squaw in here."

Still the little Fort Gila scout demurred.

"You please try think better," he pleaded. "Them Injun get in here kill us quick. You tell it sarjen," he appealed to Bourke. "You know Peaches know."

"Yeah," nodded the old soldier. "I sure do."

But they had to do something. Madden argued for it. The girl pleaded. The drifter believed they could control it and had to try. Bourke weakened. Even simple Hunker Larsen said, "Yah, we sure do something, mister. We don't, we all be where Feeny went."

The drifter eyed Bourke, and the sergeant said, "Feeny's dead. Up on the road by the gully."

"How about the nigger?" asked the drifter. "How about old Clooney Borrum?" He turned to T.C. Madden, with the last part of it, and the stage line owner shook his head.

"Dead, too, little doubt," he said. "Ain't nobody seen him. He jumped when the coach went over the edge. I guess he never come down."

"That's bad," said the drifter. "He was surely a good man." He frowned, pursing bearded lips. "Funny thing. I never had me no nigger friend afore."

"Well, that makes you both even, I'd say," growled Madden. "I reckon he never had no horsethief friend before neither." He turned his back on the drifter. "Well, sarge, how do we play it now? We got us another man but no more guns."

"Give him yours," said the old soldier. "I know a gunner when I see one." Madden grumbled but gave over the Winchester. It was one of the two they had, Peaches bringing only his old single-shot Springfield to add to the station-house arsenal. The other Winchester was up on the roof with Hunker Larsen, and Bourke turned to the drifter. "Come on, gunny," he ordered. "Let's me and you go up on the roof with Peaches and get us this here campaign laid out professional." He did not wait for acceptance but went for the chicken ladder, the others following him. On the roof, he relieved Hunker of duty and of the Winchester, appropriating the latter to himself, sending the big smithy downstairs to look after the girl again. "All right," he said to Peaches and the drifter. "Let's lay 'em all out, face up. Either we got a hand, or we ain't."

Grimly, the cards went to the gamblers.

Peaches held fast to his opinion they must never trust the Apache inside the station. Bourke could think only in terms of defending the station in military terms. Neither of them thought of the girl. The drifter, his turn coming, could think of nothing else. The girl was the entire thing, he insisted. What the hell else were they trying to do? Save the stage line for Madden? Do in young Chatto and eighteen real white-hating hostiles from Hoh-shuh Springs and Chatto's own Piños Mountain band? Save the fair name of the U.S. Cavalry? Keep himself from going back to the juzgado as a horsethief? What the hell! If they were thinking of anything in that damned place worth dying for other than that poor little lady down there with her wrong-way baby, they were thinking upside down, backward, sideways and, moreover, could go fornicate themselves as far as he was concerned; he was going to make his own dicker with that damned cat-bodied squaw over there across the road and they could kiss his ass till it bayed like a turpentined bluetick hound with his butt in a barrel of hot ash.

Peaches, understanding no more than every sixth or seventh word of the outburst, nonetheless perfectly assessed the spirit of its delivery.

"Goddamnsumbitch," he said admiringly. "Peaches say with you."

"Shit," said Bourke helplessly. "He didn't say anything."

The drifter gave him a look with the ice-blue eyes. "Wrong again," he murmured. "I said let Peachy stand up here and holler over to them devils that we got work for a squaw over here and fifteen head of good horses to pay for same. What you say, Peachy?" The drifter did not get his answer at once. In the waiting time, the girl cried out again and began to weep. "Now what you say, Peachy?" asked the drifter.

The little Apache stood up behind the parapet.

"Do best," he said and cupped his hands and called out into the desert night for the Apache of Chatto.

His answer was an instant, withering blast of repeating rifle fire from the chaparral across the stage road, and a yelling rush of unshod ponies and shadowy riders full for both station walls, flank-and-flank.

"Take the right bunch," said Bourke calmly.

"They're took," vouchsafed the drifter, as calmly. "Peachy, go on down and fetch up some fresh shells; this is going to be an ammo waste for damn sure."

Working his own Winchester, Sergeant E.J. Bourke managed a sideglance at the lanky horsethief he had guessed to be a gunner. What he saw brought only an old soldier's nod of satisfaction.

"Yep," was all he said. "I thought so."

Then the rooftop was inundated by the thunder of two short-barreled Winchesters firing in levered cadence at the whirling ghostly horsemen below.

The fight for Sifford Wells was on.

The Tucson Road

32

Indian battles with entrenched white forces seldom drew out into genuine siege, much less developed into persistent serious assault. The classic maneuver of the red cavalry was the showy flanking sweep.

Erratically as flights of nighthawks, the Chiricahua now raced firing along both walls of the station compound. Aiming at moonlit riders swirling by in combers of raised dust, the white marksmen atop the roof emptied their magazines more in prayer than real hope. The assault fell away, nonetheless, and apparently with some appreciable damage. Peaches, returning with the ammunition, reported there appeared to be an argument in the camp of the enemy. The Hoh-shuhs were angry with Chatto and his woman over such wild risk for a white woman's child which was not even born yet and might never be or, worse yet, might prove to be a girl-child.

There was loud talk of defection among the Chiricahua ranks and, listening intently from the rooftop of the station, the little White Mountain scout told Bourke and the drifter that now was the time to propose a compromise. He, being fluent in Spanish as well as Apache dialects, was at once nominated for the mission. Again at parapet's edge he called for Chatto. There was a stir this time, and old Nevado rode his scrubby mustang out into the middle of the now moonlit Tucson road.

"Is that you, lying little rat?" he called up.

"No," denied the scout. "My name Peaches cavalry scout San Carlos."

"That is the rat I am talking about," said the old man. "And San Carlos you say? Hah! Old Red Beard would not permit your kind to comb the coyote burrs from his horse's fetlocks. Fort Gila, you mean."

"Yes. These people in here want to make a deal."

"What deal?"

"The woman is in wrong labor. We need Estune in here, or mother and child will both die surely."

"What deal?" repeated the old man.

"We can discuss that," smiled Peaches, waving down to him. "Do not worry. These are good fair men. Will the squaw come in?"

"We have you, you know. When we tested you just now, not one of our men were hit. What deal?"

"Well, we counted eight riders hit and seven ponies," said Peaches cheerfully. "What deal did you have in mind?"

Old Nevado made a signal and rode back into the brush. He came back out a moment later accompanied by Estune and Gah-chilzin, with young Chatto hanging behind them at the edge of the brush, ever wary.

"Chatto says we need horses. You did not hit a one of our ponies but they are tired from too much riding. We will want to go away from here fast. We have four sound ones from those teams on the stage wagon. How many do you say you have in there? Fifteen, that skinny White Eye said. The one with the dirty beard. Fifteen. Is that the number?"

"Thirteen," Peaches corrected. "Skinny man did not know the real number. He did not know you killed those four other soldiers in the big wash."

"Name them. What horses are they?"

"Eight trooper horses and one officer horse, one team stage-wagon horses, good ones, a strong bay from Pima Bend, and my own scout pony. Thirteen."

Another conference ensued and hesitation seemed forming up as other Indians shadowed in from the brush to clot about Chatto and the negotiators. Peaches strained to catch the low voices but could not.

Across the road some of the Indians laughed jarringly.

"Sumbitch," scowled Peaches.

"What?" said the drifter, coming alert.

"Last time Peaches hear 'Pache laugh, eight white people die down Verde River next day."

"Yeah," nodded the drifter. "They never toldt me no jokes that busted my ribs neither."

Now angered words arose in the Indian meeting, and Estune came striding to stand in the moonlight of the road, holding up a buckskin medicine bag, saying she would come in now and bring the baby, saving the mother.

To the drifter she seemed proud, wild, beautiful.

To Peaches she was an Indian sister, not pretty.

"Wait," he said. "What price do you want?"

The woman tilted her head. "I want nothing. I want to save the baby. That is all I want."

"Yes," said Peaches cynically. "All you want is the baby. Will you lie to me who saved your life?"

"Will you deny me, who saved yours?" countered the woman. "Open the way, small scout. I want that—I want to save that baby. Do you not want to save the mother? Ask the White Eyes with you."

Peaches made as to discuss the situation with his companions but in reality repeated his stern warning about taking the Apache word for anything. With their own kind they were as honorable as any men. But with any enemy, Mexican or Gringo or other Indian, they were the most treacherous of people. The squaw would ultimately demand the child. Nothing would change this red thought of hers. She had taken it in her mind that Ysun meant her to have the white child to replace her Indian child slain by the white soldiers. If she entered the station house and brought the child alive, they would never deprive her of it. They had two courses, as the Apache scout saw it. They could admit the woman, letting her deliver the child, then seize her as hostage, take her with them in a retreat through the Chiricahua surround to Pima Bend, promising to release the squaw when they were safely in sight of town. Chatto's love of this woman made this course the only possible choice in Peaches' Apache mind. The other course would be to simply give the yellow-haired girl's baby to the wife of Chatto and let her go as the price of their own freedom to run for Pima Bend or Tucson tomorrow.

Now, said the small scout, could they all agree to pay this last price?

Could they agree, each one after each one, to let the Chiricahua have the white baby?

Peaches looked at Bourke and the drifter.

Below, Estune grew impatient, calling up to them that they must decide, and quickly, or lose the child. Chatto spurred his pony forward, adding his voice to his woman's. If the White Eyes wanted to get out of Sifford Wells station with their hair on, they must not delay the mission of his woman.

The young chief's words seemed to carry a peculiar urgency without bluster or heat. He appeared to be in the role of advocate, not adversary. He was advising the white enemy that the sane avenue for them to avail themselves of lay open before them if they would but take it, and quickly. All things hinged on the live delivery of a healthy child in there. The Chiricahua of Chatto would guarantee that, he promised. Also, he concluded earnestly, he, Chatto, gave his word that they would accept even a girl-child in the matter.

"Is it clear to you?" he called up to Peaches, in Apache. "Let the woman in, and we will go peacefully."

Peaches, speaking for his white companions, was not at all easy in his Indian understanding of Chatto's real mission. "For example," he challenged the young chief, "you give guarantee for the Chiricahua of Chatto. Yet where are these Chiricahua of yours? All that I see behind you are Hoh-shuhs and the old man, Nevado. Where are your five other men?"

"They are back in the brush with their riflebores watching you in this good shooting moonlight," answered Chatto. "Do you now admit my woman while there is yet time, or do we attack again?"

Peaches did not believe him as to the whereabouts or occupation of the missing five. But he sensed that a conclusion was required. He turned to his white companions with a gesture of finality.

"Not just woman want baby," he told them. "Chatto same thing."

"Chatto wants a *white* kid?" said the drifter, disbelievingly. His mind went back three bitter years and more. "I remember one he didn't want," he said softly. "He's a goddamn liar; he'll kill the baby sure."

"No," denied Peaches. "Woman take."

"Yeah," muttered Sergeant Bourke. "And raise it a goddamn Apache. It's better off dead." Wearily, he added. "Get Madden and the Swede up here; let's get it over with."

"What over with?" puzzled the drifter.

"What to do about the kid," said Bourke with exhausted dullness. "Either we let the squaw in and take our chances, or we turn her back right now and call the chief's raise."

"We got to let her in," said the drifter.

"No," said Peaches flatly. "Only if take hostage."

"My God," Bourke objected. "We can't take her hostage."

"Why not?" demanded the little Apache. "They no got hostage us."

Bourke blinked and thought it over. The drifter did not blink but narrowed his intensely blue eyes.

"That's a mortal fact, they ain't," he said.

"It's a hell of a chance," worried Bourke. "If we get them Cherry Cows stirred up enough, they'll fly apart. Once they blow up there ain't no heading them. They get crazy, like a shot animal."

"Already crazy," nodded Peaches.

"But that woman ain't. That Estune, she's smart as they come. She ain't no Apache neither." The drifter eyed the scout. "You know that, Peachy?" he charged. "I suspect you do, you little bastard."

"Yes," admitted the scout unexpectedly. "Know long time. Mother Absaroka, Crow Injun. Father Cheyenne, Chatto get from Comanche. My two wife tell me."

Madden and Hunker Larsen, summoned by Bourke as they talked, came crouching over from the traphole. When advised of the situation, both sided with the way the bearded drifter saw it:

In the final thing of it, it would be inhuman, even for an Indian, for Chatto's northern wife to insist on taking the poor girl's baby. Surely another and more realistic Apache price could be arranged with the young chief. For damned sure they had all those good horses to dicker with. The Apache had not been whelped who would not put a good horse before a good woman. And they had horses to spare, and the chief had already admitted earlier that the band needed fresh mounts.

The hell with the hostage idea or any of the rest of it; all they had to do was let the squaw in and then give her all the help she asked for in getting that little old baby out of that poor little old girl of a mother down there below.

That was the entire thing of it—getting the baby brought alive and the mother safe through the birthing.

Eight or ten good horses was a hell of a price to turn down for any redskin hostile on the run from a massacre like that of Lieutenant Kensington.

Chatto would no more refuse such a deal than he would eat goat in preference to mule.

Those damned Cherry Cows *had* to take the horses. The best bet the white people in Sifford Wells station would ever make would be to, right now, lay it all on the fact that Chatto was the chief and Estune just exactly no more than his woman in the Apache way. Which meant she would do what the chief said. *Ahora mismo!*

It was so decided, Peaches saying nothing.

He had done his best.

More than that, the white friends did have a sound Indian argument about those horses. Peaches knew the Chiricahua horses of Chatto's band to be worn to their last good mile. They had been pushed for two days on a diet of hard whipping between water holes. Those cavalry mounts of his dead patrol, then, became worth the new white baby's value a dozen times over to the hostile Apache over there beyond the road. All of them, both Hoh-shuh and Chatto's Piños Mountain people, had to be thinking like Indians now. They had to be thinking of getting far away from where they had killed nine pony soldiers and burned a stagecoach and then killed four more pony soldiers, leaving but one old sergeant and the patrol's Apache volunteer scout alive from the whole Fort Gila column sent out to punish them for five *other* white murders before that.

Anh, yes: For once, the white people were probably right on an Indian argument.

Chatto would not be able to resist the horses, and all would come out well in the end.

The scout now broke his scowling silence. Hunker and Madden were returning below. It was the time.

"Peaches say one thing," he warned Bourke and the drifter. "You plenty damn lucky we got all them horse poor Loo'ten'an Kens'ton leave in shed."

"Don't tell us, tell your redskin friends!" snapped old soldier Emmett Bourke. "We know how lucky we are."

The scout nodded, went to the parapet.

"All right, Estune," he told the woman. "Come in."

She looked up at them, and they saw the white teeth gleam in the shadow of the station house and the darkness of her northern face.

"Tell the Thin One that Estune thanks him," she answered Peaches. "Open the door."

How she sensed that it had been the arguments of the drifter that had swayed the white decision, the small scout from Fort Gila never knew. This was a strange woman. And Peaches did not trust her. He would say nothing to the thin white man of her words for him. His Apache spirits told him this wisdom.

He turned from the parapet.

"Sarjen Broke," he said. "Woman agree."

Bourke nodded, strode to the traphole. "Madden, open up and let her in. She's covered from up here."

"All right." They could hear the stage line owner forcing up the door's bar. "Look sharp!"

The lamplight from the opened door threw its sudden startling rectangle of yellow light about the tall figure of Estune and beyond her to dimly touch the motionless ponies and dark faces of Chatto and Nevado and the eleven *heshkes* from Hoh-shuh Springs.

"Go in," called the young chief through the pin's drop stillness. "And bring your child."

33

Estune examined the white girl. She made her lie on the table top, ordering heated water brought. Into this she dipped her hands and wrists, then sprinkled them with a gray-green powder from the fringed *hoddentin* bag of the Chiricahua medicine woman. Rubbing the powder into her hands, she washed them again and washed the groaning girl where the baby was breeched.

Peaches helped her at her direction, indeed, at her insistence. This was later remarked. At the moment the men in the station house common room made only sense out of it. It was natural to seek the only other Indian as the assistant. Even Peaches, caught up in the arts of his ancient people as demonstrated now by the medicine of Estune, made nothing of the request.

Had the drifter not persuaded them, it may have been different. But again, the delivery of a baby summons powerful medicine in and of itself for nearly all men. Perhaps, even if Bourke had been on the rooftop, rather than simple Hunker Larsen and still desperately scheming T.C. Madden, the end would have been another way.

But it was not. The sergeant had asked the drifter to remain below with him to watch the Indians working—he was in command, and this was his decision.

The squaw told Peaches to bring a cup of warm water, and into this she mixed a leafy broken desert herb and forced it down the gagging mother. She then told the little Fort Gila scout to take both wrists of the white girl and pull them over the girl's head, stretching her arms and her body. Meanwhile, the woman of Chatto put her own body between the legs of the girl where the table ended, calling for Bourke to bring the dishpan with the steaming water and wet feedsacking. Making sure only that this compress was not scalding—she put it to her own naked belly first, pulling her squaw-skirt up to do it—she told the sergeant to place it on the girl's abdomen and press down and toward Estune with it, hard. *"Ahora!"* cried the squaw and went to the opening with both of her hands.

The girl, even in those few moments, was already into a spasm of expellations induced by the herbal draft. She made maximum, spine-arching effort, and Estune, long fingers sliding into the dilated vaginal orifice, seized the infant and literally turned it in a grasp of amazing power and dexterity, bringing it into an unblocked breech presentation and pulling it out of the mother all in one unending, incredibly skilled rhythm of natural force and instinct.

The child gasped and squalled. It was a writhing mass of blood, membrane, broken waterbag shreddings, and the globlike repulsiveness of the placenta. The squaw, holding child in one hand and afterbirth in the other, bit and sawed off with her white teeth the umbilical cord, clamping its bleeding in the severing as neatly as any surgical instrument might ever have.

Bourke gave a weak cheer. Larsen and Madden, drawn from the parapet to the traphole in the roof, joined in when they saw the living child.

Peaches started at once for the roof, but the squaw called him back and handed him the baby.

"A girl," she said in the language of their people. "A man must hold it first and give it to the true mother."

"Anh," said Peaches. "Do not tell me. I have been cursed the same way four times." He took the child, made as though to present it to the yellow-haired girl, now mercifully fainted away.

"Dah!" rasped Estune, lean face contorted. "To the true mother, I said; to me."

Peaches' deep-set eyes darted from the squaw to the two white men. Bourke shook his head helplessly. The drifter seemed to nod as if to commend the transfer of the small child. But the Apache scout did not hesitate, now. Something Indian was warning him. Swiftly, he lay the baby on the bench by the fireplace, out of the way and with neither its natural or its savage mother. When he turned to face Estune, it was with his old Springfield rifle in his hands and its long barrel pointing into the belly of Chatto's wife.

"Do not move!" he said to her in Apache. Then, to Bourke

and the drifter, in his abrupt English, "Take look horses! Peaches hear something out there."

Instantly, the squaw threw back handsome head and bayed like the bitch-wolf that she was. From the outer yard came answering lobo yowling of the male pack and sound of hooves pounding and driven animals snorting.

Peaches reversed the old Springfield in his hands too quickly for the eye to follow. He struck the tall woman in the side of the head with the swung butt of the weapon, felling her without a sound. As her body went down, Bourke and the drifter leaped over it running for the rear door and the corral horse shed in the mud-walled station compound. Unarmed except for the sergeant's cavalry Colt, they were much, much too late.

They were in time only to see the last of the U.S. Cavalry mounts of the massacred Kensington patrol disappear *through* the adobe wall.

Chatto's five missing henchmen had done their night's work at least as well as Chatto's woman.

The baby was alive, and the mother would live, and the bargaining horses, to guarantee this miracle of Estune's Indian medicine, were gone.

The old sergeant emptying his sidearm in pure frustration, Bourke and the drifter broke into the moonlight beyond the ramada and came to that instinctive, stunned halt of the first moment of a tragedy's realization—not seeing detail but comprehending disaster.

The Indians, using knotted rawhide lariats as cross-cutting instruments, had cut down through the mudbrick barricade— one man inside, one man outside on each lariat—and sawed out a section exactly wide enough to pass one skillfully handled, hand-led animal at a time. The cavalry horses being all haltered and stall-tied could not have been deliberately better prepared for the Apache theft. It was only because the newly broken mustang of Peaches had spooked that they did not get every head of stock in the Sifford Wells corrals. As it was, the mustang's nervousness had caused the stage team to act up, jamming the narrow exit and creating the disturbance Peaches had heard.

These same four animals still ran loose in the open corral.

The drifter, sometime working horsethief himself, sized up the situation before Sergeant Bourke did. He sprinted to block the lariat-sawed hole in the wall. To be entirely afoot in Apacheria was suicide. Four horses loomed big as life itself. For his part, Bourke tried hazing the remaining stock away from the escape route, meanwhile bawling for Peaches to come out and help him collect the spooked animals and get them short-tied in the horse shed. Inside the station house, the Apache scout glanced down at Estune, decided she was sleeping soundly. His eye was distracted by the white girl, however, who was now stirring on the table. He ran to her and assisted her to the fireside bench where her baby lay. Picking up the infant, Peaches gave it to the confused mother. "Hold tight watch squaw!" he ordered and was gone in answer to Bourke's call.

Up on the roof, Madden and his faithful blacksmith blasted away at nothing. Bourke yelled up for them to stop wasting ammunition and watch the front of the station for any Indian rush. The drifter, jamming the hole in the adobe wall with loose shed lumber, saw that the sergeant and his Apache scout had the horses safely bunched and moving nicely for the shed. "I'll go check the squaw," he told them, loping past in his bow-legged horseman's gait. "You sure fetched her a skookum belt in the head with that riflebutt, Peachy."

"Split gunstock," complained the little Apache.

"I hope you split her goddamn head, too," puffed Sergeant Bourke, but the wish was not father to the reality. They all heard it in the careless pause of their exchange: high, wordless, torn from the stomach pit of terror—the yellow-haired girl screaming inside the station.

34

Of the three men in the loose stock compound, only the drifter reacted instinctively. "Block the back door!" he shouted and raced around the little building ten feet at a bound. Coming to the front of the station house, he was forever grateful for the intuitive thing which drove him not to go through the building. Even so, he was barely in time to make a desperation dive at the squaw of Chatto. The woman was just coming out of the front door when he rounded the corner. Had she imagined any of her enemies would run around the house she still would have reached the stage road with the infant, and thus the safety of her tribesmen. But Estune was thinking only of the child clutched to her savage heart. Only of that and of reaching the road and her waiting fellows.

The drifter dove at her from behind knocking her to her knees. She gave a surging twist, uttered a screeching cry for help. Next instant the drifter was astride her, the squaw still clutching the white baby. He seized her by the long hair with the left hand and drove the right hand full into the pinioned face. The blow stunned her. She lay moaning in some Indian tongue other than Chiricahua Apache. The drifter took the child from her. In this instant, he heard the pounding of Indian pony hooves. Half a dozen of the watching Hoh-shuhs were racing at him, leaning far down from their mounts to help the dazed squaw to a double mount.

From the rooftop above, Madden and Hunker Larsen who, as roofguards, had been assigned the two Winchesters, belatedly opened fire. They hit nothing but scattered the onrushing braves like quail, and the drifter, tucking the yellow-haired girl's child under one arm, took the squaw by the hair and began to drag her bodily back into the station. It was here that Chatto returned from visiting his horse-thieves at their work.

The young chief, coming down the stage road from Little Dipper Wash, saw his woman being pulled by the hair. He saw and heard the frightened infant under the white man's arm. The sight inflamed his Chiricahua brain. It was the *hesh-ke* fever, the uncontrollable rage to kill.

As any red wolf might, the Apache drove his pony not for his prey, but to cut that prey off. He sent the little animal lunging for the open doorway toward which the white man dragged his woman. He reached the opening just as Peaches and Bourke did, from the inside, blocking them. Chatto saw that only Ysun might prevent him from killing the white man who had Estune. The defenders on the roof could not fire down for fear of hitting their own fellow. The same applied to the Fort Gila scout and his sergeant. The young chief whirled his pony to ride down his enemy.

But his mustang flared at the sight of the woman's body on the ground. It leaped high and to the side, as a deer would leap, twisting away from under its rider. Chatto came down heavily in the sand of the stage road but was at once upon his feet, scalping knife in hand.

Bourke's service revolver was empty. Peaches could not fire

the old Springfield without hitting the drifter or the white girl's baby. "Down! Down!" he yelled at the white man. But the drifter had read the madness in Chatto's eyes. If Peaches should miss, the Chiricahua's knife would be in the drifter's guts the next jump.

He put the baby aside in the sand, jumping away from her to draw the Apache from that place. He had no weapon save his two hands. Yet his were no ordinary hands and no ordinary weapons. They were hard-taught weapons of bone and sinew and skill unknown to any red man.

As Chatto struck snakelike with his ten-inch blade, the drifter feinted and stepped floatingly away, pulling the Apache chief off balance for the fraction of time required to drive the right fist into the belly. This blow turned the Indian toward the white man, who then, all in one seeming motion, followed the right with an exploding left hand into the liver of the Apache. Chatto cried out as though lanced, and the third blow, another right hand, aimed and timed and driven this time with the full body of the drifter behind it, went once more into the pit of the gut. Chatto was destroyed.

He retched and humped in the dust in the manner of a rattlesnake run over by iron-rimmed wagon wheels.

The drifter would have killed him and tried to with three kicks to the head. But the target was moving and the light was bad, and now the Hoh-shuhs *were* coming in earnest back to the fight. The kicks thudded into arm and ribs and shoulder blade, and Chatto lived. The white man, his comrades in the open doorway screaming for him to "Get in! Get in!" bent double and ran for the lamplight. Ahead of him, Bourke was just hauling the squaw in. Peaches had the Springfield shouldered aiming past the crouched drifter. In the thunder and flash of its discharge, the drifter made the door and was inside barring it and standing, back to its bleached timbers, his face still wild with battlelight.

But suddenly the light changed. The black brows arched helplessly. The blue eyes swept the common room. "God amighty!" he cried. "Where's the baby? I thought one of you picked her up!"

Peaches and Bourke had no time to reply. The agony of their fearful glances was broken by the muffled tiny cry from beyond the barred planks of the station-house door. The three men stared at one another sick with what had happened.

Each of them thought the other had picked the child up. But none of them had done so.

The yellow-haired girl's baby was still out there in the dust of the Tucson Road.

35

The situation was now as stark as it might be.

They had Chatto's woman. Chatto had the white girl's child.

But that was not all Chatto had.

He had nine of their thirteen horses. He had eighteen guns to their four. He had apparently unlimited supplies of ammunition to their few remaining rounds. And more. Chatto had greed and fear and prejudice working for him inside the white fortress.

The values of Estune and the white baby as counterhostages did not balance. The squaw did not have to have the child, but the child had to have the squaw. It no longer made sense to imagine they might hold Estune to guarantee a safe retreat for them all to Pima Bend. The Chiricahua reply to that would remain simply what it would to any other suggestion of holding Chatto's woman with her mother's milk; if the baby did not nurse it must die: There was not any way in which the Apache men might give it suck or, indeed, care for it upon the trail in any way to insure its survival.

The grim meeting about the plank table in the common room of the beleaguered relay station, try as its members repeatedly did, could not escape this bond. It would not yield. It would not go away.

"It's back to the kid again," said the drifter, thin face pale beneath its heavy stubble of beard. "It ain't no place elst to go."

T.C. Madden scowled. Hunker Larsen blinked. Sergeant Emmett Bourke looked down at the table shaking his head. Over on the fireplace bench, the yellow-haired girl began to sob hysterically. "Quieten her," the drifter said to Hunker, and the blacksmith answered, "Yah sure," and went to the girl. Doing so, he passed Estune, bound hand and foot to a supporting beam of the small-log roof. The squaw cursed him and spat at his face. The spittle dribbled from the big man's shirtfront, and he stared at it and at the woman. Hunker did not comprehend hatred of this order. He was a man without serious enemy or substantial friend. A lone man, he accepted all humanity. That an Indian would spit on Lars Larsen no more occurred to him than it would occur to him that Lars Larsen would spit upon an Indian. He shook meaty, round head. "Yah sure, poor t'ing," he apologized for the glaring squaw and went on to kneel solicitously beside the weeping white mother.

The cherubic face of Peaches appeared above in the roof's traphole.

The scout pleaded with the all-white jury at the plank table to come up, *ahora mismo!* with its verdict. There was more trouble in the Indian camp. The Hoh-shuhs wanted to kill the baby, leave Chatto's woman, ride for home.

As an Apache himself, Peaches was most apprehensive for the child's life. The Hoh-shuhs had all the arguments:

What of Indian value remained to be won? they were demanding to know of Chatto. They already had all of the cavalry's *thlees,* all of its horses. They had, as well, all of its *besh-e-gars,* its rifles, and its *beshes,* its long-knives. Now, the Hoh-shuhs continued, had the baby been an *ish-ke-ne,* a boy-child, why any Apache would understand a childless man such as young Chatto taking all these risks. In that case, too, the squaw's milk, hence the woman herself, would have real meaning. But all of this ridiculous night-firing for a *day-den?* A stupid girl-child worth absolutely nothing in Arizona or Mexico or any other market? It was preposterous. Someone was apt to get hit! Even badly wounded. And three first-rate ponies had already been injured with wild bullets!

Enough of this rushing at the damned *kinh,* the damned white man's house.

Let there be a vote on it right away: Who was going home to Pa-gotzin-kay, following Lucero and the other Hoh-shuhs with the good brains in their heads, and who would stay with this lovesick young Chatto bargaining with the white people—and those two very rapidly working Winchester rifles—for his damned northern woman?

"Peaches go back listen," the scout called down, concluding his report. "Better decide quick down there."

"Yeah," the drifter answered him. "Madden?"

The stage line owner was perspiring a virtual soak of sweat. His heavy face did not look good. "They win," he said, low-voiced. "They got to win. I got to get on down to Tucson. I can do it yet tonight, if they clear out of here.

Otherwise, I lose everything and we don't save the kid anyways."

"How you figure to get on to Tucson tonight?" It was Sergeant Bourke scowlingly. "I count four white men here and four horses. That leaves us a white woman and a damned good little Apache Indian on foot. Where you see two horses in that for you alone?"

"That spare team is mine and that bay is mine. Three horses," said Madden. "One for me, one for my man Hunk, one for packing the gold-bags. We don't figure it three horses like that, we won't get the gold down there in time. Two won't cut it. And they *are* my horses."

"What you propose the rest of us do?" said Bourke.

"Wait for Bill Jimmie."

"Who the hell is Bill Jimmie?"

"My Navajo stocktender here at this station. He turnt the relay teams loose when's he heard the Cherry Cows was out. Him and that stock will be drifting back in here soon's the damned Cherry Cows pulls out."

Here the drifter nodded. "It could be," he said. "I believe that coach up yonder, and its cut harness, can be patched to run as far as back to Pima Bend. It would get the lady out thataway."

"But you're gambling on a damned Injun stocktender to come back and to know where his loose stock has went, meanwhile, and a few dozen others damned big maybes."

"You don't put down on the squares," shrugged the drifter, "you don't pick up the chips."

The old sergeant eyed him. "Seems you've changed your tune mighty swift," he accused. "It was you and your arguing for the missus yonder that got us where we are. We'd still have the kid, weren't it for you."

The drifter grimaced, then nodded. "I know," was all he said. "Hunker, how you vote?" he called.

The blacksmith had not been listening. He was holding the sleeping white girl in his great thick arms. "Shhh!" he warned, finger to lips, "Poor t'ing sleeping."

"I can see that!" snapped the drifter. "You vote to give in to the Injuns, or not, you dumb ox?"

The gentle-voiced smith nodded toward T.C. Madden.

"Whatever mister says," he answered. "He be the boss."

"That mean you vote with Madden?" demanded Bourke, breaking in. "To go for the gold?"

"Yah sure."

It was down, then, to the old soldier himself.

"Well, sergeant?" said the drifter.

"Well, hell," said Bourke wearily. "I don't know what to say. My duty lies in getting back up to the fort. Pima Bend is my vote. I guess that means waiting it out. Setting here until them red bastards leave and this here Bill Jimmie Navajo shows up with the relay stock. Or enough of it to move that coach back over Querecho Mesa."

The drifter chilled him with the frost-blue eyes.

He shook shaggy head.

"No," he said. "It means you're voting to let Chatto have the baby and his squaw to nurse it for him."

"Ah, Christ," sighed Bourke. "I know that."

It came to the veteran noncom as he admitted the uncomfortable fact, that the questioner had not himself voted yet. The battered Irish face wrinkled to challenging glower.

"How about you, Mister Horsethief?"

A passing smile briefly lit the hollow-eyed face.

"About me," admitted the drifter. "I don't know either." He paused, looking at the yellow-haired girl, looking away from her out toward the stage road and the waiting Chiricahua. "I ain't rightly got no place to go." Again, he hesitated. "I remember an old, old piece from the Book of Matthew," he said. " 'The foxes has their holes, and the birds of the air has got their nests; but the Son of man hain't not the where to lay his head.' " The fleeting, luckless grin once more lit the shadowed face. "I go back to Pima Bend, it's five years in Yumer Prison. I don't go, it's my lifetime riding on from here with her haunting my trackline," he gestured with an inclining of the head to the sleeping girl. "I already got one yellow-haired gal follering me wherever I go. Yeah, and another little blonde-haired baby-child, too." For the last time he looked up, nodding. "I reckon it's Pima Bend for me, same as for you, sarge. We ain't no other choice."

Sergeant Emmett Bourke stood up.

"Two for Tucson tonight, two for Pima Bend tomorrow," he said. "Jury's hung."

"*No it ain't,*" answered T.C. Madden. His chair scraped, and his hand came away from inside his coat and they all saw the big holes in the .44 derringer staring at them.

"My God," said the drifter. "You cain't do it."

"By God," replied the stage line owner. "I got to do it. Hunker. Grab the Winchester yonder—"

36

Hunker, true, dumb, simple Hunker, picked up the second Winchester. He did not want to hold a gun on another man, but mister had told him to do it.

Madden moved around behind the cavalry sergeant, put the derringer under the Irishman's ear, and called aloud. "Hey, you, Injun up there. Get down here."

Unsuspecting, Peaches peered obediently through the traphole. He did not ask what to do. He saw the pistol at his sergeant's ear, and he saw the hand that held the pistol shaking badly. He came down the chicken ladder, and Madden took the first Winchester from him. He tossed the weapon to Hunker. "Lay it on the mantel," he said. Then, to Bourke and the drifter. "You get one, we get one. It's fair. Besides," he muttered. "Me and Hunk ain't going until the redskins clear out. So we ain't dangering you none, meanwhile."

Neither Bourke nor the drifter said a word. Both were watching Madden. And both were deciding that to jump him was not worth it. One of those big .44 slugs could open a man up forever at that range. And the gun had two barrels and two slugs. One for each of them.

Hunker Larsen?

He might or might not fire the Winchester. Probably he would not. But they would have to get by Madden to try the big Swede. And the stage line owner was thinking of his gold. The look on his broad face was unsteady. He really was already on the road to Tucson. There was no question of it in his motions or his words. He saw what he had never expected to see again—a remaining good chance to beat the bankers to the territorial capital and his beloved Southwest Stagelines. So Hunker was no good bet either. Not with T.C. Madden shaking so visibly in the derringer-hand.

"Hunk," said the latter. "Cut the squaw loose."

The blacksmith did as he was bidden. This time the Indian woman did not spit on him. She merely stared at him slowly shaking her head. This one was a crazy. He was not right in his mind, and the Indians had always made special place in their tribal rankings for the bereft of reason. "*Schichobe*," she said to the smith.

Hunker smiled at her and grunted, "Yah sure," never knowing the wife of Chatto had called him "old friend."

When freed, the woman stood tall a moment against the post, gathering herself for whatever was to come.

"Tell her she can go," Madden ordered Peaches.

The scout made a handsign to the squaw and lied as well as any Apache. "These people say you are free. They say your life for their lives. They say you take white baby and go. You and Chatto and all the Hoh-shuhs, everyone. Right now they say. Do you agree for Chatto?"

The woman frowned, compressed her dark lips, nodded her understanding.

"Then go!" cried the scout. "There is trouble in both our camps. Let there now be an end to it."

"*Anh!*" said Estune. "*Ugashé.*"

She glided to the door but did not quite reach it. By the fireplace, the white mother had awakened. She saw the Indian woman departing, knew at once that with her went all hope of having her baby returned.

"No!" she said, starting up. "No, no—!"

She staggered toward Estune, and the drifter caught her, restraining her. "Got to be, lady," he told her. "It's the onliest way we can save your baby."

The yellow-haired girl became incoherent. It was all the drifter could do to hold her against injury to herself. He started a string of obscenities toward Chatto's tall woman. Without thinking, the profanities came in a stream of fluent cowpen Spanish, the common tongue of the *monte*. His Apache companion laughed, the squaw was impressed. She nodded to the drifter and made a sign which only Peaches knew the meaning of. The drifter's pale face was dark with blood for a moment, then he returned a sign to the woman which Peaches did not understand. Estune smiled the quick summer-lightning smile. Unbarring the door herself, she was gone through it, never looking back upon its lonesome creaking in the rise of desert nightwind.

With a last ounce of frenzy, the white girl tore out of the drifter's relaxing grasp and ran to follow the Indian woman. Peaches' catlike quickness brought him to the door ahead of her, but it was only Sergeant Bourke's burly strength that overwhelmed her. After a moment she broke and wept, and then was herself.

"Oh, my God," she kept saying, "oh, my God—"

They rebarred the door, Madden still in command with the

derringer. "Injun," he said. "Get up on that roof and see what they do." He swung the derringer. "Rest of us just going to take it easy," he said. "Hunk."

"Yah, mister?"

"Gimme the Winchester. Take the other one with you. Go get the horses saddled. Don't waste no time."

The blacksmith departed and had no more than done so when Peaches was calling down that the Chiricahua were pulling out. The Hoh-shuhs were already mounted and moving. Chatto's woman, the young chief himself, and old Nevado were down in the roadway calling up to him that they wanted to see the thin-boned man; they had something to tell him and something to show him.

Madden decided the drifter might go to the roof. Unarmed, it was a certainty he would not go over the edge again. He gave the nod, aimed the derringer at Bourke anew. Any nonsense up above he warned would earn the sergeant a .44 caliber hole in his uniform. The drifter went up the chicken ladder and to the parapet puzzling over the request of the Chiricahua.

Had Chatto's keen desert eyesight spied him out well enough in the moonlight to remember him from the long-ago raid on his ranch?

Was that bitch Estune up to some new deviltry?

Some last Indian cruelty?

"*Qué pasa?*" he asked Peaches, crouching below the parapet. "What the hell they want?"

"Want talk you. Stand up. They no shoot."

"Yeah, well thanks," drawled the white man. "Ain't nothing like a Injun g'arantee to get you strapped on your hoss, toes down."

"Thin One," called the squaw, in Spanish, from below. "Let me see you."

"Ah, Christ Jesus," groaned the drifter and stood up.

The woman, still speaking soft *monte* Spanish, told him directly that she thanked him for the child, knowing it was his counsel that had given it to her. She promised him to care for it as though it were a man-child, and to remember him always in her heart. He was to remember something else, too. He knew what it was. She would remember that, also, in her heart.

That was the end of it for her.

But as always with the Apache there was the hidden card; not the ace, but the assassin in the hole.

Chatto kneed his mustang forward. He spoke into the shadows behind him, and old Nevado rode out into the moonlight of the wagon ruts leading a spare mount. On this mount was a man, feet bound beneath the little animal's potbelly, hands free, and black head held high.

Clooney Borrum!

"Hey, Jesus, Clooney friend!" cried the drifter. "It's you! Big as a bloat-steer and twicet as ugly!" He lost the glad note. "I'm sorry, old stage driver," he called down. "We'll do everiest thing we can to get you free."

Clooney waved long dark arm. There was no sadness in the way he straightened upon the Indian mustang, no sorrow in the bass voice and grateful words.

"Gawd love you, old hossthief man," he answered. "I'm already free! Cain't you see that? Soon's we're away from here, they's gonner cut loose my feet and leave me ride with em, fullblood brother!"

The drifter tried warning him but to no avail. He was convinced of his captors' sincerity and convinced of the first true freedom of his life, running with the red brother.

"Christ," insisted his white debtor. "You cain't truly believe they spairt your life becaust yer black!"

"No, hell no, it's caust I ain't white," laughed the Negro stablehand. He waved again, calling a sober promise to look after the "leetle white chile" as if it were his own and begging the drifter not to come after him. "These here is free folks," he said, "and true ones. They knows that Injun and nigger is the same word spelt different. Goodbye, old shotgun man!"

He was gone, with old Nevado, back into the chaparral before the drifter could reply further. Chatto waved his rifle to the white man on the roof and said his black friend had spoken truly except for one small thing: If there was any pursuit within two days, the *amigo negro* would be shot through the head *before* his feet were untied. With that, the young chief and his tall wife were gone, and all the Chiricahua were gone.

Peaches and the drifter were left alone with the long empty run of the stage road through the moonlight and with their own thoughts, red man and white, there upon the parapeted rooftop of the Sifford Wells relay station. It was the small Apache who spoke first.

"Morning come we think it over," he consoled.

"Yeah, we sure will," said the drifter softly.

Then, to himself, more softly still.

"And *every* morning, from here to the last hitchpost."

Madden and Larsen, with the spare coach team and Madden's bay saddler, went out through the Apache-sawed hole in the adobe corral wall less than a half hour later. The drifter was permitted to go with them on his request that he had something "total personal" to impart to the stage line owner. This, of course, was to inform him where his gold was buried and how the spot was marked. "You cain't miss it," the bearded wanderer said, and Madden, after a hard stare, answered, "For a hossthief you're a middling strange one. We get through to Tucson, you're down for a full share."

The drifter smiled wistfully.

"Give mine to the lady," he said. Then, frowning quickly, "I wisht you'd hold off, Mister Madden; it ain't bright to push out so clost ahint them. Better yet, hang here with us for the night. We need the gun."

"Get out'n the way," growled the other, cocking the Winchester. "It's all been said."

"*Adios*," nodded the drifter, stepping back.

There was no sound after the thudding of the horses' hooves died away across Little Dipper Wash. No outburst of rifle fire. No wolf yelps. Nothing. The drifter went back up on the roof to sit with Peaches and the remaining Winchester watching the night and listening to it.

"Guess their luck heldt," said the white man, after several minutes. "I was hunchy as hell abouten them going on. But I don't hear a thing, not nothing at all."

Peaches cocked his head, Apache bangs hiding round face. "Peaches hear," he said. "Luck hold bad."

The drifter stiffened. His eyes automatically went to the run of the stage road west to the wash. Thus it was he saw the moonlight shadows of the running horseman in the same instant that the hammering of unshod and shod hooves grew loud enough even for his white ear.

"Sonofabitch!" he grated and jacked a round into the chamber.

"No!" warned the scout. "No shoot."

A solitary Indian horseman, very large for an Apache, came on muffled gallop down the road from the wash. Behind him, flanking his pony really, were the two stage horses on short rope leads. Bringing up the rear of the eerie caravan came Madden's bay saddler running loose.

The stage horses were bearing burdens but not of T.C. Madden's gold. The Indian horseman's knife winked in the moonlight, slashing free the silent riders of the coach team. Their bodies flopped suddenly not twenty feet from the station house. The Indian galloped on, leading the now riderless spare team, followed yet stupidly by Madden's fine bay saddler. As he ·.ent, he fired into the air, with joyous yelps and desert-echoed claps of rifle lightning, the full magazine of Madden's Winchester. "Do-klini!" cursed Peaches. "Goddamn."

He dropped over the parapet to the ground below, the drifter following. Behind him, Bourke was unbarring the door. The yellow lamplight found what had been T.C. Madden and Lars Larsen—Madden with five, Larsen with seven arrows driven to the fletching through belly and back. There were no arrows in the heads because there were no heads. The big brother of Dust Devil had them slung in an old sack across the withers of his war pony. The moonlight had glinted upon the gold front tooth of T.C. Madden making it seem to Do-klini as a nice thing to own. He had hacked off the head of Hunker Larsen only so that the first man's head would have company in the sack, would not be lonely or afraid in there. It was a courtesy-thing, no more.

"All right out there?" called Bourke.

"All right," said Peaches.

He touched the kneeling drifter on the shoulder.

"Bad thing," he said. "We lose gun."

He was thinking of Madden's Winchester, and the drifter knew it. What he could not believe was that any human being could think like that staring down at two beheaded men warm with life not a quarter hour gone. In his three years of living on their trail winter and summer he had learned nothing of the Apache Indians. Or of any Indians. Would any white man ever?

"Peachy, you're a beaut," he said. "Thanks for reminding me."

"Remind you what?" asked the small red man.

"That me and you *ain't* brothers," said his companion. "Come on, let's get inside."

37

While the drifter stayed with the girl, Sergeant Bourke and the Apache scout Peaches found shovels in the corral horse shed. They shallow-buried T.C. Madden and Lars Larsen in the loose sand just beyond the hole the Chiricahua had cut in the corral wall. Upon their return, all went up to the roof. The girl was made as comfortable as possible, a bedding of feedsacks being made for her beside the wind shelter and warmth of the fireplace chimney. Across-roof, the three men sat and smoked the night away watching over the parapet, unable to sleep, unable, in their minds, to resolve either past or future, much less comprehend the present.

The questions were easy:

Would they stay where they were, awaiting military or other relief sure to come eventually? Would Bill Jimmie come home with enough of the horses he had loosed to make up a stage-hitch capable of pulling the overturned Concord to Pima Bend? If he did, would the coach really roll soundly? Would they find the harness repairable? Did they dare, even, meanwhile, to go up there to Nine Soldier Gulch and scout coach and rigging? Or would some other band of hostile Chiricahua come by before any help arrived? Should they, fearing and weighing the latter chance, start out on foot with the girl on Peaches' pony? Should they leave right now so to be well on the way to Pima Bend with daylight? Or were some of the vicious Chiricahua still out there waiting for just such a tomfool venture?

Ah, yes, the questions were simple; it was the answers which made the blood run a bit chill.

Every query they put to each other, or to self unspoken, came fast-circle back to the headless bodies of Madden and his faithful blacksmith.

The conclusion, individually and full company, was the old-line noncommissioned officer's dictum voiced by thirty-year soldier Emmett J. Bourke: When in final doubt, do nothing. So they sat the darkness away, listening to the fitful, exhausted slumber of the young mother, the noises of the desert, the rustle of the nightwind, the uneasy, sleepless voices of their consciences.

Maybe old Bourke was right; maybe tomorrow would furnish its own inspirations, bring its own solutions.

Peaches and the drifter knew one thing:
He had better be right.

The day came clear and green-skied and hot, as the
preceding day had departed. In the earliest yellowing of the
sun still hiding behind Querecho Mesa, a sound fell thinly but
stirringly from the western distances, and old soldier Bourke
was right.

That was a U.S. Cavalry bugle blowing out there toward
Mount Piños and the permanent rancheria of young Chatto's
Chiricahua people.

Half an hour later the cavalry column moved in from the
desert. It was under command of a stern captain, numbered
forty troopers, with a second lieutenant, noncoms, cook, and
drivers for supply, feed, and cookwagons, to a total of fifty-
five personnel exclusive of three Tonto Apache Scouts and a
brace of Scottish staghounds belonging to the column commander. This was a reconnaissance in force on the face of it,
far beyond the power of any Chiricahua raiders to menace or
to impede. When they saw its numbers, equipment, and, most
of all, the uncompromising professionalism of its officers, both
Bourke and the drifter knew their big problem was answered—
adequate care and safe custody for the girl.

It only sweetened their pleasure to learn the column would
turn about immediately for Tucson and Fort Lowell. The
troops had camped nearby. They had come from Chatto's
rancheria, found deserted, had seen the buzzards wheeling
over Nine Soldier Gulch, found the naked corpses up there,
left a burial detail, and come on to Sifford Wells, their
original destination.

There was more. The wires had been restored to Fort Gila,
Pima Bend, and generally throughout the command area.
Kensington's unauthorized extension of orders beyond Pima
Bend was known via the sheriff there having reported the
patrol lost and exhausted on Querecho Mesa.

Justifiable official alarm had arisen. Crook, from San Carlos, seeking to repair Captain Herritt's error in choosing
Kensington to command the lost patrol, and guessing in his
shrewd way the trouble looming, had ordered the Fort Lowell force to Sifford Wells by way of Chatto's permanent camp
to intercept and if necessary rescue the headstrong, twice
reprimanded lieutenant.

The Lowell column had yet other news. As the drifter had
learned in his cistern spying, and Peaches confirmed by his

information from both the Hoh-shuh Springs and Na-koo-say encampments of the hostiles, Geronimo and the subchiefs of the warring Chiricahua were heading for Mexico raiding, burning, and killing as they went.

Much to the interest of both the white horsethief and the red cavalry scout, the stern captain in command reported that the chief pillager was a young murderer named *Chato,* or Flat Nose, who alone had been credited with killing eleven friendly non-Chiricahua Apache Indians and twenty-two whites of all ages. The strength of the Flat Nose party had been put at no more than thirteen, one of which was a woman and one a nursing babe. Even for the villainous Apache, the captain assured them, this was a modern record of butchery.

It was not only modern, the drifter decided for himself, exchanging an astonished look with Peaches, it was miraculous. Especially, considering that the Chatto they knew had only left a few hours ago and would have had no more than time to get decently out of sight of the troops sent to probe for him. But neither the small scout nor the tall lanky white wanderer made any mention of discrepancies. Indeed, as both were wanted men, they hung well back, letting Sergeant Emmett J. Bourke represent them and trusting the old soldier not to betray them. Bourke was true to the charge. He introduced them as *hombres del monte,* men of the country, known to him and of good character within the purview of his personal knowledge. The Apache had done some good work for Captain Herritt up at Fort Gila. The white man was merely traveling through from Pima Bend, riding shotgun for Southwest Stagelines, to Tucson.

There was a bad moment when the second lieutenant, ever eager, as was his grade, for ingratiating self with a superior, remembered that this same Captain Herritt up at Fort Gila was looking for an Indian scout; what the devil was the rascal's name?

"Oh," said Bourke, "you mean Peaches, yes. This fellow here is called Tzoe. He's no Chiricahua."

"Oh," scowled the lieutenant.

There might still have been something to come of this, except that the captain, a widower of but six months and a fine figure of a man on a horse, was beginning to take note of the bereaved young mother of the stolen white child, now lost to Chatto's squaw.

For her part, the girl was distraught at leaving with the

troops and had not yet taken note of the captain. Going away
from Sifford Wells meant saying true farewell to her baby. It
would be the acknowledgment that she would never see her
child again and that not only the three strange men who had
shared her ordeal with her, but these fine officers and brave
men of the United States Cavalry considered the matter
closed. It was final. Over with. Done.

The goodbyes were simple, brief, awkward.

Bourke and Peaches shook hands. The old sergeant would
be returning with the troops to Fort Lowell to be mustered
out there. He planned to stay on in Arizona, and, should the
Apache ever get down near Tucson, he would always be
welcome in the home of Emmett J. Bourke.

It was not that easy for the little scout.

He tried to tell the sergeant that he, himself, would still
serve the cavalry. He felt, he insisted, responsible for the bad
end of Lieutenant Kensington and his patrol. After all, that
had been Peaches' patrol. Those were his soldiers who had
died up there. And he was not with them. It was in his
Apache heart, he told Bourke, that he must make a balance
for this. He must do something for his adopted people and
for the cavalry that would repay them. He had, he said,
gripping the sergeant's hand for the final time, such a thing
already in his mind. He would not burden his old friend with
it, but it was a considerable thing.

"Make people remember Peaches," he said. "Make cavalry
proud. Bring peace all Chiricahua people."

Bourke was not really listening. He rather liked the little
runt but, after all, he was a damned Apache.

"Sure lad," he answered, not even looking at the small man
as he took his hand. "Good luck to you."

Peaches stepped back and saluted.

Bourke, easing up to share the seatbox of the horsefeed
wagon, said to the driver, "We ain't a thing to worry about. I
was just told the Cherry Cow war is over."

"Huh?" grunted the driver.

"That halfpint Injun yonder," the old sergeant said. "He's
going to bring peace to all the Cherry Cow people. With full
honor to the U.S. Cavalry."

"My," said the trooper. "Ain't that grand!"

"They're crazy," said Bourke. "Every damned one of them,
ours or the hostiles."

They were interrupted by the drifter working his way
cautiously up from the rear of the wagon, away from the

captain and his lieutenant who were mother-henning the loading of the "poor dear child" into her prepared bed in the supply wagon—the only one with a canvas tarp over its skeletal ribs.

"Psst!" said the drifter. "Sarge, I got to thank you for everything you done just now. It went clean beyondt any call of duty, or whatever. Uh, I—"

"It wasn't nothing," Bourke cut him off, sparing further agony of gratitude. "There wasn't no duty to it, partner. Remember that."

"Well, sarge, you're a soldier of the U.S. of A. and, well, you know." The drifter hung head, stood there. He was a man who had to have a debt stated.

"I *was* a soldier," he said. "Up until sundown last night. My thirty years run out at 6:00 P.M."

The drifter nodded, relieved. He reached up and their hands met firmly.

"What will you do?" Bourke asked him.

"Keep drifting," grinned the bearded nomad. "I'll wind up against a fenceline somewheres."

"See that you don't get strung up on one somewhere," advised the older man. "You got a running start, now. Keep going and don't look back."

"Funny," grimaced the drifter. "That's precisely what old Clooney Borrum toldt me."

"That was a smart nigger," said Bourke. "Up until he voted himself a volunteer Injun. He'll wish he'd got blasted with his friend off that old Concord before he's halfways to Mexico with them goddamn Chattos."

The drifter frowned.

"He was allus talking about being free," he said. "I hope to God he makes it this time all the way."

"So long," said Bourke suddenly. "Yonder comes the lieutenant. Get going, and keep Peaches out of sight till we're gone." He waved. "Luck, *hombre*."

"*Vaya*," said the drifter and slunk behind the wagon again.

He thought that he was safely away, not only behind the wagon but behind the flank of the mounted column waiting for the sick woman to load, but a corporal flagged him down. "You J.D. Drifter?" the young soldier asked. For a moment the question stumped him and he started to deny it. Then he remembered. Old Madden must have told the yellow-haired girl about that stupid name. "Yeah," he admitted to the trooper. "What's the charge?"

"Mrs. Carter asked to see you," the youth replied. "Come on along. We're moving out."

"Hold up," objected the drifter. "I don't know no—oh," he recovered. "That Mrs. Carter. Why'n the hell didn't you say so. Whereaways is she at?"

They came up to the supply wagon, and the yellow-haired girl was lying in it in a nice bed of clean hay and freshly unrolled army blankets. Under the airy shade of the canvas tarp and in the cleanness of the morning sun, he saw freckles and eye flecks and marvelously white pearls when she smiled. All that had been hidden or smudged or dingied-out by smoky lamplight and moonshadows before. "Gawd," the drifter said under his breath. Then, pulling off his filthy hat and holding it to his breast, as though in church or at a burying. "Yes, ma'am. Thank you, ma'am."

He stood there not knowing what else to say.

They were alone just for a few seconds, the troops all busied getting the column formed up, the officers likewise employed. If the wanderer did not know how to use seconds like these, the lady did. She beguiled him with her eyes and the squeezing of her pink hand and the genuine feeling she put into the words she had for his steadiness and courage at the station house, and, lastly, she thanked him for the kiss he had given her and which he would never otherwise have known she knew he had given her. "Here!" she said, and with surprising strength pulled herself up to the wagon's sideboard and touched her soft lips to his grimed cheek before he might move a muscle to evade the gesture. "A kiss for a kiss," she murmured, and then, as suddenly, the tears were brimming the long black lashes, and she was thinking of her baby. The drifter wished that the desert would open up and swallow him entire.

"Ma'am," he managed. "Mrs. Carter."

She dabbed the eyes, steadied herself. "Yes?"

"I purely wisht there was ought I could do to get her back for you. They'd never have had her but for me, and—"

The girl gripped his arm, again raising herself urgently. "No!" she denied. "That's not so. I would never have had her but for you. That Indian squaw saved my baby, and you—you—"

"Please don't weep no more, Mrs. Carter, ma'am."

He struggled, wanted to go, but had to stay, had to get it said.

"Ma'am, I don't rightly know where I'm agoing from here. I reckon one day 'fore long, though, that I'll ride Tucsonway, maybe just a'passing through, but I'll be there. Where will you be, ma'am?"

It was out. He had not the nerve left to look up at her, once he had said it. But he had gotten it out. And she smiled. And the pink fingers touched his arm again.

"I will be in Tucson," she said. "I'm to stay with Lieutenant Gatsby's family, and Captain Marlin has said they could dearly use help in their infirmary at the fort. You know, a nurse, or well, you know, something."

The drifter nodded.

"I'm sure of it, ma'am," he said. "Certain sure."

The cornflower eyes, flecks of sunshine and all, found his own strangely blue eyes. "You will look for me down there?" she invited. "Promise?"

The drifter felt heart beating fit to burst out past bone-thin ribs. He held up his hand in the sign language motion of attestment.

"Promise," he murmured. "Injun honor, ma'am."

She lay back, then, happily, he was certain, and he himself felt as though he were seven feet tall. But he heard the approach of booted feet and, not even looking back, he slid around the tailgate of the supply wagon; when a frowning Captain Frederick Marlin strode up next moment to demand, "Who was that shabby rascal?" of the resting Mrs. Carter, he was gone again behind the mounted column of twos. Whether the captain might have taken the matter further became academic the moment the pale and lovely girl smiled at him and answered, "Oh, Captain Marlin! Are we to start now? How grateful I am to you, sir. You will never understand what it meant to me when I saw you riding in with your men. I, I—"

"There, there," comforted the officer "Yes, Mrs. Carter, we are starting at once. Is there anything you wish before I give the order? Anything at all?"

The girl denied it and lay back. The column commander spun his horse smartly, took him on the flying gallop to columnhead. "Ho!" he barked at his first sergeant, and he himself led out his forty men, three vehicles, pale passenger, and two Scottish staghounds. Through the dust, and looking back at Sifford Wells station, the yellow-haired girl waved to the lonely figures of Peaches and the bearded white man who had so moved her emotions, so altered the very fabric of her young life.

"Goodbye," she called to them. "Oh, goodbye—!"

Hoh-shuh Springs

38

Peaches and the drifter stood alone.

Far off down the Tucson road the dustsnake of Captain Marlin's column crawled away into the chaparral and was gone.

"Where you go now?" said the scout.

"Dunno, Peachy." The white man scanned the vastness of the silent land. "It won't be too damn far, nor too overwhelming swift, without a hoss."

The Indian nodded. He knew the feeling of the horseman stranded in that burning immenseness. Especially of that horseman who was sought by the law of the white man as well as the lance of the red man. "We get you horse," he said. "Me, you, we come same place in trail."

The drifter grinned. They had indeed come to the same place in the trail. Wanted men, and unwanted men.

"Where you going from here, Peachy?" he asked.

With rare emotion for one of his stoic race, the small Apache told his white companion of the vow he had hinted about to Sergeant Bourke: The scout had been in Pa-gotzin-kay, the secret stronghold of the Chiricahua in the Mexican Sierra Madre, and he could guide General Red Beard Crook to that legendary retreat, thus enabling Crook to capture all the main bands and scatter the wild Chiricahua *hesh-kes* for all the springs to come.

"Only way come true peace," the little man concluded. "Peaches know. All Apache know. Red Beard know."

The drifter nodded thoughtfully. "All right, where's this here Pa-gotzin-kay?"

The other pointed south. "Plenty far Sonora. Five day journey past Casas Grandes."

The drifter eyed him suspiciously. "Casas Grandes is in Chihuahua," he said. Peaches shrugged off the charge.

"Sonora," he repeated. "Trail go in either way. Chihuahua east side Mother Mountain, Sonora west side."

"Ain't that grand," said the white man dubiously.

"Don't worry," reassured Peaches. "We find easy."

The drifter had to laugh. It made a strange sound in the loneliness of that deserted place, but this little Indian was nutty. "*We* find?" he said. "You got a cactus owl in your saddlebag, or something? You ain't meaning me, Injun. You want to find me something, find me a hoss."

The Fort Gila scout frowned. Behind him, his roach-maned pony whickered low in its throat. Both men knew that horse sound. They did not have to wait for the answering whicker from the other horse.

"Company," gritted the drifter. "And we ain't even cleaned up after the last bunch yet."

"You got gun," suggested the little scout. "You turn around first."

The drifter prepared to do so. It had to be either friend or enemy. There was not anybody neuter left out here in Apacheria. But the approaching animal's nickered reply to the greeting of Peaches' mount was not accompanied by human hail, friendly or otherwise. "Something funny," muttered the white man and made his turn. Peaches turned with him, and the two stared in disbelief. "Not funny," said the little Apache.

And indeed it was not.

It was the steeldust gelding, with the dead and fly-blown body of Deputy Pinky Suggins dragging from the right stirrup.

And more.

In the saddle-scabbard of the dead deputy was a gift well-nigh as rare as the race-bred horse itself: the oiled walnut and blued steel beauty of Sheriff Jules Hoberman's 44-40 Winchester carbine.

The drifter whistled, and the dust-caked animal came forward hopefully. When he caught the scent of the drifter, the gelding tossed his head and whinnied in glad recognition, moving on up to the two men and the Indian pony. The drifter caught up the trailing reins, let the horse nuzzle and bump him. The action caused the blowflies to lift in a cloud from the corpse of Pinky Suggins, and Peaches said uneasily, "Bury body quick; old Apache law."

"Hmmm," said the white man, pointing. "Good law."

The Apache looked and saw the vultures circling over

from Nine Soldier Gulch to take up their black-winged watch over the dead deputy. "Peaches hold horses," he volunteered anxiously. "You get shovel."

"White man dig, Injun stand around. Old Apache law, eh?" said the drifter.

He got the shovel and put Pinky where the friendly steel-dust had brought him, under the wagon ruts of the Tucson stage road. He knew the Indian horror of any corpse and worked quickly as Peaches had asked him to do. And as common sense told him to do. The next cavalry to check out those buzzards might not be white; it could be any shade of Cherry Cow red.

"Sorry, deputy," he said, giving the unmounded grave a last slap with the shovel. "It ain't very much, but then neither was you. Amen."

He took only Pinky's gunbelt, full of the same shining 44-40 ammunition that the sheriff's Winchester chambered. Whatever of identification or personal property the Pima Bend deputy carried would be on him for whoever dug him up out of the road. The drifter was a horsethief, but not a common one. Professional courtesy, that was all.

He handed the other Winchester to Peaches.

So they were down to it, he thought, he and the halfpint Apache Scout. Even up on horses. Even up on guns. Even up on chances to ride out alive.

He swung up on the steeldust. Peaches also mounted.

He was not, in his view, the kind to shake hands with any Indian, and this was an Apache Indian. But the little bastard had stood true, and six foot tall, and no man could take that away from him.

He did put out his hand.

Strangely, Peaches did not take it. Instead, he looked at it and then looked beyond it into the blue eyes of the strange white man.

"You don't go me show General Crook trail?"

The drifter lowered his hand.

"No, goddamnit," he said, amost angrily. "Me don't go you show General Crook trail. Why the hell ought I? I ain't lost nothing in Pa-gotzin-kay."

"You sure?" said Peaches.

The Fort Gila scout dug in a pocket of his faded denim shirt. "Here," he said. "You read on back."

Unthinkingly, the drifter put out his hand. Into it the little Apache dropped a stage line ticket.

"Read," he repeated flatly.

The pale bearded face flushed. The bony fist closed about the ticket, crumpling it.

"I don't need to read what's on it, goddamn you," he said. "I know what it says." He reined the gelding into the Indian's pony. "Who the hell gave you this, anyways?"

"Peaches promise not tell."

"It was the girl, wasn't it?"

"Peaches promise."

"I'll break your Injun ass!" the drifter threatened.

The little man only shook his head.

He had turned Indian on his white companion, and the drifter understood that immediately. It was right down where it was before on the goodbyes—except for that goddamned ticket. Helplessly, almost as though he must do so, he read the blurred print on the back of the punched stub. He glared a final time at Peaches.

"Who told you what was on here?" he demanded.

The scout shrugged. "Sarjen Broke. Peaches hear him lady talk."

"Then nobody give you this damn thing, by God!"

"Girl cry, throw away," Peaches said. "Me find."

"Son of a bitch," declared the drifter slowly. "You find, eh? And you give to me. A goddamn redass Injun putting shame on a white man. Christ Jesus."

They looked into one another's faces. Finally the little Apache asked soberly, "Now me you shake?"

"On what, for God's sake?"

"I go you bring back yellow-hair girl's baby. You go me show General Crook trail to Pa-gotzin-kay." He paused, pursing dark lips. "What you say, skookum deal?"

The drifter shook his head incredulously. He jammed the ticket into the pocket of his cavalry jacket.

"Peachy," he said to the sunny-faced small deserter of Chatto's raiders, "you're entire crazy; let's go."

"Sure!" laughed Peaches happily. "*Ugashé!*"

They put the potbellied mustang and the clean-limbed steeldust gelding up the wash-trail toward Na-koo-say. Here, at the ancient Apache camping place, Chatto would have halted to rest and water his people and his animals before starting the long, swift retreat to Mexico. Here the tracking down of the Chiricahua would begin, to end Ysun alone knew where.

From here the drifter and Pa-nayo-tishn would ride after the baby of the yellow-haired girl.

After that, Peaches would ride into history.

39

Up at Na-koo-say, Peaches became very excited.

The Chattos had built breakfast fires and departed only just before daylight. The ash moundings were yet warm and smelling of dripped meat juices. Those Indians had not left this water more than one hour before the Fort Lowell soldiers came into Sifford Wells.

The drifter shrugged, made laconic comment that this sat well with him. He would not have cared to share the young chief's breakfast. Now his blankets might be something else altogether. That tall squaw was a real *mujer*.

"No, no!" the little Apache objected.

His white friend did not understand the excitement. Peaches had thought Chatto would use the entire night to continue riding for Hoh-shuh Springs to take advantage of Geronimo's promise to wait for him one day. Any time longer than that would mean Chatto had run into trouble in his vengeance on the soldiers who had murdered his women and man-child. Trouble for Chatto was trouble for all of them. So if he did not return in the one day, Geronimo and the main band would be gone.

That was the exciting thing.

The drifter still did not get it and said so.

"Listen good," advised Peaches and went on to describe the true story of the present raid into Arizona.

To begin with Chatto was not up from Pa-gotzin-kay to support Nah-tez at Fort Gila. He had already been killing white people and Indians and burning ranches and jacals on this raid before he ever came near Fort Gila. The same with Geronimo. The great chief was not at Hoh-shuh Springs on his way to bolster the noble Nah-tez. He was there resting his stock and his people from all the running and killing they had been doing for the three days of the raid before that halt. Yes, and resting them, too, for the days of killing yet to come on the return sweep to the border.

The truth was that Geronimo was readying Chatto to replace him as head of the *hesh-kes*, the wild Chiricahua who would never surrender. The great fighter grew old. He had chosen his heir. It was Chatto; and now the thing was to complete the killing and slip back over the border so swiftly that the Americans would have no time to give them true chase, or even to alert the Mexican troops waiting for them on the other side.

All this, and much more, Peaches had heard from Do-klini and the others at Hoh-shuh. Indeed, even the great fighter himself, Geronimo, had told some of it to the round-faced little friend of the white man, thinking to influence him to renounce his desertion of the Chatto band and join up again with all his old friends from Pa-gotzin-kay. A man like Peaches, who knew the white man's tongue, and who was known as a friend by the white man, whose women and children and old mother lived not ten miles from San Carlos, why such a *nan-tan*, such a scout, could prove invaluable as a source of spying. Moreover, Geronimo knew that his little friend had not been named Coyote for nothing. The white man might call him Peaches and think he was his friend. Geronimo and the Chiricahua knew better. Peaches was an Apache. He was Pa-nayo-tishn, The Coyote Saw Him, and he was not stupid. He would surely be able to see the wisdom of Geronimo's proposal.

Here Peaches paused in his narrative to grin at the drifter. "Him know goddamn good Peaches see wisdom," he said. "Peaches don't see wisdom, Peaches don't see nothing."

"So Peachy saw, eh?" the drifter nodded.

"You bet. Swear spy good both sides."

"And?"

"Geronimo say maybe. He say me go long by Chatto and if live come back, they make council on Peaches."

"Meaning?"

"Three thing. Leave Peaches Arizona scout for cavalry, spy for Apache. Take Peaches back Pa-gotzin-kay. Leave Peaches Hoh-shuh Springs."

"Meaning dead," the drifter said.

The small scout only nodded. All the while he had been talking, he had been rekindling the Apache fire and searing some strips of horsemeat left behind by the departed Chiricahua. Now he and the white man chewed in silence, watching their horses drink and graze beyond the dying fire. Finally the drifter frowned.

"I may be dense," he said. "But all this palaver ain't getting us that baby back, nor sending you on your way to bend old Crook's hairy ears. What you really getting at, Peachy? I know goddamn well it's something."

"You good man," the scout said. "Peaches like."

"But," nodded the other.

"Not smart," said the little Apache.

The drifter laughed softly. "Go ahead on," he said.

Peaches then told him, growing excited once more, that all of this meant one thing to them—the chance, and the best chance they would ever have, to steal back the yellow-haired girl's baby.

Beyond Hoh-shuh Springs, he said, the next water was forty miles. The next stop after that would be the border of Mexico, one hundred miles by the Apache trail, from Hoh-shuh. In two days, then, the retreating Chattos would be over one hundred miles away. But! and the little man sprang the word out delightedly, Hoh-shuh Springs itself was only three or four hours' hard ride from where they now sat waiting for their horses to eat and be ready.

"For Gawd's sake," said the drifter. "Get to it."

Peaches clapped his hands in a rare gesture of almost childlike pleasure.

Listen! he said.

He knew that Chatto would go to Hoh-shuh Springs. It was just too far to the next water without making the stop at Hoh-shuh. As well, if no cavalry pursuit developed along the way, Chatto would rest out that present day at Hoh-shuh. He would at very least wait there until darkness gave him cover to strike for the next water at Forty Mile Tank.

He also knew that when Chatto got there Geronimo and the main band would be gone on.

This gave Peaches and the drifter their chance!

They would go right now, by a path known to Peaches and not to the Chattos—a path which could bring them to Hoh-shuh ahead of the young chief and his band. It was, like everything in life, a gamble. It was a game, such as *monte*, *con quién*, *tzi-chis* or *mushka*, white man's and Apache's games together. So as he and the drifter were red man and white man together, let them play the game together. Win or lose.

"*Qué dice?*" the small White Mountain scout grinned, in Spanish. "*No hay tiempo que perder!*"

"No time to lose, eh?" scowled the white man. "Only our hair, or maybe our *huevos*."

Peaches said if they got to the camp before Chatto it

meant they could find the proper place to hide-up with a full view of the place. There they could watch the Chatto people arrive, see where each one bedded, how the ponies were put out, where the guards were posted, everything. They would have the great advantage, too, of the Chiricahua having no reason to expect pursuit from Na-koo-say, as they had departed before the Fort Lowell column arrived. Certainly they feared no pursuit by poor Lieutenant Kensington or by the cravenly behaving group in the relay station, people so frightened and confused as to leave the baby lying out in the dust of the road.

"Peaches sorry," the little man said. "But Apache think like this. Not what Peaches think."

"Thanks," said the drifter acidly. "Makes a man's heart swell plumb up to know his real friends don't care if he's a coward or not. Plus a damn fool."

"Sure," said Peaches, grin spreading. "Peaches don't care." Then, proud of his English, "Peaches don't give shit."

"Thanks again," nodded his companion. "Let's go."

Peaches went around the spring and caught up both mounts. Watching him, the drifter marvelled 'anew at the Apache spirit and hardihood. Here was a little Indian runt no bigger than a boy and looking about as tough as a custard pie. He had been a prisoner far down in the Apache mother-camp. He had gotten away from Chatto's murderous band. Been recaptured by them. Gotten away again. He could have simply lit out on his pony from down at Sifford Wells, leaving the drifter standing in the middle of nowhere, and gone on to San Carlos and no doubt been a big hero with his "story for Redbeard."

But no. Here he was, not alone ready but cheerfully willing, to risk his life the third time against his maniac erstwhile Chiricahua pals of Chatto's band. And for what? A damned, dirty-bearded, horsethieving drunk and drifter of a white man who called him everything from red shithead to Injun scum and who wouldn't, ordinarily, lift one finger to help any Indian, let alone a goddamn murdering Cherry Cow Apache.

The drifter knew Peaches did not care about the baby. He was an Apache. The girl-child of a white woman meant nothing to him. It was himself, the drifter, that the little bastard wanted to help. When he grinned and said, "Me you friend," he was not playing any of those Indian-white man games he had talked of.

No man of any skin color ever had more than his head to give for his friend.

And if Peaches missed on this Hoh-shuh Springs gamble, that is what he would be giving; his head would be in that sack with Madden's and Hunker's and, like as not, with Mr. J.D. Drifter's.

The scout was back with the horses. The drifter mounted up. Peaches vaulted, Apache-style, to the back of his snorting mustang.

"Don't worry," his small comrade assured him, sober-faced now. "Peaches find."

"That," nodded the white rider, "is what I'm worried about."

40

The ride to Hoh-shuh was by a wild burro track that was high, hot, unsafe but direct. The final approach to the historic springs was blind, as were the other two maintrail approaches. That is, all trails came up to the site, not down into it, the precise reason it was always scouted ahead. It was a perfect camp, once into it. Coming into it, the traveler had best watch himself.

"*Cuidado*," said Peaches. "Tie horses here."

They were in a little pocket of pine and grass and a rockseep of water from above. The drifter nodded and got down. Moments later, they were belly-wriggling into the rim of rocks guarding the lovely pools of Hoh-shuh. And the drifter was sucking in his guts and hissing underbreath to Peaches, "*Más cuidado!* Look who's here."

Peaches looked, Peaches hit the red dirt again.

"Sorry," he whispered. "Peaches forget him."

The drifter nodded. "*Mierda!*" was all he said.

They were in a very bad place. Geronimo and the main band were gone, exactly as Peaches had predicted. But another Chiricahua band had come to Hoh-shuh Springs before Chatto. That was Lucero and the *hesh-kes* camped down there beside the beautiful water. Now young Chatto would have to ride on by, or make a fight of it; he could not share that camp with his enemy. As for the drifter and Peaches, caught squarely between the two killer packs, the one blocking their way in front, the other coming up on their rear from Na-koo-say, they were in hock-deep trouble.

The drifter did not blame Peaches.

In fact, waiting with the little Indian for their chance to slip back down the trail to their horses, the white man's mind was filled with doubts of himself and of his entire vengeance trail. Peaches had taught him that Indians took more figuring than he had ever given them. And it was not just the volunteer Fort Gila scout, either, who bothered and dug at his memory.

When the Lord had let him take that close-up look and listen to Chatto and the Chiricahua raiders from the Overland cistern, the red men had not come off the same foul murderers as they did when judged over a distance of ground.

One singular thing had ridden with him away from Sifford Wells; it was a thing sown in the soil of his hate. Listening to Chatto and Lucero in their confrontation in the Overland ruins, he realized that the voices of the two men were extremely similar. Without looking at them as they spoke, it was well-nigh impossible to say who was talking. Even then, this striking sameness of voice had taken him back to that awful night when he had ridden in late to catch the Apache just pulling away from his burning cabin. He had not sighted any one as the leader of the yelping pack of several horsemen dashing away into the outer darkness. All that had taken him on the three-year trail of his hate was the remembered timbre of that deep bass voice shouting above the others and *seeming* to be in command; that and one other thing—the solitary red horseman that his desperately emptied Winchester had knocked from his pony unseen by his fleeing comrades.

This devil, feigning death, had struck upward at him with his knife when the drifter ran to him on foot. But he was still then near enough to his old lawman's habits to have made his run-up with drawn Colt. The Apache's thrust had earned him a full cylinder in the guts at powder-burning, point-blank blast. Even so, he was yet conscious when the white rancher had pulled him up out of the bloodied earth and shouted wildly, "*Quién es, quién es?*" The man had answered between gritted teeth, gray with death, "*Chiricahua—Chato, Chato—*" and spat with a puke of frothing lungblood into the bending face of the enemy above.

The drifter had buried his own dead and taken the corpse of the Indian into the army at Fort Apache, thinking he had the body of the real Chatto. But the many scouts at the fort had identified the man as Nautizo, an older man by years than young Chatto but nonetheless a known member of the rising young chief's small rancheria.

The acceptance of Chatto as the object of his blood-hate had followed.

Now, those untold miles and three years later, he lay in the broiling heat of the rimrock bounding Hoh-shuh Springs, belly-down and tongue-lolling like a lizard frying on a willowspit, one sneeze or a tumbled pebble from eternity—for the first time wondering, deepdown, *who was* the Indian he was looking for?

"Bad thing," frowned Peaches. "Lucero do on purpose. Try make Chatto fight. Make him look coward."

"I gathered that," replied the drifter. "I mean that night I was down the cistern. So what do they do when Chatto pulls in? Toss a buffalo chip?"

They were back quieting their horses. The young Chiricahua chief had not yet appeared from Na-koo-say, and they had sneaked down Peaches' trail to keep their mounts from becoming restless. Indian ponies were very close to their masters. The little mustangs were like dogs in their devotion and affection. The Apache treated them like dogs too. They beat and kicked and, if necessary, cooked and ate them. Their horses were one thing, transportation. So the visit was business.

It was cooler in the shaded nook. They decided to rest there from the heat of the higher rocks. Refreshed, or if meanwhile hearing Chatto's arrival, they could return to the rim and spy out what the unexpected reunion of the declared enemies might provide them of opportunity or danger.

As lonely men will, they small-talked the time away.

And grew a little closer, red man and white.

Summing up, Peaches, to be understood in more detail and with greater simpatico, spoke in Spanish.

"Is it not a thing *más maravillosa*," he said, "that we do not believe someone of a different skin color may know the things we know? If a man lives in a jacal or in a white man's or a Mexican's hacienda, he will still sneeze and blow snot on his shirt if he catches a cold. Is that not truly a remarkable, a memorable thing, *Vagabundo?*"

"Could be," mused the drifter, letting the Fort Gila philosopher sort out his frontier English. "I still say Injuns ain't pure human. But it's a fact your folks got the same problems as us real people. I seen the identical puzzle come up betwixt me

and old Clooney Borrum, and everbody knows niggers ain't
regular human beings."

Peaches agreed and made other comparisons. Such as
Apaches and Americans making the same *yerros malditos*.

In example, he gave Lieutenant Kensington speaking grand-
ly of the Chiricahua Nation, when the most innocent Apache
child knew that all of the Chiricahuas in all bands going down
to Pa-gotzin-kay numbered but seven hundred souls. And that,
of these, only a hundred and fifty were able fighters, old men
to young boys. If one wished to speak of real fighters, Geronimo could mount perhaps seventy-five full warriors. That was
the Chiricahua Nation. *Santa!* was that not ridiculous?

But yet wait. There was a man like Geronimo thinking he
could defeat the White Eyes with those seventy-five Apache
riders. And another Chiricahua man like Lucero believing he
could lead the *hesh-kes* into a new rising of all Apache
peoples, such as had destroyed the blackrobe missions so long
ago.

Peaches gestured spontaneously, lapsing into English for
purpose of effect on his final summation.

"Man damnfool any color," he declared. "Sumbitch."

El Vagabundo, unable to counter such an irrefutable pro-
nouncement, surrendered the field. The flies buzzed, the
horses cropped browse and grass, the languor of the pine-
scented shade closed in. The drifter dozed.

Next thing Peaches was shaking him.

"*Vamonos!*" whispered the latter. "Chatto come."

The scene in the Chiricahua encampment was a welter of
confusion. To the drifter it looked like bedlam, but Peaches
motioned for him to wait. The little scout had some old army
field glasses and could of course read all signs being made
below. As well, some of the words of louder talkers carried
on the wind to the hidden observers. Gradually, the clamor
sorted itself out.

Chatto had been delayed by the necessity to circle far
around a fifty-man troop of San Carlos enlisted red scouts
moving swiftly. The force was southeasterly bound, apparently angling to cut off any such raiding parties as their own.
Once arrived, he could not share the camp with Lucero unless
he violated ancient tribal codes. Nonetheless, due to the
delay, his people needed rest and water for the animals
before going on. The compromise was typically Indian, hence
realistic: The small knot of Chatto's original Piños band—

Do-klini, Dust Devil, Tubac, Bosque, Noche, Nevado, and Estune—huddled to the east of the beautiful tank. To its west were the rejoined Hoh-shuh hostiles, those of Lucero and Chatto, together with a handful of warrior women of the Hoh-shuhs who had been waiting for their men after the departure of Geronimo to serve as message bearers from the great fighter who, as always in his career, had proved as well to be pretty great at fleeing.

Sitting upon a high flat rock above the small Piños group and with his back to them—thus not at the camp in techni-cality—was young Chatto.

It was the sort of practical arrangement that made the drifter certain that he had been correct all along and that the Indians were crazy. To Peaches it made eminent sense. It solved the problem with dignity.

Moreover, he pointed, his white friend could see for him-self that Chatto was not crazy. A long way from it. Had the white friend not noted the handsome willowy young Hoh-shuh girl who had detached herself from her people to put the eyes upon the lonely young Piños chieftain? See her there, now? Carrying water and good food up to Chatto? See him take it from her without looking around? And see her hunching down to face him on the rock—and thus face the camp below—so that the young rascal might, in fact, inquire of her anything he wished as to activity among Lucero's band and never come close to turning his head?

Crazy?

Not this day.

The drifter received this instruction with a nod and a point of his own.

His Indian friend, he whispered, might also note those black-eyed darts that the not so young but likewise hand-some and willowy Estune was firing up at her small husband and the young squaw on the flat rock.

"He ain't too smart in my tallybook," said the drifter. "Iffen he was, he sure as green dung don't smell good wouldn't be messing around with no young girl and his old missus fresh-sucking a new-stole white baby not fifteen feet below. That don't even make Injun sense."

Indian sense, Peaches insisted, is precisely what it did make.

The young chief had been in a bad situation back at Sifford Wells when Estune admitted Lucero's intrusion. His reputation was at stake. Had he admitted either the rumor or his squaw's confirmation of it, it would have meant Estune's nose *and* Lucero's life. An entire other war could have arisen. But his saying he believed the woman stayed true to him in her heart was an Indian masterstroke. It disarmed Lucero and spared Estune.

But did the white friend for a moment think Chatto was not human? That the betrayal did not gall him?

Hah! The Indian sense of the thing was that the young chief avoided bloodshed and more bitterness among the Chiricahua. The woman, Estune, was not forgiven. She had been reprieved nothing more. Peaches knew young Chatto. The latter had purchased this woman from the Comanche who held her in slavery and paid a high price. That was three years ago. Now it was over. He would pay no more for his love of Estune, his strange northern woman. The young girl up on the rock knew that. All the Hoh-shuhs knew it. Most of all, Estune knew it.

And Lucero, that damned studhorse, he certainly understood all about it. He would be prancing shortly.

Watching Estune boiling coffee for the Chatto men, the drifter felt he could not blame Lucero. He would be prancing too if he had a shot at this tall northern. He was stirred again by her grace of figure. She was what her name said in Apache, *estune*, the full-grown woman.

Interrupting his thoughts, Peaches pointed at the base of the rock upon which Chatto sat. Squinting, the drifter could see nothing. Peaches gave him the field glasses. Then he saw. It was Clooney Borrum, hunkered in under the overhang's deep shadow. The Negro stablehand was taking his first taste of Indian freedom; he wore a set of ancient Spanish leg-irons padlocked with a chain. About his neck was a thick leather dog collar. From collar to leg-irons a second chain ran to the huge lock. The black man's face and shoulders were a mass of welts and contusions, some still bleeding.

"Slave," was all that Peaches said.

The drifter returned the field glasses. "What will they do with him?" he asked, the blue eyes going cold.

"Take back Pa-gotzin-kay. Use haul firewood, water. Kick, beat, starve. Just like pack horse."

"All that trouble to lug him clean down inter Mexico just for to make a hand about camp?"

"Apache hunt, gamble, steal, kill Mexican on raid," Peaches said. "Not work."

"Yeah," said the drifter. "The nigger works."

"Good slave worth five horses."

"Wisht old Clooney knowed that. He'd bust with pride."

"Nigger slave worth ten horses," said Peaches.

"You're joshing. A nigger worth twicet what a white man's worth?"

"Woman like," explained the little scout.

"Poor devil. He thought they spairt him because he weren't white. They was his brothers. They was going to cut him free."

"Cut free when dead."

"You come from fine stock, Peachy."

"Peaches White Mountain. These people Chiricahua."

"Same difference," grunted the drifter.

"Sure," grinned Peaches. "Don't worry. We set free."

The drifter scowled. "The hell you say."

"Sure. Squaw own both. We take all everybody."

"What you mean, you little red sonofabitch?"

"Don't get baby without squaw. Don't get squaw without nigger. So we take baby, take squaw, take nigger."

"Name ain't nigger," said the drifter. "It's Clooney."

"Sure. Clooney Nigger."

The drifter sighed and gave up. It was small wonder there was no way to make a treaty stick with these people.

The white man's blue eyes closed against the mean slant of the westering sun. In an hour it would be riding dark. Whatever they were going to do had better be fast.

"Peachy!" whispered the alarmed drifter. "The Chattos are pulling out!" It was fully dark now, the murky, thick time before moonrise. "We're going to lose 'em sure."

"No," denied the little scout. "You watch."

There was no firewood at Forty Mile Tank, he explained. Any coffee boiled down there, or horse meat roasted, would come from wood packed down from Hoh-shuh—and the woman had not yet gathered any sticks. But right now, while Chatto's men ate what she had prepared for the nightmeal, Estune would take her new slave out into the rimrock to pick up the firewood for Forty Mile. She would bring the baby absolutely. If Peaches and the white friend picked the place in the rocks where Estune was coming, and the baby did not cry out, and Estune did not cry out, and the black man did as he was told, why, *quién sabe*? they might just bring it off nicely. If not, well, everything had to have an ending somewhere.

The drifter winced in real pain. "I suppose you know right where the squaw's coming, eh, Peachy?" he said.

"Sure," smiled the red friend. "Where wood is."

"Oh," said the drifter. "Sure."

He looked around into the glooming shade of the night. There was wood everywhere that he could see.

"Peachy," he vowed, "when the shooting sets in, I'll center you fust. Keep it in your mind, iffen you got one."

"Don't worry," said the little man, patting his cramped arm. "Peaches fix."

"Oh, Christ. God help us."

"No. Clooney Nigger help us. You see."

"If I look fast mebbe," growled his companion. "My head feels like it's already in Do-klini's gunnysack."

"Be quiet," ordered Peaches. "Dark coming. Watch woman. Peaches be back."

He made to leave and the drifter seized him with a raking grasp of the right hand. "Holdt it!" he gritted. "Where you think you're going?"

"Steal horses from Injun," shrugged the Fort Gila scout. "We need two more horse. Listen."

He laid it out in a half dozen of his jerky sentences, but nakedly plain and precise as any sheaf of military orders might make it: The white friend would capture the squaw and the baby and the black man, taking them to the nook where their two mounts were; the red friend would lift the two new mounts and meet them all at the nook in ten minutes and, from thence, the ride-out.

"All right," said the drifter. "I belt the squaw a solid lick and she don't peep. I get the kid's head snuffed in that backsling of hers so's it don't yip. Then what? Supposing old Clooney don't aim to go?"

Peaches spread his small red hands.

"We all stay here," he said.

41

Fascinated, the drifter watched the northern woman move toward him. She came as Peaches had said she would, driving poor Clooney Borrum ahead of her with a stout cudgel, the baby slung upon her back and hip. There was one other member of the little procession which had not been foreseen by the Fort Gila volunteer, an ancient bone-pile of a pack mare. This brute, panniered on either side with big Apache baskets to receive the firewood Clooney would forage, was tied by its lead rope to the Negro's waist. This animal, should she spook, could of course wreck everything. One more big maybe, the drifter thought.

He flattened himself to the house-sized boulder behind which Peaches had stationed him. Lordy! the woman seemed to have overheard him and the little bastard planning it. Heading for quite another section of the rimrock, she suddenly fetched her black forager an echoing thwack across the rump with the knobby stick. "Ummph!" said Clooney in honest injury and changed directions to come shuffling and clanking straight for the big boulder hiding his one-time co-worker for Southwest Stagelines.

Behind him, the tall woman crooned a low song to her child which was fretful. The old pack mare stumbling with the woman reached over and nuzzled the whimpering baby. Startled, the babe cried out. Immediately, several of the Hoh-shuhs, past whom Estune had come with her strange caravan, glanced out toward the wife of young Chatto. But the latter merely cursed the mare in Apache and struck it with the stick, and the Indians of savage Lucero looked away and back to their suppers.

Perfect! the drifter sighed, tensing.

He heard the rock sliding under Clooney's climbing feet. Next instant the panting Negro rounded the big rock. All he knew subsequently was that a muscled forearm, mean and hard as a snake, had his throat barred, and a remembered soft voice was hissing in his ear that the owner of the arm was his shotgun rider from the Pima Bend jailhouse—and he better remember it!

Neither Clooney Borrum, nor any other Negro on the frontier in that time, survived to an intact middle-age and a good-paying decent job in the white settlements by being slow in the head. Any black man in that society had to be part fox, part catamount, part hooty owl, and part whipped dog to get by. This experience now bore fruit. Clooney, freed by the drifter, went on past him along the face of the boulder. When the squaw and the old mare rounded the big rock, her black slave was already gathering sticks.

The woman came on to follow him. The drifter came out behind her, circled her throat, put Peaches' borrowed knife in her lower ribs. "Don't do anything," he told her in Spanish. "I am your friend; we looked at each other back there at the stagecoach station. Do you remember?"

"The Thin One?" she said in the same tongue. "Yes, I remember." He felt the magnificent body tensing against his and did not know if she would twist away, or stand.

Clooney was back then. His hands sought the squaw's belt and came away with an ancient brass key. This he employed to unlock his fetters, ankle and neck. "Holdt her tight!" he admonished the drifter. Before the woman might guess his intention, he scooped the baby from its hip sling, put black hand over tiny mouth. *"Favor!"* said Estune. *"No injuria la pequeña, negro!"*

"No, hell no, I ain't going to harm her none." The stable-hand had forgotten himself in English. Without a second's loss, he repeated himself in the Chiricahua dialect. The drifter cocked head. He had heard him talking to his stage teams in Apache, but not like this.

Neither had the squaw heard him use the tongue before. At once, the drifter could feel her easing in his grasp. But Clooney said, "Watch her! Don't leave up on her gullet. She'll squawk certain."

He ran over to the old pack mare. In one of the woven panniers Estune had put her beautiful nickel-plated Winchester. The Negro stablehand returned with this and poked it into the woman's lean belly.

"Take off your clothes," he told her in the Apache tongue. "You will wear mine. I will keep the baby with me, wearing your dress and boots. If you make one sound, or try to escape us, I will kill the baby."

The drifter understood not a word of this, was hence amazed to see the pantherine squaw begin to disrobe. In a moment she was pagan naked in the cover of the boulder. My God, the white man thought. Was there ever a settlement woman with a body like that? If his black companion was similarly stricken, he gave no sign. Handing the baby, now fretting again, to the drifter, Clooney slid the squaw-dress over his head, fought his big feet into the slim squaw-boots. Meanwhile, Estune had donned his dirty rags and work brogans and even the shapeless stable hat.

"Take the pack mare," the Negro driver ordered the woman, then had a second thought. "Better we ought stuff a gag inter her mouth, shotgun man," he said to the drifter. And suited action to suggestion by wadding the baby's small coverlet into Estune's mouth and girding it cruelly tight there with the squaw's own braided rawhide belt. Then he nodded, "Now you take the mare. And remember. I am right behind you with your shiny Winchester and your yellow-haired baby-child, your little white *day-den. Anh,* you hear what I am saying?"

Desperately, the tall woman nodded her understanding.

"You think I will kill the white *day-den* if I must, woman?" growled Clooney.

She nodded again, the fear in her dark face a thing of mother's eloquence.

"Keep believing it, then. Be very careful, *mujer!*"

Clooney Borrum turned to the drifter. "Hey, old shotgun man. I forgot to ask. Whar we going?"

"Yonder." The drifter pointed across a considerable opening between their huge rock shelter and the hidden entrance to Peaches' trail.

"Hoo, boy! You got hosses hid?"

"The Injun has. The little cavalry scout was with us at the station. Talked to this here squaw and Chatto and the old man, Nevado. Down that track a mite."

"Ummm!" Clooney compressed lips, studied the hundred feet of open, firelit rock litter of the rim which they must cross in full view of the camp. "Narrer doings."

They were in fact narrower than he imagined.

As he turned to motion Estune to move out ahead in his own ragged clothes, a tawny, leonine figure came crouched around the boulder. "*Qué pasa?*" said Lucero in his beautiful bass and came on past Estune to confront Clooney in the squaw's dress. In the same instant that the *hesh-ke* leader realized this was not his erstwhile paramour driving the pack mare, he saw the bearded white man hiding behind the animal's offside. Clooney, who had picked up Estune's cudgel, answered him with a terrible blow where the shoulder tendon joined the neck. It paralyzed Lucero long enough for the drifter to come under the pack mare's belly and explode two splintering punches on the chin. Lucero went down, eyes glazing.

Instantly, Clooney seized up the clanking leg-irons and dog collar of his own enslavement. Fastening them upon the stunned Lucero, he turned and flung the ancient brass key as far over the high rim of Hoh-shuh Springs as vengeful black arm was able. "Whee-ooo!" he said, cupping his ear. "Listen to that far-off tinkle."

Seconds later, with the drifter again hiding on the pack

mare's offside, and Estune, in Clooney's clothing, leading the animal, they set out over the open space toward Peaches' trail. The baby was by then squalling lustily. Clooney, in his squaw dress, did awkward best to imitate the petting and coddling of an Indian mother. The Ho-shuhs, some of them, looked up into the rocks in curiosity. But they saw Estune mothering the child and once more cudgeling the old pack mare, and, Ysun being with the departing masqueraders, that was all the Indians saw.

It was not, however, all that the drifter and Clooney Borrum saw. Over on his rock, the young girl had spoken something to Chatto. And Chatto was calling down to his Keeper of the Rules, old Nevado.

Clooney, trying both to walk quickly and yet like the graceful squaw Estune, translated over his shoulder to the crouching white man behind the bony pack mare.

The young girl, daughter of Gah-chilzin, the Hoh-shuh who had stayed loyal to Chatto down at the stage station, had evidently said *anh*, yes, to the young Piños chief's proposals. The protocol now was, since Gah-chilzin's wife was among the handful of Hoh-shuh women who had decided to wait at the springs for their men, that old Nevado must go over to the damned Hoh-shuhs and try to get the mother to also say *anh*, and the father, and to persuade both of them to come with Chatto now.

"My God, I hope the old folks is agreeing!" prayed the drifter. "Keep pushing on that damned old mare!"

"They'll say, they'll say," assured Clooney. "That Chatto's a mighty big ketch. They get at least forty horses for that gal. Chatto, he give thirty for this here old one we got going with us yonder."

"Don't blame him," said the drifter. "Keep moving!"

They were almost into the broken face of the rim which hid the *puerta escondida*, the secret door, to Peaches' trail down the sheer drop of the bench to canyon's floor eight hundred feet below.

"Oh, Lawdy!" said Clooney, alarmed. "Old man, he's a'heading over thisaway. Gal's folks say yes so fast Chatto's done yellt at Nevado to go on and round up Estune and the firewood. That's us, shotgun man!"

Ahead, up against the rockface of the rim, Estune had halted. She did not know of the hidden crack in the rock. She stood looking back at Clooney and the drifter as if to say, what must I do now?

Clooney spun the nickel-plated Winchester in his free hand, cocking it. The other hand raised the baby, its tiny head held to the muzzle of the rifle.

"Stay there. Do not run. We are coming," he told the woman in Apache. "Thin One will show us the way."

The drifter looked behind them.

Old Nevado, grumbling as usual, was just puffing up the grade to the rimrock by the giant boulder behind which lay Lucero. As they saw him reach the rim and turn to come after them, they saw him stop and look back toward the boulder. At the same time they heard the faint calling of Lucero for help. Nevado shouted something at Estune and turned back to see to Lucero.

The drifter waited no more. He leaped out from behind the pack mare and yelled to Clooney to come on. In an instant all were at the *puerta escondida*, and the white man was leading them in behind the face rock that screened the opening. It seemed to the arousing Apache camp as though Estune, the black slave, the pack mare, and a white man who had appeared out of the absolute nowhere of the spring night, had simply disappeared from the saucer of the high bench of Hoh-shuh Springs. It was as though the rocks had opened to swallow them up.

"*Unn-unn-ahuh!*" The strange sound of their uneasiness spread like a low growl through the encampment, Hoh-shuhs and Chattos alike. Men began to get up from about both supperfires. They looked to the places where they had leaned their rifles. They glanced toward the lower amphitheatre of the bench where the older boys held the horse herd of both parties. It was at this moment that old Nevado came stumbling out from behind the great boulder, hobbling as swiftly as he might to report back to his young chief.

Out of wind and shaking, he came to halt beneath the high rock of Chatto. He was in time to meet the latter coming down to get his pony.

"Listen!" said the old man. "Lucero is over there behind that big rock. They have put him in the chains of the black slave. In a minute he will come out of there!"

"Well? Well?" frowned Chatto. "What are you saying?"

"The woman," gasped Nevado. "Your old one. She is gone. She has run away into the blind rock with the new white baby and the black stagedriver slave, and, wait! I have more to tell you; with them is the bearded dirty white man who was with Peaches in the stage station!"

"Ysun!" cried the young chief. "I do not believe it! You have hidden some *tizwin* in your saddlebags. You are drunk, old man."

"The hell with you!" yowled Nevado spiritedly. "All you do lately is play with women. If you don't believe me, ask your friend Lucero. There he comes now!"

Chatto did not need the rumble that came across the camp from the Hoh-shuhs to tell him that Nevado was sober.

Lucero was in the Spanish leg-irons over by the big boulder. The other chief had been wounded, and nowhere in reach of his eagle's eye did young Chatto see his elder woman Estune and the yellow-haired *day-den*.

"She is gone," he said, surprisingly. "So be it."

"What?!" shouted Nevado. "You will not go after her?"

Chatto regarded him with a great calmness, a great coldness. "Would you?" he asked disdainfully.

His young squaw had now slid down from the high rock and stood by him, her soft hand in his.

Nevado glared at her.

"I would if I were your age!" he raged at Chatto. "I would not give you five mules for that new one!"

"Watch your mouth, old jackass!" warned Tubac, coming up with the other Piños men. "You are not too ancient to do away with."

"Pah!" said Nevado and spat at him. "The Chiricahua are nothing anymore. That northern woman is worth—"

"Be still," said Chatto quietly, his deep voice unhurried but terse. "We are going on to Forty Mile Tank now. Bring the horses. Here come Gah-chilzin and his woman with their ponies. This is a bad place to be. I leave it to Lucero and my northern woman. *Ugashé*."

Two young boys came galloping up, driving the Piños horses ahead of them. Chatto and his men seized their mounts. They were short one pony for the new squaw, and Tubac grabbed Nevado and threw the old man from his good warpony to the rocky ground. The girl took the little horse, and, with a shout from Chatto, the small band of Piños Chiricahua whirled their horses and were gone from Hoh-shuh Springs riding into their appointment with Red Beard Crook in Pa-gotzin-kay.

Old Nevado tottered to his feet unsteadily.

He shook clenched fist after his departing tribesmen and hurled in their company, too, the deepest curses a Keeper of

the Old Ways could be the custodian of; yet he also assured
them with final defiance:

"*Mierda* upon the heads of all of you. I was going with
Lucero after the real woman anyway. *Bastardos!*"

With which he hobbled over to beg a mount, any kind of
a mount, of the Hoh-shuhs.

The hell with the youth.

He would go with the old Apaches, the real killers.

42

Mind and body restored by immersion in the icy waters of
Hoh-shuh Springs, Lucero was brought to the fire and
spread-eagled over it to heat the chain of the leg-irons for
hammering apart. As this embarrassment went forward, its
victim snarled for the *hesh-ke* horses to be brought up; a
pursuit of Estune and her captors must be mounted the
moment he was freed. Just here, however, a sensible counter-
proposal to chasing off after Chatto's unfaithful wife was
advanced by Na-tishn.

Na-tishn pointed out that he had remained loyal to Lucero
up at Sifford Wells. He had not deserted him as had Gah-
chilzin. But now things were very different. Some of the men,
Na-tishn among them, had found their women waiting for
them at Hoh-shuh, bravely remaining after Geronimo had
departed for Mexico and safety.

In this business of safety let it also be remarked that
Chatto had barely eluded a strong column of cavalry coming
down from Na-koo-say. And there was that friendly Tonto
Apache camped with their women at Hoh-shuh, who had
seen many other soldiers from Fort Lowell on the Tucson
road but the day previous. It was plain that Geronimo's
injunction to raid not more than six days before leaving
Arizona was prudent battle judgment.

"As for myself," concluded Na-tishn, as the first of the
horses were being hazed up, and as the leg-iron chains yielded
to free the *hesh-ke* leader, "I am not going with Lucero. I am
going after Geronimo, as young Chatto has so wisely done."
Here Lucero, broken chain dragging from each ankle-iron,
clanked up from the fire. But Na-tishn faced him squarely. "It
takes more than killing to be a warchief," he told him. "I
don't think you will ever understand that."

Shouts and threats ensued, interrupted by the pathetic figure of old Nevado limping through the welter of men and animals pleading for a mount. He was rudely shoved aside by Lucero, and again by Durango, when he persisted in trying to explain that he, Nevado, wished only to go with Lucero.

"A horse!" he cried. "All I ask is one horse to ride!"

No one listened to him, and the confusion increased. A youth came running up to Lucero and Durango, where they were rallying the men who would go with them, to report two horses missing from his personal herd-charge; they were Lucero's prized appaloosa Matadero, Durango's famed black Compadre.

These thefts served only to hasten the cleaving of the people. There was suddenly something very wrong going forward at Hoh-shuh Springs. Squaws and slaves and horses were simply disappearing. *Un-huh!* Time to go.

There were twenty-five Chiricahua warriors and women remaining after Chatto's departure. Of these, only eight, the very worst of the tribe's *hesh-kes*, gathered their ponies behind Lucero and Durango. The remainder were mounting up and leaving, *ahora mismo!* for Pa-gotzin-kay. In the dust and shouting of all this, old Nevado yet wandered in and out of the angered Hoh-shuhs pleading for an animal to ride. "A horse, a horse," he croaked, but all he was given was a rageful cudgeling by two old "he-squaws;" the beating drove him to seek the cover of a nearby pile of jumbled rock. Hovering there, he was suddenly seized from the shadows by his white Apache shirt and hauled unceremoniously into the deeper hollow of the boulder pile.

"You want a horse?" said the small Indian who had speared him. "Take this one."

Nevado peered hard through the poor light. He saw the squat kinsman leading two horses, both of which were skillfully nose-wrapped with their own lead ropes. Of a sudden the old eyes widened. "You, little fart!" he gasped. "I can't believe it!"

"Believe it," advised Peaches. "And take the black."

The old man hesitated. Things had been happening to him too rapidly and at cross-purposes.

"*You* ride with Lucero?" he said, scowling.

"Sure," lied Peaches cheerfully. "I just want to show him the way through the rocks over there. Take the horse." The old man now sprang to the back of Compadre, agile with excitement and importance. "Now, listen," ordered Peaches. "Do exactly as I say. As we ride by them, full gallop, shout to Lucero and Durango, 'follow us, we know the way!' You understand that?"

"A good idea," the old man agreed. "It will save time. They won't have a chance to argue about it."

"Exactly," nodded the little White Mountain Apache. He quickly patted the old man's shoulder. "It is not for nothing you are Keeper of the Rules," he told him. "What a brain of cunning you have. In your time I will say such as Lucero could not pare out your pony's feet!"

"You would say precisely right. Yes, and I am sorry about the 'little fart' word. I used it in fatherly praise. I can see you are one for the Old Ways."

"*Anh*," said Peaches. "Are you ready?"

"Ready," nodded Nevado, old White Hair. "*Ugashé—!*"

"*Anh!*" cried Peaches and drove his heel into the nervous flanks of the beautiful appaloosa.

Out sprang Matadero. Out sprang Compadre.

Both had to be swerved sharply by their riders to avoid collision with the departing followers of Na-tishn. Past these surprised Indians, and past the startled men of Lucero and Durango by the pool, pounded the two stolen horses and their yelping riders.

"Follow us! Follow us!" shouted old Nevado. "We know the way they went!"

The admonition, the invitation, were without need.

The ten Chiricahua *hesh-kes* were to horse and after them almost as the old warrior's words left his lips. Dust and rocks flew. Wolf yelps arose. The people of Na-tishn halted their bucking and badly spooked mounts to stare after the strange flight of their fellows chasing Matadero and Compadre. It seemed to them that not fifty feet separated pursued from pursuers when the entire pack of them, prey and hunter alike, vanished into the rearing face-rock of the northwest rim.

Un-huh! Unn-unn-ahuh!

There was nothing waiting for all their friends and their running horses over there, except eight hundred rocky feet of sheer drop to the jagged floor of *Cañón Escondido*, the hidden canyon.

They were gone, they were *dah-e-sah*, all of them.

Yet their wolf yelps and chase cries could still be heard! That was a very bad thing. Dead men should not be crying

out like that. *Ugashé!* Here we go! Far away from the
sounds of ghosts and old friends gone.

In seconds, only, the waters of Hoh-shuh Springs flowed
alone. Geronimo's people came no more to that place.

Apache Leap

43

Peaches and the old man opened their lead going down the single-file track of the Hidden Canyon's wall on the east, or Hoh-shuh side. Peaches, after all, knew the way.

As well, Lucero and his wolfpack saw no reason to believe their quarry might escape them. True, this White Mountain trail had been a secret well kept from the warring Chiricahua. But once that fact was accepted, it did not improve in any other aspect the chances of the fugitives. That a squaw and sucking child, a despised Negro, Peaches, Nevado, and the reported strange white man with the fleeing group might elude ferocious Lucero and Durango was a thought beyond their thinking.

They had had their little surprise of the unsuspected third trail out of Hoh-shuh Springs, and that was that.

From here on, they would come to learn that the rest belonged to Lucero.

"Ease back a little," the handsome subchief called to Durango, whose borrowed mount was sliding up on the braced rump of Lucero's borrowed mount. "Tell the others. No use putting a good man or horse over the side."

Durango turned and repeated the order to Kiyutaneh, following him. Kiyutaneh barked it back to Jumano, who passed it on uptrail to Uklenni and in such manner to the last of the men and lunging, foreleg-braced ponies in the descending line. "Lucero says to slow down. He says, where are those people going? If they get down off this wall, where will they be? *Anh*, yes, in the bottom of that dark canyon, that is where. And who will be down there with them, only in two times their number? Lucero says there is no hurry. We do not want to fight them on this wall anyway."

Counseling themselves in this very certain way, the *hesh-kes* were not merely talking aloud to comfort themselves. Up ahead, around the very next hairpin turn in the clifftrack, back in the pine-tree pocket where the steeldust and Peaches' mustang were tied, the drifter and Clooney Borrum were asking themselves the same thing:

After they hit bottom, then what?

They were but slightly cheered by the sliding arrival of the little scout and old Nevado with the two beautiful new horses.

This made them still short a mount, unless one of them volunteered to tie his life to the creaky pack mare. Nevado at once and gallantly suggested that Peaches hand over to Estune the great appaloosa stud, an animal with which she was familiar. As quickly and unselfishly, the little White Mountain scout pointed out that the woman could not handle so much horse *and* her baby on the wild kind of ride they were to make out of where they were, *más pronto!* The old man would have to surrender his fine black, rather.

The choice did not excite Nevado.

He complained that Lucero was an imbecile to take a studhorse on a raid and Peaches a double imbecile to then steal that studhorse when he had his pick of the ponyherd.

Not so! defended the little Apache. He would have taken geldings if such were to hand. They were not, and he had seized these two because they were separately staked and had hackamores on.

The argument ended here because a spill of loose rock cascaded down from the trail up above the little pine cove, announcing the nearness of Lucero's wolves.

The drifter, with loose rockchips still showering down, broke out his best cowpen Spanish to inform Nevado that options were no longer open; Lucero's men would not kill such an old fool. Nevado could convince the *hesh-kes* he had only been trying to help them. Had he not already assured them he wanted to go with them, rather than the mouse-livered Chatto? Nevado might prolong his life by a convincing portrayal. They, on the other hand, were done for, everyone, if the *hesh-kes* caught up with them.

Nevado was not convinced. But Clooney had maneuvered into position on the other side of his mount and, with the drifter, bodily lifted the white-maned brave from his fine horse. The animal was at once seized by the alert Estune and the old man deposited upon the bony spine of the pack mare. All went to horse, now, Peaches leading the way. They were barely clear of the pine cove when Lucero and Durango rounded the hairpin up trail.

It was too close. Much, much too close.

But old Nevado solved everything.

Abandoned by both sides, he could merely have hung back in the conifers and let the *hesh-ke* pursuit clatter past his hiding place, then go back up to Hoh-shuh and follow the tracks of his people to Pa-gotzin-kay.

Perversely, he decided he would still rather ride with the *hesh-kes* than to go home on such a shameful horse as the rickety mare. His fortunes on the wartrail must improve. Moreover, this was his last raid. He was too old to come again up into Arizona.

"*Hai!*" he shouted, jumping the old mare out of the scrub squarely into the path of the oncoming Chiricahua brothers. "Wait for me!"

Whether they heard him is not remembered. That they obeyed his plea is in the tribal lore. Both Lucero and Durango, having no other place to go save over the edge, slammed full downtilt into the pack mare. Behind them, their eight men, with the same option, fought to keep their snorting mustangs on the narrow ledge of the trail.

All succeeded. But, beyond all question, their party would wait for the Keeper of the Rules, at least *un poco*.

Cursing murderously, Lucero dragged Nevado off the pack mare and would have flung him over the edge but for Durango's reminder that the old dodderer was not alone a tribal elder of repute but, much more importantly, he was godfather to Geronimo.

Spared, old White Hair was nonetheless thrown bodily back into the pine scrub and his old mare kicked out of the trail to join him. The *hesh-kes* rushed on past, but the difference had been made. The drifter and his ragtag band of misadventurers had gotten away around the next down hairpin. Ahead of them lay canyon's floor and its seeming certain trap.

In his mind the bearded white man was preparing for the end. He could recall nothing of that dry, boulder-choked bottoming which could mean anything but a shoot-out. In that, they would surely get some of the Chiricahuas, perhaps even most of them. But some of their own party would go under too.

Suddenly, he did not want that.

He wanted to get on out, to carry that blue-eyed darling girl baby down to its yellow-haired mother in Tucson, to deliver this tiny last passenger to where her ticket was punched and paid for. And then to see what the unwed girl would have of him. To find out if she would take a man who wanted her, and her nameless baby, to fend for and make a new home somewhere.

Unconsciously, his hand went into the pocket of his cavalry jacket. His fingers closed on the crumpled ticket. Yes, it was still there, still good. By God, he would make it good too. He had to. If he did not do that, he might as well never get up out of this canyon again. The thought made him yell out loud in anger and determination. Clooney, riding ahead of him, looked over shoulder through ever-deepening canyon night.

"Hey, Mister Hossthief!" he called back. "I ain't had time to thanken you proper. Wants to say I'm total beholden."

"For what, in Christ's name?" yelled the drifter.

"Taking away my 'Pache freedom," Clooney yelled in turn. "Man cain't absorb only so much liberating."

"We're all going to get liberated, happen we don't fort-up somewheres," shouted the white rider. "Hey, Peachy! There's going to be lead splashing around here thick as smoked bees in a minute. Where you heading?"

"Peaches got place!" the small man waved. "Keep horse running where my horse run!"

"Tell it to the squaw," answered the drifter. "She's the new hand around here."

Peaches turned in the saddle to bark in Apache at the tall woman. She replied in the same tongue.

"Everything skookum!" the little scout informed his white friend. "She ride our side now. Keep baby. Go home her own people."

The tall woman turned upon the lunging back of the black. She was riding without reins or hackamore rope. The baby was held to breast in both arms, the graceful body moving as one with the straining mount. It was incomparable horsemanship, and the drifter again marvelled at this red squaw's power and mountain lion's supple motion. She caught his eyes upon her and called to him the single Apache word, "*Ugashé!* we go!" and the voice went into him and he believed her, Indian or no.

Down below those dry rocks waited, and the hell's dark of the canyon bore, and God alone knew if the runt Fort Gila

scout truly had a place to run to. And behind them—right
behind himself riding last in line—came Lucero and his Chiricahua crazies, six wolf yelps and a one-handed Winchester
shot from catching them in the open rocks of the chasm's
floor. But of a sudden it did not matter what true or dangerous hole the *hash-kes* crazies were driving them into, nor how
late and dark the canyon night had grown.

Estune's decision to ride with them had changed the
game. The Indian odds were now altered past any Chiricahua recall.

Lucero was going to lose.

44

The moon was now papering the higher walls of the
canyon with its white light. But down in the depths there
was blackness still, and it was through this blackness that
Peaches now guided his friends. He did not, however, cross
the canyon to the trail he and the drifter had traveled
coming down to Hoh-shuh. That trail went up the western
cliff to topout in the high country on the Tucson side. It was
a much straighter, far less hazardous track than the one
down the eastern wall from Hoh-shuh, and, when the little
scout turned away from it to push up the narrowing, very
steep rise of the canyon to the north and east, the drifter
immediately challenged him.

Peaches was not in the mood for white man's questions.
This was Indian business; they were not being hunted by
white men.

"You want go other way, go!" he told the drifter.

Relenting when the other cursed him and called him
Indian bastard and Apache son of a bitch, Peaches pointed
out that the upper reaches of the easy, wide eastern trail lay
in the full light of the moon. The men of Lucero and
Durango would not need to follow them up that straight
road to shoot them down. They could just stand on the
bottom of the canyon and fire up at them all the way across
the wall, beginning at a range under a hundred yards "where
the moon began."

"Yeah, shotgun man," grinned Clooney Borrum. "Down
here in the plumb dark we all gotten a better chancst,
specially me!"

"*Mierda!*" answered the drifter, reining the steeldust

around loose boulder and up over rockledge. "I cain't wait. What happens when the floor of this here canyon has clumb itse'f up to where the moon hits?"

The black stablehand laughed chucklingly. "Then old Clooney gonner loom up like a fly in the buttermilk," he said. "Whee-oool"

"Keep quiet," Peaches called back. "Baby sleep."

"Oh, Jesus Christ," groaned the drifter. But he made no more noise.

An hour later they neared the edge of the moonlight, having climbed less rapidly than the lower canyon would indicate. After the first abrupt rise, it leveled off and became less boulder-strewn. The small stream, dry in the lower reaches, was here running several feet in width. They appreciated, too, its noisy rush and tumble among the rocks and over the gravel of its spreading riffles. The sound muffled or diminished entirely those other noises the fugitives did not care to hear—the clatter of unshod hooves on rock behind them, the clank of Lucero's ankle-chains striking brush and boulder, the cruel laughter and mocking cries of the *hesh-kes* who had not been fooled by Peaches' leaving of the main trail, and who now pressed so relentlessly upward, driving ever harder on their trail.

The drifter, now riding with Peaches in the van, the stream bed widening to permit double passage, saw that another five minutes would bring them into the glare of the moon. The doubt which burst from him was a natural one, pent-in the full time of the four-mile flight up the canyon's shallowing floor. How in the name of God, he demanded of the Apache, was it going to be any different getting shot in the moonlight up here than down yonder on the east wall? The Chiricahua crazies were even closer behind them, and, moreover, it looked to a white man almighty like a blind, or box canyon terminal, waiting for them up ahead.

"*Anh*, yes," agreed Peaches readily. "Box canyon you bet."

The drifter thought of braining him with his riflebutt. He also thought better of the thought. He was learning that this little Indian only seemed flighty and daft. The canyon might turn blind but not the small White Mountain man with the San Carlos tag about his neck. "Peachy," he said. "Come on, for Gawd's sake! you got another secret hole up here?"

They were within a hundred feet of moonlight's beginning. The drifter could see nothing ahead that resembled sanctuary

of any least prayer. Yet Peaches only called past him to
Clooney and the squaw that they hold in their horses *por una
vuelta escondida* straight in their path. "*A la derecha, a la
derecha!*" he stressed sibilantly. "It will be to the right."

With the words, he grinned at the drifter riding on his left.
"Watch dumb Injun sumbitch disappear," he said. And
heeled his mustang hard to the right.

The drifter gasped. It was as though the small man and
potbellied horse had in fact vanished. But they were in the
full blaze of the moonlight here, and he could see, after the
first astonished blink, what had occurred. Peaches' *vuelta
escondida* was literally that—a blind turn to the right. Without question he put his mount after the Apache scout's, and
behind him came Clooney and the squaw on equal faith.
What greeted them around the corner of the canyon's cliff
was another name for salvation.

It was a mineshaft heading.

A fortress.

Moated on all approaches by the flat-topped tailings of the
ore dump spilling to block canyon below and dam small
stream into considerable sump-lake for water to run the
stampmill leaning weirdly in ruin beyond the sun-bleached
boards of the heading shack, it was a place to fight off
Apaches from then till Chiricahua hell froze over and thawed
again.

"Gawd, oh Gawd!" breathed the drifter to their silent
guide. "You done busted the bank, Peachy."

"Sure," nodded the scout impassively.

And, with that, led the pounding rush of the four horses
over the flinty ground of the ore dump.

45

The Chiricahua came around the blind cliff onto the desolation of the dump. They were met only with stillness. Lucero
halted them. They sat on their winded ponies studying the
ancient, warped buildings, the long spill of the tailings down
into the canyon. First Lucero, then Durango, put testing
shots through the heading shack. Nothing. Another probe of
several rounds went ricocheting through the gaunt skeleton
of the stampmill. Again nothing. Lucero put down his Winchester.

"Where are the horses?" muttered Kiyutaneh. "They cannot disappear two times."

"No," Uklenni agreed. "We were too close to them this time."

"Nevertheless," scowled Jumano, "they have found some hole to hide in."

At this, Durango straightened. "The hole!" he pointed. "See it there where the timbers make its frame?"

They all saw just beyond the heading shack the gaping mouth of the drift tunnel into the cliff. Durango had solved the riddle. The people and the horses were in that mining hole over there.

The Chiricahua went behind a protective slide of talus rock nearby. They secured their ponies by picket rope to a pine snag in the cliff, built a small fire, rolled corn-husk cigarettes, and put the question of, what next? to their leader.

Lucero made his talk with *hesh-ke* passion.

Their opportunity here was a rare one. It all hung upon taking back to Geronimo in a sack the head of the deserter Pa-nayo-tishn, Coyote. The entire fabric of the Chatto and Geronimo great raid had been torn asunder by the White Mountain traitor guiding that patrol that had murdered the Chiricahua women at the Killing in the Rocks. It was impossible to imagine what power might fall to the band that killed those people in there and took the head of Pa-nayo-tishn. They would be heroes to the wild Chiricahua. Even Geronimo and bloody old Juh, his second-in-command, might be risen above without waiting for their winters to overwhelm them.

As for himself, he concluded dramatically, he wanted only the woman Estune.

Of course if, upon their triumphant return to Pa-gotzin-kay, the people should demand his leadership, he must bow. But it would not be for himself. It would be for the power of the *hesh-ke*. And if that power should come to them through Lucero, they all knew what it would mean: No surrender to the white man; *dah-eh-sah* to all enemies of freedom—death to any Apache who would not kill to protect the Chiricahua people!

"For all of this," he said emotionally, "we have but to bring the head of Pa-nayo-tishn to Geronimo."

It was an inspiring talk.

Only one of the men who heard it shook his head.

"I don't know," said Uklenni, who had known Peaches

down in Pa-gotzin-kay. "The fox goes to earth and does not intend to die. Why not the Coyote?"

Lucero went from noble leader to bad-tempered Apache killer in the blink of glittering eye. "What are you saying? You think he has a plan in there?"

Uklenni shrugged. "Does a mare lift her tailroot to the stud's nose? Does a weanling squat to stale? Does a new foal wobble? Of course he has a plan; I know him, remember. He is named for a bad animal."

From somewhere on the cliffside above the black hole of the drift, an owl hooted dolefully in the silence.

"You hear that!" challenged Kiyutaneh, a supremely superstitious man. "Speak of bad-name animals, eh? I do not like this, at all. Bû is on their side. That is a terrible omen. We ought to get out of here."

Some of the men nodded vigorously. Others held their heads still.

"*Mamarrachada!*" rasped Durango, the Mexican Apache. "What nonsense! That is the dung of your ancestors. You sound like old Nevado." He wheeled sharply on Lucero. "As soon as the moon sets and it is dark," he said, "we must take only the knives and go into the mining hole after them and that head we need for Geronimo. Agreed?"

"Let me think," frowned Lucero. "I do not want the woman harmed. Who touches her must kill Lucero."

"Bah! It is that woman who will kill you. She hates you. Do you not understand that yet?"

"She loves me," said the other killer softly. "She bore my man-child."

"*Mierda!* She is a northern. She despises the Apache. She cared only for Chatto. She told the truth about that. You were nothing to her."

"*Callate!*" The handsome face of Lucero writhed in ugliness. "No one harms my woman!"

Durango wisely went away from him to squat against the cliff with Kiyutaneh and Uklenni. The others stayed with Lucero peering across the talus slide trying to think how to get the Coyote to come out of the hole so they could take his head back to Geronimo without crawling in after it. No real suggestions were heard.

The moon sank. The darkness followed. Wore away into the dawn. The day came pink-flushed upon the western rim. Still they had thought of nothing.

The sun climbed. It got into the canyon. The heat of it

made the rocks shimmer. The deer flies drew blood along the picket line. Ponies squealed, nipped, kicked one another. Tempers among the men began to fry. The sun westered, blazed down against the talus slide. Ysun! but it was hot.

Jumano, who had a square of baconside in his saddlebag— the only food among them—went to cut some for broiling and found the entire slab sun-melted into a slush. He threw the glob upon the ground, cursing it.

From the minedrift someone laughed.

Jumano cursed the laughter and kicked at the blob of ruined bacon. But his ire took him unthinkingly beyond the shelter of the talus slide and cost him the top of his left ear knocked off by an instant rifle burst from the tunnel mouth.

"My shot!" called a remembered throaty voice from the dark mine, and the *hesh-kes*, hearing it, knew who had laughed and who now spoke from in there. As one, they put their eyes upon Lucero. It was Estune who laughed at them and fired that shot.

Lucero's face was blank as a rock.

This was the end of it. They all knew it. No more squaw talk now. Durango was right. The woman was not Lucero's woman. All such *mamarrachada* was behind them. The waiting was over.

"All right," said Lucero to Durango. "Tonight we go in with the knives."

46

In the mine tunnel Peaches, watching the talus slide and the blind cliff turn beyond it, knew that the Chiricahua had not departed. The afternoon wore on as uneasily for him as it did uncomfortably for the *hesh-kes*. Being an Apache himself, he knew how the minds of such killers as Lucero and Durango worked. Accordingly, when they had not ridden away that morning, that noontime, or even this late nearing sundown, he knew they were waiting for darkness and for him.

With the grim knowledge darkening his sunny features, he called his companions to join him at tunnel's mouth.

It was time, he told them, for his last plan.

"Gawd he'p us," said the drifter, but he saw at once that the small White Mountain man was not his customary self, and he added quickly. "Excuse it, Peachy. Plow ahead on."

The little scout nodded, revealed his fears:

It was himself, whom the *hesh-ke* called Pa-nayo-tishn, Coyote, that Lucero and his pack were after. All of the woes that had come upon the Chatto and the Geronimo raids must, in the Apache mind, stem from the defection of Peaches to the cavalry of Lieutenant Kensington. The fact that Lucero had precipitated the massacre of the Chiricahua women by the killing of the ranchwife and her two children up near Fort Gila only made it the more necessary for that same Lucero to extract penalty from another, specifically Pa-nayo-tishn.

"Lucero want Peaches' head in sack," he said with Indian prescience. "Take trouble from self. Make people in Pagotzin-kay forget. Think Lucero big hero."

The drifter objected. What about the squaw? he asked. Was he expecting them to believe that Lucero was really after him? With the cat-bodied tall woman in the tunnel with them? Bushway!

No, insisted Peaches. The woman was a personal matter, a thing between Chatto and Lucero. The others, Durango especially, would never be with him on a mere squaw chase. Runaway wives were not unknown to the Apache. Estune was of no actual importance. The *hesh-kes* badly needed something to put the final cinchstrap tight about the great killing of cavalrymen they had made at Nine Soldier Gulch. "A little something in the sack," as they say among the Chiricahua, he concluded.

He had been speaking in Spanish, so all might follow the conversation, and for a browknit moment no one said anything. Then Clooney Borrum turned to the drifter.

The little red man was right, he said. Clooney knew Apaches and Apache thinking. In that regard, he had a small confession to make to his shotgun man. When he had told him at Sifford Wells that he was happy to be going with Chatto's raiders, and that they had promised him his freedom because he was not white, and that black man and red man were as brothers, it had all been a high pile of horse manure. Before landing in Pima Bend, Clooney had been a captive of the Texas Lipan Apaches for six years. He knew what he was going into that night at the Wells. But he had not wanted to drag his new white friend along with him. He knew that was hopeless too. No use both of them winding up "Apache-ed." So he had lied to the drifter, not being noble or anything in

the world but plain decent to somebody who had been kind
to him and who did not know what Apache freedom meant.

"Gawd amighty," breathed the drifter.

He put his hand out and just squatted there with it on the
stablehand's shoulder, unable to find his words. Clooney
reached up and patted his hand and said, "It weren't much,
old shotgun man. You'd favor me to fergit it." He paused,
earnest black face wrinkled. "Thing is now to bend ear to this
here leetle Injun. Taken my swore word fer it. He knows."

The drifter looked over at Estune, as though to give her
the chance to be heard. The squaw only looked back at him
and said something in Apache to Clooney.

"She want me to tell you it weren't her putten all these
here lumps and cuts on my hide and haid," he told the
drifter. "Meaned to tell you anyhows, but fergot. She just
fetch me enough licks on the haunch to make it look good
to the 'Pache sisters. They're the ones hurt me. This here
Estune, I ain't never see'd a Injun liken her afore."

"Nor me," agreed the drifter. "Not anything like."

The squaw, watching him intently, smiled.

The drifter touched his hatbrim. "You betcha," he said and
turned back to Peaches.

"Peachy, she's yourn to say what goes. You tell us what's
got to be did, and she's done. Long as the squaw and the
baby ain't in the line of fire, fire away."

There was a thing in the Old Rules, the little scout told
them, which Lucero would not dare deny. It was the challenge to personal battle. The thing where two men fought to
settle a matter for all parties concerned.

As with most ideas Indian, this one was designed to the
practical side; it let something be decided at the cost of but
one man's life, where several or many other men's lives might
otherwise have been wasted.

This explanation was in Spanish again, and the drifter
noticed Estune leaning forward showing her first intense
interest. The northern woman's luminous eyes were darting
from Peaches as he talked to the drifter as he listened. But
the scout was continuing, and the white man returned his
attention to him.

Of them all there in the mine tunnel, Peaches said, his
was easily the strongest right of the challenge. Lucero had
killed Peaches' soldiers up there in that terrible fight. The
soldiers would never have been in that place if Peaches had
not been guiding them. It was a blood debt owing between

him and the *hesh-ke* leader. Only blood would wipe it away; Peaches was going outside now, he would like to touch the hands with each friend.

He arose with the words, but Estune flung up a dark hand. "Wait!" she said. "You are not the one!"

The hand pointed at the startled drifter.

"He is the one," she said. "It was Lucero who killed his yellow-haired wife and child."

The story, simply told, was that Estune had been with the Piños Apache band of Chatto returning from the Llano Estacado, land of the Comanche, after the occasion of her purchase by the young Chiricahua chief from the Kwahadi Water Horse people of Quanah Parker.

The Comanche had supposedly long been conquered and their ancient customs suppressed. Estune knew better. The Kwahadi who had bought her from the Comancheros, those nomad merchants of the buffalo country, had treated her well—for a Comanche—but had hesitated not in the least to sell her to Chatto like a head of *wohaw,* or agency steerbeef. The price had been a lot of good horses, many head beyond reasonable price, for young Chatto had looked at her and was undone.

At the time, his men, on a trading not a raiding trip to visit friends in the Kiowa-Apache band that roamed the Staked Plains with the Comanche, did not want their youthful leader—not yet a full chief—to take her.

It was against the Old Rules to bring in alien blood, although it was done all the time with both white and Mexican women. Indeed, it had been the same crusty old Keeper of the Rules, old White Hair, old Nevado, who had persuaded the others to accept Estune, as she was clearly of high blood and strong, if not as young as one might desire for their leader, then but twenty-three summers in age. So they had started back to Apacheria.

With the band had been an older subchief, not more than early middle years, however, vain, fiercely handsome, a real *macho* rumored to be a secret brother of the dread *hesh-ke* sect of Chiricahua assassins, who controlled the Apache people through terror and murder. At this time, however, he was only a member of the visiting Mount Piños party and considered Chatto's nearest friend and first lieutenant in battle. The two were indeed so inseparable that whispers of man-love were made about them, but these were lies. No suitor could have been more attentive than Chatto upon the return trip.

One thing marred that journey to Estune's new home in the rancheria of her young husband.

Lucero, the headstrong *macho*, would not obey Chatto's injunction to travel swiftly in peace through New Mexico seizing only such horses and supplies as necessity might demand. No killing was a strict order. It was a time of uneasy peace, and the risk of the long ride to the Kiowa-Apache cousins was sufficient without making war.

But Lucero repeatedly made side-strikes with his half dozen malcontents and young men simply spoiling to take hair and cut white throats while up in that land where they did not live and would not need to answer for their depredations. It was upon the last of these side-killings that Lucero had struck the drifter's ranch near Fort Apache to the north of the Chiricahua homelands down near Cochise Stronghold, Fort Bowie, and Apache Pass.

One man had been killed by the white rancher. Estune would now give that man's name, so that the white brother listening to her story might believe it had been as she said: It was Nautizo.

Her words ended as abruptly as that, but the drifter believed, and had to believe, that the tall Ute-Cheyenne woman had brought him to the sudden final ending of his three-year vengeance trail.

Not knowing how else to convey to her his feelings, he offered her his hand. She took it, and he was surprised to note that she did so with shyness. Yet while their fingers were yet pressing together, she looked up at him with those luminous, strange eyes that had disturbed him from his first sight of her.

"*Schichobe*," she whispered to him in Apache.

"*Anh*," he answered her, learning a little of the Chiricahua tongue. "*Schichobe*, dear friend."

He felt awkward as a schoolboy, knowing Peaches and Clooney Borrum, both Apache experts of hard education, were watching the exchange—watching and waiting.

But when he let the squaw's hand go, his mind was already running back to that nightmare darkness at his small ranch on the Tonto Rim. Of a sudden, he was not thinking of tall squaws, or small scouts, or rescued black friends; he was seeing again the way that he had found Aura Lee and the little girl within the burning cabin, and he got up and said in a flat voice more menacing than any rage: "All right, Peachy. Go out and make your dicker for me to fight him."

The small friend of the U.S. Cavalry nodded quickly.

"Peaches do best he can," he said.

And he went to the full opening of the drift tunnel calling for Lucero to come out and hear him.

There was to be a *mano-a-mano*.

The very thin white man would fight Lucero to the death, hand-to-hand. He, Pa-nayo-tishn, was invoking the Old Rules. The referee would be whoever from his own ranks Lucero might appoint. Both sides would stand with ready rifles in the open, guarding the Old Rules. Either fighter who broke those rules would be shot and his defeat made forfeit to the other. Terms would be as ever—all spoils and privileges of war to the victor, any mercy or generosity to the vanquished's people made only by the surviving fighter.

"*Qué dice, hombre?*" the small White Mountain man demanded. "Who will be your referee?"

Lucero, who had stalked from behind the talus slide to stand magnificently to the challenge, was not permitted time to name his candidate. Ysun, or as the grim drifter put it more pungently, outhouse luck, provided the answer from behind them all.

"Ah! you bastards!" screeched old Nevado, limping into view around the blind cliff turn. "I have finally caught up to you. What's going on here?"

47

The hesh-kes stood in front of the talus slide, rifles in hand. Before the drift and by the heading shack waited the enemy: Peaches, Estune, Clooney Borrum, all with Winchesters at the ready. Between the forces stood the drifter and Lucero. And between them stood old Nevado in the highest moment of his long life as Keeper of the Rules.

It was late and very still in the canyon.

High above the last of the sun pinked the eastern rim.

The agreements of the *duelo* were made.

Beyond Lucero his second, Durango, held for him the great warhorse Matadero, returned to the *hesh-ke* leader in fairness for the fight. Behind the drifter was his second, very small man holding very small horse, Peaches and his roach-maned mustang, which animal the White Mountain defector from Chatto's raiding party had strongly counseled that his white friend ride, rather than the powerful black of Durango or his own stolen steeldust.

This was an Apache fight, Peaches had insisted vehemently. His little pet knew the drifter. The black and nervous proud-cut stud did not. The steeldust race horse was worse than useless in a cut and slash and spin and wheel contest from horseback. "Put faith in Gatito," he pleaded with the drifter. The Little Cat.

So now Little Cat and the rangy big Matadero, the Slaughterer, waited for their riders while old Nevado repeated for the final time the instructions.

The weapons were warclubs alone.

No guns, no blades, no flighted shafts.

This was in fair consideration of the dirty-bearded and wasted thin white man. It was the weapon of least advantage to Lucero. A club was a club. And men of all skin colors had swung the primitive cudgel.

The combatants were to begin on horses and continue whether ahorse or afoot until one man was dead. Any natural weapon was allowed, a stone, another timber or stick, dust in the eyes, all and any trickery of deceit, anything at all except the gun, the blade, the lance, the ax, the arrow, any man-made weapon. A horse might stomp to death a dismounted opponent, very fair. Everything was fair so long as only nature's weapons and the weapons of the brain—cunning, cheating, feigning—were employed.

Did the two enemies understand it?

"*Anh!*" rumbled Lucero, in that voice that again returned the white man to the night of his sorrow. "Let him join his pale-haired woman and sickly girl-child."

"*Comprendo,*" said the drifter, memory turning dark within him.

There were a brief few moments then while the old man searched both fighters for hidden blades, and each adversary had opportunity for last estimates.

Lucero saw across from him a man thin to the look of starvation. He was perhaps six feet and three or four fingers tall. Grizzle-bearded, ragged, flop-hatted, cavalry-jacketed, flat-booted, he looked as a scarecrow in the rancheria corn rows. In fierceness he had the effect of *enh*, the prairie dog. For menace, his entire appearance as well as attitude seemed like *penole*, cornmeal mush. The tattered hat, shading the white man's face, did not show Lucero the peculiar blaze of the deep-set blue eyes; and the cavalry jacket hid a certain steelspring flatness of muscle not compatible with mush, or scarecrows, or barking prairie dogs. But the *hesh-ke* nodded, and he knew it would be a short fight. A far better thing than going into the tunnel at night with the knives. There was no white man he feared in single combat, or any enemy. Lucero and fear did not know one another. Only death was his brother and his business.

The drifter was nervously aware of this murderous eying. In return he sought in vain to discover some flaw in his opponent. Lucero was as tall as he less perhaps an inch or two. He was much heavier yet without three ounces of spare flesh. He was all solid bullneck and wide shoulders with flat belly and small buttocks, long muscular arms, short bowed legs covered now by the mid-thigh reach of the Apache riding boots. He was otherwise naked, except for breech-cloth, the copper of his body gleaming in the deepening shadows of the canyon.

The clubs were three feet long, rawhide wrapped around ironhard mesquite or Comanche orangewood, dense as pig-iron, and unbreakable.

Nevado was finished with his search.

He stepped back.

"Find your horses," was all he said.

Matadero and Gatito came together.

Lucero swung the beautiful appaloosa to collide with scrubby Gatito. But Little Cat was too quick and went sideways like a puma, so that the appaloosa and he only brushed rumps. And then the potbellied mustang turned in a spin so fast that he had the drifter up behind Lucero in club's reach. The white man swung meaning to end it all with a brain-blow. Yet Lucero twisted on his mount's far side, sensing the blow, and the club struck Matadero in the flankribs only grazing the clamping calf of his rider. Next instant the *hesh-ke* had recovered and was back rearing his trained warhorse on his hind legs working him in upon Gatito without once giving the white man another club opening at Lucero. Little Cat had a strange counter for this.

He dashed in under the much larger appaloosa at the highest upfling of the latter's forefeet, so that the belly of the appaloosa actually came down upon the sturdy rump of Gatito, causing Matadero to struggle and kick aimlessly to free himself from this unheard-of beaching or stranding. Lucero, forced to fight to stay on his frenzied mount, missed his vicious cut at the white man's skullbase. Instead, his club thudded sickeningly into the drifter's back muscles. But Little Cat got him free, gave him time to clear his head and come back at Lucero.

Again and again the men and horses rode at one another, now the one and now the other clubman landing bruising, dizzying, blood-letting but non-lethal blows of the cruelly wrapped clubs.

Finally it happened.

Both clubs met in full-arc and with crunching impact. That of Lucero stayed in the *hesh-ke's* hand. The drifter's flew cartwheeling forty feet away.

Lucero hurled Matadero at Little Cat.

There was nothing the white man might do save to attempt to seize in midair the whirling club of Lucero. To break its force, even if hand or arm broke in the process. But as the appaloosa drove into Peaches' insignificant scrub, Gatito squatted down immediately in the path of thundering Matadero. The mustang went down like no other horse in the species will or can. He went into the ground like a hunching rabbit, and great Matadero could neither leap him in time, nor swerve aside. The appaloosa went knees and fetlocks into the squealing little scrub, cutting his feet from under himself as though running into a stretched rope. Over Little Cat he flew, crashing to the rocky surface of the dump, where he lay on his side, as though killed.

Lucero, of course, as had the white man, abandoned mount in midair, going straight over withers to collide with the drifter just leaping free of the squatted Gatito. In the matter of a drawn breath both men and both horses were on the ground, all except for the unfair Little Cat who, with a grunt and a whicker of purely Apache derision, got up and galloped over to true master Pa-nayo-tishn, the pudgy Coyote.

But Lucero, dumb with his fury now, still had the warclub. And more. He gained his feet before the white man did. It was over—or was it?

No! by Ysun. That skinny Winchester shooter from Sifford Wells and the stagecoach station managed at the utter end moment to scoop up a large flat rock and hold it in both hands where Lucero's murder-club was coming with a *hesh-ke* killing cry down into his unprotected face. The warclub rang upon the rockshield with a bounce and a vibration which literally burst it from the hands of Lucero, and, for the moment, those hands were too benumbed for the subchief to pick the weapon back up.

He reached for it, and the fingers went about it, but when the hand came away the club was not in it but still lay on the ground. In that second, the white man had struck for the club like a snake, never leaving the earth but driving the heavy wood into both long frontbones of Lucero's bent legs. The pain of it was sufficient to drive the *hesh-ke* leader back three uncontrolled steps.

The enemy was upon his own feet then.

And coming savagely with the club.

They were near the skeletonized stampmill now by the drift of their battle. Lucero, not in cowardice but in tactic, wheeled and dove over the waisthigh foundation of the ancient building. He was in throbbing pain. He must gain time. The drifter spared him little, following him at full leap.

But the Chiricahua raider was steady again, and to hand in the ruins of the mill were weapons of endless kind. The two men closed in final strength and wile.

The fight went up onto the high platform of the ore vat above the crushing rollers. It raged down the checkman's ladder. Up the vatman's stairway. With pipe and scantling and heavy belting, rusted ancient wrench and pickstaff and mucker's shovel handle, it spread its wounds and left its cloutings of shed blood.

The two neared exhaustion with neither the clear victor nor even the superior *hombre* or *macho* or *honcho* of the extended cruel brutality. It was the *mano-a-mano* of living memory among the *hesh-ke* Chiricahua, and, in the end, it was fortune and not supremity of arms that decided it.

A hand rail gave way behind Lucero as the white man drove him by a flailing of terrible blows of the fists to bones of the face and guts of the body into that restraining timber. The *hesh-ke* leader plummeted helplessly a full twelve feet onto a floor of earth packed by the snows of winter, baked by the suns of summer, into a surface like swept rock.

The wonder was it did not kill him outright.

The drifter followed him, dropping from the platform by his hands, running to him with a red-rusted shard of angle-iron raised to brain him if he moved.

But Lucero lay in last defeat.

He could not rise.

All that remained was for the dirty-bearded white man to

crush the leader's brains out upon the floor and to stand astride of the lifeless body to claim of the Keeper of the Rules that victory which was rightly his.

The Chiricahua and the drifter's people all came silently in about the central figures of the combat, waiting for the white man to make the claim, watching him and old Nevado whose hands were poised to issue the killing sign when he had done so.

But the thin white man in the cavalry jacket did not drive the rusted angle-iron into the head of his enemy. He stopped its swing and looked at it and put it aside with a clanging toss against the crusher bin.

"I cain't do it," he said.

Then softly, shaking blood-caked head to himself and to those wasted miles and days and years of his hatred for this fallen murderer and his cruel people.

"It ain't in me no more."

48

There was a strange silence in the old stampmill.

The drifter, trembling with fatigue, looked about him. The Chiricahua, standing with dark, brooding Durango, did not move, either to take up their fallen leader and restore him or to go away from him. Clooney and Peaches and the northern woman waited also and uneasily.

Old Nevado, it was, who came toward him scowling.

"It is not permitted," he said. "One must die. If not, nothing has been settled." He spoke in Spanish for the white man, and the drifter nodded wearily.

"Por favor, Patron," he said. "How is this?"

Nevado shrugged. He rather liked this dirty, shaggy fellow. He did not want to see him hurt by things which were old with the Apache before there was anyone called American living in Arizona.

"Having won," he said, "you must kill your enemy. If you do not, then we who judge the fight must kill you. It is our way. As I told you, only one may live."

The drifter could see the Indian sense to it.

Brutal or not, it worked.

It was not like the settlement or the military law where, often as not, the guilty dragged the innocent down with them. Or worse. Where the guilty went free.

"Nevertheless," he said to the old man. "I cannot do it. It is murder to kill a helpless man."

"No," said Nevado. "It is justice."

He raised and cocked the outside hammer on his old-model 1866 Winchester. "I am the judge," he said.

There was no doubt in the mind of any Indian present that the drifter was to be executed. Clooney, moving impulsively to come in and stand beside his white friend, was instantly ringed by aimed Chiricahua rifles. Peaches, knowing when fate hovered, did not try to move.

"Listen!" he pleaded to the white man. "You do! Do for Peaches. No good you die."

But the drifter crouched back in desperation.

His eyes were the eyes of an animal measuring the way out, ready to run for it, gunfire or not.

"No!"

It was the squaw, Estune. She came gliding swiftly between Nevado and the white man.

"There is a rule," she told the old Chiricahua. "I know you will remember it. The victor may give the life of the defeated to another."

Nevado nodded soberly, frowning.

"Only if that other then kills the defeated one," he clarified. "Will you kill Lucero?"

"Will you give me the courtesy rule?" she countered.

"Go ahead," said Nevado. "You may talk ten breaths."

Estune went to the drifter and said in Spanish that he must give to her, by touching her on the shoulders with his two hands, the life of Lucero. Trust her not to kill the *hesh-ke* leader, or not trust her. But give the sign now as she stepped back. If he did not, he was finished. And she, Estune, she said, did not want that.

The drifter had no escape.

He was not, finally, going to be shot down for the likes of Lucero, or any other red Indian.

He reached forth and touched his hands on Estune's shoulders.

The squaw at once turned back to Nevado and received from the old man a knife. This weapon she bore back to the now groaning but still half-conscious Lucero. Before anyone might guess her real intention, she bent over the *hesh-ke* who had been her lover and used the knife.

Even though barely aware of his surroundings, Lucero gave a strangling cry and came halfway to his feet.

They all saw his face.

Estune, going again to old Nevado, held out her hand, fist clenched, to the Keeper of the Rules.

"I have taken more than his life," she said and placed in Nevado's trembling hand that which she had taken from the savage chieftain of the *hesh-ke* killers.

The old man stared at her in disbelief.

He turned to the Chiricahua and held forth his hand, unfolding the gnarled fingers to show them what lay within his palm, still weeping serous blood.

It was Lucero's nose.

49

The Chiricahua went away from the tailings dump of the ghostly minehead with the twilight. They bore no seeming ill-will to the drifter, or to the others, save for the tall northern squaw. Toward her, they made no sign whatever. The thing she had done to the leader was worse than taking his life. Every Chiricahua knew of what had been between them; for a squaw to exact from a warrior the penalty for adultery that tradition placed upon the woman was monstrous. Yet the woman had not lied. She had done more than killed Lucero.

In a last moment old Nevado was torn whether to go with the wild Chiricahua back to Pa-gotzin-kay or to cleave with the scheming Coyote and run with him in safety and service to the white man. Finally, he knew that he was too old to change. Old Nevado, old White Hair, would die wild. He would go home to Pa-gotzin-kay. He would never surrender.

Unlike the others, he went to face the people of Pa-nayo-tishn. He made the sign of peace to the white man and touched the hands with him in the American grip. He did the same with the black man. To Peaches, he said that he believed the little scout had chosen the right path for a young man. He wished him well. He would never have thought that a small fat White Mountain could bring down the great Lucero. Coming to the tall squaw, he looked into her dark face a long moment, then nodded.

"I still say Chatto was right," he told her. "If I were but fifteen winters younger—" He broke off, shaking the snowy locks. "Raise that girl-child to be a good Indian," he said gruffly. "The hell with all of you."

He put the old pack mare, limping still but serviceable,

after the slowly moving horses of the Chiricahua following Durango toward the blind cliff trail.

Watching from the mine drift, Winchesters yet in hand, all horses behind them and in control, Peaches and his people watched the silent exodus. The small man with the San Carlos neck-tag was moved to emotion.

"It is almost sad," he said. "The wild ones are going away. Their kind will come no more. Chatto, Geronimo, Lucero, Juh, Nachez, Durango, Ka-ya-ten-na, Nana, Zele, Bonito, Chihuahua, Hieronymo, Loco, all will be but names soon. An Apache must feel this changing thing *¡Qué tristeza, qué tragedia!"*

Clooney Borrum, who had known so much of sorrow in his own past, said softly, *"Lo siento mucho, hombre."*

Peaches thanked him with gesture.

Estune and the drifter said nothing. They had known their sorrow, too, and it had come from these same wild people, and too lately from them. Surely each felt something of the pathos in Peaches' farewell to those with whom he would never ride again. Yet each also remembered the Chiricahua in another way.

Who had killed the white man's wife and child?

Who had *really* brought about the murder of the northern woman's man-child in the bloodied rocks beyond Fort Gila?

Estune knew, the drifter knew.

The Chiricahua were nearing the awesome vertical drop of the blind-turn ledge. Peaches raised an arm in impulsive goodbye to his former comrades of Pa-gotzin-kay. None of them, not even old Nevado, replied to him. The Chiricahua had their memories too.

At the narrowing of the ledge where it went around the blind corner, Durango, bearing Lucero mounted double behind him, pulled his horse out of line. The others went on around the turn and were gone. Nevado and the pack mare limped after them. Only Durango and Lucero remained visible to the watchers from the mine drift.

Durango slid from his horse's back, giving over the nervous mustang to his first friend and war brother.

Lucero mounted the animal. He reached down and touched the Mexican Apache on the shoulder. All watching from across the ore dump knew the single spoken word was *schichobe.*

Then Durango was gone walking like a chief proudly erect around the blind turn of the hanging ledge.

Lucero, reining in the horse, looked back in the final moment at the people who had destroyed him. He flung up a dark arm, saluting them all. Then he spurred the warpony of Durango, spoke an Apache word to him, and turned him suddenly from the trail in a long neighing leap over the edge.

Fort Lowell

50

It was the advice of Peaches to delay one week in the safety of the high canyon mine. This was to give the country about them time to quiet down when it was learned that Chatto and Geronimo had gone back into Mexico. Right now, and for several days yet, Ariozna, in this southeastern corner of the Chiricahua raiding, would be a hornet's nest of cavalry, of militia, and, as always, of aroused settler bands out to kill anything that looked or smelled or spoke or took the skin color of an Apache Indian. The best thing that they all could do was to lie low. That was the Coyote's counsel, and he urged his friends to abide by it.

The latter needed scant urging.

They knew there was no danger of the Chiricahua returning. Durango and his *hesh-kes* were already two days late in fleeing after Geronimo. They would be fortunate to escape with their lives, let alone their honor, intact. Moreover, Durango had been born and grown up in the Sierran stronghold of his Chiricahua people. He had never been on an American reservation, and his entire heart would be driving him to reach Mexico and the homeland in Pa-gotzin-kay.

Clooney and the drifter voted quickly enough to wait it out where they were. Meanwhile, Estune, hearing the decision, lit the early nighttime with the peculiar luminosity of her smile. It would be good, she said, to be here with her men and her pale-haired girl-child.

For different reasons, and each surprised by his pleasure, Clooney and Peaches and the drifter looked at one another in a smug manner as if to say that he understood very well the other two were not included, except by courtesy, in the tall squaw's man-felt smile and throaty words. As old Nevado had said, this was some woman: They could agree with the snowy-haired Keeper of the Old Ways that Chatto had been right about her.

The three men sharing guard duty, just in case, the night passed quietly, the first day came up clear and cooler. Spirits rose and hands grew busy.

At her own insistence, Estune accompanied Peaches down the mine's tailings slide into the canyon to attend in the Indian manner to the burial of Lucero. Also while down there they would butcher the horse for meat, find the dead man's rifle, seize anything else of nomad value.

Upon leaving, she gave the baby unexpectedly to the drifter. Clooney Borrum laughed. The drifter scowled.

"Well," explained Clooney when they were alone, "you is aiming to give the baby back to its white mama, right?"

"Damn right that's right! What the hell elst?"

"This elst," said Clooney, sobering. "Who you going to give the squaw back to?"

"Goddamnit!" began the drifter, then decided better.

The only thing in the territory that mattered to him was seeing the yellow-haired girl again down in Tucson. She had said she would be there, and so had he.

"Whar you going from here?" asked Clooney softly.

"Tucson, I reckon. Then back to Pima Bend and square it with that old sheriff. Man cain't ask no gal to marry up with a hossthief."

Far down below Clooney watched the graceful swaying of Estune's figure leaping from rock to rock.

"Got to keep her with us tills the baby's delivered," he frowned. "No way 'round that."

"Nope," said the drifter. "No way."

They fell silent. When Peaches and Estune climbed up out of the canyon, both men were sound asleep, back-to-back, the baby bubbling peacefully on the ground between them. The drifter's hand held one corner of the child's blanket sling, the black man's grasped the other.

The two Indians looked at one another.

"Maybe we are all the same under our separate skins," Peaches said in Apache to the northern woman. "Look at that."

Estune smiled down upon the sleepers.

"*Sikisn*," she murmured. "Brothers."

At week's end they went down the canyon to Peaches' trail, topping out in the high country of the Tucson side without incident. Their luck, however, had frayed its twine thin. At San Pedro River crossing, they ran into scores of settlers, miners, townfolk, and general frontier riff-raff gathered into an amorphous posse northbound for San Carlos Reservation. This was the ill-famed Tombstone Rangers, formed around two wagon loads of whiskey with a common resolve to march up and clean out every redskin under Crook's protection. The posse was straggling for miles over the country, and any one clot of its members would fire first at whatever humans were abroad without benefit of white skin. Only because of Peaches' endless skill and the fact that the avengers were drying up their supplies of inspiration, did the drifter's party bring its two Indians safely past Tombstone to the dry course of the Babacomari River, above Fort Huachuca.

From there, they had a narrow brush with capture by prowling cavalry troops, eluding this force only because of their superior horses, Lucero's appaloosa, Durango's black, the steeldust gelding, Peaches' wiry mustang, and because of the flooding of Pantano Wash by a flash storm between them and their pursuers.

There was a third ugly incident when, nearing exhaustion from the four sleepless days and nights of the run from Hidden Canyon, the drifter was brought to go into a ranch much too close to settled neighbors begging for food and water.

The ranchers were Christian people, a minister of God, his good wife, and young only son. They not only bade the drifter welcome within their humble home but, guessing from the mercy in their hearts that he had companions, pleaded with him to bring them in also. Not alone food and water but rest would be theirs, the charge the ordinary one in that lonely land, nothing, and no questions asked.

It was unthinkable to bring in Estune with a white child at her dark breast. But Peaches was safe with these gentle souls because of his San Carlos tag, and Clooney was only a poor colored man wherever he went.

The squaw was hidden up in the chaparral, the three comrades going in to the ranch house for their first hot coffee and home food in weeks. Here it might have ended, too, with God still in his rightful place and the Reverend and Mrs. Hickenberry due the gratefulness and blessings of their Samaritan kind.

The difference was that Estune was not a Christian and so

did not understand the merciful significance of the young
Hickenberry son who, only minutes after the driven guests
were welcomed, took secretly to his cowpony out behind the
homestock corral to pound off in a race toward the four-mile-
distant lights of the cattle town of Cienega Creek. Simple
Estune imagined that the youth had been dispatched to
bring enemies down upon her men, and so shot him out of
the saddle on the full gallop and ran her own black gelding
into the front yard of the ranch house shouting in Apache of
the attempted betrayal.

The mount-up and ride-out were made without argument,
but the damage was done in part, no matter.

The good couple had had a fine look in flooding lamplight
of the tall squaw and her blonde baby, and that posse
from Cienega Creek would be on their heels now regardless of
young Hickenberry's sudden halt.

"Bless you, Reverund," called the drifter, last to leave the
lamplit ranch yard. And with the words, and his Winchester,
shot out the lamp, profaned its bearers, wished them well in
hell, and rode off with his dark-skinned friends.

Nearing Fort Lowell at last, the drifter understood fully the
dangers—to Estune and Peaches as Indians—of the final approach. He understood, as well, the risks that he and Clooney
Borrum ran of being seen together. There was no way to
know if the Hickenberry shooting had come this far ahead of
them. The only thing they could know was that, of them all,
only the white man among them might go into the military
post and come away again. Preparations were made to this
end.

One precaution the drifter did not mention.

He knew he could not leave the baby with Estune in the
chaparral of the Tanque Verde foothills where they were
hiding. The northern woman knew why they were here. She
had been desperately clinging to and crooning to the child
the past three hours. She could not hope to hold it for
herself. But with the savage mother, as with the caged wild
one, the life of the young was not safe. Hence, with all in
readiness for himself to mount up and go down to the fort,
he had made his decision. Clooney Borrum would ride with
him and hold the child in the brush just outside the post. In
that way Estune could neither harm nor flee with the white
mother's child. Yet she would be held waiting at Tanque
Verde with Peaches as no other bonds might hold her. With

a last word to Peaches in English on watching the squaw, he and Clooney rode down the draw and out upon the flat below. Neither looked back. Both heard the soft moaning of the Indian mother behind them.

"Goddamnit," said the drifter. "It ain't somehow the right come-out. It just ain't."

Clooney Borrum compressed wide lips.

"You done right," he said, cradling the sleeping, breast-full babe. "She'd have kilt it sure, happen you'd have left it with her, knowing you was going in to have it tooken away from her."

He shook weary head, let wide shoulders slope.

"It don't allus comes out liken it ought, old shotgun man. What matters is that you done right."

The drifter nodded grimly.

"Yeah," was all he said.

The drifter stood outside the infirmary door at Fort Lowell, flop hat in hand, praying that he could get it all said straight to the girl, and quick, then go bring her baby in and let the Lord handle it from there. Taking a last deep breath, he opened the door and went in.

"Yeah?" said the corporal at the desk within.

"Mrs. Carter. I'm looking for—"

"Who?" frowned the corporal.

"Mrs. Carter. Young lady brung in from up to Sifford Wells bouten ten, twelve day gone. Mighty purty and sorter slim. Yeller hair and—"

"Oh," said the soldier. "You mean Mrs. Marlin; Cap'n Marlin's wife. She ain't here no more. Been transferred up to Fort Apache. Old Crook's sent Lieutenant Britton Davis, you know he was C.O. up to Fort Apache, well, Crook's got him over to San Carlos now and Cap'n Marlin he's taking over up to Fort Apache. Crook's down to Wilcox on the S.P. Railroad. Getting set to take out after old Geronimo. Anything else?"

"When'd they get hitched?" asked the drifter.

"Hell, I don't recall. Couple, three days after she come in with his column from up yonder." The noncom shrugged. "It was kind of a hurry-up thing. He was getting sent out, and all."

"Did she leave word about the baby?"

"Baby? You being cute, mister? I just told you they ain't been married a week."

"She never sayed nothing that you heard bouten the baby?"

"Look, old man, we're busy around here."

The drifter nodded.

He turned and went out.

It was a gray day and growing grayer. He got on the steeldust and sat a moment looking at Fort Lowell.

Very slowly his hand went into the pocket of his cavalry jacket. He brought forth the stub of paper, tore it in bits, sifted it on the wind—the stage line ticket.

He turned the trim gelding away, walked him dust-plopping down the road along officers' row. He did not see if the guard waved him past at the gate; he was seeing a far piece of country past Fort Lowell.

He picked up Clooney and the baby in the brush and they rode quickly now, watching behind them. Within an hour they came to the mouth of the draw and went up into the Tanque Verde hills. Peaches and Estune were waiting for them. When the northern woman saw the white baby, she uttered a low, piercing cry and swept it to her breast. "It's yourn now, Estune," the drifter said. "Yourn and mine."

Peaches told her what the white man had said.

The squaw put down her head and wept.

"I reckon," said the drifter, "that it's time to go." He looked away from his fellow drifters, all of them feeling what he felt. "Peachy," he said. "Whereaway for you?"

The little man who would above all things be an enlisted scout of the United States Cavalry told them that he would go now to the jacal of his White Mountain mother and his two Chiricahua wives near San Carlos. There word would reach Lieutenant Britton Davis that an Apache who had been in Pa-gotzin-kay was hiding nearby. The soldiers would come and arrest him. They would put him in jail for riding with Chatto and for killing the Mescalero Bobbie with his riflebutt. Then he would plead to be taken to General Crook, saying that he could guide Red Beard and the cavalry from Willcox to Pa-gotzin-kay without losing one soldier, or more than three pack mules.

The drifter pursed lips, frowned dubiously.

"Luck," he said. "*Vaya.*" Then, concern still shadowing the blue eyes, "Clooney friend, how about you?"

The Negro stablehand shook his head. "Don't rightly know," he said apprehensively. "How abouten you?"

The drifter showed his little inside smile.

"Well," he said, "I reckoned me and you might go up yonder to the Wells and see if we could tip that burnt coach onto her rims, splice the harness back together and hope that there Bill Jimmie Navajo has done come back with the spare team stock. Happen he has, I figure we could hook 'em up and roll that old rig back to Pima Bend wheres we stoled it from, squaring us with that old sheriff."

Clooney looked at him in sheer admiration.

"You mean with me and you up top like we was, driver and shotgun man? With the gold still in her and everything?"

"Why not? We ain't afraid; man's got to stand plumb square with the law, don't he?"

Clooney studied him a moment to be sure the other meant it. Then he said gladly, "Sure he do, old shotgun man! Whee-ooo, me and you together!"

"As ever was," said the drifter in all soberness and turned to Pa-nayo-tishn, the small White Mountain Coyote who had guided them so craftily and well.

"Peachy," was all he said, and he put out his hand.

The Apache took the hand, obviously with some emotion. He did the same with Clooney. Overcome, he said no word to either man, white friend or black. It was not the way of his people to show weakness.

Wheeling his pony, he kicked the disreputable animal up the rocky incline. He waved once to them from the top of the draw, then sent Little Cat over the ridge, away from Tanque Verde, into history.

For Clooney Borrum and the drifter, however, and for the tall northern woman with her tiny blue-eyed baby girl, one more ride remained.

51

Clooney rode Lucero's beautiful appaloosa stallion. The drifter was on the stolen Fort Gila steeldust. Estune had the black gelding of Durango. Wary and watchful, they enjoyed a lovely springtime desert night ride up along the Tucson road to Sifford Wells. By turn, the men carried the baby to rest the squaw. They flattered themselves that the infant was beginning to know both of them, while seeming to be particularly partial to the black stablehand. Clooney, who could handle either a wild Chiricahua studhorse or a cooing days-old white child with equal aplomb, accepted his new role of

nursemaid as he did everything in a hard life—gracefully.
"Gots to be, gots to be," he crooned to the tiny child and
held it close, humming lullabies unknown to white drifters or
Ute-Cheyenne squaws.

Estune and the drifter rode a good part of the way
side-by-side. Clooney could hear them talking in low-voiced
Spanish but did not try to listen to their words.

He hoped mightily that he knew what they were telling
each other. He felt, as well, that he knew for certain that the
tall northern woman would get it said for her part, with or
without words. It had to follow that his white horsethief friend
could understand *that* Indian language without Clooney, or
anybody else, interpreting for him. "What's going on back
yonder," he told the baby in his arms, "is spoke the same
anywheres."

They came with the clear green dawn into the Wells and
old Ysun must still have been attending them, even though
his own red children were scattered from Sonora to Chihuahua in great trouble.

The Navajo Bill Jimmie was back from the brush and he
had two good teams of the spare stage stock there with him.
Moreover, Bill Jimmie had much happiness to see them
appear. Now he could turn over the stage company stock to
Clooney Borrum—known to him in person as a most trusted
employee of his own dead benefactor T.C. Madden—and
depart permanently to live with his Navajo people up north
of Holbrook and Winslow, where the Hopi and the Zuni
might be seen but seldom the Chiricahua.

They persuaded the nervous stocktender to tarry long
enough, with their assurances that the Chiricahua were everywhere fleeing south to Mexico, to help them put the coach
and harness in rolling trim. He proved an excellent mechanic
and, the considerable skills of the drifter and Clooney aiding,
something recognizably like a stagecoach was pulled back to
the Wells late that afternoon.

At this point Bill Jimmie "went home."

Taking his departure, at the last minute he recalled a
small detail of some possible interest to his friends who had
also worked for the good man, Mr. Madden: The old sheriff
from Pima Bend had come out to Sifford Wells and gone on
up to Nine Soldier Gulch some days back to search the old
coach for the company gold it carried.

He had found it gone and had felt very bad about it

because it gave the murdering Cherry Cows mint coin enough to buy new Winchesters for the next ten years.

Bill Jimmie had felt bad about that part of it too.

In fact, it was the principal reason behind his decision to leave Apacheland and go raise angora goats and a few children up in the Painted Desert.

The drifter patted him on the back, told him they appreciated his help, wished him a good journey home.

"Don't worry about the Cherry Cows getting all them guns," he told him. "It'll be a spell. You'll see."

Bill Jimmie did not seem convinced, and set off toward Holbrook in an appreciable hurry.

With Clooney Borrum still cocking an eye at him over the assurances of the Chatto and Hoh-shuh raiders not buying guns with Mr. T.C.'s gold, the drifter said he believed they ought to rest-in at the stage station until about midnight. They had none of them had any decent sleep for days, none at all the past two nights.

"Meanwhile," he said, "I'm a'going up to the gulch for a last look-see." He bowed his head. "You know how it is, Clooney friend. The good Lord spairt me up there, and I reckon that's where I'd ought to go to set right my proper thanks 'twixt Him and me."

"Sure it is," said Clooney. "You go on along."

It seemed to the black man and to the anxious squaw that the drifter took uncommonly long to get himself square with his Maker, as darkness came on and he still was not back. However, in a bit he came in from around behind the station, claiming to have traveled down the gulch to Little Dipper Wash just scouting the country to make sure everything was as quiet as it sounded.

Clooney noticed a couple of other things, such as the steeldust being lathered somewhat over the withers, but he said nothing and agreed with the drifter that it was likely the safest thing to do to park the coach in back of the station, just in case, and for the two of them to take guard turns until leaving time.

He was grateful, actually, when his white friend offered to take the first shift. The drifter shrugged aside his thanks and in minutes both Clooney and the weary squaw were deep in slumber. The next thing either knew they were being shaken awake, the moon had moved to a midnight set, and the drifter was bidding them all aboard for Pima Bend, or wherever.

The time remembered was shortly after eight o'clock the morning of April 8th, 1883.

It came in from the north, down main, tilting three feet out of plumb. It was scorched, splintered, colandered with bullet holes. The axles were sprung, thorobraces sprained, wheels lumping out of time. It lurched, pitched, swerved. It could not possibly run another forty rods, but it had already rolled thirty-six night miles from Nine Soldier Gulch, and it would make it those final three hundred feet to the Pima Bend jail.

Schoolbound children ran and called to other lagging scholars. Old men, caning down the boardwalk, shaky-legged it across the dirt street to spraddle and stare. Merchants opening shops, dropped pushbrooms. Housewives abandoned the breakfast skillet, left the eggs unbroken.

Piney Newbold, snapping up the oilcloth window roller, could not believe what he saw past telegrapher's sounding receiver and through unwashed panes of what had been the front office window of the Southwest Stagelines & Fast Freight Company.

That was Clooney Borrum sitting high and mighty for a nigger on the driver's box of the burned-out Tucson stage. And if Piney's steel-rimmed spectacles did not betray him, that was the Fort Gila horsethief sitting up there with him riding shotgun in a U.S. Cavalry jacket. For the love of God! where had these ghosts come from?

The Fort Lowell cavalry had reported Clooney captured by the Apache. There had been no escaped horsethief mentioned among the relay station survivors, only a local man and a San Carlos Indian both known to and vouched for by Sergeant Emmett Bourke. And the company livestock and the shell of its fire-gutted coach had been declared salvage and abandoned along with the station itself. The gold cargo had patently fallen into the bloody hands of the Chiricahua butchers of brave Kensington and his gallant eight. Whence then these apparitions from the massacre at Sifford Wells?

Piney flipped up his green eyeshade, sprinted up the boardwalk to join the clot of curious thrombosing about the wounded stagecoach now parked in front of the town jail. As the bald-headed telegrapher ran, he saw that the cindered coach was not the only wheeled vehicle curbed there. Behind the Concord was old Jules' big Murphy freight wagon loaded to the tailgate with the worldly and human possessions of an honest lifetime.

Now this was something too!

Piney drew up in time to witness the exit of Sheriff Hoberman from his ancient adobe bastille. The old man came grumping out, took in the ruined Concord, its driver, its horsethief shotgun rider, the stolen steeldust race horse tied to its boot, all in one practiced glance.

He also spotted Piney on the crowd fringe, assessed the complete potential for frustration of his own private and personal plans, took instant decision to let nothing stand in the way of either justice or Jules Hoberman.

"All right, folks," he said. "Clear out and let me and Piney sort this out. Piney's the receiver, due and legal, for all Southwest properties. These other birds belongs to me. You ain't going to get cheated out of nothing."

The citizens were reluctant to depart.

They noted their sheriff was not in official garb. He had on traveling clothes, and that was sure his wagon parked behind the bent-up Concord. Moreover, his fat old roan saddler was tied to the back of the Murphy, and even his sick bluetick hound puppy, Ranger—obviously over the epizootic—was lying in the dust between the rear wheels, ready to trot. On the seat his fat wife and daughter waited, two lumps of chattel clay in sunbonnets.

"What in tunket's coming off here, sheriff?" queried an overalled burgher of the Pima Benders. "Ain't you laying it on a mite powerful ordering people around? Ain't nobody been murdered is they?"

"You want to join these boys in the juzgado, Link?" Old Jules was sharp with it. "If not, clear out. All of you. Piney, call a meeting for the folks."

Taking his cue, Piney Newbold assured the citizens that as soon as he and their duly constituted lawman had straightened out the case of the returned property, and its returners, a town hall assembly would be called in the Tecolote Saloon for purposes of full disclosure.

"Sure!" piped up Hayes Jacobs, owner-bartender of the Tecolote. "Come on, friends—first one's on the house. Got to let the law operate free and clear, ain't we? This here ain't Tombstone, is it?"

A chorus of local pride welled up in response, and the crowd broke away. Adult males headed for the Tecolote. Adult females took their yowling offspring by the ear, marched them on their delayed ways to the clapboard schoolhouse in the opposite direction.

The minute they were gone, old Jules reached in his coat pocket, pulled out a big padlock, snapped it shut on the jailhouse door, gave over the key to Piney Newbold, and said, "Come on, we'll hear this case in your office; it ain't in my jurisdiction."

"It ain't in your *what?*" said Piney, hesitating.

Old Jules reached in his other pocket, pulled out his battered star, handed it to the little telegrapher.

"There ain't no law no more in Pima Bend," he said. "I just resigned."

"Good Lord!" gasped Piney, looking to be sure no tarrier among the crowd had heard. "Come on!"

Jules Hoberman waved up to Clooney Borrum.

"Wrap your lines, Clooney. Come on, hossthief."

The four men went quickly down the boardwalk into the telegraph office of the defunct stage line.

Clooney and the drifter pleaded in vain that they had returned in good faith to give themselves up and to square themselves with the legal law.

Piney Newbold, like all sniffy little men, proved quite big for the letter of the law, but the trouble was that Jules Hoberman, in the strange role of amicus curiae for the two miscreants, insisted flatly that, until a new election was held and another lawman voted in, there simply was not *any* law in Pima Bend that could, would, or should hold these men.

The old sheriff did better than that.

He advanced good legal briefs in both accounts.

Clooney Borrum and the one-time horsethief were not sitting on or driving stolen property in the matter of the abandoned coach and team stock. Company receiver Piney Newbold had himself so declared these properties as salvage, of no known or demonstrable value to the bankruptcy settlement of Southwest Stagelines.

Bill Jimmie had caught up the missing horses and given them of his own free will and generous redskin heart to the defendants. The coach belonged to anybody with brains enough, and being fool enough, to want it.

Bill Jimmie was way back in salary owed as stocktender at Sifford Wells, so the horses were his to give. Clooney Borrum was eight months overdue on pay from Southwest, and there went horses, harness, coach, the shooting match. Sheriff Hoberman's recommendation to Piney Newbold was that he make out a bill-of-title to all of it in the name of Clooney Borrum, free, black, and twenty-one American citizen.

For himself the departing sheriff of Pima Bend wanted only his Winchester, which he had spotted in the scabbard of the steeldust, and that brought the judgment down to the Fort Gila horsethief.

Old Jules gave the drifter one mean long stare, but there was a glint of twinkle behind it which Piney Newbold did not see, and the sheriff made it sound stern as though handed down by the U.S. marshal's court in Prescott. "Ipso facto," he began, "you cain't hold a man for something he ain't done. To begin with, this here rummy was a sure enough hossthief. But he has made restitution by bringing in the stole animal, and, moreover, old man Steinhower and his son and the son's missus and both little ones, God rest their souls, was wiped out by the Cherry Cows, and there ain't no knowed next-of-Steinhower-kin. Now where a animal's been stole from somebody and brung back and there ain't nobody, that there animal ceases to litigate or exist; it's what we lawfolks calls *Nolan's Contender*, meaning this here hossthief ain't no hossthief."

Neither the innocent pair, nor receiver Piney Newbold, could fault this presentation. Grudgingly, Piney made out the bill-of-title in Southwest's behalf to Mr. Clooney Borrum, long and trusted employee of the firm. Piney was dispatched to the Tecolote to keep the citizenry involved in debate, old Jules hustled his clients up the boardwalk to the hipshot Concord.

Here, he retrieved his Winchester, asked quite seriously if the two would not accompany him and his family to his father-in-law's fine horse ranch—way over east in Chihuahua where the Chiricahua never came—as both men were masters with horseflesh, and the *estancia* of his Mexican *suegro*, his wife's *padre*, could surely use such first-rate gringo help. To this well-meant offer Clooney answered that he would have to go where his white friend went. The drifter, in his turn, said he was heading the other way. His luck had not been too impressive in the south country, and he believed he would try it for a change up north.

Old Jules allowed that this was a fresh thought, a horse-thief running away from Mexico, and just fitted in with his original assessment of his former prisoner.

"I never thought you was the real thing," he said.

He put out a big hand and both men shook it.

"Now," he said, "you had better light your shucks. These folks in Pima Bend ain't the brightest to ever come down the trail, but that lawyering I gave Piney Newbold ain't going to last past the first few bottles. My advice is climb on that old coach and wheel her out of here *ahora mismo*."

Clooney and the drifter clambered up to the box, kicked off the parking brake, hauled on the lines, turned the teams, short-swing in the middle of Main Street, and headed north out of Pima Bend and into local legend.

Two miles out of town they picked up Estune and the Apache horses, where they had been left to avoid Indian trouble with the local citizens. The squaw with her blonde baby got into the coach. The drifter tied the appaloosa and the black to the boot, rejoined Clooney on the driver's box.

Clooney clucked-up his four horses, wheelers and leaders, and the Tucson run was rolling again.

But not for Sifford Wells.

52

"Whereaway?" said Clooney Borrum.

"We'll head up through the Injun nations," answered the drifter. "I promised Estune we'd get her back to her folks."

"Whee-ooo! She done toldt me her people was Crow and Cheyenne. That's past the nations a considerable piece."

"Yep. Wyoming."

"Hmmnn. Sure to be cold up there."

"Yep," said the drifter.

They went along enjoying the fine morning. Somehow the battered coach was rolling more easily. The four horses, which ought to have been bone-tired, were pulling like colts. It did not seem so far to Wyoming, or wherever they were bound.

Down in the coach, Estune suckled the blue-eyed baby and looked about her in wonderment. To an untamed horse-back Indian woman who had never seen the inside of any stagecoach, even the charred interior of the old Concord was a palace of miracles.

The child, full-fed and drowsy, fell away from the ripe thrust of the big brown nipple. Estune put her carefully upon the opposite seat in her wrapping blanket, continued her curious examination of the wonderful "goddamn" which her white man had found for her.

The *goddamn* was in itself an index of the northern woman's nomad innocence of her new mate's world. It was the Sioux and Cheyenne appellation for any of the white man's wheeled vehicles, taken from the habit of the early white teamsters to use the word in constant endearment of their freighting teams, horse, ox, or mule.

So Estune poked and pried at everything about her, from smoke-stained leatherette window curtains—which still worked!—to horsehair upholstery, leather tug-straps for passengers to cling to on rough western roadways, beautiful gold-gilt scrolling on door panels of finest hickory hardwood, the shreds of burned canvas headliner hanging down like Spanish moss, ah! it was all truly a miracle of the white man's magic and power.

Beneath her own seat, the rear seat facing thus forward, the squaw's strolling fingers came upon a slotted groove which seemed, naturally, to trap her grasp. She leaned over tapping speculatively at the freshly fingered panels that showed the dusty prints of other digits than her own and, her tracking eye informed her, most recent in their making.

Again the red fingers tried the slotted groove, this time with astonishing result. The wood moved! Was that not remarkable? Indeed, it slid all the way to one side, disclosing a hollow place under the seat upon which she rode.

Well, it was not entirely hollow.

It was partly filled.

The squaw examined and poked at the heavy saddlebags. She cocked interested ear to the musical metal clinking they gave forth when she reached in with her squaw-booted heel and delivered them an inquisitive kick.

That was pretty.

For about a quarter-mile she amused herself keeping time to the horses' hoofthuds by heeling the clinking saddlebags. Then, tiring of this, and her heels becoming tender, she closed the underseat panel, picked up her blonde baby, lay back, and closed her eyes.

The white man was not always so smart.

He could have had that hollow place full of good food, or some tobacco, and sugar, and salt.

Above her, outside upon the swaying driver's box, Clooney Borrum and her bearded squawman slowed the teams to splash them through the shallows of the Pima crossing. Hauling out upon the far side, the drifter looked back the four dusty miles to the Bend and began to laugh.

"I rode in flush and I'm riding out busted," he grinned to his companion. "Believe me Clooney friend busted is better!"

Clooney nodded. He hawed the teams to the left and to the north.

"Iffen you say, old shotgun man. Alls I know is that we is both a hunderd times richer than we was afore I doused you in the Pima Bend horse trough."

The drifter's blue eyes danced. The black brows eased at last.

"Oh, at least," he said softly. And laughed and laughed and laughed.

Clooney Borrum never did find out how a man could be so happy over a burned-out Concord coach, a third-hand Cheyenne squaw, somebody else's little blonde baby girl, four scruffy stage horses, two biting mean Indian ponies, a horsethieved steeldust gelding, and one getting-old and out-of-work nigger friend.

Epilogue

No story truly ends where the writing stops; its people do not cease suddenly to be, for reasons of convenience or farewell, nor do its events and places disappear. As always, where little-known beings cross lives with the famous, or the infamous, rough spots develop in the trail. The result is what Apache rancher Peter Iklani, of Sonoita, quotes his grandfather as calling, "Potholes in the stage road of all journeys between tribal lore and the white man's hard history."

It is a simple thing to recommend published journals of white men who were there. Bourke's *An Apache Campaign* and Davis's *The Truth About Geronimo* are primers for the military view, handbills for the great and famous players. Bourke's *On The Border With Crook* is a definitive work of white frontier reporting, again star-billing the Geronimos, the Crooks, the Cochises, and the John Crums of the Main Act. These books, with Frank Lockwood's superb *The Apache Indians*, should be studied intently by anyone interested in the red man yesterday, or today. But they cannot and they do not tell what happened to the bit players, known and unknown, whose brave or craven or merely ordinary roles made possible the grand entry of the leading actors.

What of Peaches himself for instance?

Did the small, sunny-natured scout just ride off into the Arizona sundown that long-ago day when he parted with his friends at Tanque Verde, near Fort Lowell, to seek out Crook and tell his story of the trail to Pa-gotzin-kay?

Not really: He did exactly what he said he intended to do, and the army did exactly what he had intended it to do, no more, no less.

When Lieutenant Britton Davis's troopers arrested Peaches at his mother's jacal near San Carlos, he told his story, and Davis wisely relayed it by telegraph to Crook who had by that time moved his forces from railside at Willcox on down to jumping-off base at San Bernardino Springs, in Arizona's extreme southeast corner. Crook, with that canny genius of his for seeing Apache truth, immediately ordered Peaches

239

brought down to his camp on the border. He spoke briefly with the chubby Pa-nayo-tishn, told him he believed his report, assigned him—on the purely personal assessment of that single half-hour interview—to guide the entire command.

This duty Peaches discharged by so skillfully approaching Pa-gotzin-kay through the terrible canyons and cliff-falls of the Mexican Sierra Madres as to capture every one of the Chiricahua main and subchiefs, including the notorious Mexican Ka-ya-ten-na, Looking Glass, who had never even been in America. The list read like an Apache *Who's Who* of the Chiricahua war leaders: Loco, Nachez, Nana, Geronimo, Juh, Benito, Chatto, Mangus, Zele, Ke-e-te-na, Chihuahua, Hieronymo, the entire red hornets' nest of the dreaded Cherry Cows and their Warm Springs Apache allies. Purists on the Apache ethic will at once and loudly wail that none of these warriors was actually captured, that they all surrendered in their own ways and times. The disclaimer is academic. When Peaches cornered the Chiricahua and Warm Springs wild ones, and old Red Beard called them in, they *came*.

If any Bucky O'Neill-style horseback bronze has been erected to the memory of pudgy Pa-nayo-tishn, the White Mountain Coyote, it has been installed beyond reach of motorcar or reasonable muleback. But then all that Peaches did was to break up for all time the wild Chiricahua hostiles in a matter of brief weeks, something the awesome military machine of the United States government had proved unable to do in thirty years.

Well, what the hell; he was only an Indian.

His epitaph, so far as any man knows, was written as follows by Frank Lockwood:

I MET AND INTERVIEWED TZOE IN THE SUMMER OF 1933 AT HIS HOME ON CIBICU CREEK. HIS HUT, A SORT OF COMBINATION RAMADA AND SHACK, WAS LOCATED ON THE SITE OF THE BATTLE OF CIBICU FOUGHT IN AUGUST, 1881. "PEACHES" WAS THEN A VERY OLD MAN AND WAS ILL. HE DIED ABOUT A YEAR LATER. HE WAS ABLE TO GIVE INTERESTING DETAILS CONCERNING HIS PART IN THE EVENTS HERE NARRATED. . . .

And so what of the others in the story—Peaches' friends of the U.S. Cavalry and the fight at Sifford Wells, the flight from the Hoh-shuh hostiles and the parting in the hills at Tanque Verde?

Well, ancient Tazati, a ninety-seven-year-old White Mountain crone living alone out near Chiricahua Butte in the bleak Natanes Mountains of San Carlos, says that the old sergeant, Emmett J. Bourke (no relation to famed Captain John G. Bourke), was living "over in the winter country on the big river at Yuma" as late as 1939. He would then have been over one hundred years old, but Tazati insisted he was "hale and of clear unclouded eye."

And Chatto? What of the young warchief who, Lockwood says, "rode four hundred miles in the six days of the raid into Arizona and triumphantly back into the mountains of Mexico" without once being blooded along the way? What of Chatto who, leaving Sifford Wells and Hoh-shuh Springs, swung into New Mexico to commit the notorious McComas killings on the road between Silver City and Lordsburg, carrying off Judge McComas' small son Johnny who in his own time became an Apache legend?

What of this Chatto the cruel? Chatto the bloodthirsty? Chatto the monstrous?

Ay de mi! He came meekly back to San Carlos of his own will, foreswore the raiding trail, became "one of the two best Apache farmers on the reservation," subsequently rose in rank to senior sergeant of scouts, "and ever afterward proved a most efficient and trustworthy man."

Do-klini, Dust Devil, Noche, Bosque, and Tubac, his fellow Fort Gila raiders, fared less well, all being involved in the abortive revolt of Ke-e-te-na at San Carlos after the surrender. Ke-e-te-na, a half Chiricahua, half Warm Springs minor chief with no reputation to approach wild young Chatto's, was in the end the truer savage. He was tried by a jury of his Apache peers and sentenced to three years in prison on terrible Alcatraz Island in faraway California. Yet alas! even untamable Ke-e-te-na saw the white man's light. Upon release "he became a changed men—learned to read, and write, and to desire peace. He became the warm friend of Crook, and was later of great service to him." It is presumed, since they were not at Alcatraz, that Do-klini and friends went free.

Bobbie, the Mescalero enlisted scout? The one whom Peaches brained with his riflebutt? Bobbie did not "brain" so easily, it seems. He regained consciousness in two days, was back on active duty the entire time of Peaches' flight from the "hanging rope." Somehow, they say, the friendly Coyote never forgave his Mescalero brother for this oversight to inform of recovery. When, a few springs later, Bobbie was shot through the back of the head while leading a charge on a gang of Mexico-based horsethieves in the badlands south of Cazador, some of the Apache Scouts present with Peaches would not eat with him for a week. But then they forgave him by agreeing that perhaps, after all, it was only Ysun's way of evening up Bobbie's part in the murder of the Chiricahua women on the tragic Day of the Rocks during the great Chatto Raid.

The Kensington Massacre? Well, it is not on any map as Nine Soldier Gulch. Nor is it outside Sifford Wells. Neither does it appear in the published military record. Much does not. But awhile back a state highway crew grading for a new roadside rest area on two-lane blacktop off the beaten throughways, turned up a dry-rotted piece of ponderosa wagonboard. It looked like a marker and had originally, at least, been inscribed with two lists of names, thirteen above, and three below. Legible among the larger list were its heading name, *Kensington, Lt. Harry C.;* then randomly, *Moriarity, Dennis J.; Peabody; Schermer; Werner;* and *Crockett.* The separate three-name list was completely eaten away except for the last name, *—den, T.C.*

Since the road crew were all Apaches and not in tune with the possibility the old slab was a tallysheet for their side, they happily threw it aside where, for a few years more, it lay out behind the little block building marked MEN in a small gully which was certainly not then, or since, called Nine Soldier Gulch.

Madden's gold?

People still dig for it out there where they think it is. But all they have yet unearthed is an old Civil War issue cavalry sabre, without scabbard, dug out of a drywash bank by a government wolfer denning for bounty cubs in the spring of 1951.

Mrs. Carter?

As Mrs. Frederick Marlin, the lady wound up the wife of a full general of the U.S. Army, bore him six fine sons, not one of whom, any more than their dashing sire, was ever permitted to know that he had a sister born at Sifford Wells, Arizona Territory, the twenty-seventh day of March, 1883.

Much less did any of them come to know that Aura Lee Wandermere, the celebrated actress, born and reared in remote Wolf County, Wyoming, only daughter of a millionaire pioneer Hereford cattle breeder and a full-blooded Wind River Cheyenne Indian squaw (and oddly enough a blue-eyed blonde!), was, in fact, co-heir to the lordly Marlin mansion upon the Hudson, in New York State.

It does not matter. As Peaches so often assured his white friend, "Don't worry, we find."

So it might seem that the drifter did find his fenceline and come to lodge against it. What account that it was thirteen hundred miles north and many a hard winter after?

If he who doubts would seek to firm the word not here called history, let him ask at the post office in Twosleep, Wolf County, Wyoming, for the star route and box number of C.J. Borrum, Jr. the eighty-six-year-old and only colored member of the Appaloosa Horsebreeders Association.

Should the seeker be so fortunate as to find this wonderful snowy-haired and wealthy gentleman at home, ask him, for openers, if the name "Matadero" means anything to frontier history or to him.

It will be an interesting afternoon.

The Bloody Texans

Kent Conwell

Trapper and scout Nathan Cooper returned home to his cabin in East Texas, only to find a sight he would never forget—his wife, his young niece and his niece's intended, all slaughtered. With his heart broken and blood in his eyes, Nathan buried his family in the cold ground. Then he made an oath. He swore that the men who did this would pay. Nathan would use all of his skills to hunt the murdering scum, and he would see them suffer. One by one, he will track them and kill them, even if he has to break down the gates of Hell to do it!

ISBN 13: 978-0-8439-6066-2

MAX BRAND®

Luck

Pierre Ryder is not your average Jesuit missionary. He's able to ride the meanest horse, run for miles without tiring, and put a bullet in just about any target. But now he's on a mission of vengeance to find the man who killed his father. The journey will test his endurance to its utmost—and so will the extraordinary woman he meets along the way. Jacqueline "Jack" Boone has all the curves of a lady but can shoot better than most men. In the epic tradition of *Riders of the Purple Sage*, their story is one for the ages.

ISBN 13: 978-0-8439-5875-1

FIRST TIME IN PAPERBACK!

Max Brand

"Brand practices his art to something like perfection."   —*The New York Times*

Sequel to LUCK

CROSSROADS

"There's bad luck all around me."

Jacqueline "Jack" Boone couldn't say she didn't warn him. But Dix was a man who made his own luck. And he couldn't resist a beautiful woman who, according to tales told round the campfire, had bested one of the most notorious gunmen in decades. Except the people who were after Dix for a murder he didn't mean to commit are now after Jack too. Relentlessly stalked by a man known as El Tigre, the pair can only ride headlong into danger and hope that in the end their luck holds out.

ISBN 13: 978-0-8439-5876-8

ANDREW J. FENADY

Owen Wister Award-Winning Author of *Big Ike*

No mission is too dangerous as long as the cause—and the money—are right. Four soldiers of fortune, along with a beautiful woman, have crossed the Mexican border to dig up five million dollars in buried gold. But between the Trespassers and their treasure lie a merciless comanchero guerilla band, a tribe of hostile Yaqui Indians and Benito Juarez's army. It's a journey no one with any sense would hope to survive, or would even dare to try, except...

The Trespassers

Andrew J. Fenady is a Spur Award finalist and recipient of the prestigious Owen Wister Award for his lifelong contribution to Western literature, and the Golden Boot Award, in recognition of his contributions to the Western genre. He has written eleven novels and numerous screenplays, including the classic John Wayne film *Chisum*.

ISBN 13: 978-0-8439-6024-2

"When you think of the West, you think of Zane Grey." —*American Cowboy*

ZANE GREY

THE RESTORED, FULL-LENGTH NOVEL, IN PAPERBACK FOR THE FIRST TIME!

The Great Trek

Sterl Hazelton is no stranger to trouble. But the shooting that made him an outlaw was one he didn't do. Though it was his cousin who pulled the trigger, Sterl took the blame, and now he has to leave the country if he wants to stay healthy. Sterl and his loyal friend, Red Krehl, set out for the greatest adventure of their lives, signing on for a cattle drive across the vast northern desert of Australia to the gold fields of the Kimberley Mountains. But it seems no matter where Sterl goes, trouble is bound to follow!

"Grey stands alone in a class untouched by others." —*Tombstone Epitaph*

AVAILABLE JUNE 2008!

ISBN 13: 978-0-8439-6062-4

✂ ❏ **YES!**

Sign me up for the Leisure Western Book Club and send my FREE BOOKS! If I choose to stay in the club, I will pay only $14.00* each month, a savings of $9.96!

NAME: _____

ADDRESS: _____

TELEPHONE: _____

EMAIL: _____

❏ I want to pay by credit card.

❏ **VISA**   ❏ **MasterCard.**   ❏ **DISCOVER**

ACCOUNT #: _____

EXPIRATION DATE: _____

SIGNATURE: _____

Mail this page along with $2.00 shipping and handling to:
Leisure Western Book Club
PO Box 6640
Wayne, PA 19087
Or fax (must include credit card information) to:
610-995-9274

You can also sign up online at **www.dorchesterpub.com**.

*Plus $2.00 for shipping. Offer open to residents of the U.S. and Canada only. Canadian residents please call 1-800-481-9191 for pricing information.
If under 18, a parent or guardian must sign. Terms, prices and conditions subject to change. Subscription subject to acceptance. Dorchester Publishing reserves the right to reject any order or cancel any subscription.